W9-AIB-505

"An extraordinary novel. Poignant, moving, rich in character and deeply emotional. A keeper."
—*Romantic Times*

"YOU'RE BEAUTIFUL, KATIE," HE WHISPERED

"Zachariah, don't do this to me," she pleaded in a tremulous voice. "I'm not quite ready for this."

"You will be," he promised softly.

The sensations he elicited were so acute, so tantalizing, that Kate could scarcely breathe. He touched her as though he meant to sculpt her, fingers whispering over the flesh of her arms, tracing the curves and hollows, lingering, then moving on, only to stop and hover again as if to memorize each line. By the time he reached the slope of her shoulders, Kate couldn't form the words to ask him to stop.

"Please don't be frightened, my darling Katie," he murmured.

"I'm not frightened, Zachariah. I just don't know what to expect," she said shakily.

"Ecstasy," he said. "Ecstasy."

Also by Catherine Anderson

Comanche Moon
Comanche Heart
Indigo Blue

Available from
HarperPaperbacks

Harper
Monogram

Coming Up Roses

CATHERINE ANDERSON

HarperPaperbacks
A Division of HarperCollinsPublishers

This is a work of fiction. The characters, incidents, and
dialogues are products of the author's imagination and are not
to be construed as real. Any resemblance to actual events or
persons, living or dead, is entirely coincidental.

HarperPaperbacks *A Division of* HarperCollins*Publishers*
10 East 53rd Street, New York, N.Y. 10022

Cover photography Herman Estevez
Cover illustration by R.A. Maguire

First printing: August 1993

Printed in the United States of America

HarperPaperbacks, HarperMonogram, and colophon are
trademarks of HarperCollins*Publishers*

❖ 10 9 8 7 6 5 4 3 2 1

To my sons, Andy and John, who have filled my life with love and laughter. There was a time when my hand steadied you as you took your first steps. Now each of you offers me an arm, and I walk between you. I do so with a great sense of pride.

1

Oregon, 1890

Compliments of an overcast sky, a shaft of anemic afternoon sunshine came through the window of the otherwise cheerless kitchen. Even on fair-weather days, the unpainted plank walls, floor, and ceiling made the room seem bleak.

Leaning sideways to avoid getting smoke in her eyes, Kate Blakely shoved another chunk of laurel into the fire and settled the range lid back into place. Strings of pitch ignited, sizzling and snapping inside the belly of the stove. The merry crackling had always brightened Kate's mood, and, despite everything, she still loved the sound.

As she walked back across the kitchen, Kate craned her neck to look out the window at the old willow in the yard. The tree's dense canopy of trailing branches swayed in the light breeze, an indication that it would probably be dark before the storm blew in. From the looks of the clouds hovering over the mountains, they would bring thunder and lightning, too, unless the wind picked up. A real sky ripper.

The thought made the back of Kate's throat prickle. She forced the tension from her shoulders. There was nothing to do but put a bright face on it and pretend the darkening sky didn't worry her. Her little girl, Miranda, became agitated enough during thunderstorms without Kate adding spice to the stew.

Darned weather, anyway. Central Oregon always got a lot of rain, but this year beat all. Here it was mid-June already.

She glanced at the lantern that hung from a ceiling beam above her. During the storm tonight, she would have to light the lamps to keep Miranda calm, and that would deplete their weekly ration of fuel. If she expected to save enough from her egg and milk money to make Miranda some school dresses and buy paint for the kitchen, she couldn't use a lamp every time the mood struck.

With a sigh, Kate picked up the dog-eared journal and carried it to the trickle of feeble sunlight over the sink. As she circled the slop bucket, used to collect food scraps for the hogs, the swirl of her black cotton twill skirt disturbed a fly. The insect, sluggish from the unseasonably chill weather, buzzed around her head and then swooped down to land on the open pages.

"Confound it."

She waved the fly away and leaned into the light but still couldn't tell how many tablespoons of rolled sugar the recipe called for. By all rights, she should know the recipe for her grandma's crullers by heart, but her husband had never allowed her to make them. Joseph claimed sweets were as addicting and bad for the moral character as alcohol, especially for females who were feebleminded and more easily led astray than men.

Since Joseph's death, the one luxury Kate spent money on was sugar. Other children had sweets several times a week, and Kate was determined Miranda's childhood, from here on out, was going to be as normal as she could make it. As far as Kate could tell, neither she nor Miranda had been led astray by their frequent consumption of sugar, or suffered any other ill effects. Unless, of course, one counted the weight each of them had gained. Kate didn't. Miranda needed meat on her bones, and her own figure was no longer of great importance. If her waist became too thick to be spanned by a man's hands, so be it. The only time a man would have call to grasp her waist would be to help her out of her wagon when she went to town, and not then if she could avoid it.

"Ma, you're squintin' again. If you don't stop, we'll need another milk cow to keep you stocked with wrinkle remedy."

"The devil take wrinkles. What worries me is that I must need spectacles." Kate held the journal out as far as her arm would reach. "If I don't stop reading by candlelight, I'll be blind as a mole before I'm thirty."

Just the thought of having to give up her nightly reading time made Kate feel anxious. For five endless years, her husband Joseph had never allowed her to open a book, save the Bible, and now that she could read whenever she wished, she couldn't get enough of it. Two-month-old newspapers. Outdated catalogs. Yellowed issues of *Harper's Bazaar*.

If her eyes failed, she'd have to give up those moments she set aside for herself every evening. She didn't know why, but over the last few months, she had come to need that solitary time even more than she needed sleep, which was saying something.

Selfish, selfish. What if she truly did need spectacles? She had more important uses for her eyes than reading. Sewing, for instance. She couldn't afford to dress Miranda in ready-made. She shifted her gaze to the crockery bowl on the icebox where she kept her meager savings. Nearly every penny in the bowl was targeted for other expenditures, and she had hoped to save those that weren't to buy prune trees to start a small orchard next year. Prunes were proving to be a very profitable crop in the Umpqua Valley, and since they didn't require the back muscle that so many other crops did, Kate felt she could raise them.

If she had to buy spectacles, how much would they cost? Unless she missed her guess, they were frightfully expensive. It was yet another worry to add to her list. Feeling overwhelmed, Kate forced her mind back to the moment. Without a husband to provide the necessities, getting by had become enough of a struggle without thinking ahead to disasters that hadn't even happened yet. Besides, she had to think of Miranda. The child had seen long faces aplenty in her short lifetime.

Giving up on the recipe, she laid down the journal and narrowed an eye at her daughter who sat atop a stack of books on a chair at the table. It took her a moment to recall what Miranda had been talking about. No small wonder. The child chattered like a squirrel gathering winter nuts. "Where did you hear that milk was a remedy for wrinkles?"

Too short to see into the array of green baking canisters before her, Miranda was engaged in a touch-and-taste exploration of the ingredients Kate had set out on the table. Having just sampled the sugar, the child licked her finger again, stuck it in the baking soda, tasted, and shuddered. Kate hadn't the heart to scold. Not long ago, Miranda wouldn't have dared do such a thing. The change in her was nothing short of a miracle.

Her small face still contorted with distaste, Miranda shuddered again before she answered Kate's question. "When we was in the general store, I heard Mrs. Raimer talkin'. She says Abigail Snipes, the dairyman's wife, has the purdiest confection in town 'cause her man has so many cows."

"Complexion, not confection," Kate corrected. "And keep your fingers out of that saleratus. I don't mind you sneaking sugar, but the saleratus isn't to eat."

"Pa ate it."

"Only for indigestion." Feeling a little apprehensive at the mention of Joseph because she was never quite sure how Miranda might handle the memories, Kate approached the table with a brisk step and added eight tablespoons of sugar to the ingredients in her bowl. "The recipe be hanged. The sweeter the better, right?" Flicking her daughter a teasing glance, she added, "And I'll remind you not to contradict your elders, young lady. You're only four years old, and I guess I know better than you if saleratus is good to eat."

Miranda swiped at a streak of flour on her cheek. "Do birthdays make people smarter?"

"So they say, which means I'm seventeen birthdays smarter than you, so mind what I say."

With a dubious glance at the baking soda tin, Miranda said, "I'm not so sure your birthdays made you too smart, Ma. If saleratus ain't to eat and it tastes so powerful bad, how come are ya puttin' it in our crullers?"

Kate smothered a laugh. "If you don't like them, the more for me."

"If our crullers taste like that saleratus, I don't want none anyhow. It's nastier than hog slop."

"You been dipping in the hog slop again? I declare, Miranda Elspeth Blakely, first thing I know you'll be stealing the chickens' worms. And it's *isn't,* not ain't. If you don't learn to speak properly, what'll you do next year when school starts?"

"I ain't—" Miranda broke off and wrinkled her delicate nose. "I isn't been eatin' slop, Ma. I was just imaginin'."

Kate chuckled. "If you *isn't* been eating slop, then you aren't sure how it tastes, are you? And in answer to your question, saleratus is added to sweet doughs for rising." She gave the ingredients in the bowl a stir. "Without just a dash of it our crullers would be flat as dollars and twice as hard."

Miranda watched the rotations of Kate's wooden spoon. "Will I like school, Ma?"

Kate missed a beat. "Of course you will. I loved school when I was a girl."

"Will you come with me?"

Kate's mouth went dry. "You'll be a big girl by then, sweetness, and you won't want me with you."

Miranda cast a glance downward. "Jeffrey Mullins says I ain't no bigger than a speck of grasshopper spit."

Despite the seriousness of the moment and her fears that Miranda might not fare well when she was forced to attend school, Kate had to laugh. "Grasshopper spit? What an awful comparison." She gave her daughter a conspiratorial wink. "You just wait until he sees you in your new dresses. He'll be so surprised, his freckles will pop right off his nose."

At the mention of new dresses, Miranda's eyes danced. Looking adorable even in her patched and faded gray pinafore, she strained to sit tall enough to put her elbows on the table. When she did, she lost her balance and toppled to the floor before Kate could catch her.

"Oh, honey . . ." Abandoning her mixing bowl, Kate sank to her knees and lifted Miranda to a sitting position. "Are you all right?"

Suddenly pale, Miranda glanced over her shoulder as if she thought someone had pushed her. The unconscious gesture made Kate's heart constrict.

"I reckon I'm all right," the child finally said. "Except for my ubbles."

Accustomed to Miranda's near misses in pronunciation, Kate said, "Your elbows?" She shoved up the sleeves of Miranda's blouse to see the barked skin. The injuries were slight, but Kate imagined they stung, nonetheless. "Oh, ouch. Will a kiss on each help?"

Miranda's cheeks dimpled in a weak smile. "Maybe."

Kate administered the treatment, then smoothed her daughter's hair and lifted her back onto the stack of books. As she resumed her measuring, she mused aloud, "Now, where were we?"

"You was gonna name the colors of my dresses." Miranda tugged her sleeves down. "Tell me about 'em one more time, Ma."

Kate pretended to ponder. "Let me see. One's going to be purple."

"Ugh! Not purple, Ma. Robin's-egg blue!"

"Ah, yes, robin's-egg blue. And . . . pink."

"Apple-blossom pink," Miranda corrected.

"And red," Kate finished.

"Rose-petal red. Now, say 'em all at once."

Kate made a nonsensical jabbering noise and blew air past her lips, which sent Miranda into a fit of giggles. When the child recovered from her mirth, she said, "Not all at once like that. One word at a time."

"Robin's-egg blue, rose-petal red, and apple-blossom pink," Kate recited, mentally crossing her fingers that no unexpected expenses would crop up. If any little girl deserved three beautiful new dresses, Miranda did.

"Will I git lots of icicles on my petticoats?"

Kate stopped measuring again. "Icicles? What in tarnation?"

"You know . . . like them that the Widow Darby hangs in her parlor window at Christmas. You said they was cut-out icicles, and the other day I saw a lady in town with lots of 'em on her petticoats."

"You mean eyelet lace," Kate corrected with a chuckle. "I don't know, Miranda. My egg money may not stretch far enough to buy eyelet. Maybe I can sneak a look at Mrs. Raimer's Montgomery Ward catalog and find a better buy than we can get in town. We'll see, hm?"

As Kate folded in the last ingredient, she recalled the lace on her wedding gown, which was stored upstairs in her camelback trunk. If the gown hadn't yellowed too badly, perhaps Miranda could have icicles on her petticoats after all. Envisioning how sweet Miranda would look, all decked out in her first day of school finery, Kate got tears in her eyes.

"Why you cryin'?"

Kate wiped beneath her eye. "Lands, Miranda, I don't know. I was just thinking how pretty you're going to look and how proud I'll be of you that first day of school, and there you are. My ma called them happy tears, and I reckon that's as close to an explanation as I can get."

"I never heard of a happy crier before."

Kate shrugged.

"You're s'posed to cry over sad things, or when you get hurt, but I ain't never seen you do it. Why come is that, Ma?"

"Because I don't let myself."

"So why do you let yourself cry when good things happen?"

Kate wasn't sure she could answer that. "Happy tears sort of sneak up on a body."

"So you don't know they're comin'?"

"That's right. Who expects to cry over wonderful things? No rhyme nor reason to it, the first thing I know, I'm all weepy eyed and everybody thinks I'm crazy."

"I don't."

"That's because you love me. I'm a strange one in everyone else's books. It's female hysterics, I reckon. At least that's what your—" Kate hesitated, not at all sure she should mention Joseph again. "That's what lots of folks claim, anyway."

"What's female hysterics?"

Kate pinched some dough to test the texture. "It's a perplexity to me, but I reckon I've got an incurable case. I thought about getting myself some Goff's Giant Globules. The advertisement I saw in the *Morning Oregonian* says they're the strongest female nerve tonic known."

"You gonna order some?"

Kate gave the dough a final stir. "Not likely. They cost a whole dollar for two weeks' treatment." She leaned over to kiss Miranda's forehead. "With you around, I'd lose the farm trying to cure myself of happy tears."

Miranda stretched to touch the bottle of Knight's Apple Cider. "You don't need them old globules, anyhow. Your happy tears make your eyes shine purdy, and they go away fast."

"Thank goodness for that."

Drawing the cider bottle closer, Miranda asked, "What's this for? I ain't never tasted nothin' so plumb awful sour."

Realizing that Miranda must have sampled the cider earlier, Kate snatched the bottle away. "I swan, Miranda, you'll be needing a dose of lemon milk for your upset stomach before these crullers are done. Leave off, now, and keep out of things. You can't eat sweets if you're sick."

"If crullers is sweet, how come sour stuff goes into 'em?"

The child could ask more questions than voters at an election speech. "Truth to tell, the recipe calls for a tablespoon of dry wine, which we don't have, so I'm substituting. And, once again in answer to your question, it beats the sass out of me why a dash of something so sour is called for."

"What's wine?"

"Sinners' swill, and don't be asking what that is because you don't need to know."

Curiosity gleamed in Miranda's brown eyes. "Wine is what our new neighbor is tryin' to grow, ain't it? Mrs. Raimer said."

"He's going to grow grapes. Wine is the drink he hopes to make from them."

"And wine is sinners' swill?"

"Yes, little ma'am, that's exactly what it is, and that'll be the end of the subject."

Kate wiped her palms on her white apron and stepped to the stove to check her kettle of lard to see if it was hot enough for frying.

"Is that how come we didn't take him a loaf of welcome bread? Because he come here to make sinners' swill?"

"Came, not come. And, yes, that's why. I want no truck with a drinking neighbor, which a man who plans to build a winery must surely be."

Satisfied that the melted lard was plenty hot, Kate returned to the table to fetch her dough. As she dropped dollops of it into the sizzling grease, a loud *thunk* resounded through the house. Another quickly followed. It sounded as if someone was out in their yard chucking stones at the house. Kate glanced up, and Miranda went perfectly still.

Her eyes large with alarm, Miranda whispered, "You reckon he heard you and comed over here to throw rocks at us?"

Kate smiled reassuringly as she set the bowl of dough on the warming shelf. "If he has, I reckon we'll just throw them back. Don't be a goose, Miranda. There's nothing to be afraid of."

Miranda slid off her elevated perch. "You ain't seen how big and mean lookin' he is."

"And you have? Don't tell me you've wandered over there?"

Before Miranda could answer, something struck the house again and distracted Kate. With the child following in her wake, she went to investigate, feeling a tad uneasy in spite of herself. It was bad enough that their new neighbor, Zachariah McGovern, was probably a drinking man, let alone big and mean. She had troubles enough running this farm without adding an inebriated, cantankerous, and oversized neighbor to the list.

Kate was totally unprepared for the sight that greeted her when she opened the front door. A large yellow-and-white dog was digging gigantic holes in her rose garden along the fence, the damp, well-turned earth flying in wide arcs behind him. Miranda caught her breath and gave a dismayed squeak.

"Consternation!" Kate ran across the stoop and down the steps. "Shoo! Bad dog!" The dog, seemingly oblivious to her cries, never paused in his excavations. Kate snapped her apron at him. "Shoo, I said! Confound it, look what you've done. Go home. Go on, git!"

Throwing up a thin little arm to shield her face from the flying dirt, Miranda followed Kate into the yard. "Make him stop, Ma. Hurry and make him stop before he digs it all up!"

Kate was trying, but the dog didn't seem particularly intimidated. Her pulse skittery with building anger, she raced back into the house for her broom. She'd show that ill-mannered mongrel what for, and next time he'd think twice about digging holes at the Blakely place.

2

The leather of the saddle squeaked as Zach McGovern stood in the stirrups. His sorrel gelding snorted and tossed his head in protest at the uncomfortable shift of his rider's weight.

"Just keep your shirt on, Dander. I won't be but a minute."

Zach took off his hat, wiped his brow with his sleeve, and squinted into the feeble sunlight. He hoped to spot his dog, Nosy, who was half collie, half Australian shepherd, and all ornery. Damned dog, anyway. He ought to let him run, that's what. It'd serve Nosy right if a neighboring farmer shot his no-account ass off.

Even as he thought it, Zach knew he couldn't head home and leave the dog to whatever fate might befall him. For all his pranks, Nosy was a sweet old mutt. The problem was that he killed chickens. Not maliciously, never that. It was more a case of overzealous chase and pounce, during which the chickens lost enthusiasm for the game. But Zach didn't reckon an angry farmer would care what Nosy's intentions were. The end result, no matter how you looked at it, was dead chickens, and that was a shooting offense in farming country.

Zach sighed as he took the measure of the neighboring spreads that dotted the hills along the North Umpqua River. Spotting Nosy in the thick line of oak and fir trees along the stream was hopeless, and at this distance, the odds of his being able to tell a dog from a sheep in the fields weren't much better.

If he were Nosy, which direction would he head? Going on the assumption that Nosy had probably followed his infamous nose straight into the first peck of trouble he happened upon, Zach supposed he ought to check at the closest farms first. He lowered himself back onto the saddle.

Wasn't that a fine kettle of fish? Ever since coming here nigh unto three months ago, he'd been planning to drop by and introduce himself to his nearest neighbor, the widow Kathryn Blakely. Talk in town had it that she was about as pretty as could be and badly in need of a husband since her first had got himself drowned in the river. Not a strong-natured woman, according to the gossip, and given to nervous spells, but so beautiful that no man in his right mind would give a tinker's damn once he looked at her.

Zach doubted Kathryn Blakely was as comely as rumor claimed. Well-meaning folks had a way of exaggerating a widow woman's attributes when an available bachelor was within earshot. Times were just that hard. But Zach didn't value a woman's looks overmuch, anyway. Being a widower and lonely, not to mention none too pretty himself, he considered anything on the uphill side of ugly a good prospect. He had hoped to scrub up and put on his Sunday best before moseying over to meet her, though. Nosy's escape from his pen had scotched that.

Using his fingers as a comb, Zach tried to smooth the front of his hair, not bothering with the back since that would be covered by his hat. Then he did a half-assed job of wiping his face with his sleeve. God only knew what he must look like after working behind the plow all day. Damned no-account dog, anyway.

As he drew near the Blakely farm, the sound of a dog's excited barking, interspersed by high-pitched shrieks, told Zach he had found Nosy long before he could actually see him. Judging by the noise, he also guessed that the mutt's nose had once again led him straight into trouble.

As Zach rode up the rutted drive to the weathered, two-story white house, he could finally see what all the commotion was about. Nosy had discovered a new pastime, digging holes. From the looks of things, the dog found it far more entertaining than chicken chasing, and Zach could see why. Nosy had a found a woman instead of a chicken to play with him.

Adding to the overall ruckus was a little girl, no bigger than a mite, who was dancing about, waving her spindly arms and screaming. It didn't appear to Zach that the child's shrieks were likely to make the dog leave off anytime soon. And Kathryn Blakely's swings with her broom weren't exactly what could be termed powerful dissuaders. Instead of clobbering the mutt, as he so richly deserved, she drew the broom up short every time she swung. A stranger to blows of any kind, Nosy seemed to think this new game of swing and duck was all for fun.

With all the noise and confusion, Zach's slow approach went unnoticed. He drew his horse to a stop several yards shy of the flower bed, which cut about a ten-foot swath along the fence, extending out into the yard some six feet. Just having come from his own place, where the work was piled knee high to a tall Indian, he couldn't help but notice that the Blakely farm was in equally sad shape. It wasn't just that the house needed painting. The front porch was buckled and sinking at one end, the fence that bordered the rose garden leaned and swayed in the brisk breeze, and the barn looked as though a sneeze would blow it over.

Zach returned his attention to the well-tended rose garden, which struck a strange contrast to the ramshackle condition of everything surrounding it. It was none of his concern, but to his way of thinking, a widow's time might be better spent on something other than flowers. Trying to survive out here without a man, she'd find herself rose rich and food poor come winter if she didn't get her priorities straight.

As he refocused on Kathryn Blakely, Zach's serious thoughts gave way to amazement. While he had been looking elsewhere, she had somehow managed to get her coronet of braid tangled in the thorns of a rosebush that climbed the trellis behind her.

Zach took in the damage and wondered why she persisted in darting after Nosy. True, the dog had dug some considerable holes, but none had unearthed the rosebushes or were so close they were likely to harm the roots. The dog probably wouldn't do any irreparable damage in the time it might take for her to untangle herself.

There was just no figuring women. At least Zach had never had a knack for it. She obviously held the dirt around her roses in mighty high regard, and whether or not that made sense to him was beside the point. Damned dog. So much for his chances of getting off on the right foot with Kathryn Blakely.

And wasn't that a shame? Rumor hadn't lied. Even in a threadbare, somber black dress and smudged white apron, she was just about the prettiest little gal Zach had ever clapped eyes on. Her sable hair was as shiny as hot fudge before it lost its gloss. Even narrowed in anger, her eyes were the biggest thing about her face and the softest brown he had ever seen.

A man of lofty stature with considerable bulk, Zach had always fancied taller women with more substantial builds, but Kathryn Blakely was proof that small didn't necessarily equate to less. Though delicate of frame, she was well proportioned and pleasantly rounded in all the right places.

Nosy barked and executed some more fancy footwork to avoid another swing of the broom. Set off-balance, Kathryn Blakely did a sidestep and was brought to a reeling stop by the rose branch that was still tangled in her hair. Zach winced and decided he'd better bring this to a stop before the fool woman hurt herself.

The instant Zach shifted in the saddle to dismount, Nosy spotted him and promptly ceased his mischief. With a whine of greeting, the dog dropped to his haunches, tongue lolling, his expression angelic.

Kathryn Blakely, still anchored, twisted to look up, her large brown eyes filled with surprise. A blush of what Zach guessed to be embarrassment dotted the flawless ivory of her cheeks. The little girl threw a frightened glance over her shoulder, gasped, and then skedaddled toward the barn like a pebble launched from a bean flip.

Kathryn Blakely gazed after her fleeing daughter with unmistakable longing in her expression, but held her ground. Not, Zach was sure, because courage bolstered her but because the rose branch would snatch her bald-headed if she did otherwise.

The combined reactions of mother and child, not to mention Nosy's, made Zach feel none too welcome. "It looks like my dog has stirred up a peck of trouble." He finished dismounting and looped Dander's reins around the saddle horn. "I'm right sorry about this. He got out of his pen when I wasn't lookin' and took off."

All things considered, Zach thought his opening was as good as any and neighborly. Kathryn Blakely didn't seem to share the sentiment. Still bent sideways, she held the broom as if she intended to thump him a good one if he got too close.

Zach shuffled his boots and then remembered his manners enough to take off his hat. He no sooner did than he recalled the stir his hair was probably in and clapped the hat back on, backward and cockeyed. He gave it a jerk to put it right and cleared his throat, which made Kathryn Blakely start.

Zach couldn't figure out what her problem was. He knew he wasn't very pretty to look at, but he had never scared anybody speechless. For the second time in less than ten minutes, he found himself trying to look at things from someone else's perspective, first from Nosy's, and now from Kathryn Blakely's. And damned if it hadn't been easier to think like a dog.

He guessed she must be uneasy because her farm was isolated and he was a stranger. A large stranger, by her measuring stick. She wasn't much bigger than a minute, and he stood a head taller and a good measure broader than most men.

"I'm Zachariah McGovern, your new neighbor," he tried.

She brought the broom up a tad higher. So much for polite introductions. Zach glanced around, not quite sure why. A mutual acquaintance wasn't likely to appear out of thin air to introduce them properly.

He jabbed a thumb toward his place. "That's my spread over yonder."

She didn't look in the direction he pointed.

"I've been meaning to mosey over before this, but the work has kept me too busy." He eyed her tangled hair. "If you'll set that broom down, I'll get you loose from there."

Her knuckles whitened as she tightened her grip.

Zach decided that he'd live through it if she tried to lop his head off. Slowly so as not to frighten her, he moved in. "You're in a fine fix. Let me see what I can do to get you untangled, hm?"

She jerked when he settled his hands on her hair. The splay of his long fingers could easily encompass her head, which gave him a better idea of how she must be feeling. She and the child were alone out here, and in these parts, a wise woman probably greeted strangers with a well-primed shotgun.

She smelled like vanilla and cinnamon, not exactly an intoxicating perfume, but mighty appealing to Zach, who thought of apple pie covered with dollops of fresh whipped cream. Good enough to eat, that was how she smelled. And her hair felt as soft as corn silk. He hated to jerk on it for fear it might tear, not to mention sting her scalp. He grasped her narrow shoulders to turn her slightly and felt the tension in her body. Coiled to run. He had a good mind to leave her tethered. Odds were a hundred to one that he'd never get another chance to get acquainted with her.

Something hit the back of Zach's legs. He glanced over his shoulder to discover that Nosy, out from under his master's evil eye, had resumed his excavations and was sending dirt flying. "Leave off, Nosy!" Zach roared.

At the sound, Kathryn Blakely tried to leap away, only to be brought up short by the rose branch. Zach saw involuntary tears spring to her eyes and felt bad about startling her into hurting herself.

"Mrs. Blakely, if you don't relax, you'll be balder than a peeled turnip by the time I get you loose."

"It's a little difficult to relax when my hair is being pulled out by the roots and my garden is being destroyed."

Zach liked the sound of her voice, even in anger. It put him in mind of warm honey on buttered biscuits. Realizing that this was at least the third time in as many minutes that he had drawn a comparison between her and food, he had cause to wonder if he was hungry. "I'll save your hair if you'll hold still, and I'll repair the damage to your rose garden."

"If you'll just untangle me, I can tend the roses myself, thank you."

Even with her neck in a crimp, she managed a stubborn lift of her chin. Zach bit back a smile. "That wouldn't be neighborly of me. My dog did the damage. It's only right that I fix it." As he spoke, he set his jaw and gave her braid a sharp tug. "There."

Free of the thorns and him, she sidled away, one hand clamped to her smarting head, the other still gripping the broom. Zach eyed the wispy dark curls that had escaped the strictures of her braid and decided she'd be even prettier with her hair loose and soft around her shoulders. Not that she needed much help with her looks.

"Thank you for getting me untangled," she finally said.

She didn't look too grateful. Fact was, Zach suspected her fondest wish was to have him out of her sight. Now that she could stand straight and run if the mood struck, she didn't look quite so frightened. She gave his dusty jeans and chambray work shirt a careful study, then lifted her gaze to his face. After a long moment, she seemed to relax a little, and he guessed that she must have decided he was telling the truth about who he was.

"Is your hoe in the barn?" he asked.

Zach couldn't tell if she was staring at the scars on his cheek, but he felt self-conscious anyway and tugged the brim of his hat farther down.

A muscle at the corner of her mouth twitched, and her chin came up again. "As I said, I'll tend to the damage."

Zach sighed. "Mrs. Blakely—Kathryn, may I call you Kathryn? I'd like to make amends. I feel bad enough as it is. It won't take me ten minutes to fill these holes—"

"Kate."

"Beg pardon?"

"Kate," she repeated. "I go by Kate."

She didn't look like a Kate. The name Kate conjured pictures in Zach's mind of a sturdy woman with broad shoulders and a strong back. Probably because Kate Bracken, the only Kate he had ever known, had stood five foot nine and wore a size ten man's boot. Katie, maybe. Yes, Katie suited her better.

"Look, Mr. . . ."

"McGovern."

She licked her bottom lip. "Mr. McGovern . . . as much as I appreciate how you must feel"—she swept a hand toward Nosy—"about the damage your dog has done and all, it really isn't necessary for you to fill in the holes." She cast a nervous glance at the ground. "Truly, it isn't. In fact, I'd prefer not. My daughter isn't accustomed to strangers, and I—"

A gust of wind broke over the roof of the house and came whistling across the yard to lift her black skirt. Zach got a glimpse of black high-top shoes and white muslin bloomers before she could gather the cotton twill of her skirt close to her slender legs. As the wind eddied around her, she looked toward the house and sniffed. Then a horrified expression crossed her face.

Tossing aside the broom, she dashed for the porch, crying, "My crullers! Oh, lands, I totally forgot them!"

Wondering what in the hell crullers were, Zach watched her fly into the house and disappear. The distinct smell of scorched lard drifted to him. He shot a glare at Nosy. "Damned dog."

Nosy whined and lay down, resting his head on his dirty paws.

Zach picked up the broom and leaned it against the fence. Now that Kathryn Blakely had taken the scent of vanilla and cinnamon away with her, he could smell the light perfume of the blood red roses. With a wry smile, he touched a fingertip to a delicate, silken petal and then glanced at the house. Most fragile and beautiful things had to sprout a few thorns in self-defense, he supposed.

With a shrug, he turned toward the barn, hoping to find a hoe. In short order, he did so and returned to the rose garden, his intention to right the wrong Nosy had done. Before he had executed more than three strokes with the hoe blade, Kathryn Blakely came flying from the house, for all the world as if he were molesting her person.

"I said I'd take care of it," she cried.

Grabbing the hoe, she tried to wrest it from him.

"Kate, I'd like—"

"I really don't care what you'd like! What *I'd* like is to fry up my grandma's cruller recipe in peace, and that's exactly what I intend to do. So, please, take your dog and go home."

Feeling absurd, he let her have the hoe. He'd be damned if he'd stand there fighting her for it. "No hard feelings?" He knew that was a stupid question. The woman looked angry enough to chew nails and spit out screws. "I'd hate to think Nosy's antics got us off on the wrong foot."

"No hard feelings, I assure you," she replied shakily. "Not toward you or your dog. Just take him home and make certain he doesn't escape his pen again."

Zach had never known anyone to get into such a stir over a little disturbed dirt. He stood there for a moment, gazing down at her. Standing so close, he took the measure of her height next to his shoulder and realized she missed the mark by a good half head. He doubted she'd tip the scales at much over a hundred pounds. He hated to leave her to do extra work that had been caused by his dog, but didn't see as how he had much choice.

He turned toward his horse, then paused to glance back at her. "Maybe one Sunday you and your daughter would enjoy coming for tea." Tea? Where in hell had that come from? He didn't own a teacup and wasn't any too sure he could readily buy one in Roseburg, the only close town.

"Thank you for the invitation, but I'm not much for socializing, I'm afraid. This farm keeps me as busy as yours does you."

At least she was polite when she turned a fellow down. Zach tipped his hat to her. "A pleasure meeting you."

"Likewise." She wiped her hands on her apron and scanned the churned earth around her.

Zach swung up on his horse and whistled for Nosy. As he rode along the road adjacent to the barn, a flash of movement caught his attention, and he turned to see the little girl peering out at him from around the corner of the building. He reined in to smile at her, noting that her fragile features, sable hair, and huge brown eyes made her unmistakably Kate Blakely's daughter.

"Hello," he called.

At the sound of his voice, the little girl gave a startled leap and fled. Zach gazed after her, unsettled by the stark terror he had seen flash across her face. The Blakely females were the most skittish he had ever run across, and that was a fact.

As he rode home, Zach found himself troubled by the memory of the child's frightened expression. Coming up with no explanation, Zach set the problem on a back shelf in his mind. Some people were just odd. Besides, it wasn't his concern. Even though he was her closest neighbor, he doubted he would be seeing much of Kate Blakely. Probably not hide nor hair, if she had her way, which she would. Zach was nothing if not a gentleman.

"Damned dog," he muttered.

The instant Zachariah McGovern disappeared and Kate felt assured he wouldn't come back, she dropped the hoe and went in search of Miranda. She found her child huddling behind a hay bale in the barn loft, knees drawn to her chest, arms crossed over her head. Kate's heart caught, and she sank to her knees in the soft hay to gather Miranda close.

"Oh, sweetness, it's all right. Don't be frightened."

"Is that scary-looking man gone?"

As she smoothed her daughter's hair, Kate recalled Zachariah McGovern's darkly handsome face and twinkling hazel eyes. Not everyone would agree that he was frightening. No wonder tongues in town were buzzing. In these parts, bachelors were a commodity in short supply, and McGovern was about as good-looking as a man came with that wavy, chocolate-colored hair of his and that fine set of shoulders.

In Miranda's books, any man was scary looking, Kate guessed. And who had taught her that? Kate knew she couldn't place the blame entirely on Joseph's head.

She massaged Miranda's narrow little shoulders. "He's not only gone, but I doubt he'll ever come back. He just came for his dog. Chances are the beast won't get loose again."

Miranda burrowed closer. "That dog dug in the roses," she whispered. "Great big awful holes. I was afraid you couldn't make him stop. And then that man came. He was so big, Ma. Bigger than Pa. Even bigger than Uncle Ryan."

Kate squeezed her eyes closed. "I love you, Miranda. With all my heart. You mustn't feel afraid. Do you understand? Not of Mr. McGovern or anyone. No matter what happens, I'll always take care of you." Kate tightened her arms. "I promise."

Miranda sniffed. "I know you will, Ma. No matter what."

Kate bit her lip and sent up a silent plea that this was a promise circumstances would never force her to break. Miranda, unlike many children, had only one person to protect her. God forbid that something should happen to separate them. Miranda's only other relative, Ryan Blakely, who would undoubtedly be awarded custody of Miranda if anything happened, was as mad as his brother Joseph had been.

"Some of the crullers burned, but we have half a batch yet to fry," Kate murmured. "What say we go to the house? After I've repaired the rose garden, we'll have a party, just you and me. I'll tell you stories by the stove."

Miranda looked up. "Will you tell the one about when you was a little girl and your pa bought you a kitten?"

Another ache of sadness cut through Kate, so sharp it hurt. Of all the stories Kate had told, that one continued to be Miranda's favorite, probably because it allowed her to glimpse a world she had never known, a world in which little girls were protected, and loved, and cherished by gentle fathers.

Miranda's fantasy . . . It was one Kate knew would never be fulfilled.

3

One afternoon *nearly a week* later, Henrietta the milk cow didn't come in from the fields. Henrietta supplied Kate and Miranda with milk, cream, butter, and cheese, not to mention the little bit of extra Kate sometimes made by selling surplus milk products. Left with no choice, Kate bundled Miranda up against the chill and set out in search of her.

"It's summertime, Ma. How come I gotta wear a coat?"

"Tell those clouds it's summertime, little miss. Besides, it isn't a heavy coat, just light serge."

Trying to spot Henrietta, Kate gazed off across the fields. In places the grass was so tall it could easily hide a cow. The men who first settled in the valley still told stories about having seen grass in those early days that grew over seven feet high. Kate tried to picture the orchards she hoped to plant and wondered if the stubborn grass would choke out her saplings.

"You think it might rain?" Miranda asked.

The sodden earth sucked at Kate's sturdy high-top shoes. "Just what we need, more rain. But, yes, I reckon it might."

"It's good for the roses. You watch. All this rain will make 'em grow like weeds. Purdy soon, they'll be so thick no ground will even show."

Kate settled a hand on her daughter's bent head, uncertain how to reply. Since the visit of Zachariah McGovern's dog, Miranda had become as obsessed with the rose garden as Kate was.

Miranda wrinkled her nose. "Pa'd have fits if he could see them roses. They're purdier this year than ever, huh?"

Miranda's observation made Kate's stomach knot. She tried to speak and couldn't. She knew the child needed to talk about Joseph, to purge herself of the memories, but it seemed to Kate that some things were best laid to rest.

Miranda looked up. "Why did Pa hate the roses, Ma?"

Swallowing hard, Kate said, "He felt flowers were a sinful waste of time."

"Are they?"

Kate wished the question away, but when she looked down, Miranda's big eyes were still demanding an answer. "I reckon I'm not smart enough to answer that, sweetness."

"Why? If Pa was smart enough, why aren't you?"

Kate smoothed a lock of sable hair from her daughter's cheek. "I'm a female, and females are feeble—" The words caught in Kate's throat, and an unreasoning anger welled within her. Joseph was dead. Dead! He couldn't reach beyond the grave and chastise her if she dared to speak her own mind. Kate took a bracing breath. "I guess it's a matter of biblical interpretation." For once, Miranda didn't ask what that meant. "Your pa believed anything pretty was sent by Satan to tempt us to be frivolous and sinful. I believe God made beautiful things and gave them to us as gifts to lighten our load."

Miranda smiled. "I think you're right, Ma. How could Satan make somethin' as purdy as a rose?"

"That's a good question."

"I don't think he made you, neither, Ma."

Kate fastened a startled gaze on her daughter's small face. Sometimes it was frightening to realize just how much of Joseph's wild ranting the child had overheard.

As if she felt it might be necessary to back up her statement with fact, Miranda added, "You're not a rose, but you're near as purdy. If Satan couldn't 've made the roses, he couldn't 've made you."

Kate finally gathered the presence of mind to say, "Thank you. Just remember that pretty is as pretty does and that looks only run skin deep."

Reaching up to give Kate's hand a squeeze, Miranda said, "You're purdy inside, too. I bet you even got purdy innards."

Kate couldn't help but laugh. "That's a lovely compliment, I think."

Cutting a swath through the tall grass, Miranda skipped on ahead, her dark hair streaming in the wind behind her.

"Oh, look, Ma, this is where a house was."

As Kate drew near, she saw the tumbledown remains of a foundation and brick chimney. "I'll be." She seldom walked this far into the grazing pastures, and when she had, the tall grass and the rolling lay of the land must have hidden the structure. "I didn't know this was here. This must be where the previous owners built their first home."

"I could play house here."

Kate nudged the crumbling foundation with her toe. "You stay clear of that chimney. I'm not sure it's safe."

Miranda, who, out of habit and necessity, had learned to be more obedient than most little girls her age, made a wide circle around the cascade of bricks and went skipping away through the tall grass. Kate gazed after her, wishing every moment in Miranda's life could have been like this one, carefree and happy.

Suddenly, as if she were a mark on a chalkboard that had just been erased, Miranda disappeared. Kate blinked, not quite able to believe her eyes. "Miranda?"

No answer. For an instant, Kate thought the child might be playing, that she had deliberately sunk to her knees to hide herself in the grass. But that wasn't like Miranda. And there had been something unnatural about the way she dropped from sight, almost as if the ground had suddenly disappeared. . . .

"Miranda?"

Kate broke into a run. How could she be so stupid, so careless? It stood to reason that where one found the foundation of a house, one also might stumble across an abandoned well.

Zach walked down the mud-slicked slope between two rows of newly erected vine trellises. In his mind's eye, he saw not the tender little vines on this small patch of hillside, but mature vines, what grape growers called old wood. In his imagination, he envisioned acres of them.

Someday, he promised himself. Come next February, he would harvest these vines, grade them, and put them into cool sawdust storage until grafting time next spring when the vine propagation would begin all over again. It might take a number of years and backbreaking work, but one day he'd have plenty of fruit-bearing old wood and a vineyard to rival those he had seen in France during his honeymoon with Serena.

This climate would grow grapes. Even left neglected in people's yards, vines thrived here. By God, if they could survive and bear fruit when left to their own devices, he could make a success of this venture. He just knew he could.

Not that he had his eggs all in one basket. He already

had several acres planted in wheat and several more in alfalfa hay. If the grapes failed or the market didn't support a winery, he'd have something to fall back on. He also had a substantial amount of money in the bank, if he needed it, proceeds from the sale of the first house he had built for Serena right after they married.

Serena. Zach brushed his knuckles along his scarred cheek. Now that he had moved from the Applegate Valley, he seldom thought of her.

At the base of the slope, Zach left the vineyard behind and lengthened his stride, heading for the house. This was his favorite time of day, the grueling work hours behind him, the evening ahead. He looked forward to a good home-cooked meal, compliments of his new housekeeper, Ching Lee, a Chinaman who had finally given up on mining as a way to make his living. After supper, Zach planned to indulge himself by reclining in his rocker near the fire with a book, Nosy snoozing at his feet. No matter that he usually found the big house ominously quiet and lonely at night. Sooner or later, he'd find himself a nice, homely woman who looked for more in a man than a perfect face.

As he stepped onto his back stoop, a distant ruckus made him pause before opening the door. He turned into the unseasonably chill wind and gazed across the yard, glad for the turned-up collar of his sheepskin jacket. A buckboard bounced and careened up the road to his place, and unless his eyes deceived him, Kate Blakely was driving it, doing none too expert a job. If she didn't slow down, she'd break her damn-fool neck.

Something was wrong. A person didn't run a horse like that unless she had good reason. He retraced his steps into the yard and headed for the road to intercept her. When Kate saw him, she stood and hauled back on the reins, bringing her swaybacked old mare to a skidding halt. The buckboard rocked crazily, giving Zach reason to suspect it was so rotten in the seams that it was held together by a prayer and precious few rivets. The mare, clearly unused to such an abusive pace, wheezed and blew, her lathered sides laboring for every breath.

"You'll kill that horse, pushing her like that," he commented as he drew up beside the wagon.

Kate just stood there, her face deathly pale, her mouth working but no sound coming forth. Zach was about to ask her what was amiss when she took him completely off guard by jumping to the ground. He snaked out an arm to catch her.

"Mir—Miranda," she said between gulps of air. "An old well. I didn't know it was there." She clutched his jacket, her gaze clinging to his. "Please, you have to help me. I haven't the strength to get her out by myself. I was afraid if I tried, we might both be trapped."

For a second, Zach felt as though his heart stopped pumping. A loud pounding began in his temples. He didn't have to ask who Miranda was. Kate had the look of a mother terrified for her child. A picture flashed through his mind of her little girl's pale face and doelike eyes. An old well. Oh, Jesus.

"Is she conscious?" Zach asked.

Kate's face twisted. She swallowed and made a visible effort to calm down. "I—I don't think so. I called down to her, and she didn't answer."

Zach had to pry her fingers from his jacket. "I'm going to get my horse and a rope. You wait here for me, okay?"

Kate gave a jerky nod and reached to grasp the wagon for support. "Hurry, Mr. McGovern, please, hurry."

Zach had never been much for praying, but during the seemingly endless horseback ride over to the Blakely place, he sent up a plea to the Almighty with nearly every breath. Even if he had never seen Miranda, the frantic clinging of Kate's arms around his waist and the rigidness of her body pressed to his back would have made him afraid for her child's safety. Only six months ago, this woman had lost her husband in a tragic drowning. It might be more than she could take to lose her daughter.

When they finally reached the well, Miranda didn't reply when Zach called down to her. He took a penney from his pocket and let it fall, turning his ear toward the opening to listen for a splash when it hit bottom.

"It's dry, I think," he said.

Zach wasn't sure whether it was good news or bad. Miranda could drown if there was water, but without it, the fall could have broken her neck. By Kate's expression, he guessed he needn't elaborate. She was as pale as a freshly whitewashed picket fence. He had to admire her pluck. Most mothers would be hysterical by now.

After tying the rope to Dander's saddle and asking Kate to hold his bridle, Zach lowered himself into the dark shaft, acutely conscious of the silence. The dankness of the well closed in, the mustiness so thick he found it hard to breathe.

Though the light from above provided feeble illumination at best, his eyes soon adjusted, and he spotted Miranda's pale gray coat several feet before he reached her. About halfway to the bottom of the shaft, she lay huddled on an outcropping of stone, knees drawn to her chest, head tucked. Even in the dimness, he could see how badly she trembled. She was definitely conscious, so why hadn't she responded when he and Kate called down to her?

With a quick glance, Zach gauged the distance from the surface of the well to the ledge. She hadn't fallen far. Enough to bruise her, surely, possibly even far enough to break an arm or leg. But her rigid posture didn't indicate that.

Zach groped for a foothold on the dank earthen wall to steady himself and assess the situation. From his vantage point, the ledge looked sturdy enough to bear Miranda's weight, but he wasn't any too sure it would hold his. That meant he'd have to pluck the child off the outcropping with one arm while he somehow held himself suspended from the rope with his other.

Tipping his head back, he yelled. "I see her, Kate! And as near as I can tell, she's all right."

The instant Zach's voice boomed, a buzzing sound started up a few feet below him and slightly off to the left. He froze and peered into the dimness, scarcely hearing Kate's reply. Another buzzing noise began somewhere below his feet. Then it seemed as if the sounds began to come from all directions.

Zach's first instinct was to shinny up the rope as if the devil was on his ass. He had one phobia, and that was of snakes. Even a harmless garter snake could make his blood run cold. To hell with playing hero. But then Miranda squeaked, a tiny, terrified sound, and he snapped back to his senses.

Zach drew his boot from the wall and hung there on the rope for a moment, so paralyzed with fear that he couldn't move. Only a few feet below him were rattlers, a whole goddamned den from the sound of them, and to reach Miranda he had to lower himself into their midst.

Gripping the rope with his feet, he flexed his hands. Easy does it, one inch at a time. Sweat popped out on his face. It became more difficult to breathe. The muscles in his arms and legs started to quiver as he began the descent.

Don't think. Block out the sounds. The kid is all that matters. At last, Zach drew level with the ledge.

"Miranda, honey," he whispered.

The sound of his voice set the snakes to buzzing again.

Zach expected them to strike at any second. No wonder Miranda hadn't answered her mother.

"Miranda, honey," he whispered again.

Though it was a strain to hang there on the rope, Zach knew he didn't dare make any sudden moves to set the rattlers off. He also had to consider Miranda's possible reaction if he made a grab for her before he explained what he intended to do. She might try to elude him and fall from the ledge. In a ragged whisper, he said, "I'm Mr. McGovern, the man you saw last week. It was my dog that tore up your ma's flower bed. Do you remember me, honey?"

An ominous rattling sound started up again to his left. Then another, and another. He fought back a wave of numbing, mindless panic. One wrong move, and he was a dead man. His skin shriveled, and he stopped breathing to peer into the darkness. After a moment, he made out the dim shape of a rattler coiled on a jutting lip of stone. The snake was a giant. Six feet long or better, and as thick as a man's wrist.

With the shaking fingers of one hand, Zach slowly unbuttoned his coat. "Miranda, I'm going to grab you—real fast—and put you under my coat where you'll be safe. You understand? When I do, you grab onto my neck with all your might and wrap your legs around my waist. They can't bite you through the sheepskin."

She gave another terrified squeak. Zach knew exactly how she felt, but unless he acted, and quickly, she'd get bitten for sure. Probably more than once.

"I know you're scared," he whispered. "Just trust me, okay? I won't let them get you."

Zach prayed that was a promise he could keep. Slowly, ever so slowly, he angled a leg onto the ledge to help support his dangling weight. When he moved, something hit his thigh. It felt as if a fist had slammed into him, but when he looked down, all his worst nightmares became reality. A rattler had bit him, and the goddamned thing had its fangs snagged in the denim of his jeans. A crawling, thought-robbing hysteria swamped Zach, and he nearly turned loose of the rope.

"Son of a bitch!" Freeing one hand, he grabbed the huge snake, jerked it loose, and threw it away with all his strength. The pain in his leg spread like flames licking a spill of kerosene, down to his calf, then up to his hip. "Christ Almighty! Jesus Christ Almighty . . ."

Zach's first instinct was to clutch his burning thigh, but there wasn't time for that. Instead he jerked his coat open, grabbed Miranda, and pulled her against his chest. Shaking violently, she clung to his neck.

"They're gonna git me. They're gonna git me."

Zach unclenched his teeth. "No . . . I won't let them. It's okay, honey." He drew his jacket closed around her. "See? They can't bite through all that sheepskin. Wrap your legs around me. Up high, so they're covered by the coat."

Obviously too terrified to respond, Miranda just hung there and made mewling noises. The strain of his position began to tell on Zach's back and arms, but he didn't dare put more of his weight on the ledge. If the rock gave way, the fall might kill Miranda. If not, the snakes in the bottom of the well would.

"Wrap your legs around me," he repeated. "I won't let them hurt you. I promise."

With a whimper, Miranda finally obeyed. Zach didn't have to tell her to hang on. Once he got her to move, she latched onto him like a baby opossum. The feel of her tiny body plastered against him had a strangely calming effect. His mind froze on one thought; he was all that stood between this child and death.

With numb fingers, Zach rebuttoned the coat around

her. "Duck your head, honey, and make sure you keep your legs up around my waist, as high as you can get them."

"Sc-Scared. I'm scared."

Zach felt sweat trickling along his jaw. "There's nothing to be afraid of. I've got you. Keep under my coat, and they won't be able to bite you."

Zach wished the same held true for him. Unfortunately, a great deal of his body was exposed. Once he felt certain Miranda was completely covered by the sheepskin, he gripped the rope with both hands. Now that his eyes were more accustomed to the dimness, he could see several snakes above him, curled into deadly coils on staggered outcroppings of rock. No telling how he had come past them without being bitten.

Zach eyed the sphere of light above the snakes and considered staying where he was until they calmed back down. He had the ledge to support his weight partially. If he waited it out until they grew calm, maybe, just maybe, they'd let him go past again without striking at him.

He might survive one snakebite.

The burning pain in his thigh scotched the idea of staying where he was. The bigger the rattler, the more venom. The one that bit him had been huge. He had ten, maybe fifteen minutes left before the poison took hold, if he was lucky. If he waited for the snakes to settle down, he might still have the strength to haul himself up the rope. But what about Miranda?

There were no choices. None that he would allow himself to consider, at any rate. He had lived a fair number of years. Miranda's life had just begun. Snakes be damned, he had to make that climb.

4

Zach began the ascent. He knew he'd be bitten again when he moved. But nothing could have prepared him for the agony of it. Three feet up, he felt the first impact. The burning sensation snatched his breath, and it took all his concentration to keep a hold on the rope. Two more feet, and another snake struck.

The explosion of pain blocked out all other sensation in his legs. He could no longer tell if his feet were gripping the rope. Judging from the strain on his arms, he doubted it.

One hand over the other, inch by slow inch, he worked his way toward the light. A rattler struck his jacket, and Miranda screamed. "Hold on, honey. Whatever you do, don't turn loose."

Zach thought he felt another snake get him, but couldn't be sure. Somewhere near the surface, a wave of dizziness hit him, and he nearly lost his grip on the rope. He heard Kate's voice, sounding as if it came from a distance. He threw a knee over the rim of the well, folded one arm around Miranda, and grabbed wildly for the grass. Fresh air. No snakes. Daylight.

Miranda's head popped out from under his coat like a turtle's from its shell, but when Kate tried to wrest her away from Zach, she refused to let go of his neck. With hands that no longer felt attached to his arms, he unbuttoned his jacket and searched Miranda's body for bites.

He knew he was a goner. They had nailed him three, maybe four times. He could feel the denim of his jeans stretching taut around his legs and knew his limbs were swelling at an alarming rate. But not the child. Please, God, not the child.

"Snakes." He looked up at Kate and blinked, suddenly so dizzy that he wasn't quite sure which of the three women looking down at him was the real one. "Rattlesnakes, a whole den of 'em. Make sure the sons of bitches didn't bite her."

He imagined he could feel the poison coursing through his blood stream. In his recollection, snakebite symptoms usually came on more slowly, the first hitting after fifteen or twenty minutes, growing worse after that, taking hours before the cumulative effects were fatal.

Not with him. His heart was already chugging like a steam locomotive going up a steep grade, the beats coming so rapidly, one upon the other, that his chest felt as if it might explode. His body was drenched in sweat and tingled, as if pins were jabbing him. Nausea rolled through his stomach.

Feeling weak, he passed a hand over his eyes, wincing at the intensifying ache that throbbed in his temples. He tried to focus his gaze, vaguely aware that Kate had dragged Miranda away and was frantically running her hands over his legs.

"Oh, my God, Mr. McGovern. Oh, my God. You've been badly bitten. I have to get you to the house."

Zach figured he'd just as soon die where he was. Less

effort that way. He sank back on an elbow. The sound of Miranda's high-pitched sobbing penetrated the fog around him. He clawed his way through it. "Don't cry, honey," he managed to slur. "It's over, and you're safe." He searched for Kate's face. "She is okay, isn't she? They didn't get her."

"No, they didn't." Kate's voice cracked. "Thanks to you. Oh, Mr. McGovern. I've never heard of anyone being bitten so many times. You're bleeding awfully."

He struggled to martial his thoughts. "The poison . . . It makes the blood thin."

Zach closed his eyes. He seemed to be floating, and he went with it, glad to escape the burning pain. Time passed. He wasn't sure how much, only that Kate Blakely was tugging at him. Her voice clamored inside his head. *You mustn't lie down.* And why the hell not? he wanted to ask. But he couldn't muster the energy. *Please, Mr. McGovern, you have to at least try to walk. Just to the horse. Please, please try.* If it wasn't just like a woman to pester a man when he was trying to rest.

At Kate's prodding, Zach managed to stagger to his feet. At least, he surmised he was on his feet. His legs felt like blazing stumps, and the pain obliterated all other feeling from his waist down. He felt her drape his arm around her shoulders and realized the crazy little fool was trying to carry him.

"Don't . . . You'll hurt yourself."

"I'll thank you to just keep walking, Mr. McGovern. I'll worry about what will hurt me and what won't."

Was he walking? Zach had a vague impression of the ground passing beneath him and decided he must be. She sure as hell wasn't big enough to carry him. When they reached the horse, his mind cleared enough for him to realize she wanted him to mount up. He draped both arms over Dander's saddle and dropped his head. This was as far as he was going.

"Get your foot in the stirrup."

"I'm finished."

"You'll be finished when I say, and not before. Lift your foot, dad-blame you."

Zach felt her come up on the other side of the horse and seize hold of his wrists. He struggled to lift his head. "You can't pull me up."

He felt her pull anyway, and damned if she didn't manage to lift him a couple of inches. Zach groaned and tried to sling his leg over. He failed on the first try, succeeded on the second. When she finally got him into the saddle, he lay forward on the horse, not caring that the saddle horn jabbed him in the belly. Every step the beast took was an agony. Zach gritted his teeth one second and cursed the next.

The trip to the house passed in a dizzying blur of pain. He had vague impressions of the sky, the ground, the barn, and then the rose garden. The next thing he knew she was half carrying him up the steps. He wanted to help, tried to help, but his feet felt as if they were a hundred blazing miles from his brain and weighted with lead.

She couldn't get him much farther, Zach thought. He outweighed her by a good hundred pounds, and his legs grew more useless with every attempted step. But carry him she did. Through a dark foyer. Down a long, dim hallway that spun round and round until he couldn't tell where the floor ended and the ceiling began. Then he felt the soft embrace of a feather bed come up to meet him.

In the farthest reaches of his mind, he wondered if someone had forgotten to tell Kate Blakely that a rattlesnake bite was usually fatal. He had been bitten more than once. He was as good as dead and just too stubborn to quit kicking.

He felt her trying to work his jeans down over his hips. For the life of him, he couldn't push up to help her. Damned fool woman. She didn't know when to quit any more than he did. When she finally stopped tugging on his britches, Zach strained to lift his head.

"Would you do me one favor?" he managed to ask.

For some reason, everything went clear and unnaturally bright for a second, and Zach could see her pale face. Her gaze clung to his. "Anything, Mr. McGovern. All you need do is ask."

He worked his mouth for some spit so he could swallow. God, he wanted a drink. "Toss a stick of lit dynamite into that well. If I've gotta go, I want to take those goddamned snakes to hell with me."

"You're not going to hell, or to heaven either, for that matter," she informed him in a determined voice. "You're going to live, Mr. McGovern."

"Rattler bites are fatal," he mumbled.

"These won't be. Not if I have anything to say about it."

Using her sewing scissors, Kate cut McGovern's jeans and underwear straight up the front crease of each leg and laid them open like the peeling on a banana. She counted four bites, three deep, one superficial. His last words rang in her head. *Rattler bites are fatal.* She thanked God he was unconscious. What she had to do would be excruciatingly painful. Shoving the denim aside, she sheered off his long underwear to the length of a boy's shorts and shoved the knit cotton high on his thighs.

Unable to spare a moment to comfort Miranda who stood sobbing by the bed, Kate dashed to the kitchen, grabbed the butcher knife, and sterilized it as best she could in the cookstove fire. As she exited the kitchen, she grabbed the broom. By the time she returned to the bedroom, Mr. McGovern's lips had begun to turn blue, his tanned face a pasty color. Jerking back the counterpane, she seized hold of the bedsheet and slashed off several strips to serve as tourniquets.

"Get back, Miranda."

Holding the broom at an angle, Kate struck it sharply with the heel of her shoe. The length of wood snapped in two. She repeated the process until she had several pieces broken into manageable lengths. She made fast work of making tourniquets on McGovern's thighs between the puncture wounds and his torso.

She swiped sweat from her brow and glanced up. "Miranda, I want you to go out to the barn, find the big milking bucket, and fill it with dirt for me."

Miranda dragged a frightened gaze from the fang marks on Mr. McGovern's swollen legs. "Is he gonna die, Ma?"

"Not if you hurry and do as I say."

Miranda bolted for the doorway. The instant she was out of sight, Kate went to work on Zachariah McGovern with the knife. When she had made all the necessary incisions, she dropped to her knees and placed her mouth over one of the bites. She didn't know if it was the steely muscle that roped his thigh or the tautness of his swollen flesh, but it was nearly impossible for her to get suction. She worked the skin, took a long draw and then spat. *Gently, gently.* She knew she mustn't bruise the tissue surrounding the wound or it would slough off later.

The seconds sped into minutes. In such a hurry that she scarcely paused between suckles to breathe, Kate began to feel lightheaded. She continued working. This man had saved her daughter's life, and she could do no less for him.

When she had sucked the bites as clean as she could get them, she gently worked the surrounding flesh so the wounds would continue to bleed. Then she mixed a thick mud paste with the dirt Miranda had collected, praying she wasn't doing the wrong thing as she globbed the mixture onto McGovern's legs. She recalled hearing that animals bitten by venomous snakes went to mudholes and submerged themselves. Mud had drawing properties.

If it worked for animals, pray God it would work on a man.

Exhausted, Kate rubbed her hands clean and stood beside the bed, trying to think of something else she might do. There was nothing, save go for the doctor. Just in case McGovern might still be able to hear, she leaned over him and touched his arm.

"I'm going to town for Doc Willowby, Mr. McGovern. I'll be back as soon as I can."

He didn't respond. Kate had never seen anyone so close to death yet still breathing. She half expected every rise of his chest to be the last. She gathered Miranda into her arms and headed outside to find the horse.

"He saved me, Ma," Miranda said with a sob. "He heard the snakes before he was close enough to get hurt, but he comed down and got me anyways. That's how come he's all bit."

"I know, sweetness. He was very brave."

"Will he die?"

Kate nearly lost her balance on the front steps and braced a shoulder against the post to right herself. "No. He isn't going to die, Miranda. I won't let him."

When the doctor moved away from the bed, he threw an eerie, hunchbacked shadow that danced across the

unfinished plank walls of the bedroom. Dreading his prog-
nosis, Kate dragged her gaze from Zachariah McGovern's
inert, sheet-draped body.

"Only a miracle will save him."

She was prepared for that. Wasn't she? "Isn't there
anything more that I can do?"

"All we can do is pray. So much time passed before you
got him here and sucked the poison out that—" Doc Willowby stepped to the ladder-backed chair that Kate had
drawn to the bed. Placing a hand on the small of his back,
he bent stiffly to close his satchel, then turned back to her.
The spectacles perched on his bulbous nose gave him an
alert, owlish look. "I'll go back to town and round up
some men to help me move him to my clinic. You've got
enough to handle, caring for that child and trying to run
this place. He may linger for several hours."

"I can't just give up."

Doc ran a gnarled hand over his thinning gray hair.
"Kate, you're a good woman and I'm sure you're a fair
nurse, but care won't give him an edge. A man his size
could live through one snake bite, maybe two, but not
even a horse could survive four."

"As tiny as Miranda is, she wouldn't have survived even
one. If he had been less concerned with saving her, he
might never have been bitten. I can't give up, not until he
does."

The doctor sighed, then nodded. "I guess I'd feel the
same. And one thing's for sure, he'll get more attention
here than he would in town. Since the wife passed on, I
don't have a nurse. I delivered a baby this afternoon and
have another woman in labor, which is likely to keep me
away from the clinic for several hours. He'd be left to fare
on his own." He shrugged. "I have to apply my skills
where they'll do the most good."

Kate understood. This could be hard, cruel country. Folks hereabouts were lucky to have a doctor at all. She took a steadying breath. "I'm not blaming you. Tell me what to do."

As briefly as possible, Doc Willowby gave Kate instructions, most of which she knew, to keep McGovern comfortable, to force fluids down him, to keep the wounds packed with poultices. He had never known anyone to try mud on snakebites, but he didn't see how it could hurt unless it brought on infection. "I've heard of an antivenin they've come up with," he finished. "But if it's so, I haven't seen hide nor hair of it." He shrugged again, a habit that Kate guessed he had acquired to express his feeling of helplessness when illness or injury outflanked him. "I probably wouldn't know how to use the doggone stuff, anyway."

"You've done your best, Doc. That's all I or anyone else can ask of you. If Mr. McGovern were conscious, I'm sure he'd agree."

"He may start bleeding from the nose. And maybe from other places. Snakebites can cause that. It won't be pretty." He glanced around. "It'd be wise to keep the child out of here. Where is she, by the way? I ought to check her over."

Kate knew Miranda had come through the fall with scarcely a scratch. Being examined by a strange man would do her more harm than good. "She's a shy one. She must be off hiding somewhere."

"Would you call her, please?"

"I've already checked her over, Doc, and she's fine. You have a baby to deliver, remember?"

At mention of his other patients, the doctor picked up his satchel and moved through the house to the front door. "You sure she's okay?"

"Positive." Glancing out into the yard, Kate noticed the absence of her wagon out by the barn. If an emergency arose and she had to get her patient to town to see the doctor, she would need the buckboard. "On your way to town, could you stop by McGovern's and ask whoever's there to bring my wagon back?"

"Certainly." As he stepped onto the porch, the doctor said, "I'll be back first thing in the morning to make arrangements. When it's over, just cover him and pull the bedroom door closed."

The words made Kate flinch. She remembered Zachariah McGovern's concern for Miranda's safety after he brought her up from the well, the gentleness in his big, work-roughened hands as he ran them over her small person. She couldn't repay him for that by allowing death to take him. She just couldn't.

5

As soon as the doctor left, Kate went to the kitchen and browsed through Joseph's collection of remedies. She had been meaning to throw the bottles out, for the sight of them brought back unpleasant memories. Now she was glad she hadn't. As robust as her husband had looked, he had been afflicted with frequent complaints, real or imagined, Kate wasn't sure. No matter. She had several medications at her disposal, and she intended to put them to good use.

After much deliberation, she selected a bottle of Fairdale Bitter Water, which, among its many other attributes, was supposed to purify the blood. She also chose some Swift's Specific because she had read an advertisement in the *Morning Oregonian* that claimed it to be the best blood remedy in the world, a good treatment for skin eruptions, blood poisoning, frostbite, and many types of wounds.

Then she opened her mother's journal and turned to the back where the remedies for various illnesses were listed. Hops off the vine and seeped in vinegar were good for a poultice. Kate had hops growing along one side of the barn, and the vines were already leafed out. She sent Miranda to gather some. There was also a cure for fever that called for cloves, pulverized Peruvian bark, and port wine. All Kate had were the cloves.

She went into Joseph's study and searched his desk until she found his ready-reference cyclopedia, *The Little Giant*. Unfortunately, it listed nothing about snakebite. She did, however, find the ingredients for a fever remedy, and since she felt certain Mr. McGovern would probably be victimized by such, she located the *Aconitum napellus* in Joseph's medecine cupboard and took it to the bedroom with her.

Her patient looked so pale it frightened her. When Miranda came inside with the hops, Kate put them to soak in vinegar so she could apply them later. Then she went outside for another bucket of dirt. While repacking Mr. McGovern's snakebites with fresh mud, she heard her wagon pull up out front. Well aware that Miranda would dash off to hide somewhere, Kate hurriedly finished with the mud poultices and ran to answer the door.

A thin, gray-haired man of medium height stood on her front stoop, hat in hand. Dim lantern light from behind Kate fell across his face. His skin, she noticed, was as wrinkled as the excess hide on an old hound. One look into his blue eyes told her he had heard the news. From the dust on his faded jeans, she guessed that he had come here directly from the fields.

"Are you a friend?" she asked sadly.

The man fingered the brim of his dusty hat. "Just a hired hand, but I've knowed him a long stretch. I worked for him on his place along the Applegate. Been with him goin' on five years now. The name's Marcus Stone."

Ordinarily Kate wouldn't have considered allowing a strange man to enter the house. Shoving aside her uneasiness, she opened the door more widely. "Do come in, Mr.

Stone. Five years certainly qualifies you as a friend. Would you like to see him?"

"Yes'm." He stepped into the foyer and glanced uneasily around.

Kate pushed the door closed and led him to the sick-room. She stood aside as he approached the bed. Body rigid, his hat held respectfully at his waist, he gazed for a long while at her patient. Kate knew by his expression that it pained him to see his boss in such pitiful condition. With a ragged sigh of acceptance, he slapped his hat against his thigh. "He don't look too good."

Kate had to agree. "I've done all I can." She clasped her hands. "If I can just get him through this first twenty-four hours. . . ." She could think of nothing more to say.

Marcus Stone nodded. "I'll help you. Caring for an unconscious man ain't no job for a lady. The boss'd scalp me if he knowed I let you."

Kate hadn't thought of the proprieties. She felt heat rising up her neck. "I'm a widow, Mr. Stone. You needn't be concerned about my maidenly sensibilities."

In a sense, Kate knew she was lying. Her five years of marriage to Joseph had not left her greatly familiar with the masculine form. But that wasn't important. Thus far, she had scarcely been aware of Zachariah McGovern's gender, nor would she be as long as his life was hanging by a thread. He was just a very sick man she wanted desperately to save.

"I still think I oughta take care of his personal needs. Widow or no, there's some things a man don't want a lady seein'."

Reluctantly, Kate conceded the point. "Whatever you think he'd want is fine with me." She thought of the spare bedroom upstairs and balled her hands into fists at the prospect of having a healthy stranger stay the night. Aside from her concerns about how Miranda might handle it, she had her own anxieties. A woman couldn't be too cautious when she lived alone miles from town. "I've plenty of room to put you up."

"A pallet in the barn will suit me fine," he came back. "I got me a tendency to snore, and if I stayed in the house, I wouldn't sleep a wink for fear of keepin' y'all awake."

Kate tried to hide her relief.

Stone seemed to search for words. "If he needs bathin' during the night or starts to run a fever and needs wettin' down, you can holler at me from the porch."

Kate hadn't thought far enough ahead to consider how she meant to bathe McGovern. "That sounds fine. I'll appreciate your helping me care for him, I'm sure."

He rested solemn blue eyes on hers. "I'll do better than that. Until he's well and off your hands, I'll take over your chores here. You can't be nursin' him and runnin' a farm. Tomorrow, I'll mosey back over to our place and tell the hired hands to carry on without me until the boss is out of the woods."

Kate didn't argue. On a normal day, there weren't enough hours to get everything done. She thought of Henrietta, still lost in the fields, but now didn't seem the time to worry Stone with that. "It's very generous of you."

"No more than I ought," he replied. With a polite inclination of his head, he moved closer to the bed to look into the bucket sitting there.

Kate wasn't sure how he might react when he realized she had packed the snakebites with mud. "Have you eaten?" she asked, hoping to distract him.

He seized the bucket by its handle and glanced up. "No, but I don't feel hungry, nohow."

Neither did she. Running a hand over her hair, she felt stray tendrils trailing from the braid encircling her head. Her gaze moved to the bucket, and she braced for a dressing down.

"Smart move, using mud packs," he said.

"I didn't know if it was or not," she admitted shakily.

"If anything'll save him, mud will. I've seen more than one bit dog waller in mud and pull through. If it works for dogs, it should work on him." He clamped his hat back on. "I'll git you some more makings to use during the night. As soon as the mud starts to dry, you should pack on fresh."

Kate was so relieved that he wasn't angry over her use of the mud that she nearly smiled. "While you're outside, I'll gather up some quilts and a pillow. It's liable to get mighty chilly out there in that barn before morning."

He moved toward the door. "My hide's tough. And I can sleep anywheres."

Sleep. The word made her aware of how exhausted she was. After seeing Mr. Stone to the door and sending Miranda off to bed, she gathered some bedding and returned to the sickroom to sit beside her patient. As uncomfortable as the straight-backed chair was, she opted against bringing in her rocker. If she got too cozy, she might fall asleep. Unless she missed her guess, it would be a long night. Not that she would begrudge this man a second of it.

Studying McGovern's face, she searched for any sign of life. Aside from his shallow, rapid breathing, he still looked like a corpse. Kate's chest tightened with regret. If she had it to do over again, she knew she would ride to his farm and beg his help. Miranda's life had been at risk. But she couldn't help feeling to blame for his condition.

His face was burnished and weathered from too much sun, with lines etched at the corners of his eyes and deep smile grooves bracketing his mouth. It was a face that looked lived-in, one that spoke of joys and heartaches, hopes and disappointments.

Her attention shifted to the scars along his jaw and neck. She hadn't noticed them before and suspected she did so now only because of his pallor and because his head rested against the stark white pillowcase. The glazed, drawn flesh reminded her of the scars on Miranda's right hand, caused by severe burns.

As if her steady regard disturbed him, McGovern groaned and flailed with one arm. The sheet slid downward to reveal his naked chest and shoulders. Kate blinked. While she was out of the room, Doc Willowby must have pulled off her patient's underwear. Recalling how she had slid the sheet up Mr. McGovern's thighs earlier to repack his bites with mud, she blushed in spite of herself. The man was stripped stark. A tad higher with the sheet and— She worried her lip, suddenly very much aware of her patient as a member of the opposite sex.

She scarcely knew this man, yet here he lay in her downstairs bedroom, unconscious and as naked as the day he was born. She imagined those dark eyelashes lifting, those hazel eyes turning to her. Now she was glad that Marcus Stone had insisted on staying to tend his boss's personal needs.

And if that wasn't idiotic, Kate didn't know what was. She was a grown woman with a child. A naked man shouldn't be a curiosity to her, much less an embarrassment. Memories slid unbeckoned into her mind, dark and shifting, like shadows from a dream. Joseph coming up behind her in the dark and pressing her forward over the dresser. His hands groping for the hem of her nightgown. His hardness thrusting into her. The panting sounds he made as he did his husbandly duty to beget a son.

As always, the memories filled Kate with a need to escape, and she shoved up from the chair. She set about tidying the sickroom and turned her thoughts to those first horrifying minutes after Mr. McGovern had brought Miranda up from the well. Kate had no idea how she had managed to get a man his size onto his horse and then into the house. Thank goodness there was a bedroom on the first floor.

His chapped lips working as though to speak, McGovern moaned again and tossed his dark head upon the pillow. Concerned, she touched his forehead and discovered he felt feverish. Extremely feverish. Wasting no time, she poured water from the pitcher into the basin and began bathing his face. He muttered something and made a feeble grab for her wrist.

"It's all right, Mr. McGovern. Everything's all right."

Kate prayed those words wouldn't prove to be a lie.

Before the next few minutes were out, Kate had cause once again to thank heaven that Marcus Stone had insisted on staying over. Before the man returned to the house with the bucket of dirt, Zachariah McGovern had begun to thrash, and it soon became apparent that her patient was delirious. When she tried to anchor his flailing arms, he fought her. Even in his weakened state, his strength was great, and Kate couldn't subdue him.

"Fire!" he cried hoarsely. "Jesus Christ, it's on fire!"

Kate caught his arm as it swung upward and strained with all her power to hold it back down on the bed. "Mr. McGovern, please. You're dreaming."

"Get out," he rasped. "Jump to me, for God's sake!"

Swinging with his free arm, McGovern caught Kate alongside the head with his wrist. The blow left her blinking away black spots. Left with no alternative, she threw her body across the man's chest so she could bring her weight into play. It wasn't enough. Tempered by years of doing heavy farm work, he threw her off as if she weighed no more than a child. She landed rump first on the floor, several feet from the bed. Pain shot from her abused tailbone up her spine.

She realized that her patient was now sitting up and looking as if he intended to stand. Kate scrambled to her feet. She had just started toward him when Marcus Stone reentered the bedroom.

"Help me," she cried. "He's out of his head with fever."

The hired hand quickly stowed the bucket of dirt near the door and dashed to assist. Between the two of them, they wrestled McGovern to his back. Using the leftover linen that Kate had torn into strips for tourniquets, Marcus secured his boss's wrists to slats in the headboard, his ankles to the footboard.

"Snakes!" McGovern cried. "Jesus Christ Almighty . . ."

The horror in his voice was so real and he sounded so lucid that Kate cast a frantic glance around, almost expecting to see rattlers in the bedroom. McGovern strained against the bindings that held his arms. She knew that in his mind, he was back inside the well, surrounded by vipers. The terror she read in his glazed, hazel eyes tore at her. Until that instant, she hadn't truly realized what it had cost him to go into that well after her daughter.

He gave one last violent pull against the bindings, the veins in his neck and face bulging with the strain. A trickle of blood came from his nose, and when he finally threw back his head in defeat, Kate saw watery pinkness streaming from his eyes.

"Oh, dear God."

Marcus Stone made an inarticulate sound that bespoke the shock he felt.

"It's one of the symptoms," Kate hastened to assure him. "Doc warned me. The venom thins the blood." She scooted closer and used a strip of unused linen to wipe her patient's face. "Oh, Mr. McGovern. There are no snakes. Shhhh." Kate smoothed damp waves of dark hair from his brow. "It's all right. There are no snakes."

Still winded from the struggle, Marcus Stone stood by the bed. "It might help if you called him by his first name."

"Zachariah," she said softly. "It's all right. Truly it is. You're out of the well and safe now."

The soothing tone of her voice seemed to have the desired effect. The tension eased from McGovern's body, and after a moment, he closed his eyes. Kate pushed wearily to her feet.

Concerned, Marcus asked, "You okay? Looks like he thumped you a good one."

With a nod, Kate straightened her bodice and skirt. "It's him I'm worried about. He's burning up."

Marcus touched a hand to his boss's forehead. "Ain't he just. We gotta cool him down."

Stone had no sooner spoken than McGovern suddenly arched off the bed. His body began to jerk. For a moment, Kate just stood there, frozen and mindless. The clacking and grinding of McGovern's teeth finally jerked her back to her senses. "Oh, lands, he's being taken with fits."

Marcus raced from the room. Moments later, he returned with a galvanized basin from the kitchen, which he had filled with water. Tearing back the sheet, he began wringing a wet rag over his boss's body. Kate had a vague impression of long, muscular limbs spread-eagled on the bed, of a torso roped with muscle, and of—

She jerked her gaze from the dusky juncture of McGovern's thighs. A body was just that, a body. His was just made a tad differently than hers, and now was no time to note the dissimilarities. She grabbed the cloth she had used earlier and began helping Marcus Stone wet McGovern's feverish skin.

From that second on, Kate did what she had to do, the devil take propriety. Marcus Stone made no more mention of what ladies should or shouldn't see.

They were all that stood between Zachariah McGovern and death.

6

Over the next three days, Kate learned the true meaning of exhaustion. With scarcely a wink of sleep and very little to eat, she drove herself to set one foot before the other, to do whatever had to be done to keep Zachariah McGovern alive.

It wasn't easy to cheat death.

As reluctant as she had been to let Marcus Stone stay over, Kate didn't know what she would have done without his help. He not only spelled her at Zachariah McGovern's bedside, but also kept the chores done, which included milking Henrietta, who had wandered home the second night.

As the endless vigil wore on, Kate stopped feeling nervous while Stone was in the house. She couldn't say exactly why. Maybe because he seemed as ill at ease in her presence as she did in his. It was a little difficult to feel threatened by a man who nearly tripped over his own feet when he was around her.

On the fourth afternoon, Doc Willowby came by to check on Kate's patient and finally said the words she had been praying to hear. "I don't believe it, but I'll be danged if I don't think he might pull through."

Kate stared down at her still-unconscious patient through a blur of relieved tears.

Doc smiled and sighed. "I think it's time for you and Mr. Stone here to get some well-deserved rest." He drew the sheet higher on McGovern's chest. "He's resting easy. The initial danger has passed. All we can do now is force fluids down him and pray infection doesn't set in. In his weakened condition, that would kill him for sure."

Kate turned to the doctor. "Is there any way that I can stave off infection?"

Doc pursed his lips. "Hot poultices, maybe. As hot as the skin can stand and applied for thirty minutes every four hours. Other than that, there's nothing."

Kate exchanged glances with Marcus Stone. "We can do that."

Doc clamped a hand over Kate's shoulder. "First, you get some sleep, young woman."

Marcus seconded that. "He's right, Miz Blakely. You're beginnin' to look like you was rode hard and put away wet." Glancing back at Doc Willowby, he added, "She ain't hardly let her head touch a pillow once. I offered to spell her so she could sleep, but she wouldn't have none of it."

"You see that she does now," the doctor ordered. He gave Kate a fatherly pat. "I'll come back out at the end of the week. If you need me before then, Mr. Stone can ride in and fetch me."

Kate followed the doctor from the bedroom. "You truly think he'll make it, Doc?"

Doc Willowby opened the front door and then paused. "God willing, yes. You've worked a miracle, young woman. In my line of work, I don't see many."

"Only God works miracles."

"Sometimes through good people like you," the doctor retorted. "Mind you, now, he won't be doing a jig any time soon. That poison has played heck with his system, and it'll take a spell to work its way out. He's liable to suffer more fever. And he'll be as weak as a scoured calf for weeks. Start him off on broth, then slowly add solids into his diet."

Kate leaned an arm against the door as she watched the doctor go down the porch steps. The relief she felt weighed on her body like a thousand pounds of lead. Now that the worst was over, she couldn't muster the will to move or even think why she should. She felt Marcus Stone step up behind her.

"Why don't you feed that girl of yours her supper early and git yourself some sleep? After I git the chores done, I'll stay handy this evenin' to take care of the boss."

Kate blinked and straightened. Miranda. Her mind was so numb, she had nearly forgotten her daughter.

"I'd feed her," Marcus added. "But she's as skittish around me as a preacher in a whorehouse."

Startled by the analogy, Kate glanced over her shoulder.

A flush spread up Stone's swarthy neck, and he cleared his throat. "Pardon the talk. I ain't much for parlor manners." He buried his hands in his pant pockets. "She is a nervous little thing. Even if I could catch her, I doubt she'd eat what I put before her."

Kate touched Marcus's sleeve and forced herself to move past him back into the foyer. Supper for Miranda, and then bed. She could keep going for a few more minutes.

Along about dusk, Kate clawed her way up from a fog of sleep and lay rigid in the bed listening. Something had startled her awake, but what? The house was silent. Then she heard a door slam shut downstairs. Heavy footfalls echoed across the plank flooring. Marcus? Kate heard a voice and strained her ears.

"You answer me, girl. I asked you where your ma is."

Kate bolted upright. Not Marcus. She threw the quilts back and leaped to her feet, not taking time to grab her wrapper. Ryan Blakely was downstairs, and from the sound of it, he had cornered Miranda.

Kate dashed from the bedroom and along the hall to the landing. Leaning over the rail, she looked down upon Ryan's dark head and bent shoulders and glimpsed Miranda's gray pinafore when he moved. He had her daughter by the shoulder and was giving her a shake. Anger broke over Kate in a hot wave, washing away all trace of sleepiness. Using the banister to swing her weight, she cleared three steps in a leap.

"Let go of her!"

At the sound of Kate's voice, Ryan snapped erect but didn't loosen his hold on Miranda. "Somebody has to teach her manners."

Kate descended the remainder of the stairs and squared off with her brother-in-law, refusing to be intimidated by his much greater height and the broad span of his shoulders. With a cry of fury, she wrested her daughter away from him. "Her manners are fine, and even if they weren't, you have no right—"

Ryan jutted his chin. "No right? No right to discipline my brother's child? The child he asked me to look after if something ever happened to him?"

Kate gave Miranda a little push to get her feet moving. "Go out to the kitchen, sweetness."

Miranda didn't need to be told twice. With a wide-eyed glance back at her uncle, she tore down the hall. She hesitated outside the door of the sickroom. For a moment, Kate thought she meant to enter. But then the child continued toward the kitchen, in such a hurry that she thumped into the door before she got it fully open. Kate waited for Miranda to disappear into the room beyond before she turned back to confront Ryan Blakely.

"How dare you come into this house and raise your voice at my daughter?"

Ryan's handsome features went taut with outrage. "This is a Blakely roof, Kate, bought and paid for with Blakely sweat."

"And *I* am a Blakely," Kate cut in. "Joseph's widow. By law, this house belongs to me now. You've no authority here."

Ryan drew his lips back in a sneer. "Oh, so now we're quoting the law, are we? Interesting, very interesting. Maybe I'll just pay a little call on the sheriff and remind him that my brother disappeared under mighty peculiar circumstances."

The threat snapped Kate's mouth closed. She stared into Ryan's blue eyes and read the madness there. He truly would stop at nothing, and in that, if for no other reason, Kate found cause to fear him. Not for her own sake, but for Miranda's. Like Joseph, Ryan could lose all sense of reason in the blink of an eye. He wasn't above making outlandish accusations to stir up trouble so he could have his way.

She took a steadying breath, wanting to kick herself for losing her temper. That wasn't and never would be the way to handle this man. In a cajoling voice, she said, "Ryan, please. Why do you come here and do this? Joseph's been gone nearly six months. As you can see, we're fine. You've done your duty to Miranda and me. It's time you went back to Seattle and your own life."

Kate's gentler tone had the desired effect. The tension slowly eased from Ryan's shoulders, and the mindless anger faded from his eyes. The apparent effortlessness with which he changed moods frightened Kate more than anything. His lazy smile made her nerves prickle as he ran his gaze over her rumpled flannel gown. "You and Miranda have become my life, Kate. You know that. Joseph asked me to step into his shoes if anything ever happened to him. What kind of brother would I be if I went back on my word?"

Into Joseph's shoes? Revulsion constricted Kate's throat. With his blue eyes and ebony hair, Ryan cut a fine figure, and when he chose, he could hide his true nature behind a facade of charm. Women who didn't really know him probably found him attractive. But not her. She knew how quickly that smile of his could turn to a snarl.

"Why are you abed so early?" he asked with what seemed like genuine concern. "Are you ill?"

Kate struggled to follow his change of subject. She had done the same many a time with Joseph, caught up and pulled this way and that by his mood swings, like a leaf in a whirlwind. "Ill?" She swept a hank of dark hair from her eyes. "No. I've just had very little rest these last few days."

"Why? I've offered to lend a hand any time you need it. If something's wrong, why didn't you come into town and get me?"

Ryan would be the last person Kate would ever go to for help. The less he came around her farm, the better. She glanced uneasily down the hall at the sickroom door. "Our neighbor, Mr. McGovern. He—um—" She fixed her gaze on Ryan's burnished face. His chiseled features were very like her dead husband's, unnervingly so. "He was bitten by rattlers and nearly died. I've been caring for him. This evening is the first—"

"You've what?" Ryan followed her gaze to the closed bedroom door. "You have a man in this house?"

Before Kate could reply, Ryan started toward the sickroom. She stepped into his path to bar his way. "Don't. He's far too ill to be distur—"

Ryan seized Kate by her upper arm and jerked her toward him. "As God is my witness, I should beat you," he said with a hiss. "How dare you bring a man into this house? What of the child? Have you no decency at all? My brother barely six months dead!"

"It isn't like that." Kate tried to keep the cajoling note in her voice, but this time it wasn't going to work. She knew that by the glint that had come into Ryan's eyes. "Truly, Ryan, it isn't at all like that."

He glanced at her nightgown again, then lifted his gaze to her hair. "Lewd is woman."

Coming from anyone else, the comment would have seemed absurd. But Ryan meant it. Kate could almost feel the anger welling up from within him. Despite her effort to speak calmly, her voice turned tremulous. "I tell you, it isn't like that. He saved Miranda's life! She fell into a well, and there was a den of snakes down there. McGovern went after her. He was bitten four times. How could I let him die? I had no choice but to—"

"No choice? You had a choice, Kate. If you had let me move in and take care of you, this circumstance never would have arisen." He gave her a shake. "But no. You turned me away. And now look what I've walked in to find. You in your nightdress before it's even fully dark, with a strange man in the house."

Kate tried to speak, but again he cut her off.

"Didn't I tell you that you needed me here? Didn't I? If I had been in charge, Miranda wouldn't have been whiling away time unsupervised and fallen into a well in the first place. And if by chance she had, I would have been here to fetch her out."

"She wasn't unsuper—"

"What more must happen to convince you that you should abide by your dead husband's wishes and marry me?"

Just the thought made Kate shudder. Ryan drew her closer and pressed his face near hers. "You hated him, didn't you?"

"No. Ryan, please—"

His fingers dug more deeply into her flesh. "That's the truth. From the first, he sensed your waywardness and tried to save you. Instead of thanking him, you hated him for it."

"No . . ."

"I wouldn't be surprised to learn you killed him."

Kate drew in a sharp breath. "That's madness."

"Is it? I know what a harsh disciplinarian he was. Joseph made no secret of the trouble he had keeping you and that child in line. I can't count the times he and I joined in prayer that God would give him the wisdom to save you from yourself, not to mention the strength he needed to resist your seductive ways."

Kate tried to pry his fingers from her arm. "I was a good wife, and Miranda has always been an obedient little girl."

Ryan leaned closer. "He told me about the scissors, Kate. You killed him, didn't you? All that remains is for me to find out how." Still holding onto her arm, Ryan flung her against the wall so hard that the back of her head cracked against the planks. "Where did you hide his body?"

Kate blinked away spots. Frantically, she tried to sort out her thoughts so she could reason with him. But how could she respond to such insanity?

With a sneer of disgust, Ryan finally let go of her. "God

help you, because no one else can, not if you insist on living out here alone." He glanced toward the kitchen. "At least let me remove Miranda from this near occasion of sin."

Those words pushed Kate beyond caring if she lost her temper. "How could I possibly be sinning with an unconscious man? How, Ryan? The evil way your mind works makes me sick. God forbid you should take Miranda, or even be around her."

"God forbid that she should grow up seeing her mother's harlot ways," he retorted. "You ask how you could sin with an unconscious man? In your thoughts, that's how. Read the Bible, woman! Your body is probably weeping with lust even as you stand there. You need a God-fearing man to discipline you. I'm your only hope of salvation. The day will come when you'll regret that you refused to marry me."

Kate pressed her palms against the rough wood behind her. "Get out," she rasped. "Get out of my house."

Ryan stood there, fists clenched at his sides. For a moment, Kate feared he might strike her and she braced herself for the blow. Then, as if the wildness relinquished its hold on him, he flexed his shoulders and made a visible effort to relax. "I'll leave," he said raggedly. "But you haven't seen the last of me. I'll be out of town this next week to move my things down here from Seattle. Once that's done, I'll be back. Mark my words!"

With that, he strode across the foyer and opened the door. After he'd stepped out onto the porch, Kate ran and slammed the door closed, then pressed her trembling body against it.

"Do you hear me, Kate? I'll be back!" he called from outside. "There's nothing I can do to prevent you from burning in hell, but I won't stand by and allow Miranda to become a victim. Do you understand me? Your shadow, that's what I'll be. You won't take a breath that I won't know about!"

Her mind beset by the echo of Joseph's voice and memories she tried constantly to keep at bay, Kate pressed her hands over her ears.

Zach stirred in his sleep, troubled by crazy dreams. A woman's frightened voice and that of an angry man sliced through the mists of his unconsciousness and tugged persistently at him.

I should beat you!

Zach moaned and tried to battle his way up from the darkness. He heard the woman cry out and knew she needed help.

The voices receded, then grew louder again, but jumbled. Zach strained to listen, but only a few words came clear.

Your body—weeping with lust. You need a God-fearing man to discipline you.

With sheer strength of will, Zach managed to push up on one elbow. The shadowy room seemed to rock on its axis, then go into a dizzying swirl. He pushed feebly at the covers. Then a blanket of blackness dropped over him, and he fell back onto the bed, all awareness lost to him.

Still shaking with nervous reaction, Kate moved quietly through the dimly lit kitchen, her ears pricked for the slightest sound.

"Miranda?" she called softly. "Sweetness, where are you? Your uncle Ryan is gone, darling. Won't you come out now?"

Nothing.

Kate paused by the table and gazed out the window at the gloaming that had settled over the yard. The old willow tree cast a dark silhouette against the sky, its branches dancing like eerie specters in the evening breeze. Surely Miranda wouldn't have ventured outside when it was so near to nightfall.

Panic tried to clutch at Kate, but she warded it off. Miranda was probably still in the house. All she had to do was find her. And if she wasn't, Kate could call Marcus. He would be doing evening chores. In the barn, most likely. If she asked, he'd surely help her search the outbuildings and fields.

A board creaked. Kate whirled toward the sound. The pantry door stood partially open, the enclosure beyond dark and silent. She moved slowly toward it. "Miranda?"

With a sweaty palm, Kate pushed the door all the way open and stepped into the darkness. It took a moment for her eyes to adjust. After peering into the shadows for what seemed an endless time, she could finally make out Miranda huddled on the floor in one corner. Her movements jerky, the child rocked quickly back and forth, her chin tucked against her chest.

Filled with a new kind of fear, Kate moved toward her. "Miranda?"

The child didn't answer or otherwise acknowledge that she heard. Kate sank to her knees beside her. Miranda continued rocking and didn't look up. Kate's attention was snagged by another movement, and she glanced down to see that Miranda had her right hand cupped protectively in her left, her outside fingers massaging those within.

Kate closed her eyes on a rush of rage. Damn Ryan Blakely. Damn him. She swallowed hard. Then she forced herself to grow calm. Very carefully, she drew her child's rigid body into her arms, then pushed to her feet.

"I'll rock you, Miranda, if you'd like to be rocked. Would you like that?"

Miranda's only response was to press her wet cheek against Kate's breast. Feeling leaden and helpless, she carried her daughter back into the kitchen and sat with her in the rocker by the stove. She didn't allow herself to look into Miranda's eyes. She knew what she would see. A terrifying nothingness.

Battling tears, Kate cuddled her daughter close and set the chair into motion with a push of her bare feet. "You don't have to feel afraid, sweetness. Truly, you don't. I won't let anyone hurt you. I promise. Never again."

Miranda remained rigid in her arms. Kate tried to massage away the stiffness.

"It's just you and me," she whispered. "From now on. When Uncle Ryan comes to visit, he may raise his voice, but he can't do anything bad to us. If he did, I'm sure he knows the sheriff would come and take him away. We're safe. Do you hear? Just you and me. For always."

Kate listened to the urgent creak of the rocker slats and pushed less frequently to strike a more soothing rhythm. How could she calm Miranda if she revealed fear herself?

"From now on, every day is going to be ours to do whatever we want." She forced a note of cheerfulness into her shaky voice. "We'll grow pretty flowers all around the house. Every color of the rainbow, hm? And I'll make you dozens of new dresses. With icicles galore on your petticoats. We'll bake cookies whenever the mood hits. And every evening we'll sit here by the stove and have story time. Won't that be nice? I'll tell you a story now," Kate whispered. "Would you like that?"

She didn't expect Miranda to answer, but the silence still caught at her heart so that she wanted to weep. Miranda had been doing so well these last few weeks.

Only days ago, Kate had been marveling at the transformation, and now this. With one maniacal tirade, Ryan Blakely had undone months of healing.

"Let me see," Kate went on. "I bet you'd like to hear the story about the time my pa went clear to Jacksonville to buy me a kitten."

And so the story began, and Kate was swept back through the years to the innocence of her childhood, to a time before the death of her parents, when she had been safe and loved and fiercely protected. The memories made her long to regress from adulthood, to become that child again. She yearned for her mother's arms, for the feel of her pa's whiskers scrubbing playfully at her neck.

Oh, yes, to be that child again. And to take Miranda with her. Not to have to deal with the reality in which they found themselves entrapped. Kate knew that Miranda, in her own way, was also trying to escape, not into memories but from them, by separating herself from the world around her. What terrified Kate was how successful the child seemed to be at it. What if, during one of these spells, Miranda became lost in her unreality and never found her way back?

7

The next morning, Miranda awoke bright-eyed and smiling, as though the visit from Ryan Blakely had never occurred. Kate watched her daughter closely throughout the day, but as the hours wore on, she detected nothing unusual in her behavior. It was as if the child had erased the previous night from her mind.

Alarmed on the one hand, relieved on the other, Kate could only be thankful that this spell hadn't lasted. A few months back, Miranda might have stayed hidden within herself for days, staring at nothing, constantly rocking, her eyes reflecting the nothingness into which she had taken refuge.

At noon, Marcus Stone came up to the house to eat. To avoid any possible conflict, which she feared might send Miranda into a relapse, Kate fed her daughter early and sent her upstairs for her nap so she wouldn't see Marcus when he came.

Usually a quiet man, Marcus surprised Kate by growing chatty while he ate. He updated her on how the sow's seven new piglets were doing, asked how much wool her sheep had yielded during the spring shearing, mentioned that the carrots were coming up in the garden, and then complained a while about the fickle weather, which had been sunny one day and raining buckets the next.

In kind, Kate filled Marcus in on his boss's condition. "He seems to be asleep, now," she said as she turned from the sink. Still clutching a half-peeled potato, which would go into their soup for supper, she waved her hand to convey her lack of words. "I can't describe the difference, exactly. But I don't think he's still actually unconscious. I keep expecting him to jerk awake, but he doesn't."

Marcus seemed to ponder that for a moment. "Nothing to fret over, I reckon. He almost died. His body must need the sleep to heal itself up."

"But to never awaken, not even once? It worries me."

"Maybe he has—just for a minute or two—when we wasn't around."

Kate considered that. "I suppose that's possible."

Marcus swirled the dregs of coffee in his mug and took a slow sip. As he lowered the mug, he regarded Kate with a quizzical expression. "I'd think if anything would've woke him up, that fella raisin' sand in here last evenin' would've."

Kate turned back to the sink and said nothing, not because she wished to be rude but because she didn't know how to reply.

"It ain't none of my concern, but I'm gonna ask anyways. Who in hell was that man?"

"Please don't swear, Mr. Stone," Kate chided softly. "I have a child upstairs."

"Where I come from, there's a difference between cursin' and swearin'." She heard his chair scrape across the planks. "I take it you don't wanna talk about it."

"Not really," Kate admitted.

Marcus sighed. "I heard him out on the porch, there.

Yellin' like a wild man. I seen you close the door behind him, so I knowed you was all right, and I didn't reckon I should come up and stick my nose where it wasn't wanted."

Kate dug the blade of her paring knife deep into the potato.

"Just the same, I thought I oughta say somethin'. You bein' alone and all, sometimes it's nice to know you got friends." He cleared his throat, and from the corner of her eye, she saw him put his hat back on. "If he ever comes around ag'in, and you need somebody to stomp his ass, I'm usually wearin' my shit kickers."

With that, he strode from the kitchen. The butchered potato fell from Kate's hands into the sink, forgotten. She curled her fingers into tight fists and closed her eyes.

What Marcus Stone didn't understand, what he couldn't possibly understand, was that Ryan posed a far greater threat than that of physical harm.

The next three days took on a monotonous sameness. Zachariah McGovern continued to sleep like the dead, not even rousing when Kate spooned broth down him or when Marcus bathed him. The weather lived up to Marcus's opinion of it and remained fickle, burying the valley under rolling clouds one day, then steaming it dry under a relentless sun the next.

Only one spot of excitement occurred—another visitation from Nosy, Zachariah McGovern's pesky dog. To Kate's surprise, Miranda and the dog developed an almost instantaneous and mutual attachment, and because they did, Kate hadn't the heart to ask Marcus to take Nosy home. To keep the dog out of her roses, Kate kept him tethered to the porch post during the day when Miranda wasn't playing with him and brought him into the house at night.

With Nosy for a companion, Miranda ventured out of doors more bravely than before, and Kate grew accustomed to hearing the dog's bark and Miranda's laughter echoing across the fields as they romped together. Though she cautioned Miranda not to wander, Kate still worried. On warmer days, the rattlers might leave their den, and Miranda could stumble across one.

The moment Kate mentioned it, Marcus took care of that worry, and McGovern's last request before losing consciousness was finally granted. Marcus rode to town, located a miner, bought some dynamite, and blew the snake den to kingdom come.

Though Kate felt a mite guilty because Zachariah McGovern didn't really require much nursing now, she remained indoors and let Marcus continue to do the farm chores. One never knew when McGovern might take another fever or wake up, and Kate felt she should be close at hand, just in case. Marcus agreed.

That day, Kate found herself, for the first time in her memory, completely finished with her daily household chores by early afternoon. After putting Miranda down for her nap, she deep cleaned every cupboard and shelf she could think of, scrubbed the windows, and then stood forlornly in the kitchen, wondering what she might do next. It seemed sinful to read while the sun was still out. As long as there was light to see by, she should put her hands to a useful task.

What a quandary. She had no material to sew. No seeds that she could plant. Marcus already had the garden free of weeds. She had all the mending and darning done. A stew for supper was already simmering on the stove, and four loaves of fresh bread were cooling on the rack.

Driven to find something she might do, Kate crept into the sickroom to check the toes of Mr. McGovern's wool socks, which she had washed, blocked, and left neatly folded over the tops of his boots. There were no holes in the sock's toes, none on the heels, or even any worn spots. As she straightened, she spied his jeans, which lay freshly washed and folded on the bureau. She recalled running her scissors straight up the front crease of each leg. There was some mending she could do.

Glad to have a mission, Kate carried the ruined jeans to the kitchen and sat down in her rocker by the stove to begin stitching up the legs. As she sewed, she watched the seam that grew behind her needle, the frantic path she had taken that day with her scissors. She didn't suppose Mr. McGovern would be any too pleased with the mending job, but he might wear the pants to work in his fields.

After her nap, Miranda, accompanied by Nosy, joined Kate in the kitchen, and they spent a pleasant afternoon, Kate telling stories while she sewed, Miranda listening, Nosy snoozing.

Toward dusk, the house grew suddenly dark, and Kate's poor eyesight forced her to set her sewing aside. There had been a time when she had been able to do tedious work while the light was dim, but those days seemed gone forever. She stepped to the kitchen window to peer outside. Black clouds hovered over the mountains.

"Another storm," she murmured. "My guess is it'll hit tonight sometime."

Miranda came to stand beside her. "I hate 'em, Ma. I wish there'd never be storms."

Kate bent to give her daughter a hug. "If there were never any storms, we wouldn't have an excuse to sleep together."

Miranda gave a reluctant smile. "I reckon there's one good thing."

Kate straightened and ruffled her child's hair. "Since

we know the storm is coming, we can start the night out right, hm? When I tuck you in, I'll climb right in after you. We'll cuddle. And I'll tell stories. Won't that be fun?"

Though Miranda nodded, Kate noticed that her gaze clung to the window, her huge eyes reflecting her dread.

"Can Nosy sleep with us?" Miranda asked.

Kate curled a finger under her daughter's chin and lifted her small face. "Miranda Elspeth Blakely! You haven't let that flea-bitten, mangy animal sleep on my fresh-scrubbed sheets?"

Miranda worried her bottom lip. "He only takes up just one little spot."

Kate cast a disparaging glance at the large dog. One little spot? "I have never in my life slept with a dog, and I don't intend to start now. And I don't want you letting him get into your bed again. Is that clear? He should be perfectly comfortable sleeping on the rug."

"Yes, Ma." Miranda gave Nosy a woebegone look. "I'm sorry, Nosy. I guess you can't sleep with me no more."

At the sound of his name, the dog cracked open one eye.

"I should say not," Kate said firmly.

That night, Kate fell asleep with Nosy's head beside hers on the pillow, his wet nose pressed against her neck.

Thunder cracked across the sky, and an instant later, a flash of lightning illuminated the room. Zach stared at the ceiling, uncertain where he was. It was a funny thing about ceilings; they all looked the same until you woke up to see an unfamiliar one.

There was a storm raising hell outside. He knew that much. But he didn't think the sounds were what woke him. He blinked and lay still, absorbing the feel of the room. Slowly his senses sharpened, and he realized what had disturbed him. Warmth was pressed against his side. Trembling warmth.

Zach tensed and tucked in his chin to look. A small hand was clenched in his chest hair. Attached to the hand was a thin, flannel-draped little arm. What the hell? He squinted to see better, and saw that a head of tangled, dark hair was buried in his armpit. Miranda.

It all flooded back to him. The well. The snakes. He was in Kate Blakely's house. And damned if he wasn't still alive. Zach started to move, and pain exploded in his legs. He went limp against the mattress. It felt as if a horse had run back and forth over the top of him.

Thunder cracked again, and Miranda flinched. Zach heard Nosy whine. He lifted his head once more and strained to see, finally making out the dog, who stood beside the bed, nudging the child's back. Still a bit befuddled, Zach took a second to realize that Miranda was terrified by the thunder and that Nosy was trying to soothe her. It took him another couple of seconds to assimilate the fact that, for reasons beyond him, Miranda had sought him out for comfort, instead of going to her mother.

About a half minute after coming to that conclusion, Zach registered the crisp feel of ironed linen against his bare skin. He wasn't dressed for entertaining ladies.

He considered sending Miranda on her way, but three things forestalled him. One was that he didn't want to part with any of his chest hair, and from the way she was holding on, he didn't think he could pry her loose without losing a fistful. The second was that he barely had the strength to move, let alone to make someone else. And third, the child was clearly afraid. Zach didn't have the heart to shove her away.

Instead, he let his head fall back to the pillow and fumbled with the sheet to make sure it was tucked between their bodies. The instant he curled his arm around her, Miranda burrowed closer, her bony little knees scrambling for purchase, her hand tugging sharply on his chest hair. Zach winced but allowed her to settle in, a little self-conscious because of where she had chosen to duck her head. He had never slept with someone's face pressed just below his armpit. But he decided that if it didn't bother her, it didn't him.

Thunder ripped across the sky once more, but this time the child didn't react. Zach stared at the ceiling, more than a little humbled that she had come to trust him, a virtual stranger, so completely. He recalled their nightmarish ascent from the well. Not really a stranger, he guessed. Not after coming through something like that together.

Which was probably why she had come to him. He had been her savior once, and now she felt threatened again by the storm. Even as weak as he was, he probably seemed as large and untouchable as a mountain to her.

Zach curled a hand around her side and marveled at the fragile network of her ribs beneath his fingertips. Just like her ma, no bigger than a minute.

Smiling, he went back to sleep on that thought.

A loud crack of thunder woke Kate with a start. Groggy, she reached to put a comforting arm around her daughter and found only an empty bed beside her. She opened her eyes and sat up. Both Nosy and Miranda were gone.

Alarmed, Kate slid from bed. As she reached for her wrapper, lightning slashed across the sky and filled the room with a bolt of eerie, blue-white light. She shoved her arms into the sleeves of her wrapper and ran from the bedroom.

She knew from experience that Miranda wouldn't respond to her call if she was frightened, which she undoubtedly was with a storm raging. Kate hurried along the short corridor. When she reached the landing, another clap of thunder shook the house. She gave an involuntary start and gripped the bannister.

Dear God, where was Miranda? She would be terrified. Battling her own demons, Kate descended the stairs, her skin prickling and clammy. She had to find her daughter.

After searching the entire house, Kate began to grow frantic. She had checked all Miranda's hiding places, and the child was nowhere to be found. Kate returned upstairs and looked one more time beneath each of the beds. Then she went back down to stand in the foyer, determined not to panic. Miranda would never venture outside during a storm. Never. She had to be inside the house somewhere.

Thinking she might double-check the kitchen, Kate retraced her steps along the downstairs hall. As she passed the sickroom, she noticed that the door was ajar. Kate reached to close it, then remembered how Miranda had stopped outside this door the evening of Ryan's visit. Surely she wouldn't be in there. Not fearing men as she did. Still, it was worth a look.

Kate pushed the door all the way open and stepped inside. Her daughter lay cradled against Zachariah McGovern's side. Scarcely able to believe her eyes, she moved closer and saw the way Miranda clung to their neighbor, even in her sleep. Oddly enough, it looked as if McGovern had turned slightly to accommodate her, his powerfully muscled arm bent to hold her.

Kate approached the bed, her intent to pick up her daughter and leave. But before she did, she noticed how Miranda's hand clutched McGovern's chest hair. It would take some tricky maneuvering to pry those tightly clenched little fingers loose. On McGovern's other side lay Nosy, his head on the spare pillow, belly up, paws dangling, his long tongue lolling limply over his teeth.

Between claps of thunder, the deep rasp of a snore made Kate start. She couldn't tell if it had come from man or beast, and then decided maybe from both. During another lull, she heard two distinct snores and Miranda's even breathing. A peaceful threesome, all sound asleep.

Kate pressed her hands against her waist, longing to snatch her daughter away from Zachariah McGovern, to hold her. But she knew her protective feelings were unfounded. The man had nearly forfeited his life to save Miranda's. Surely Kate could entrust her child into his care for the duration of the night. What point was there in waking any of them?

None at all. Except that Miranda's abandonment left Kate to weather the storm alone. Thunder rolled across the sky again, and Kate flinched. Ridiculous. She was a grown woman. This wasn't the first storm she had endured alone, and it wouldn't be the last. She drew the folded blanket up from the foot of the bed and laid it over her daughter. Then she backed from the bedroom, leaving the door ajar in case Miranda called for her.

Even with a storm shaking the house, the parlor would be within hollering distance, Kate decided. The horsehair settee would serve her well enough as a bed. As she stepped into the dark room, the wind caught an outside shutter and slapped it up against the side of the house. Then lightning flashed.

A pulsing flare of blue-white light came through the window and cast a magnified shadow of the coat tree onto the wall beside Kate. She glimpsed a looming silhouette with reaching arms. The specter gave her such a start that her feet came clear off the floor. She grabbed her throat and whirled, so frightened she couldn't scream. *Joseph.*

Even as she thought it, Kate saw that the shadow wasn't a man's. Going limp, she backed against the adjoining wall and closed her eyes.

Foolish. Kate struggled to breathe. Thunder clapped again, wind moaned around the house, and her damp skin turned icy. She began to shiver and clenched her teeth to stop their chattering.

"Ma!"

Kate opened her eyes and strained to hear. The call was distant and ethereal. Real or imagined? Though she knew it might be only the fluting of the wind, Kate ran from the parlor.

"Maaaaaa!"

The storm momentarily lulled, and the foyer went black. Kate planted a hand on the wall and froze to listen to the sudden silence. She nearly screamed when thunder clapped directly above the house. She felt the vibration shudder through the floor.

Then she thought she heard Miranda calling her again. On quivering legs, Kate crept through the darkness to the sickroom. Miranda still lay sound asleep, shielded by Zachariah McGovern's large, muscular body.

"Maaaaaa . . ."

Kate covered her ears and squeezed her eyes closed, tortured by the sound, praying it would stop. She hurried back to the parlor, found a pitch-black corner, and sank to the floor in a protective huddle. Carried along by the moaning wind, the child's desperate cry came to Kate again. Not Miranda, yet not imagined, a memory of her daughter's voice that came from deep within the black layers of her own mind. Never to be forgotten, never to be escaped, it would haunt her during violent storms for the rest of her life.

8

The sun was well up the next time Zach opened his eyes. His first awareness was of the starched white pillowcase beneath his cheek. Then he felt Miranda's small body pressed against his own. He blinked and focused on her. She lay quietly in the bend of his arm, her head leaned back so she could study his face.

Befuddled with sleep, Zach stared into her big brown eyes for a moment, then let his gaze trail slowly over her delicately made features. To his recollection, he had never seen such perfection. Finely arched sable brows capped her expressive eyes, their darkness striking a sharp contrast to her alabaster skin. On the tip of her turned-up nose was a smattering of freckles the color of brown sugar. Her mouth was etched in a delicate rose pink, the upper lip defined in two perfect peaks, the lower full.

She returned his regard with an unblinking intensity that soon made Zach begin to feel self-conscious. He wasn't surprised when she touched a finger to his jaw.

In a voice gone gravelly from disuse, he said, "That's a scar. A long time ago, I got burned real bad in a fire."

Miranda lifted her hand and placed it squarely before Zach's nose. He moved his head back and saw she had similar scars on her palm and between her fingers. Their angry red color indicated that the burns had occurred recently, probably within the last several months, and had been severe. Though not as it had at first, the newly healed tissue probably still pained her, for it took a long while for the nerves exposed by a burn to heal. Even now, seven years after the fire, Zach's cheek and neck were more sensitive to the sun than the rest of him.

His heart caught at the thought of such a little thing enduring the kind of agony she obviously had.

Since she apparently wanted to share her experience with him, but seemed too shy to speak, he said, "It looks like you were hurt in a fire, too. How did that happen?"

At the question, she went rigid. Before he registered that he had upset her, she scrambled off the bed and fled the room.

Only seconds later, Kate Blakely appeared in the doorway. Zach was shocked at the way she looked. In a dress of dark charcoal with a high neckline, her sable hair skimmed back from her pale face and caught in a coil of braid atop her head, she was as severe and colorless as a daguerreotype done in varying shades of gray. Beneath her large eyes, ashen shadows of exhaustion followed the contours of her fragile cheekbones.

"You're awake," she said, and promptly made fists in her gray apron.

Zach started to push up on an elbow, then remembered how his legs had hurt last night when he moved. He rubbed his jaw, expecting to feel inch-long whiskers. With one side of his face mostly scar tissue and devoid of hair, he made a pretty awful sight if he didn't shave every morning. To his surprise, those places on his face that could still sprout beard felt as smooth as a baby's behind.

He swallowed to get his voice and asked, "How long have I been out?"

She took a hesitant step into the room, her nervous hands still worrying the apron. "A long time. Well over a week."

"A week!" The words came out in a croak. Again, Zach tried to swallow.

"Would you like some water?"

She stepped briskly to the low table by the bed and lifted a willow-patterned pitcher. He watched as she filled a glass and turned toward him. When their eyes met, she hesitated, as if she weren't quite certain how to proceed. That made two of them.

Zach jerked the sheet up over his chest, suddenly conscious of his nudity beneath the linen. In his misspent youth, he hadn't minded when he had awakened in similar circumstances, naked and abed with a strange woman in the room. But this was different. As was Kate Blakely.

"Where are my britches?"

Zach hadn't meant for that to come out like an accusation, but it sounded that way. He couldn't help it. All kinds of pictures were floating through his head. If he had been out for over a week, who had been taking care of him? He had a sick feeling he knew. And all he could think was that he wanted his pants, yesterday if she could arrange it.

She cast a startled glance toward the door. "They're in the kitchen."

His voice still gravelly, Zach said. "Would you mind getting them for me?"

"I'm mending them."

"Mending them? They're almost brand new."

"Not anymore. I cut them straight up the front crease."

She broke off and tightened her grip on the water glass. "I'll have them finished this afternoon."

Zach wanted his pants now. If he couldn't get up and out of here, he wanted to be decently covered, at least. The first time he had seen Kate Blakely, he'd wanted to get acquainted with her. But this wasn't the way he'd had in mind. He glanced around. "What about my drawers?"

She slid a perplexed look at the bureau.

"No, my drawers." Zach gestured at his body, which was outlined a little too clearly for comfort beneath the sheet. "You know? My long underwear."

"Oh." Her mouth, so like her daughter's except for the hairline scar at the corner of her bottom lip, pursed in surprise. Then she blinked. "Those, too."

"Those, too, what?"

"I cut them. It was the only way I could get your pants off." Color flooded her cheeks. "To get to the snakebites."

Of course. The snakebites. Zach ran a hand over his right thigh and felt the swelling. With a light caress of his fingertips, he sought out one wound, then another. Suddenly weary, he closed his eyes.

"Who's been shaving me?" he asked raggedly.

"I have."

His worst suspicions confirmed, Zach nearly groaned. To wake up and find out that any woman had been nursing him would have been humiliating. That the woman had been a lady like her made it doubly so. Presuming that his body had continued with its daily functions, as it undoubtedly must have—Zach almost wished the snakebites had killed him. Embarrassment welled within him, but after the first rush, he didn't have the strength to concentrate on it.

"Here," she said softly.

He felt her arm slip under his neck, and with surprising

strength, she lifted his head. The rim of the glass touched his lips, and he opened his eyes. The first of the water trickled down the crevices that bracketed his chin. Swallowing quickly, he managed to down the rest. As she drew the glass away, he saw that her hand was trembling. For several long seconds, they stared at each other, their faces a few scant inches apart.

She grabbed a cloth from the bedside table and dabbed at his neck. "I didn't mean to drown you."

Zach cleared his throat. In a stronger voice, he said, "I'll dry."

He watched as she set the glass down by the pitcher. The shakiness of her hand told him that she didn't find this situation any more palatable than he did. Since he was probably the reason she had circles of exhaustion under her eyes, he felt bad about that. If he had been unconscious for over a week, she must have half killed herself taking care of him. It was a poor show of gratitude to start grumbling for his pants the minute he woke up.

That was a problem easily rectified. "I haven't thanked you for saving my life."

She looked genuinely startled. "You, thank me?"

"Yes. I have a feeling I wouldn't still be here, if not for you."

A smile touched her mouth. It was just about the sweetest smile Zach had ever seen, flashing a dimple in her cheek and transforming her face. Her eyes took on a sparkle that he realized were unshed tears.

"Mr. McGovern, if not for your quick thinking and courageous disregard for your own safety, my daughter would be dead. No thanks from you are necessary, believe me. It's I who should be thanking you."

The unmistakable adulation that he saw in her expression went a long way toward restoring his dignity. Bare-assed naked and helpless as he had been this last week, he had somehow emerged a hero, at least in her estimation. All wasn't lost.

Only he wasn't a hero. There had been an instant down inside that well when he had nearly left Miranda to her fate. It didn't sit well being touted for his courage when he knew he had a yellow streak a mile wide.

"I didn't know before I went into the well that it was full of snakes. And once I realized it, I almost skedaddled, the devil take your kid."

Though Kate was still smiling, his admission set the corners of her mouth to quivering. She lifted her gaze to the ceiling, the gesture conveying that she'd never seen his like. With a lift of her hands that spoke volumes, she said, "Don't try to make light of it, Mr. McGovern. With others, perhaps, but not with me. Miranda told me you heard the snakes before you reached them. Yet you kept going." She brushed her sleeve across one cheek. "As small as Miranda is, one bite would have killed her. If I try for the remainder of my days, I'll never find a way to repay you."

Gazing up at Kate Blakely's delicately shaped face, Zach could think of several ways. All of which made him feel ashamed of himself, and none of which were worthy of a hero. Not that he was. But if she wanted to persist in thinking so, who was he to argue?

Even in her somber clothes and with circles under her eyes, Kate Blakely was one of the loveliest women he had ever seen, and from all indications thus far, as sweet within as she was without. After getting off to such a bad start with her, he was appreciative of just about anything that would improve her opinion of him, even a den of rattlers. It wasn't as if he could count on his good looks to help him out.

The thought no sooner settled into Zach's mind than

he had cause to question his sanity. There wasn't a woman alive so pretty or so desirable that she was worth getting snake bitten for. And from the feel of his legs, his suffering had just begun.

"You just have," he said in a low voice.

"I've just what?"

"Repaid me."

"I suppose that depends on who's keeping track. You may feel we're even. I never will. If there's anything I can do for you—anything at all—just say so and consider it done."

Anything? Most widow women weren't so naive as to make an open-ended statement like that, at least not to a man. Kate's doing so told Zach a great deal about her, probably far more than she thought to reveal. He accepted the offer as he knew it was intended. "I'll bear that in mind. You can never tell when I might need a helping hand."

She took a deep breath, as though relieved, which gave Zach the impression she had been trying to think of a way to thank him and was glad it was over. "Well . . ." She pressed a hand to her waist and smiled down at him. "I'll bet you're starving. I made chicken soup for the noon meal yesterday. Would you like some of the broth?"

What Zach really wanted was to close his eyes, but he couldn't, not as long as Kate Blakely was standing there. "That'd be real nice."

She hurried from the room, her gray skirt aswirl around her ankles. Zach gazed after her for a moment. His eyelids felt heavy, but he fought to keep them open because he knew she would return in a few minutes with the broth. It was a losing battle.

The sound of his name dragged Zach up from the dark mists of sleep. He squinted to see. Kate Blakely's face hovered over him, so close he felt her breath on his cheek as she spoke. Her nearness brought him instantly awake.

"I've got your broth." She leaned across him to get the spare pillow. As she strained to lift his shoulders, her bodice brushed against his jaw. "There," she said, once she had him propped up. "Now perhaps you can eat a bite."

Her uneasiness painfully evident, she perched on the bed beside him and reached for a mug that sat on the table. Giving him a smile, she spooned some broth into his mouth. Zach swallowed. He didn't have much choice. Before she could go for another spoonful, he said, "I think I can do it."

"Mr. McGovern, I doubt you can even sit up."

Zach doubted it as well, but he felt like a fool. "I'm not used to a woman feeding me."

"You're in good company. I'm not used to feeding someone." She spooned more broth into his mouth. "Except for when Miranda was a baby, of course."

He could tell by the quick, almost breathless way she spoke that she was horribly nervous and trying to hide it. The dimple in her cheek flashed again, appearing so briefly that Zach wanted to place his fingertip on the spot to see if he had imagined it.

As if she couldn't tolerate the silence, she added, "As long as you don't do like she did and spit it on me if you don't like it, we'll manage fine."

The spoon darted in for another attack. Zach managed to grin after he swallowed. "It's delicious."

"Thank you."

Barely giving him a chance to breathe, she came at him with the spoon again. Zach nearly told her she didn't have to go at feeding him like she was killing snakes, but given his recent experience, the saying died on his tongue.

Before he could think of another comment, she shoved the spoon in his mouth again.

"How are you feeling? Marcus and I have been very worried about you, you know."

All Zach managed to get out between mouthfuls was an inarticulate grunt. He knew it was probably only because she was tense, but if she shoved much more broth at him, he was going to strangle. He thought about grabbing her hand before she dipped up more, but doubted he would be quick enough. His body felt oddly disconnected from his brain.

"For a while, I had begun to think you'd stay unconscious forever."

The spoon filled his mouth again. Amazingly enough, Zach was starting to feel full. To ward off another attack, he clamped his lips closed and let his eyes drift shut. The spoon didn't touch his lips again, so he guessed she got the hint. After a moment, he tested the water by unclenching his teeth enough to say, "Marcus? He was here?"

"From the first. He insisted he be here to—"

Her hesitation made him curious, and he lifted his lashes. "To what?"

"To care for your personal needs."

Zach let his eyes drift closed again. "I'll have to give that man a raise."

He heard her set the mug back on the table. The shift of her bottom tugged on the sheet, and he winced. When she sat back, her hip pressed against him. She grew still. Zach felt her warmth, and her sudden awareness of him. So weak he doubted he could stand, he was more than a little amazed that he was equally aware of her. Of her slightness. Of her softness. And of her scent. This morning she smelled of roses, freshly baked bread, and just a trace of vanilla. The kind of woman a man longed to taste, and savor.

He lifted his lashes again and looked into her startled brown eyes. The touch of her hip against his side seemed to burn through the sheet.

She shot to her feet. "You didn't eat much."

And not any of what he really wanted to taste. "I feel like I overdid."

She bent to retrieve the mug. "I'll bring more in a couple of hours," she said nervously. "Your stomach has probably shrunk."

The distaste she felt for him was so obvious that Zach felt heat rise up his neck. More the fool he for thinking an attractive woman like Kate Blakely might give a man like him a passing glance. He splayed his hand over his chest and forced a smile, determined not to show how that hurt.

So painfully reminded of his own scars, he suddenly recalled Miranda's. Because he needed to say something, anything, to smooth over the moment, he asked, "How did your daughter get her hand so badly burned?"

At the question, Kate gave a start. Her slender fingers lost their grip on the mug. Before either of them could react, the porcelain hit the plank floor with a resounding crash and shattered in a dozen different directions. Kate gasped and stepped back, brushing ineffectually at the splatters on her skirt.

"Confound it."

"Damn." Afraid that the shards might have cut her, Zach forgot all about his legs and shoved up on an elbow. "Are you all right?"

The room went into a spin. Zach grabbed a handful of sheet to steady himself, afraid he might pitch headfirst onto the floor. Kate caught his arm.

"Mr. McGovern, please . . ."

Zach fell back against the pillow, panting as though he had run a race. "Shit." He closed his eyes to make the spinning stop. "I've never been this weak in my entire life."

"You nearly died. It's going to take a few days."

"Are you cut?"

"No, I'm fine." She made an exasperated little sound. "Lands, what a mess. Can I trust you to lie still while I clean it up?"

Zach sighed. "I don't think I'll be going anywhere for a few minutes."

He heard her bustle from the room. Seconds later, she returned, broom in hand. He was too exhausted to keep his eyes open once she began sweeping.

"This broom is useless." Porcelain chinked. "I suppose I'll have to buy another. I ruined my good one."

Zach was too weary to ask how. A few minutes later, even though he didn't hear her leave the room, he noticed the absence of her scent and knew she was gone. As he drifted off to sleep, his last thought was that she had never explained how Miranda had burned her hand.

After leaving the sickroom, Kate leaned against the hallway wall, broom in one hand, dustpan and rag clutched in the other, her heart pounding like a kettledrum. She had been caring for Zachariah McGovern for days and had grown accustomed to seeing his large, sheet-draped frame lying motionless on the bed. There had even been times, while away from the sickroom, that she had forgotten his presence in the house. But now he was awake.

Her arm still tingled where she had touched his massive shoulders to lift him. She recalled the intense regard of his eyes, which seemed to change with his emotions, a twinkling hazel when he smiled, an arresting green when he asked a question, and then the color of flint when he thought she might have been cut by flying porcelain. Kate had the unnerving sensation that those eyes of his saw far more than she wanted them to.

She felt unsettled. Even now that she was out of the room, her legs still quivered. Knowing he was in there, that he would frequently awaken, that she would have to care for him, all the while suffering his intent scrutiny, made her stomach knot.

Kate closed her eyes, disgusted with herself. *Admit it, Kate. You find him attractive. That's why he makes you so nervous.* To admit that, even in the farthest reaches of her mind, made Kate want to give herself a good kick. Was she out of her blooming mind? Zachariah McGovern stood a head taller than Joseph had and was half again as broad at the shoulders. Talk about jumping from the skillet into the fire.

She was grateful to him, that was all. Grateful and beholden. He had saved her daughter's life, and her maternal instincts were all in a stir. In a few days, those feelings would diminish. Once she was her old self again, she wouldn't be affected when he looked at her with that speculative twinkle in his eyes. She wouldn't.

9

For Zach the next week passed as slowly as an ant walking across spilled honey. The flesh around his snakebites sloughed off, and the sores became infected. He suffered recurring bouts of fever, which set him back and drained what little remaining strength he had. As he drifted in and out of delirium, he was vaguely aware of Kate caring for him, of her gentle hands, her soothing voice, and of her eyes—always of her eyes—the biggest thing about her and constantly filled with worry.

Sometimes Marcus was there, his visits marked by the strength in his hands as he rolled Zach this way and that to bathe him. Even in a haze of fever, Zach wanted to tell him thank-you, but the words wouldn't come to his tongue. Other words did. Unbidden from the black, secret parts of his mind, they crawled up his throat. The most awful part was, he knew he was rambling, but couldn't stop. His brain seemed divided in half, one side aware yet powerless, the other crazy with fever.

Even if he hadn't been aware that he was talking out, Kate's gentle responses would have told him. "Shhh. It's all right," she would whisper. Though soothed by the touch of her cool hand on his forehead, Zach felt ashamed. What was all right? What had he just said? Why did he hear that note of sympathy in her voice? "I'm here. It's all taken care of. Don't worry."

So sick, so awfully sick. Zach couldn't make sense of things. In the back of his mind, he knew she was comforting him as she would a child. That stung his masculine pride. But even so, the softly spoken reassurances calmed him.

Morning became night, night became morning, and Zach marked the passing of each day with a vague awareness, slipping in and out of sleep, swallowing what was poured into his mouth, turning his face to accommodate the cool cloths that caressed his skin.

Katie . . . Somehow, he came to think of her as Katie. Kate sounded so sturdy and practical and plain. She was none of those. Even while he slept, she lingered in his mind, as light as a whisper, her touch like gossamer, her voice a delicate scale of musical notes that lulled and soothed him. Katie . . . Her image became a pallet of shades behind his closed eyelids, light pink and deep rose on alabaster, her sable hair the perfect frame for her fragilely sculpted face. An angel who floated between him and the clutching hands of death.

When Zach finally awoke one morning to clarity, he not only felt on the road to recovery, but knew exactly where he was. Though he couldn't recall staring at them, the unpainted plank walls around him had become as familiar as the palms of his hands, every crack between the bare boards memorized.

He wasn't surprised to see Miranda sitting on the straight-backed chair beside his bed. Even in his semiconsciousness, he had sometimes sensed her small presence in the room. Nosy lay curled around the legs of the chair.

Both child and dog were watching him as though they'd been keeping an endless vigil.

Miranda stiffened when she saw that he was awake. Without a word, she slid off the chair, nearly tromping on Nosy's plumed tail as she fled. Nosy wagged the uninjured appendage and pushed up to lick Zach's face.

"Leave off, Nose." Zach didn't have the strength to shove the dog away. "Leave off."

"He likes you."

The unexpected observance startled Zach, for he thought Miranda had gone. He tucked in his chin to see that she was standing at the foot of his bed. She was so short that her face barely showed above his toes.

"Right now, I wish he didn't. Give him a swift kick for me, would you?"

Her vulnerable-looking mouth curved in a smile that showed tiny, squared-off teeth with gaps in between. "You don't really want me to."

Victimized by Nosy's enthusiasm, Zach batted weakly with his wrist. Miranda came around the bed and pulled the dog back by his ruff. Once Nosy ceased his mischief, she stood there staring at Zach, her gaze inescapable and disconcerting.

"If I was to kick him, he wouldn't like me no more," she observed.

Zach ran a shaky hand across his mouth. "Then I'd be stuck with him, so don't."

"He likes you a lot."

This was the second time she had noted that, and it dawned on Zach that the revelation amazed her. Why, he couldn't guess. After all, Nosy was his dog, and dogs usually liked their masters. He squinted to study her. "Maybe I should start kicking him, then. I don't care to have a dog licking my mouth."

"It's how he kisses."

"Hm." Still a little groggy, Zach tried to read her gaze. "Does he kiss you?"

"Yep, and I kiss back. It ain't nice not to." Her attention shifted to his lips, and she wrinkled her small nose so the freckles ran together. "It ain't nice to scrub 'em off while he's lookin', neither. Nosy'll think you don't like him."

Zach let his offending hand fall to his chest. Duly chastised, he said, "I'll remember that. I wouldn't want to hurt his feelings."

"Me neither." She smiled again and her eyes grew as bright as polished buttons. "My ma won't let him kiss her on the mouth, but she lets him on her ear."

Zach didn't think that sounded like such a bad trade-off. Nosy was one lucky dog.

"It gives her shivers. She says since Nosy come that she's got the cleanest ears this side of—" She broke off. "I can't remember where, but it's a long ways."

"Texas, maybe," Zach supplied.

She nodded. "You been there?"

"No. That's why folks say this side of Texas, because it's so far."

She shrugged a frail shoulder. "Me and Nosy been waitin' for you to get well. We been comin' to see you near every day. You talked sometimes."

Zach didn't want to be reminded. Morbid curiosity got the better of him. "What did I say?"

"Funny stuff. One time you said a spider was on the ceilin', and you kept yellin' for my ma to smash it." She leaned forward slightly. "Ma finally got the broom and pretended, only she said not to tell 'cause you'd be barest."

Zach figured out what she meant and silently agreed; he was embarrassed. "It sounds like I've been a handful. Yelling, was I?"

"Real loud. You said—" She caught her lip in her teeth. "I ain't s'posed to say it."

"What?"

"If my ma hears, she'll soap my mouth. She won't soap yours, though, 'cause you're bigger than her. You still shouldn't oughta say it, though."

Zach cringed. He had a way with words when the mood struck, but he tried never to blackguard in front of children. He seldom did in front of women, either. "I'm real sorry if I've been saying things I shouldn't."

"Ma told me not to listen. I poked my fingers in my ears, but when you think a spider might get you, you can yell mighty loud." She rolled her eyes. "When Ma whacked the ceilin', you thought that spider fell in your bed and you near had a fit."

Zach didn't want to hear this.

She grew quiet for a moment, then added, "I wasn't scared."

"Of the spider?"

She giggled. "No. There weren't no spider. I wasn't scared of your yellin'. Know why?"

Zach hadn't a clue.

"'Cause Nosy wasn't. Ma says a dog can't talk, but Nosy does. He ever talk to you?"

"Not the same way a person would talk."

"But clear as rain in dog talk."

Zach knew how expressive Nosy's face could seem and understood what the child meant. "What does he say to you?"

She wrinkled her nose again, this time in thought. "Lots of stuff." Her gaze settled on Zach's. "I used to think you looked big and mean. But Nosy says you ain't."

"He does?"

She nodded but didn't elaborate. "That's why I wasn't scared when you kept yellin' for Ma to come kill the goddamned spider." Her eyes widened, and she clamped a small hand over her mouth. After shooting a glance at the door, she spread her fingers to whisper, "I said it."

Zach was glad for the slip. Given his colorful vocabulary, he had been imagining far worse. Evidently Kate had never been around a man who could curse until the air turned blue. He would have to watch his language. "I won't tattle on you."

"Promise?"

Feeling drained, Zach managed to smile. "I promise. I think we both better try not to say it again, though."

"You goin' back to sleep?"

Unaware until that moment that he had closed his eyes, Zach blinked. "I reckon."

He felt her small hand touch his. "Don't worry about spiders gettin' you. Me and Nosy won't let 'em come in here. If one does, I'll fetch Ma's broom and smash the shit right out of it for you."

Zach took that promise with him into the black layers of sleep.

Kate stood outside the sickroom door and thought of a dozen reasons not to go in. There was bread to be put in the oven, dishes to wash, lunch to start. But if Zachariah truly was awake as Miranda claimed, she couldn't ignore his existence.

Look on the bright side, Kate. When he grows strong enough, he can leave.

As far as she was concerned, that would happen none too soon, and for more than one reason. For days Miranda had been spending hours at his bedside, her large eyes intent on his dark face, her own aglow with adoration. Kate knew it was natural for her to develop an attachment. Zachariah McGovern had saved her life, and in the child's mind, that made him a man of heroic proportions, someone she could love and trust. That would be fine if Miranda were a normal little girl, but she wasn't.

Not that Kate believed McGovern would deliberately set out to hurt her child. It was just that Miranda expected and needed far more than he could ever understand or be prepared to give.

Taking a deep breath, she pushed open the sickroom door. As she stepped inside, she sensed that her patient was indeed awake, just as Miranda said, even though his eyes remained closed. She couldn't say exactly how she knew. The rhythm of his breathing didn't change. His dark face looked relaxed, as though in sleep. His large hands, which rested at his sides atop the sheet, were loosely curled. Yet she knew.

As silly as it was, Kate decided the air in the room seemed different. Charged and heavy, like right before an electrical storm, it made her skin tingle. Wondering why he didn't acknowledge her, she stepped softly toward the bed.

The faint sound of Kate's footsteps and the whisper of her skirt had become as familiar to Zach as the rhythm of his breathing. Unsettled by the feelings that swamped him, he kept his eyes closed, trying to come to terms with his reaction to her.

Could a man fall in love while he floated in and out of delirium? A month ago he would have answered that question with an unequivocal no. But he couldn't deny his emotions. Katie, sweet, gentle, beautiful Katie. During his illness, he had absorbed the essence of her as a sponge did water.

Right now she smelled faintly of laurel smoke and Pyle's Pearline Washing Compound, which told him she had done laundry that morning. Without any clear recollection to explain it, Zach knew he'd be smelling a hot iron on starched cotton before the day was out. She usually tried to do her ironing on the same day she did the wash. How odd that he knew that about her, yet had no memory of how he knew.

Now that he thought about it, he realized that wasn't all he knew about her. To make her store of potatoes stretch, she often baked camas root, a bulb that grew wild in these parts and had once been a mainstay of the local Indians's diet. She served salmon caught in the Umpqua far more often than she did venison or pork. She also loved onions and added them to nearly everything she cooked, and she frequently baked sweets.

How could he possibly know all that? Zach struggled to recall and couldn't. He guessed that maybe he had registered the kitchen smells and stored them away as memories.

His sense of smell solved several mysteries, but there were a multitude of others. He knew that ice was delivered only once a week, and that even in summer she could afford to buy only two blocks, which never lasted her. She pretended not to like Nosy, but gave him a scratch behind his ears every time they met and allowed him the run of her house. Reading was her favorite pastime, and she indulged in it every chance she got, poring over the same old newspapers and periodicals, night after night. Had he seen her pet the dog? Had she sat by his bed to read?

Zach couldn't say. He could only accept that there were unexplainable facts about Kate stored away in his mind. When disconcerted or frustrated, she made an inarticulate little sound in the back of her throat and followed it with a whispered, "Dad-blame," as if it were a cussword she wanted no one else to hear. She kept Pear's Soap readily at hand somewhere in the house, probably next to the kitchen sink, and washed her hands so frequently that its distinctive but pleasant scent always lingered on her skin. She hated the rain. She loved flowers, and she was saving her pennies to make Miranda school dresses.

Her pennies . . . They were pitifully few, and she collected them in what she and Miranda referred to as the savings crock. Kate was using the pennies to teach Miranda her numbers, and of an evening, their voices rang through the house as they counted from one through twenty until Miranda got it *almost* right.

Almost was one of Kate's favorite words when dealing with her daughter. Miranda could *almost* write her first name. She could *almost* make the bed by herself. She could *almost* drink her milk without dribbling any down her chin. Kate was one of those rare mothers who had a knack for ignoring failures and made a big to-do over minor successes.

Yes, he knew so many things. Like right now he knew she was standing at the foot of his bed in a gray or black dress, her large brown eyes concerned but wary. When he lifted his eyelashes, a touch of pinkness would flag her cheeks and her hands would begin to worry her apron, which would be gray or white because she owned only two.

He slowly opened his eyes. And sure enough, there she stood. The moment his gaze met hers, she began to pluck at her white apron, and her cheeks turned a comely pink. His gaze shifted to the right corner of her bottom lip, searching for a hairline scar, faded to an almost imperceptible white, that he knew was there. There was another at her temple, but the flyaway tendrils that escaped her severe coiffure usually concealed it.

Today she wore the black shirtwaist, which had seen better days. The simple lines of the pleated bodice and flared skirt did little to conceal her slender figure, which was temptingly well rounded in all the right places.

"How are you feeling?"

Like hell, but he didn't dare say so for fear she'd run and get the Pear's soap. "I've felt more spry. But I'm a darned sight better than I was."

"I'm glad."

As if she realized she was wringing her apron, she pressed her palms against her skirt and forced her fingers to be still. Zach considered assuring her that he didn't bite, but she looked so delectable he didn't. If he got a chance, he'd happily nibble on that neck of hers. As if an opportunity might arise. He was in no condition to pose a threat. At least not yet.

As he studied her, the blush on her cheeks deepened, and she lifted a hand to her waist. He followed the nervous ascent of her slender fingers up the line of black buttons on her bodice. As she splayed her hand on her chest, he realized where his gaze had come to rest and forced himself to look away—at the chair, the wall, the ceiling. When he finally glanced back, he saw that her blush had turned crimson, and he wanted to kick himself.

Say something, you idiot. Zach searched his mind but couldn't come up with a single thing. For a delicately made woman, she had lovely breasts, just the right size to fill a man's hands, but that wasn't an observation he could make aloud.

"A-Are you hungry?" she asked.

Zach placed a hand on his belly and blinked in surprise. He had lost so much weight that his navel was damned near buttoned to his backbone. "Jesus H. Christ."

It was Kate's turn to blink, Zach's to blush.

"Sorry," he muttered. "That just shot out."

She stared at him for a moment. "For the remainder of your stay, please try not to take the name of the Lord in vain, Mr. McGovern. There's a child in the house."

For some reason that Zach couldn't readily recall, he had always believed that the *H* between Jesus and Christ had somehow made the expression acceptable. Kate clearly didn't agree.

"Sorry," he repeated. "But it's not every day I wake up to find I'm nothing but skin stretched over bones."

He didn't look like "nothing but skin stretched over bones" to Kate. Her gaze dropped to the dark mat of hair on his well-padded chest, then shifted to the bulges of muscle in his bare arms. If anything, the weight loss had more sharply defined the powerful lines of his body.

When she glanced back at his face, she saw that his eyes had closed. He looked indescribably weary, with deep lines etched in his cheeks. "It'll take a while to regain your strength, but you will." Concerned by his sudden withdrawal, she moved closer and touched a palm to his forehead. Though it made no sense, she felt something akin to relief at the heat of his skin. No matter how powerful he looked, he was still an extremely sick man who needed tending. "You're a bit feverish again. To be on the safe side, I'd best get another dose of *Aconitum napellus* into you."

Zach heard a bottle and spoon clink. Then cool metal touched his lips. Trusting her, he parted his teeth, and the most horrible stuff he could recall ever tasting filled his mouth. His throat convulsed as he tried to swallow, and he choked. Burning liquid bubbled into his sinuses. He reared up on one elbow, gasping and coughing, tears streaming. When he got his breath, he croaked, "Son of a bitch! What're you trying to do, kill me?"

"I'm trying to help you," she cried as she dabbed his face with a cloth.

Zach grabbed the cloth and scrubbed at his lips. "Warn a man before you pour shit like that in his mouth. I damned near choked to death."

She made that inarticulate little sound in the back of her throat that he had come to know so well. "Mr. McGovern! A bit of bitter medicine is no excuse to use filthy language like that. For shame!"

Zach looked up into her startled brown eyes and realized what he had just said. Before he could apologize, she plunked the bottle and spoon back down on the table, then swept from the room. As he sank weakly back onto the bed, he wondered if she had gone to get the Pear's soap and decided just about anything would taste better than *Aconitum napellus,* whatever in hell that was. He'd rather have the fever, thank you very much.

He took another swipe at his mouth, then threw the cloth in the general direction of the bedside table. When it landed, it hit the bottle of medicine, and before he could react, both bottle and cloth fell to the floor. Glass shattered, and the bitter remedy geysered.

Zach pushed weakly up on an elbow to gaze down at the mess. She would never believe in a million years that he hadn't spilled it on purpose.

The sound of his voice resounded in his head. So much for watching his language. In the space of a minute, he had already used half the cusswords in his vocabulary. He fell back on the bed, groaned, and angled an arm over his eyes. Damned if he couldn't give lessons on how to drive off females.

10

Just as Zach feared, Kate had as little as possible to do with him from then on. Oh, she saw to his needs, and she was unfailingly kind. He had no complaints there. But she didn't prolong her visits to his room a second longer than was absolutely necessary.

In all fairness, he knew the scarceness of her appearances in his room probably wasn't by design. Now that Zach was better, Marcus no longer felt Kate needed his help, and he had gone back to Zach's place to oversee the hired hands. That left her with all the farm work. The few moments of leisure time she did manage to steal were spent with her daughter, which was as it should be.

Each evening Marcus came by for short visits, helping Zach to bathe when he needed it and updating him on the goings-on at his farm. Zach began to yearn for the company like a thirsting man did water. He wasn't accustomed to inactivity, and the endless, empty hours of the day nearly drove him mad. For some reason, little Miranda never came to his room anymore. Zach laid it to her age and the fact that a sick man probably wasn't very entertaining company for a four-year-old.

As though she sensed how restless he was, Kate started leaving her precious store of reading material on his bedside table each morning. As much as Zach appreciated her thoughtfulness, he had never been much of a one to read the Bible, and he didn't cotton to studying *Harper's Bazaar* dress patterns or leafing through last year's issue of the Montgomery Ward catalog. That left two Portland newspapers she had in her possession, and he soon got sick to death of poring over those.

He memorized every event reported in Portland on the nineteenth and twentieth of June. Copper sales were booming, but who gave a fig? After three days, he could recite the ball game scores at any given inning. He knew a trout fisherman could pick up a dozen superior quality flies at Hudson's Gun Store for fifty cents, that the telephone number to Henry Weinhard's brewery was 72, and he drank an entire bottle of Swift's Specific in one afternoon, praying it was as miraculous a restorative tonic as the advertisements claimed. It wasn't.

Kate, convinced that he had consumed such large quantities of the remedy for its alcohol content, was none too pleased when she learned what he had done. During their discourse that evening, Zach filed away two more important facts about Kate Blakely; she was dead set against spirits of any kind, and she considered the wine he intended to produce to be sinner's swill.

Two more marks against him.

This new discovery about Kate pretty much dashed Zach's hopes that once she got to know him she might develop a fondness for him. In order for a woman to fall in love with a man despite his exterior flaws, she had to see something noble in his character. As far as Zach could tell, his only saving grace in Kate's eyes was that he had braved a den of rattlers to rescue her daughter.

Not a man to beat a dead horse, Zach accepted Kate's indifference and set his mind to regaining his strength. The problem was, his body didn't seem to respond to the messages from his brain. When he sat up on the edge of the bed, he broke out in a sweat. The one time he tried to stand, his legs folded beneath him as if they were hinged and well-oiled at the knees. He had a hell of a time dragging himself back up from the floor and into the bed, and when he managed, he was so drained he slept straight through supper and didn't awaken until the next morning.

When Miranda and Nosy appeared in his doorway one afternoon looking forlorn and bored, Zach was so glad for the company that he wished he could lasso the pair and tether them to his bedrails. Since that morning over a week ago when he and Miranda had discussed the spider, he had caught only glimpses of her. And since Nosy seemed to have become her unshakable shadow, Zach had been deprived of the dog's loyal companionship as well.

"Long time, no see," he said lightly. "I thought maybe I'd made you mad at me or something."

Miranda wrinkled her nose and shook her head. "Nope."

"Then why have you been such a stranger?" The puzzled look in her guileless brown eyes told him she had never heard that expression. "If you aren't mad, why don't you ever come see me?"

She caught her lip in her teeth and wrinkled her nose again. "I ain't s'posed to."

"Oh."

She studied him for a moment. Then her gaze shifted to his mouth. "How come do you lick dirt? Does it taste good?"

Zach blinked. "Lick dirt? What gave you that idea?"

"Ma said."

"You must have misunderstood, Miranda."

"Nope. Ma said it straight out."

"Well, she's mistaken then. I don't lick dirt."

With her hand riding Nosy's back, she stepped into the room and drew up at the foot of Zach's bed. Peering at him over his sheet-draped toes, she said, "Let me look."

"At what?"

"Your tongue."

Zach stared at her. "My tongue?"

"Yep. So's I can see if it's filthy like Ma says."

He swallowed a laugh. "Ah—so that's what she said." Feeling absurd, he slid the body part in question out between his teeth so Miranda could take a gander at it. "Is it dirty?"

She shook her head. "Not the brown kind of dirty. But it's got icky lookin' white stuff on it."

Zach felt a flush of embarrassment rising up his neck. "That's because I've been sick. Your ma works so hard that I hate to send her on extra errands. But if you'll go get me some saleratus, I'll give my teeth a good scrub."

Without a word, she ran from the room, Nosy bounding behind her. Seconds later, she returned with a fistful of baking soda. After drawing up beside his bed, she unfurled her fingers. Her hand was none too clean, but Zach had eaten so much dust behind a plow in his lifetime that he didn't figure a little more would kill him. After retrieving the toothbrush Marcus had brought him from the nightstand drawer, he leaned over to get the pitcher and bowl that Kate kept on the tabletop. While Miranda looked on, he set about cleansing his mouth. She giggled when he tipped his head back and gargled.

"You're so silly," she informed him.

He gave her a wink. After emptying his mouth, he said "How's that?" and stuck out his tongue again for her inspection.

"Clean as a bleach-scrubbed floor," she announced.

Zach returned the pitcher and bowl to the table. "I feel like a new man. Thank you, Miranda."

She hitched up her skirt and climbed onto the edge of his bed. "I reckon Ma won't care now if I visit."

Zach made a mental note to speak with Kate. He'd happily promise to watch his language if Miranda could come visit him.

Taking care not to bump his thighs, she settled herself cross-legged and brushed at a streak of dirt on the knee of her black cotton stocking. Zach's recollections of his boyhood were as clear as if they had happened yesterday, and despite all of his mother's efforts, tidiness had never been one of his concerns. He supposed little girls were just naturally more conscious of their appearance. As well as graceful. The fluttery way Miranda moved was distinctly feminine. He had always assumed the vast differences between males and females manifested themselves in puberty. Not so, he guessed.

Instead of brushing away the dirt, she smudged her stocking with some of the baking soda that still clung to her palm. Her forehead pleated in a frown, and her rosy little mouth pursed. "Consternation," she whispered, sounding very like her mother.

He lifted the corner of the bedsheet and rubbed at the spot, careful not to exert too much pressure on her bony little knee. Like Kate, she wasn't sturdily made. "Now we're both clean."

She smiled at that, flashing a dimple that also put him in mind of her mother. Nosy nudged his nose under her arm and persisted in jostling her until she scratched behind his ears. Zach had a feeling he had lost a dog. "It looks to me like you two have become fast friends."

"It didn't take long," she agreed.

As much as he yearned for children of his own, Zach had never been around them much. Being with Miranda made him realize that little girls her age took most of what was said to them literally. He felt a smile spreading warmth through his chest. What, he wondered, did little girls like to talk about? If he didn't think of something, and fast, she and Nosy would leave, and he'd find himself staring at the walls again.

"I'm glad you're here. I've been feeling lonesome."

She fastened her big eyes on his. "Did you cry?"

Zach circled that. "Men don't cry much, and if they do, they don't admit it."

"Would you be barest if I saw you?"

He recalled their first conversation. "Embarrassed? Yeah, I reckon I would."

She nodded. "Folks'd think you was crazy, huh? But you don't need to worry. Me and Ma wouldn't. She says tears can sneak up on a body sometimes. Them happy tears is the worst. My ma has spells of 'em. She don't never cry otherwise, but them old happy tears'll get her ever' time." With a shrug, she added, "We don't got enough egg money to order a cure."

"A cure?" Zach couldn't see the necessity.

"Yep. Them globules cost a whole dollar for two weeks, you know. So my poor ma just gots to stay hysterical."

Miranda was proving to be a font of information. Zach settled back against his pillows. "Hysterical?"

"That's what some folks call it, female hysterics. That's 'cause they think it's odd-turned to cry when you're happy."

"Do you think your ma's odd-turned?"

She wrinkled her nose again, a habit she seemed to have whenever she pondered something. After a moment, her expression cleared and she sighed. "I reckon. My ma says she is, and she's seventeen birthdays smarter than me. That's why she's so careful to hide her happy tears most times. She don't want folks thinkin' she's crazy. When she can't hide 'em, she says she's got somethin' in her eye. Most times they ain't drippy tears, you see, just the kind that make her eyes shine purdy. And they go away if she blinks real fast."

Her gaze grew intent on Zach's. "You won't go tellin' I told, will you? Ma's barest about it, just like you."

"It'll be our secret."

She apparently liked the idea of sharing a secret. With a smile, she leaned toward him. "You wanna see her do it?"

Zach arched an eyebrow. "Cry, you mean?"

"I can make her."

"You can?"

She gave an emphatic nod. "All's I gots to do is hug her and say I love her this much." She spread her arms as wide as she could stretch. "She gets happy tears ever' time."

A tight sensation crept up the back of Zach's throat. "She must love you very much."

"Yep. That's 'cause I make her so happy she could bust."

"You're a very lucky little girl."

Her radiant smile faded. "Except for I don't got a pa."

"I'll bet you miss him," Zach said softly.

She gave him an odd look. "How can I miss him if I ain't found him yet?"

Zach started to explain that he had been referring to her real father, but then he thought better of it. She obviously hadn't recovered enough from her grief to speak of him, and he respected that. "Good question."

"My new pa'll be somethin'. At night when he comes in, he'll be so glad to see me he'll tickle my neck with his whiskers and throw me way up high in the air and then catch me."

"I see." He repositioned one leg and winced. It'd be a spell before he had strength enough to toss a little girl in the air, much less catch her.

"And he'll 'prise me with a kitten someday, too." She watched him closely as if to gauge his reaction. "He wouldn't have to go clear to Jacksonville for it, though. Not if there was kittens in Roseburg."

A silken curl fell forward over one of her eyes, and it was all Zach could do not to smooth it back. Her hair, which was still too short and silken to be confined in braids, lay against her cheeks in a dark cloud of ringlets. She had such a precious little face that his fingers itched to trace its shape. "So you like kittens, do you?"

"I reckon. Mostly I just want me a pa that'd ride a long, long ways to go get me one."

From the sound of it, Joseph Blakely would be a hard act to follow. Not that Zach was in the running. "I hope you all the luck. It's not easy to find a good pa."

Her gaze clung to his. "I know. My ma says even if I was to find one, he might not be in the market for a little girl."

"Maybe not."

After watching him for several seconds, she asked in a thin little voice, "I don't s'pose you want a little girl."

The question made Zach feel as though he had just stepped off into open air. He searched her gaze and read the naked hope there. Until that instant, he hadn't realized where she was heading with this conversation.

"I'd love to have a little girl," he said cautiously. "But wanting and having are two different things. First off, I have to find a wife."

Lowering her head, she fiddled with the hem of her gray pinafore. At last she looked up. "Does it always gots to happen that way?"

"Does what have to happen what way?" he stalled.

"What if you was to find a girl you liked who was already borned? If she didn't have no pa, why couldn't you be her pa?"

Careful, Zach. "I never thought of that. I reckon it could happen that way."

"I ain't got no pa, and I'm already borned."

Feigning a thoughtful frown, he crooked a finger under her chin. Turning her face, he pretended to look her over for flaws. "And you're pretty as can be. I reckon if I were to go shopping for a little girl, I'd pick one just like you."

A beam of happiness lit up her face. "Then you'd like to be my pa?"

"I'd love to be your pa. But about the time I tried to cart you off, your ma'd probably take after me with a shot-gun."

"Cart me off?"

"If you were my little girl, you'd have to live with me."

A stricken look crossed her face. "But why can't you be my pa at this house?"

Zach could only wish. "I'm not married to your ma."

"You could go see the preacher."

"A lady has to like a fellow a lot before she'll go with him to the preacher. I'm not sure your ma likes me quite that much."

"Except for your filthy tongue, she likes you fine."

Zach couldn't hide his smile. "Who knows? Maybe if I scrub good with saleratus everyday, she'll take a shine to me."

She nodded enthusiastically. "I'll bring you some, faithful like. Besides, I been makin' magic wishes."

"Just remember that sometimes, no matter how hard we wish, things don't happen exactly the way we want."

She looked unconvinced. "Even magic wishes?"

Zach wished there were such a thing. "I'm afraid not."

"But—" Her lips quivered, and she caught the lower one between her teeth. After a bit, she said, "You mean not ever?"

He had the horrible feeling she might start to cry. "Well, maybe magic wishes come true—sometimes. Let's not count on it, though. If your ma doesn't take a shine to me, you and I can still be friends. Wouldn't that be almost as good?"

Judging from her down-turned mouth, mere friendship with him wasn't what she had in mind. "I reckon."

"Best friends," he amended, hoping that might sound more appealing. "I've always had a hankering for a best friend, and I've never been lucky enough to find one. Have you?"

"Nosy."

He glanced at the dog. "Yeah, he makes a good best friend, all right, but he's not a person. That's different."

"How?"

After thinking a moment, he replied, "Well, if I were your best friend, as soon as I got well enough, I could throw you high in the air and tickle you with my whiskers. It's not just a pa who can do that."

Her face brightened. "And would ya s'prise me with a kitten, maybe?"

"Maybe." He held out his hand to seal the bargain. "What d'ya say? Best friends, or not?"

"I couldn't call you Pa."

"No, but you can call me Zach."

"Nope. My ma says I gots to say mister."

"Mr. Zach, then."

Still she didn't accept his handshake. "What would you call me? Seems like it shouldn't oughta be Miranda, 'cause that ain't special."

That one was easy. Miranda had always struck him as too long a handle for such a little thing. "I think I'd call you Mandy. Yeah, Mandy. I like the sound of that."

Apparently she did, too, for she smiled.

He glanced down at his outstretched palm. "Well, will you shake with me on it?"

"What's shakin' do?"

He smothered a chuckle. "It makes it official."

"Official?"

"Kind of like a promise. When two people shake on something, they give their word to honor the bargain."

Her smile turned brilliant, and she placed her tiny hand in his. "You and me, official best friends."

For some reason, Zach had to swallow before he could speak, and even then his voice sounded tight. "You and me."

He closed his fingers around hers, marveling at how small they felt enclosed in his palm. As he regarded her fleeting expressions, he could see why Kate Blakely was afflicted with spells of happy tears.

That night when Kate brought Zach his supper, he asked her if she could stay and talk to him for a moment.

"About what?" She looked instantly defensive, and more than a little nervous. "You aren't taking a setback, are you?" She leaned forward to place a palm on his forehead.

Zach drew back, wishing that just once she would think of something besides symptoms when she looked at him. "I'm not feeling sick. Fact is, I'm getting a bit stronger every day. There's just something I need to discuss with you."

She straightened. "Miranda . . ."

"That's right. I take it she told you about our little visit this afternoon?"

"Yes."

Zach didn't like the wariness that had crept into her eyes and he wondered at the cause. "While we were talking, I learned that you've forbidden her to come in here and see me."

Her gaze chased off toward the window. "I didn't exactly forbid it. Discouraged would be a better word."

Zach sighed and set his untouched plate of food on the bedside table. Salmon, again. Much more fish, and he'd grow gills. "Kate, I . . ." He waited until she looked back at him, then met her gaze head-on. "I apologized for using bad language. Are you going to hold it against me forever?"

A flush stained the graceful curve of her neck. "Of course not. You can speak in any fashion you wish, Mr. McGovern. Just not around my daughter."

"I give you my word. I won't say a single cussword in her presence. If I promise you that, what harm is there in letting her visit me?"

She stepped briskly away from the bed. "I just don't think it's a good idea, that's all."

"But why? Can't you at least give me an explanation?"

"I don't feel it's necessary to explain my reasons. I'm her mother. I know what's best for her. You'll simply have to accept my judgment."

"Kate, wait. Don't leave. Can't we discuss this?"

Back rigid, she continued on toward the door. "I can't see any point. You won't change my mind."

Incredulous, Zach watched as she disappeared into the hall. Recalling his bargain with Miranda and wondering how on earth he would explain this turn of events to her, he felt a wave of anger surge through him. Since he was helpless to follow Kate, other measures were called for, and in that split second, only one came to mind. "Goddammit, come back here. I saved her life, for Christ's sake! You owe me at least five minutes to plead my case. Short of that, you should at least give me a reason."

Just as he knew she would, she reappeared in the doorway. Brown eyes snapping, she swept into the room, grabbed the door, and slammed it closed behind her with a resounding crash. "Keep your voice down!"

"Not on your life."

"Not one single cussword? Ha! You wouldn't be capable of speaking with a clean tongue if your life depended on it!"

Zach relaxed against the pillows. "At least I've got your attention."

Watching her, he knew the precise instant when she realized she had been had. The flush of anger on her neck turned blazing crimson. "I don't find this the least bit amusing."

"Well, I'm not having a barrel of fun, either."

She turned back toward the door.

"Walk out, and I'll yell what I have to say. They'll hear me all the way to Roseburg. You can bet your sweet little ass on it."

She stopped midstride, doubled her hands into fists, and slowly pivoted to face him. Anger became her, Zach decided. She walked back to stand at the foot of his bed. Folding her arms around her waist, she threw a fierce glance at the clock, then turned the glare on him.

"A half minute of your time is used up," she finally said.

Zach grinned. "Did anyone ever tell you you're beautiful when you're mad?" It was an age-old line, but judging from Kate's flustered reaction, she had never heard it.

She hugged her waist more tightly. "Now it's a minute. You've only four left."

Zach gave it up and forked his fingers through his hair. Lowering his gaze, he tried to think what to say. In the end, he came straight out with it. "I'm lonely as hell. What possible harm can it do if she spends a little time with me?"

She rolled her eyes. "Listen to yourself."

Zach went back over what he had just said and groaned. "I wouldn't say hell in front of her."

"Filthy talk shoots out of your mouth like peas from a pod."

"Filthy talk?" He could only wonder at her definition. In his estimation, colorful would have been a better word.

"Yes, filthy talk. So much that I'm not at all certain you're aware of it. If not, you can't possibly correct it."

"I will," he promised.

She shook her head. "No. I'm sorry, Mr. McGovern, but I truly don't think—"

Zach shoved up on one elbow. "She's a precious little girl. Do you really believe I'd do or say anything that might change that? At least give me a chance. Whether you realize it or not, she needs me as much as I need her."

"Don't presume to tell me what my daughter needs."

"Then open your eyes. She misses her father. I know I can't take his place. But I might help ease the ache a little."

In her urgency, she leaned forward. "You tell me to open my eyes? She wants more than friendship. Can't you see that?"

Zach saw tears fill her eyes. "Katie . . ."

She raised a fist at him. "Don't call me Katie. It's Kate! And don't you dare start calling my daughter by your pet names, either. Mandy!" She clucked her tongue. "Oh, yes, she told me about that, and I won't have it. Do I make myself clear?"

Too late, Zach realized there was a whole lot more

worrying Kate than the language he sometimes used. "I think maybe we should start all over. It's not my cussing that's the issue here, is it?"

She dug her teeth into her bottom lip and stared at the ceiling. When she finally looked back down at him, she had managed to blink the tears from her eyes. "I don't want her hurt. She's building a castle of dreams around you. Are you truly so blind you haven't noticed? You're right up there with fairies and elves and mystical unicorns. Miranda's hero. Can you live up to that, Mr. McGovern?"

Zach had no idea how to answer. Miranda's hero?

Her gaze clung to his. "If you can't, you'll destroy what few little-girl dreams she has left."

He licked his lips. "I'm not perfect, Kate. But I don't think Miranda expects me to be."

"She's falling completely in love with you," she whispered. "In her eyes, you *are* perfect. No one can measure up to that."

"No, and I won't try, if that's what's worrying you. I'm not cut from hero cloth. But I don't think she's looking for a hero. She just wants a friend, someone to fill the empty places in her life now that her father's gone."

"She's looking for magic," she insisted in a tremulous voice. "I know you can't possibly understand, but—" She gave her head an emphatic shake. "You won't be here forever. Before we know it, you'll be gone, and that castle of dreams she's trying to erect will be absolutely shattered. I can't stand by and allow that to happen. Don't ask me to."

"She knows I won't be staying here. We discussed that."

Surprise filled Kate's large eyes, which were nearly as guileless as her daughter's. "You did?"

He held up his hands. "I realized right off that she was hoping for things that could never happen, and I explained to her why they couldn't. We settled on being best friends. I live nearby. When I leave here, there's no reason we can't continue to be friends. What's the harm in that?"

"The harm will come when you forget she exists."

Zach snorted.

"It'll happen," she assured him. "You'll marry eventually and have children. You won't have time for someone else's little girl. You probably won't even think of her. But she will you. And she's suffered enough grief."

He fell back against the pillows. "What do you take me for, a heartless bastard? If I tell the kid I'll be her best friend, then I damn well will be. You have my word on that."

She stood there staring at him, her indecisiveness etched in rigid lines upon her face. "You make promises very lightly, Mr. McGovern. How are you at living up to them?"

For a fleeting instant, Zach nearly backed off, not because he feared he might disappoint Miranda, but because all his instincts told him there was far more boiling beneath the surface of this discussion than Kate was letting on. Far more. She wasn't just concerned about her child; she was terrified. The question was, why? She didn't strike him as the type to grow this frantic without reason.

"Is there something you aren't telling me?" he asked softly. "If so, you'd better be up front with it."

At his question, the color drained from her face. Zach had his answer. As she often did when feeling shaken, she pressed a palm to her waist. "No, there's nothing. Miranda's just a very sensitive little girl who's lost her father. I don't want her hurt. I know you mean well, but—"

"I do mean well," he interrupted. "If you'll give me half a chance, I'll prove it."

Even as he spoke, Zach wondered why he was persisting this way. Then a picture of Miranda's small face flashed through his mind. *I don't s'pose you want a little girl?* The memory made his heart catch. What if Kate was right? What if he did hurt her? Maybe, in their innocence, children didn't see things the way adults did. When the day came that he had to leave, would Miranda view his departure as abandonment?

"I wish you had talked to me sooner," he said softly. "As it is, you're a little late. This afternoon, Miranda and I agreed to be best friends. We even shook hands on it. I don't see how I can go back on that without disillusioning her, which is apparently what you've been trying to prevent."

Her lips thinned into a tremulous line.

"Kate, I won't hurt your daughter. Now that you've explained your concerns to me, I'll go out of my way to make sure she doesn't build false hopes. Trust me."

"I pray not. Because if you do, I'll take every tear she cries out of your miserable hide."

With that, she turned and fled the room.

11

Over the next few days, Zach felt as though he were on trial. To Kate's credit, she no longer tried to keep Miranda away from his room. But he didn't kid himself. One wrong move, just one, and she'd forbid the child to see him. He couldn't count the times that he glanced up while playing with Miranda to see Kate in the doorway, her watchful gaze reflecting emotions he couldn't read. Dread? Fear? Perhaps even a bit of jealousy? Try as he might, he couldn't figure out what her problem with him was.

She wanted him on his feet and out of her house, the sooner the better; she made that as clear as rain. Not intentionally, he felt sure. He didn't believe Kate had it in her to be unkind. But the message came through. The moment he was strong enough to don his jeans and sit on the edge of the bed, she looked happy enough to bust and began encouraging him to try his legs. Though he complied and managed a few shaky steps, he couldn't help but feel like a bad case of influenza she couldn't wait to be rid of.

What kind of man did she think he was, anyway? Only

a monster would steal a child's heart and then callously break it.

As perverse as he knew it was, Kate's fierce protectiveness of Miranda and her suspiciousness of him only served to make him more determined to befriend the child. If it was the last thing he did, he'd make Kate admit his relationship with Miranda was one of the best things that had ever happened to her.

And so it was that he deliberately set out to capture Miranda's heart. Bad move. Before he knew exactly how it happened, he was the one who had fallen hopelessly in love.

Miranda . . . She was laughter and magic and sweetness, all rolled up in a tiny bundle. When she settled in the circle of his arm and cuddled close, he felt a sense of contentment and purpose. Listening to her talk held him spellbound for hours. Her endless questions about the world and everything in it gave him a new outlook on the everyday things he took for granted.

Some of her questions he was able to answer, others he wasn't. Either way, he was left pondering things that had never concerned him. Why did the wind blow and then stop? Why did folks say "I beg your pardon" when they hadn't done anything wrong? Why was it all right for husbands to have fat stomachs, but ladies had to wear corsets? Why did cream separate from milk? Why were religious folk referred to as God-fearing if they weren't afraid of God? Why did some plants make flowers and others didn't? If the rain was in the clouds, why did the whole sky turn dark before a storm? What made lightning? And why did the air feel prickly before the lightning came?

One of Miranda's unanswerable questions troubled Zach. Why was it that parents could be bad to their children and that was okay, but when children were bad, they got whipped? Not spanked. Not thrashed. Not punished. Not scolded. But whipped? The expression on Miranda's face when she asked that question made a cold shiver run up Zach's spine.

When Miranda wasn't asking questions, which took up a great deal of their time, Zach entertained her by telling her stories or teaching her games. She spent hours playing oops, a game of dexterous skill Zach constructed that involved catching a ball in a cup. When her interest in that waned, he sent her to find two sticks and an embroidery hoop so they could play graces, the object being to catch the hoop with the sticks.

Since Miranda was a girl, Zach knew it was inevitable that she'd eventually ask him to play with her dolls. That was where he intended to draw the line. But when the moment finally came, he didn't have the heart. For one, the armload of rags she held were the most pitiful excuses for dolls he had ever seen. Kate had fashioned them from worn-out socks. Their button eyes didn't match. Their yarn hair was so sparse they looked as though they had a bad case of mange. And, like the quilted counterpane on his bed, their dresses had been fashioned from old clothing scraps, all in shades of mourning. Even so, Miranda held them with reverence and touched them as if they were beautiful.

Zach played dolls. What the hell. Only a man who wasn't very sure of his own masculinity was afraid of being sissified.

"This is our secret," he warned Miranda. "If your ma comes in, the dolls go under the bed. Agreed?"

Miranda's first response to that was a giggle, but she finally conceded with a nod. Zach settled down to play dolls. The first crack out of the bag, Miranda complained that Zach's doll, Suzanne, was a girl doll, and therefore she didn't "talk scratchy." Feeling absurd, Zach tried to speak in a high-pitched voice. His efforts sent Miranda into fits of laughter. They finally decided that Suzanne had a sore throat.

In one afternoon of playing dolls, Zach learned more about Miranda than he had in all their previous hours together. The first thing he noticed was that her doll families always had a ma, but never a father. When he suggested they remedy that, Miranda's favorite doll, Sarah, promptly hid beneath the sheet.

"Where did Sarah go?" Zach asked carefully, not liking the bloodless pallor of Miranda's face. "Is she tired of playing?"

"She's in the cupboard," was Miranda's reply.

"In the cupboard?" Zach circled that. "Why, Mandy?"

"Because her pa comed home, and she don't like him."

That stopped Zach dead. "Then let's give her a new pa."

"She can't get a new pa if the old one just comed back."

That made sense. He guessed. "So she's hiding in the cupboard? That isn't very fun."

"She likes the cupboard. She can't do nothin' bad in there. And she knows her ma won't tell where she's at, so her pa can't find her."

"Oh, I see." Only, of course, Zach didn't see at all. An ache filled his chest. "Mandy, are you—is Sarah afraid?"

She fixed wide, wary eyes on his. "Not when she's in the cupboard. Not unless her pa calls her and she don't answer. Then she gets afraid. 'Cause he'll get mad if she don't come."

"What'll he do if he gets mad?"

A muscle at the corner of her small mouth began to quiver. "He'll hit on her ma." She glanced furtively over her shoulder, almost as if she were afraid someone might be behind her. "That makes Sarah cry. 'Cause her ma's gettin' blue spots, and if Sarah unhid herself, her pa'd give her the blue spots instead." A haunted look came into her eyes. "Sarah's ma says blue spots don't hurt grown-up ladies like they do little girls. But Sarah thinks her ma's fibbin', and she feels sad."

"Does Sarah's ma get lots of blue spots?"

Zach wasn't sure he wanted to hear the child's answer. And as it happened, Miranda didn't exactly give him one. Instead, she brightened and said, "Let's make her pa go away again. On a trip. He can go to—" She wrinkled her nose. "What's that faraway place where nobody goes?"

"Texas?"

She gave an emphatic nod.

Zach phrased his next question cautiously. "Why don't Sarah and her ma go on a trip instead? That way they'd never have to worry about her pa coming home."

"They don't gots enough money to go on trips, and her pa always finds 'em if they try to walk. One time Sarah's ma saved her pennies for train tickets, but the 'ductor and sher'ff made 'em git off in Medford and wait till her pa got there. After that, Sarah's pa hid all the pennies."

"I see," Zach said softly. "Well, in that case, we'll just have to send Sarah's pa away, then. Clear to Texas so he won't come back for a long, long time."

She agreed with another emphatic nod.

Texas it was. And Zach never again made the mistake of conjuring up a father for Miranda's dolls. That didn't prevent an ugly suspicion from forming in his mind. Miranda was a bright child, and he knew from playing dolls with her that she had a vivid imagination that often amazed him. But how inventive could a child her age possibly be? Unless she had firsthand experience, how could she know so much about bruises and trains and conductors and the town of Medford?

A couple of times he considered asking Kate about her

deceased husband. What kind of man had Joseph Blakely been? Was he the reason Zach sometimes thought he saw fear in Kate's and Miranda's eyes? In the end, though, he kept silent. After all, Joseph was dead. If he had once been a threat, he wasn't now. Zach had no more right to pry into Kate's past than she did his. It wasn't as if he didn't have a secret or two of his own that he didn't want to share.

Kate seldom mentioned Joseph, but when she did, her features always settled into a grim stillness. Her memories of him clearly brought her pain. Now Zach was no longer certain that her pain stemmed from grief.

About a week after Kate began letting Miranda visit with Zach, he was awakened one morning shortly after dawn by the sweet sound of the child's voice.

"Today's my ma's birthday."

The announcement dragged Zach up to consciousness. He turned his head and opened one eye a crack. Miranda stood beside his bed, her small form a gray blur. He blinked and tried to focus.

"Say what?" he croaked. Squinting at the shaft of sunlight on the window, he surmised it was morning since it had been dark outside the last time he looked. "What time is it?" He tried to see the clock. "Whose birthday?"

She held up handfuls of twisted paper, her eyes glistening with what he suspected were unshed tears. Mouth atremble, chin quivering, she repeated, "My ma's."

"Your ma's?" Zach ran a hand roughly over his face, blinked again, and stifled a yawn.

"I wanna make her a paper rose, but I forget how."

In Zach's estimation, unshed tears were nothing to mess around with. He sat up a little, finger combed his sleep-tousled hair, and shook his head to clear it. "A paper rose?"

She heaped the twisted paper on his bed. "Can you fix it?"

Zach stared down at the mess. "Honey, I'm not much of a hand at making flowers."

Her mouth drew into a tremulous pout.

"I can sure try, though," he quickly amended. After all, how hard could it be to make a flower from paper?

Ten minutes later, Zach had the answer to that question. Damned hard. He held up his attempt at a rose, which was pretty pitiful looking even in his books, and upon seeing it, Miranda promptly let out a caterwaul to wake the dead. It certainly brought Zach wide awake, at any rate. Then she burst into tears.

He tossed aside the paper and drew her onto his lap, wincing at the press of her weight against his sore thighs. "Hey, now. It's nothing to cry over."

Her sobs gained force. "I wanna give her somethin' nice."

"You will. We'll think of something."

After enfolding her in his arms, he propped his chin on her head. Her silken hair smelled of Pear's soap and little girl sweetness, a scent he wasn't at all sure could be defined. Since meeting Miranda, he only knew it existed. Perhaps innocence had an essence all of its own.

"Honey, please don't cry. I said we'll think of something."

"But I don't got a present to give her!" she cried. "She'll come back from the barn 'specting somethin', and I don't gots nothin'."

"We'll just have to surprise her. We'll make her wait all day, thinking we both forgot, and then we'll give her something tonight. Those kinds of presents are the most fun, anyhow, because you don't think you're going to get anything."

"But what?"

Without a cup of coffee to clear his head, Zach wasn't very inventive. "You could pick her some real roses. A great big beautiful bouquet. She'd love that."

"But *she* made them roses, not me! I wanna give her somethin' I did. Somethin' purdy that she can keep. She don't got nothing that's purdy, Mr. Zach. Not a single thing."

He had noticed that, yes. The only beautiful things in this house were Kate and Miranda. "Maybe you could pick her some wild flowers. That'd be something you did, and she'd be real surprised. When they start to wilt, she can press them in her Bible so she can keep them a long time."

"Alls we got is danderlions."

He smiled in spite of himself. "Dandelions are pretty."

"They're weeds. Ma jerks 'em up ever' time she sees one."

So much for that idea. Zach searched his mind. Suddenly he recalled a gift for his mother that his father had helped him make years ago. "I've got it. Let's carve her a plaque."

That clearly stirred Miranda's interest. "What's a plaque?"

Zach wondered if she had any idea how weak in the middle he felt when she regarded him through puddles of tears. A man didn't stand a chance. "It's kind of like a picture. Made out of wood. Ladies hang them on their walls. We could carve her a rose in the center and darken the etching with charcoal. It'd be something pretty that she could keep forever."

Her swimming eyes brightened with pleasure. Feeling relieved, Zach lifted a corner of the bedsheet to dry her cheeks.

"Okay, let's do it."

He chuckled. "Can I have my coffee and breakfast first?

It wouldn't be much of a surprise if your ma came in to feed me and caught us making her a present."

"Okay," she agreed reluctantly. "You can eat first."

Immediately after breakfast, Zach sent Miranda to the barn for a suitable piece of wood. Since she had never seen a plaque, suitable turned out to be the operative word. She made four trips before she returned with a flat board that held any promise. Since Zach was afraid she might cut herself with his pocketknife, he had to do the carving while Miranda did "the most important part" by holding one end of the wood.

When Kate came in from doing chores, a mad scramble ensued to hide the newspaper full of wood shavings and the half-finished plaque. Zach ended up with the shavings dumped in the bed, which was uncomfortable, to say the least.

After lunch, he shooed Miranda from his room long enough to don his jeans. Then the two of them cleaned out his bed. Once that was done, they set to work again. By late afternoon, the carving part of the process was complete, and all that remained was to darken the etching with charcoal. Zach had looked forward to this stage all day, for the coloring was something Miranda could do by herself.

"How about getting me some charcoal?" he asked.

She went perfectly still. "Charcoal?"

"Yeah. You know, a chunk of the black stuff that's left over after a fire. There should be some in the fireplace grate."

At the suggestion, Miranda turned absolutely white. There was no mistaking that look in her eyes. He shifted his gaze to the scars on her hand. At last he knew how she must have gotten burned. She wasn't the first child to have played with fire and suffered catastrophic consequences.

Though still horribly weak and shaky on his feet, he swung off the bed and stood. "Now that I think on it, there's no reason why I can't go and get it myself," he said lightly. "Point me in the right direction."

"The closest fireplace is in the room by the kitchen," she said thinly. "There's another one in the parlor, but you'd have to walk longer."

"And where is the kitchen?"

Zach expected her to lead the way, but she remained on the bed, face still pale. He didn't have much strength, but if she grew this upset just thinking about the fireplace, he had no choice but to explore until he found it. The house wasn't that large, and he knew the kitchen had to be on the first floor.

"Sit tight," he said, grabbing the footboard of the bed for support as he moved toward the door. "I'll be right back." A few faltering steps across the floor and he amended that. "Well, maybe not right back. But don't give up on me."

Several minutes later, he returned to the bedroom, charcoal in hand, feeling as exhausted as if he had run a five-mile race. When he reached the bed, he collapsed. Further work on Kate's plaque had to wait until he had caught his breath and rested.

Despite the delay, the gift was finished by the time Kate came in from doing the gardening and evening chores. A work of art, it definitely wasn't. Without any way to sand its surface, the wood was still rough, despite all Zach's attempts to smooth it with his knife blade. But Miranda was ecstatic over it. Between the two of them, they concocted a plan to surprise Kate with her present when she came in to serve Zach his supper.

Their careful plans went off without a hitch—until Kate leaned over to set Zach's supper tray on his lap. Miranda chose that moment to pop out from under the bed, yelling "Surprise!" a little more loudly than they had rehearsed. The shout startled Kate so badly that she nearly dumped Zach's meal all over him.

"Oh, my!" she cried, pressing a hand over her heart. "What is this?"

Miranda beamed up at her and shoved the plaque in her hands. "Your birthday present. I made it for you."

Kate's eyes went wide as she examined the patterned edge Zach had carved. Then she ran shaky fingertips over the rose, looking more impressed than the artwork warranted. He silently applauded her for giving a fine performance.

"Oh, Miranda," she whispered, "how lovely."

"Mr. Zach helped. But only a little bit."

Kate's mouth curved up at one corner in a smile that he suspected she was trying to squelch. "It's—oh, sweetness, words can't describe it. You made this for me? All by yourself, with only a little help? I can't believe it."

As she spoke, Kate's eyes filled with tears, and she sank to her knees to embrace her daughter. "I've never received anything so lovely. Most times everyone plumb forgets my birthday!"

"Not me," Miranda chirped. "I'll always give you a present on your birthday, Ma. Just you watch."

"I know. How lucky I am to have such a thoughtful little girl!" As if she suddenly realized she had tears on her cheeks, Kate swiped with her sleeve and fluttered her eyelashes. "I seem to have something in my eye. A bit of wood chip, maybe."

Miranda threw Zach a secretive I-told-you-so look. Then she used her sleeve to help her mother mop up. Zach fixed his gaze on his supper plate. *Happy tears.* He camouflaged a grin by filling his mouth with salmon.

"This calls for a celebration," Kate announced shakily. "After our supper, what say we have a birthday party?"

In her excitement, Miranda jumped up and down. "Can we have it in here, so Mr. Zach can have fun with us?"

Kate pushed to her feet, still holding the plaque in one hand. "Of course. It wouldn't be fair to exclude him after he helped you to make me such a lovely gift."

The sincerity in Kate's voice brought Zach's head up. She was turning the plaque in her hands, testing its surface and once again tracing the design with her fingertips. He studied her face, searching for any sign of artifice. All he found was an unspoiled sweetness. That silly etching of a rose, humble and imperfect as it was, meant the world to her; it truly did.

Zach looked away again, this time not to save her feelings but to hide his own.

Shortly after supper, Zach smelled cookies baking. A few minutes after that, Kate and Miranda came to his room, each bearing a tray, the child's filled with freshly baked sweets, Kate's with three mugs and a pot of hot cocoa.

"It's time for our party!" Miranda informed him in an excited voice. "Are you ready?"

Aside from eating, Zach wasn't too sure what they might do to celebrate. He hoped the child wouldn't be disappointed. He needn't have worried. Kate was nothing if not inventive. She told stories. They sang songs. Then they capped off the evening by playing charades. In all his life, Zach had never laughed so much or so hard. When the hour grew late, Kate gathered Miranda onto her lap and ended the festivities with another story, which she told in a low voice that made Miranda start to nod off.

Thinking the child was asleep, Kate let her voice trail off. Miranda immediately jerked awake. "Then what happened?"

"I'm sorry, sweetness. Your eyes were closed, and I thought you were snoozing."

Miranda snuggled back down. "My eyes goes to sleep before my ears does."

Kate resumed the story. Zach thought she looked ready to nod off herself. She'd been going full tilt since before dawn, doing work that would exhaust a man. Most mothers would have accepted the plaque, said thank you, and gone to bed.

But not Kate. Her child was clearly the most important thing in her life, and no sacrifice was too great if it would make Miranda happy. Such love, so very much love.

The lamp on the bedside table threw out a warm glow that created a nimbus of gold around her and the child. Watching Kate's face and the emotions that played upon it, Zach found himself wishing she'd look at him that way. Just once.

Though he knew he had overstayed his welcome, he didn't want to leave. The thought made him feel desolate. Yet the day was bound to come soon, and there was nothing he could do to stop it.

From beyond the open window, the sounds of the summer night drifted to him, a dreamy backdrop for the gentle cadenu of Kate's voice. The harmony of crickets and frogs floated on a soft breeze that rustled through the trees and over the tall grasses. So peaceful, just the three of them like this. It felt so right, so absolutely right. If time had substance, Zach would have grabbed this particular handful and stuffed it under his pillow. But, alas, the ticking of the clock didn't falter, and the precious moments swept by, forever lost to him.

After she finished the story, Kate smoothed Miranda's

hair and whispered, "I'd best get her tucked in." She lifted luminous eyes to his. "I'll come back down to clear up the mess."

He couldn't help but note the shadows that lined her cheekbones. "Leave it till morning. You look plumb tuckered out."

"It's a very wonderful kind of tired," she said with a smile. "All women should be so blessed."

Blessed? She slaved every waking moment of every day, yet still had trouble making ends meet. Because she refused to take money, Zach had commissioned Marcus to bring over food—flour, sugar, potatoes, smoked and dried meat, anything that would keep and in far greater quantities than Zach could ever consume. But that wasn't enough. She needed a man to look after her. Most farm widows set out lickety-split to find a new husband, a period of mourning be hanged. Survival, that was what it boiled down to. Surely she realized that. Yet never once had she indicated that her thoughts were running along that line.

If they had been, he was the perfect candidate, scars or no. He loved her child. His property bordered hers. He was well-set financially, and nobody could say he didn't have the muscle for hard work. He could give her everything a woman could want.

At the thought, his throat tightened. He wanted to give her so much. Did she realize that? Was that why she seemed so unsettled every time their gazes locked, because she sensed what he was thinking?

She pushed to her feet, cradling Miranda in her arms as though she held a precious treasure. "If I leave the cleanup till morning, it'll throw me off stride the whole day. As tempting as it is, I reckon I'd better do it tonight."

"I wish I could help."

"Nonsense. It won't take me more than a few minutes."

She turned toward the door. "I'll be right back."

While she was gone, Zach got out of bed and started cleaning up. Each step was an effort, and before long, his hands started to quiver. Even so, he managed to gather the cups and put the plate of cookies back on the tray. Afterward, he lay on the bed in a pool of sweat, resenting his weakness, yet acutely aware that it was his only excuse for remaining here.

Excuses. He had been making excuses for days, trying to put off the inevitable. Deep down, he knew his time here already should have come to an end. With the help of Marcus and Ching Lee, he could manage to get along over at his place now.

He closed his eyes, hating to make the decision yet knowing he had to. This woman and child didn't belong to him. They never would. It was time to pick up the pieces of his heart and get the hell out of here.

"You shouldn't have, Zachariah! I could have picked up."

At the sound of her voice, he opened his eyes and raised his head. "It's my contribution to your birthday celebration."

She moved toward the bed, her eyes aglow. "You contributed plenty by making that beautiful plaque. Thank you for devoting so much time to it. You made the day for Miranda."

"It wasn't much of a present." He managed a grin, even though smiling was the last thing he felt like doing. "If you had dropped a couple of hints a few days back, I could have helped her make something nicer."

"Yes, well. I didn't have any more warning than you. It isn't actually my birthday, you see."

Zach narrowed one eye. "Say what?"

She lifted her hands and gave a little laugh. "It isn't my

birthday. I can't imagine where she got the idea—" She broke off and chuckled again. "Well, actually, I can. I thought about it all evening, and I finally concluded that she misunderstood something I said this morning."

"And what was that?"

A blush touched her cheeks. "Something silly." Her gaze moved to the window. "The dawn was so lovely this morning. When I came in from gathering wood, I felt uplifted, and I said something about feeling reborn. I remember her asking if that meant it was my birthday, and I said yes, in a sense, it was."

He understood exactly what she meant about the dawn and the sense of newness. Baptism in the first rays of morning light, a feeling that nothing before that moment mattered. Ah, yes, he understood. He had felt just that way a thousand times.

It was his turn to chuckle. "And she took it from there? Why on earth didn't you just tell her? As tired as I know you are, why the party and all?"

"I couldn't disappoint her like that, not after she'd worked all day to make me a gift. She's so small that she won't realize a whole year hasn't passed by the time the actual date rolls around."

"You're a marvel, Katie. Just take care that you don't push yourself that extra step once too often. You're only one person, and working too hard can wear anyone down."

She bent over the bed to grasp one of the trays. "As I said, it's a very nice kind of tired."

As she stacked one tray atop the other, the sweetness of her scent filled his senses, and he felt the misty warmth of her breath on his jaw. He felt like a fist had just been buried in his guts. He closed his eyes on an urge to touch her.

"Are you all right?"

Hell, no, he wasn't all right. He wasn't sure if he'd ever be all right again. "I'm fine. It's just been a long day."

He lifted his eyelashes, praying she'd move away. Instead, she touched a hand to his forehead. Annoyed, he grabbed her wrist. The contact was nearly his undoing. Only the wariness he saw in her eyes forestalled him from pulling her toward him.

Just once, he wanted to taste those tremulous lips of hers to see if they were as warm and moist and sweet as they looked. Just once, he wanted to see how her body felt pressed the full length of his. Just once, dammit.

He released his hold on her. And his heart broke a little at the nervous way she grabbed up the trays and hastened away from him. When she reached the doorway, she glanced back.

She knew. He could see it in her eyes. She knew, and the realization terrified her.

12

Right after breakfast the next morning, Zach rose from bed and got completely dressed. Pulling on his boots left him feeling weak, but he was determined. No two ways about it, he had to get his strength back and hightail it out of here.

It wasn't healthy to lie about, bored nearly to tears, watching a woman and child, yearning to call them his own. Time to go, time to get his life back on track. Once he could return to work, he'd feel better. No more foolish dreaming. As if he had a chance in hell, anyway. Not with a beauty like Kate. No maybe to it, she could have her pick of the unmarried men for a hundred square miles.

When Zach stepped out on the porch, he wasn't sure if it was the wavy flooring or him, but he felt dizzy. He leaned a shoulder against the porch post, tempted to go back to bed. But desperation drove him. He'd take it easy and just mosey along. To the barn and back would be enough for today. Each morning, he'd push himself to go just a bit farther.

Damn. How far was the barn, anyway? Halfway past

the rose garden, he had to stop for a rest. The perfume of the blossoms filled his nostrils. Needing the support, he rested a hand on the fence, which was so wobbly he wasn't sure if it was holding him up or the other way around. The place was falling down around Kate's ears. No fault of hers, that. He had never known a woman who worked harder or more ceaselessly.

Judging by the delicious smells wafting to him on the breeze, he guessed she was inside baking. Vanilla and cinnamon, yeast and melted butter. Touching a fingertip to a rose petal, he smiled at his memories. The first time he had seen Kate—the wonderful way she smelled—the way he had kept comparing her to food. It seemed a lifetime ago.

She still smelled delicious. Good enough to eat. His smile turned sour, and he turned from the fence to finish his walk. It felt good to be outdoors. He filled his lungs with the fresh air, loving the taste of it on his tongue. This was where he belonged.

The stalls in the barn needed to be mucked. He sniffed and shook his head. Kate would get to it, bless her heart. He reached the barn and leaned his back against the weathered wood. The morning sun bathed his face, and he lifted his chin to enjoy the golden warmth. It made him feel alive, really alive, for the first time in weeks. The smell of the earth, of the animals, of the green grass. Everything that he was came from the land. Now he'd get back to it. He'd be okay.

The first thing Zach noticed when he came in from out of doors was that the house smelled like Kate, with faint traces of vanilla, yeast, cinnamon, and roses. Not exactly what he'd call sensuous. Hell, no. Give him a velvety neck dabbed with lilac, and he was a happy man.

That was his problem. It had been a spell since he'd been with a woman. A long spell. As soon as he got his legs under him, he'd ride into town, buy himself a jug of sinner's swill, Kentucky bourbon if he got his preference, and take care of that little matter. Someone with big blue eyes, and big everything else. Someone who smelled like a woman instead of—he sniffed and scowled—a damned cinnamon roll in a rose garden.

With that thought to cheer him, Zach opened the sick-room door. As his gaze settled on the bed, he froze mid-stride. Miranda sat there holding his open pocketknife. The blade glinted wickedly in the sunshine that shot through the window.

Without thinking of the consequences, he closed the door with more force than he should have and cried, "Mandy!"

She jumped. His heart took a leap with her. Even after the punishment he'd given the knife yesterday, it was still sharp enough to shave whiskers. He hurried across the room, grabbed the child's wrist, and prized the weapon from her tiny fingers.

Still reeling from the fright she had given him, he cried, "What possessed you to touch my things without asking?"

Miranda stared up him, her pupils dilated so that her eyes looked nearly black.

"Don't *ever* get into my stuff again without asking me first! Do I make myself absolutely clear, young lady?"

She gave a jerky nod. Her gaze moved to the knife, and the color washed from her face. Zach immediately saw that he had frightened her. Tossing the knife onto his pillow, he bent and gathered her into his arms.

He ran a hand over her hair, trying in the only way he knew to soothe her. She held herself rigid and shrank from his touch. With a moan of regret, he rested his cheek atop her head. "I didn't mean to scare you, honey. But you can't touch my things when I'm not here. Don't you know what can happen to little girls who play with knives?"

At the question, she started to tremble. The next instant, Zach felt something warm and wet seep across the waist of his shirt and jeans. For a moment, he couldn't think what had happened. Then realization jolted through him.

As if she suddenly realized what she had done, Miranda jerked back. He looked down at her small face. If possible, she had turned even paler. Her mouth began to work, but no sound came out. Watching her, seeing her terror, Zach knew his unthinkable suspicion the other day had been correct. *Sarah, hiding in the cupboard.* Oh, Jesus.

Feeling sick, he hugged her close and sat on the chair. Instinct guided him, and he began to rock her, slowly, gently, using his hands to ease the rigidity from her tiny body. "Mandy. Oh, Mandy, honey." His voice didn't sound like his own. "I'm not mad. Really I'm not. When I saw you with the knife, it just scared me. That's all. I yelled without meaning to."

She worked a hand between them and touched her sopping pinafore. A pitiful little whimper came up her throat.

Sensing her concern, he whispered, "You can wet on me any old time the mood strikes. We're best friends, remember? I know it was an accident. And even if it wasn't, I don't care. Really I don't. Marcus brought me other clothes. I can change."

He felt some of the tension ease from her. Pressing his face into her hair, he closed his eyes on a wave of helpless rage. Heaven help him, he could kill whoever was responsible for this. Joseph Blakely . . .

The name etched itself across his mind in blazing red. If only the bastard weren't already dead. What in God's name had he done to this child?

The time to get an answer to that question would come later. For now, Zach's only concern had to be for Miranda. He continued to rock her. No words came to him. What was there to say? That he was sorry? That his heart bled for her? Jesus, how pitifully inadequate words were. The only message she might comprehend would come from the way he held her. And from the silence. In that, there was a measure of peace.

He threaded his fingers through her silken curls, painfully aware of how small her head felt beneath his palm. As God was his witness, no one would ever hurt her again. Not as long as he had breath left in his body.

The seconds slipped by and mounted into minutes, and still Zach rocked her. Time became meaningless. There was just the child. He wondered what she was thinking. Or did fear such as this wipe the mind clean? Mindless terror. That was what he had seen in her eyes.

It seemed to Zach that an eternity passed before Miranda finally stopped shaking. When she reached an arm around his neck, tears stung his eyes. Trust always came dearly, but from a child like Miranda, it was priceless. He tightened his arms around her.

"I'm sorry I yelled at you. I'll try never to do it again," he whispered raggedly.

She shinnied up his chest to hug his neck with both arms. "I won't be bad no more."

"Oh, Mandy, you weren't bad. Just curious. Someday, when you're old enough, I'll give you that knife and teach you how to use it. Just don't touch it until then. Okay? I don't want you to get cut."

"I was just lookin'."

He cupped the back of her head and pressed her little face against his shoulder. "You can look at it all you like when I'm with you. But never when I'm not. Is it a deal?"

She nodded and clung more tightly to his neck. "I love you, Mr. Zach."

The tears that had stung his eyes earlier spilled over onto his cheeks. He sniffed and glanced down. "I'd say you and I are wet through to the skin. You should probably go change your drawers."

She remained cuddled against him a while longer, then finally nodded, gave his neck a last hug, and climbed down from his lap.

Zach found Kate in the kitchen pantry. She was reaching for a jar of green beans from the shelf, and when his shadow fell across her, she started. It seemed to be his day for frightening females. So be it. This confrontation was bound to get worse before it got better.

"Somebody has been mistreating your daughter," he blurted. "I want to know who. If the bastard's not already dead, he'll wish he was by the time I get done with him."

Kate gasped and stepped back against the wall. The blood drained from her face, leaving her skin a translucent white.

Zach took her hand, led her from the pantry, jerked a chair out from the table, and pressed her down onto it.

"I want answers, Kate. Who abused your daughter?"

Strength quickly flagging, Zach pulled out a chair for himself, and not a second too soon. As if possessed of a will of their own, his legs folded. A clammy sweat sprang up all over his body. He needed to rest. Desperately.

White lipped and big eyed, Kate stared at him, making no attempt to give him the answers he was determined to get.

"I asked you a question. Neither of us is leaving this room until you answer me."

She curled her fingers over her knees. Zach could

almost see her thoughts racing, and he had the sick suspicion that she was trying to think of a lie to pacify him.

"It was Joseph, wasn't it?"

She flinched as if he had slapped her. "No," she whispered. "What gave you that idea?"

She looked as frightened as Miranda had a few minutes ago. Recalling the little girl's story about Sarah's ma and the blue spots, he couldn't help wondering if Kate was afraid he would strike her. Later, he might ask her about that, but for now, his main concern had to be for the child and her immediate safety. Someone had abused her. If not Joseph, then who?

As if she read his thoughts, Kate hugged her waist and cried, "I promise you, it'll never happen again. There's no need for you to meddle."

"Meddle?"

"Yes, meddle. She's my daughter and therefore my concern, not yours."

He jackknifed forward and caught hold of her chin. "I'm making her my concern. Understand that. If you think I'll turn my back on this, not knowing for certain that she's safe, you've got another think."

The rasp of his own voice filled Zach's ears. He sounded like a man within inches of turning violent. Calling upon all his self-control, he released her and settled back in the chair. Struggling to speak in a calmer tone, he said, "Someone mistreated that little girl. You can't blame me for wanting to know who." He held her gaze, relentless in his pursuit of answers. "It must have been Joseph. Who else?"

She swayed slightly, looking as if she might faint. "No, it wasn't Joseph. I—I'm the one to blame. And I swear, it'll never happen again."

With that she lurched up from the chair and darted past him. He shot out a hand and captured her wrist, spinning her back around to face him. If ever he had doubted how slightly built she was, he didn't now. He nearly jerked her off her feet and had to check her fall. She staggered toward him until their faces were scant inches apart.

"Don't say something like that and then run out."

She tried to wrench away from him. Afraid that the grip of his fingers might bruise her wrist, he relented and let her go.

"I said I was the one to blame," she cried. "Just leave it at that and trust me not to let it happen again."

Her words still ringing, she left the room, slamming the door behind her. It was Zach's second shock of the day. Kate had been abusive to her daughter?

Kate?

He didn't believe it. She didn't have it in her to harm anyone. She hadn't even been able to clobber Nosy with her broom, for God's sake. Yet she expected him to believe she had hurt her own child?

He went back over their conversation, recalling how pale she had become when he mentioned Joseph's name. If he didn't know better, he'd think she was terrified of a dead man.

The next afternoon, after taking a short walk to the barn, Zach happened into the kitchen for a drink of water and caught Miranda sneaking a dipper of cream from the pail of milk Kate had left sitting on a tripod in the corner.

"Ah-ha! I caught you red-handed," he said teasingly.

The child gave a violent start, dropped the dipper, and fell back against the wall. As she moved, her elbow bumped the pail. It rocked precariously, gravity gained the upper hand, and before Zach could move, milk went everywhere.

One look into Miranda's eyes told him how terrified

she was. An awful paralysis gripped him as well. For a moment, he was afraid even to breathe for fear of frightening her more.

"Uh-oh," he said softly. "Now we've got a mess to clean up. If your ma sees this she might scalp us both."

As he stepped ever so slowly toward her, Zach saw that she was quivering. *Easy does it. No sudden moves. Act like it's nothing.* He set the bucket upright, drew two towels from the rack over the sink, and hunkered to mop up the spill.

"This brings back memories. When I was a boy, I dipped in the cream every time my ma turned her back." He wrung the towel over the empty bucket and flashed her a smile. "I could never figure out how she always knew what I'd been up to."

Some of the fear ebbed from her eyes.

"Can you guess how she always knew?" he asked.

Clearly too frightened to think, she glanced at the milk.

"Because I had a mustache," he admitted with a low chuckle. "Clear up to my nose. I was about ten before I finally caught on, and then I started wiping my lip with my sleeve."

A bit of color returned to the child's cheeks. Her gaze moved to his mouth, and her own pursed as if to speak. At first no sound came forth. Zach's heart broke as he watched her.

At last, she said, "Wh-What h-happened then? D-Did you st-still get caught?"

"My ma was one smart lady. She took to grabbing my wrists and jerking my arms up to check my cuffs. If she found smears of cream, she tweaked my ears."

She moved away from the wall. "Does tweaks hurt?"

Oh, Mandy . . . Zach had to speak around a lump in his throat. "My ma didn't tweak hard. Mostly it was a game between us, me sneaking and her trying to catch me at it." He handed her a towel. "Want to help?"

Though she was still quivering, she timidly accepted the cloth. After watching him for a moment, she finally gathered her courage and squatted to blot up some milk. Working in tense silence, they finished cleaning up the mess. When all was set right again, Zach was so exhausted he made a beeline for a chair.

When he was settled, Miranda asked, "Do you still like cream?"

He winked at her. "Sneak a sip every chance I get. But now I'm careful not to get it on my face. There's a trick to it." He braced his elbows on his knees, feeling as shaky as she looked. "You have to stick your chin out and kind of lean your head back. And don't tip the dipper too much."

A faint smile curved her precious little mouth. "I gots a long tongue. I can lick clear up to my nose."

Zach assumed an incredulous expression. "Ah, go on. Nobody's tongue is that long."

Her expression still grave, she nodded, stuck out her tongue, and touched the tip to her nose.

"I'll be." He studied her intently. "I've never seen the like. Do it again."

She obliged him, face contorted, eyes crossed to look at her nose. Zach couldn't help but laugh, and she rewarded him with another timid smile. Ghosts still lurked between them, though.

"My ma says I gots a tongue that'd put lizards to shame."

"I should say so." He straightened and braced an arm on the table. His elbow bumped a plate of chocolate cookies, leftovers from Kate's birthday party, he guessed. Inspiration struck. "You know what sounds good to me right now? Milk and cookies. But I guess I'm out of luck. We spilled all the milk."

"Ma's got other milk, but she says I shouldn't eat cookies right afore supper 'cause it ruins my—" She wrinkled her nose. "My hungry part. What's it called?"

"Your appetite," he supplied, and glanced over his shoulder. "Does your ma keep a running count on the cookies?"

Looking bewildered, she shook her head.

Zach winked. "Then as long as we eat a good supper, she'll never know if we have some, will she?"

Her eyes widened. "You mean you wanna sneak?"

"I won't tell on you if you won't tell on me."

A mischievous twinkle crept into her eyes. She dashed to the icebox and opened the lower left door. Straining under the weight, she removed a half-gallon pitcher from the shelf. Weary though he was, Zach rose to help before they ended up with more milk on the floor. He located the shelf where Kate kept her glasses, filled two, returned the pitcher to the icebox, and then joined Miranda at the table. After reseating himself, he snagged four cookies from the plate, giving the child two, keeping the others for himself.

"You know how to dunk?" he asked, then promptly showed her how. "Cookies never taste so good as when they're dunked in cool milk."

She wiggled around to get on her knees so she'd be tall enough to dunk her own. Zach smiled to himself when she cupped her hand under her chin to catch the drips as she took a bite. There was definitely a world of difference between little girls and little boys.

"Mmmmmm," she murmured appreciatively.

They settled down to some serious eating, grinning at each other like partners in crime. After finishing her cookies, Miranda drank nearly all her milk and then contemplated the remaining inch of liquid in her glass. A distant expression came into her eyes. "Did you know you can get drownded in milk?"

"Drownded? Drowned, you mean?" He thought it a rather odd observation but pretended to give it due consideration. "I reckon a person could. It'd take a powerful lot of milk to do the job, though."

Miranda glanced across the kitchen at the milk pail on the tripod. A bruised look came into her expressive eyes. In a tremulous little voice, she said, "Nope. Alls it takes is a bucketful if somebody sticks your head in it."

A piece of cookie lodged in Zach's throat. He struggled to swallow, then turned his gaze toward the milk pail. *Dear God in heaven.*

Before Zach could think of anything to say, he heard a distant screech. Kate? He cocked his head. Another shrill cry drifted through the house. It sounded as though she was out in the front yard.

Moving more slowly, Zach followed Miranda from the kitchen. When they spilled out onto the front porch, he sagged with relief. Nosy had been digging in the rose garden again, and Kate had taken after him with her hoe.

Bending at the waist, Zach rested his folded arms on the wobbly porch railing. Instead of whistling for the dog, as he knew he should, he simply watched for a moment. As she had once done with her broom, Kate drew the hoe up short every time she swung at the dog, coming close but never actually hitting him.

Kate Blakely had never laid a hand on her child. He would go to the bank on that.

That night when Kate came to the sickroom to get Zach's supper dishes, she didn't rush to leave as she usually did. Instead, she hesitated before picking up the tray from his bedside table, her face drawn, her hands plucking at her apron.

"I—um—I've noticed that you've been venturing outdoors yesterday and today," she started.

Though stretched out on the bed, Zach was fully clothed. Two days ago, he might have been amused by her nervousness. Now it made him feel sick. She was so young, so very young. Yet he could only guess at the trials she must have endured.

She clearly wanted to talk with him about something. Since that suited his purposes, he forced a smile.

"Why don't you sit down? Our conversation yesterday didn't end very pleasantly." He patted a spot beside him on the bed. "No hard feelings, I hope."

To his surprise she sat where he indicated instead of on the chair a safe distance away. "No, no. None at all. I know you meant well." She fell silent for a moment. "I take it that you must be feeling stronger?"

He wondered where this was going. "Yes, a bit stronger."

She clasped her hands in her lap. Late evening light came through the nearby window, casting the shadows of her long eyelashes onto her cheeks. Whatever it was that she wanted to say, she was having a devil of a time getting it out.

Zach didn't mind the silence. Because she was in it. And, God, how that realization hurt. How had he come to care so much? The more fool he.

Her small white teeth tugged at her bottom lip, depressing the blood so the almost unnoticeable scar at one corner turned pink. Had Miranda been the only one abused by Joseph Blakely? Once the question entered his mind, he couldn't turn it loose.

She's looking for magic. Are you truly so blind you haven't noticed? Miranda's hero. Can you live up to that, Mr. McGovern?

The words whispered in his memory. He had indeed

been blind. Time after time, he had searched Kate's gaze, troubled by an elusive something that shadowed her lovely eyes. Now he realized he had been unsettled, not by what he had seen there, but by what he hadn't. *Trust.* His Katie no longer believed in heroes. Magic existed for her only in the stories she told her daughter.

Zach wished he could change that. If he could, he would build her a castle out of clouds and turn her wishes into rainbows. But he was just an ordinary man with both feet rooted deeply in reality, as imperfect within as he was without.

She finally looked up. The shadows veiled her expression. "I suppose we should both be thinking in terms of your leaving soon," she said softly.

So that was it. Not that he didn't have it coming. He had butted in where he wasn't wanted and pressed for answers she had no wish to give. Besides, it wasn't as if he hadn't already drawn the same conclusion himself. Wishes weren't rainbows, and the time had come for him to go.

In a husky voice, he offered, "I'll gather up my things in the morning and be ready to leave when Marcus stops by tomorrow night. I'd light out sooner, but I should probably have someone riding along with me my first time back in the saddle."

She nodded and averted her gaze. "I don't want you to think I've minded having you here. I haven't. It's just—" She shrugged. "I'll always be indebted to you. If you ever—" Her eyes sought his. "Anything. All you need do is ask, and it's yours. You'll always have a friend in me."

He wanted much more than friendship. He sensed she knew it. He settled his hand over hers where they rested in her lap. Judging by her expression, even that much contact unsettled her. What would she do if he kissed her or drew her into his arms?

"You say anything." He hated himself for this. But what did he stand to lose? "And all I need do is ask? What if I asked you to marry me."

"Pardon?"

"I think you heard me."

With both her hands trapped beneath one of his, he was free to touch her, and he did, running a fingertip across her lips, then along her cheek to her ear. She shivered and shrank away.

"Don't, please, don't," she whispered.

He grasped her chin and leaned toward her. "You act stunned. I can't believe I've caught you by surprise. I haven't made a secret of my feelings—not for you or for Mandy."

She didn't move, didn't blink. He couldn't be sure, but he suspected she had even stopped breathing.

"Katie?"

He touched his lips to the spot on her cheek where her dimple always flashed. She drew in a shuddering breath.

"Sooner or later, you'll be forced to remarry," he whispered. "You can't make it on your own here. Why not me? I know I'm not much to look at, but there's more to a man than—"

"Stop it!" she cried. She wrenched away from him and lunged from the bed. Coming to stand before the window, she clamped her hands against her waist, looking for all the world as if something vile had just upset her stomach. "I can't marry you. I don't intend to marry anyone. Miranda and I will get by."

He studied her pale profile. Lord, how he wanted to make pretty promises he could probably never keep.

"Kate, this place is going to rack and ruin. You work from dawn till dark, and you still can't keep up with it. One hard year of needing loans to get your crops in, just one, and the banker will be on your stoop, serving you eviction papers. Where will that leave you and your daughter? Out in the cold, that's where. If you won't think of yourself, think of Miranda."

"No! Prunes. I'm going to raise prunes and—"

"Prunes!" he said with a snort. "You'll be the prune, dried up and in the grave long before your time." He swung his feet to the floor and sat up, bracing his arms on his denim-clad knees. "If you married me—"

"I can't marry you. Not you or anyone else."

"Why? Because the last time around you tied up with a son of a bitch?"

She gasped and whirled to face him.

"It's true. You asked me once if I was blind. The answer is no." He pushed slowly to his feet, acutely aware that she retreated a step when he stretched to his full height. "Miranda wasn't the only one Joseph Blakely mistreated. Look at you, shrinking away from me." He came to a stop several feet from her. "What happened in this house, Kate?"

At the question, she turned deathly pale. Her distress was so obvious that Zach nearly backed off. He, of all people, knew what it was like to be haunted by the past, and he had a couple of secrets of his own that he'd never find it easy to divulge. The difference was that he had learned to live with his, and Kate clearly hadn't.

He plunged on. "Where did you get that scar on your lip?"

Her fingertips flew to the spot.

"Did he backhand you? Or worse? And that place on your forehead. What happened? Did you tangle with a door? Let's hear how good you are at inventing quick, believable lies."

"I haven't been telling you lies."

He leaned toward her. "Haven't you? Look me dead in the eye and swear you were the one who abused your daughter."

She moistened her lips and glanced frantically around the room, as if she might find answers there. "It wasn't Joseph. You have to believe that. As for the scars on my face, I had an accident in the barn. I—I fell. Coming down the loft ladder. My shoe got caught on my skirt."

"And pigs can fly."

Her eyes went stormy dark. "You choose not to believe me. That's your choice. Either way, I really don't care. My daughter and I are none of your business, anyway."

"Whatever else I may feel for you, Kate, I also think of you as a friend. I don't turn my back on people I care about. In a nutshell, I've made you my business."

She made fists in her apron. "As I said, I think it's about time for you to leave."

With that, she moved toward the door.

"I can't turn off my feelings quite that easily."

His words stopped her dead. She slowly turned to face him again.

"If there's someone or something you're afraid of," he tried, "why not let me help? Do you really think I'll be able to sleep nights? What if I'm wrong, and it wasn't Joseph? That question will haunt me. You're terrified of something. It's written all over you. Why won't you trust me with it?"

For a fleeting instant she looked as though she might confide in him. He saw the longing in her eyes, along with another emotion he couldn't identify. Then her chin came up. "Tomorrow," she whispered. "Don't wait for Marcus. Get your things, saddle your horse, and go. I'm sorry to have your stay here end with unpleasantness, but it seems you're bent on it. As long as you are, then stay away from me."

"And Miranda?"

"Miranda, too."

She whirled, flung open the door, and rushed out into the hall.

13

Zach folded his coat around his extra change of clothing, then swept the small pile of his personal belongings off the bedside table and stowed them in one pocket. His supper tray still sat on the table, a silent reminder of all that had passed between him and Kate last night before she fled the room. In all the time he had been here, she had never once left his tray until morning. Her doing so now was testimony to how badly his proposal of marriage had rattled her.

As he started to roll the sheepskin, his fingertips grazed a rough spot, and he paused to examine two puncture holes. Fang marks. Those horrible moments down inside the well rushed back to him with harsh clarity.

Thanks to his damned mouth, things were in a dandy fix. If he'd had a lick of sense, he would have eased off Kate last night. But he'd kept pressing. And she'd fought back the only way she could.

Now what? He had no choice but to leave. But how would he explain to Miranda that he couldn't come back? Zach sank onto the edge of the bed and cradled his head in his hands. He could apologize to Kate. Not that it would do much good. Once a man admitted his feelings to a woman, it either drew them together or wedged them apart.

He sighed and rubbed his temples. Then a strange sound made him look up. Voices. He turned his head to listen. A man, and from the sound of it, he was fit to be tied.

Zach stood and moved slowly into the hall. The voices became clearer. He heard Kate cry, "That's preposterous!" Then the man roared, "You're acting like a Jezebel. Everybody in town is talking."

It sounded as if Kate had her hands full. Zach strode along the hall, acutely aware of how weak he still was. *Nothing like going to a gunfight armed with a slingshot.* When he reached the foyer, he paused. Maybe he'd get lucky and the guy would stand five foot three and weigh no more than a hundred pounds. With that thought to bolster him, he opened the door.

There was no God in heaven.

The man who stood at the bottom of the steps was a strapping six feet if he was an inch. Even in a serge double-breasted sack suit, he looked broad across the shoulders, narrow of hip, and powerfully muscled. At six five, Zach was seldom intimidated by another man's size. But then his legs didn't usually feel as limp as wet straw, either.

The man's fedora hat, made of gray felt to match his jacket and neatly creased trousers, sat crookedly on his head, the dip of the crown angled over his temple instead of his brow. He didn't pause in his ranting when Zach stepped out onto the porch.

"I told you once, and I'll tell you again, I won't stand by and watch you ruin that child. I can't force you to marry me. But I can get custody of the girl. And that's exactly what I'll do if you won't listen to reason."

Kate stood resolutely on the top step, looking small,

defenseless, and totally unnerved. Not that Zach blamed her. As far as he could tell, the man hadn't made any threatening moves toward her, but his blue eyes glittered with rage. Leaning a shoulder against the porch post, Zach folded his arms, not at all certain it was his place to interfere.

The man's voice rang a bell. He frowned slightly. Then a vague memory came flooding back. A dream? Surely it had been a dream, conjured during his delirium.

"Who, may I ask, is this?" the fellow demanded to know and gestured toward Zach.

Kate's voice rang as shrilly as chiming crystal. "This is the neighbor I mentioned the last time you were here. Mr. McGovern, the man who was bitten by rattlers while rescuing Miranda from the well." She glanced at Zach. "Mr. McGovern, my brother-in-law, Ryan Blakely."

Zach inclined his head. As if from nowhere, memories popped into his mind. *I should beat you.* Then other words filtered in. Insane, all of it. Kate's body, weeping with lust? He'd happily await the moment, but he wouldn't hold his breath. If ever he'd met a woman with too much starch in her bloomers, Kate was it.

Knotting his hands into fists, Blakely moved up a level on the steps. Zach pushed erect. Weak or not, he'd have to take over if the stupid ass got any closer.

"So the rumors are true? He's still staying here? I can't believe it. Have you no sense of shame?"

Two bright spots of color flagged Kate's cheeks. "He's been ill, Ryan. Surely you can see that. Why, he can scarcely walk!"

Oh, joy . . . Nothing like having his handicaps pointed out to his opponent right before a scuffle. Zach shot Kate a look. She didn't intercept it.

"Tell him how weak you still are, Zachariah. He thinks—Well, it's obvious what he thinks." She finally met his gaze, hers filled with appeal. "Say something, won't you? Tell him his accusations are groundless."

Zach shifted his gaze to Blakely's fists. Women. Sometimes, he didn't think they had the brains God gave a gnat. "I've been in better shape," he offered.

"Better shape?" she wailed. "You can barely stand." She lifted her hands. "Ryan thinks we've been—that I've—that you and I have—" She broke off and blinked. "The very idea is outlandish."

Zach met Blakely's gaze. Possessiveness shone in the other man's eyes. They slowly assessed one another. Blakely straightened his shoulders and tightened the muscles across his chest. After so many weeks in bed, Zach was none too sure he had any muscle left to flex.

Kate made an exasperated little sound. "Zachariah? Say something! Tell him nothing indecent has occurred between us, that we haven't even entertained the notion!"

Maybe Kate had never entertained the thought. Zach had. On more occasions than he cared to count. And he felt fairly certain Blakely knew it. "You heard the lady."

Clearly frustrated by his lack of support, Kate cried, "That's all you can say in my defense?"

"A lady doesn't need defending. Her word should be enough." Zach glanced at Kate, then back at Blakely. "And a finer lady I've never met."

Blakely curled his lip and shook his fist. "You'd better think over what I've said! I won't turn my head and ignore this! I'll take that child away from you, as God is my witness."

Kate flinched. Zach stepped closer. "It might be a good idea if you calmed down a hair, Mr. Blakely."

Nosy came running out onto the porch, lip snarled, teeth bared. As much as Zach could have used some reinforcements, he didn't want the dog getting hurt, and ordered him to sit. The animal growled, but dropped obediently to his haunches. Zach glanced toward the open doorway, hoping Miranda wasn't hiding nearby and overhearing all this.

"And you!" Blakely cried, leveling a finger at Zach. "She's got you fooled. A lady? It amazes me how blind all you people can be."

Seeing as how he had just implied that the entire town was gossiping about Kate, Zach found that observation interesting. Clearly not everyone believed the worst of her.

"Well, you can't fool me." As Blakely spoke, he thumped his chest. "I know what kind of woman you *really* are. Just like I know what really happened to my brother. People will laugh out the other side of their faces when I find proof! And so help me, I will. If I have to dig up every square inch of this property!"

Kate's face went bloodless. If it hadn't been for the fact that he could see how upset she was, Zach would have laughed. What was this lunatic accusing her of, anyway?

He couldn't stand by and let this continue. "What the hell are you saying, mister?"

"I think that's obvious!" he retorted.

"Damned right, and I'll tell you something else that's obvious. You're crazier than a coot." Zach gave Kate a measuring glance. "She couldn't kill a man if she tried. Even if she had it in her, which she sure as hell doesn't, she isn't big enough to do it."

Blakely snorted. "Naturally, you'd defend her. As far as I know, you might have helped her hide his body." To Kate, he said, "Is this the kind of sterling character you allow to be around your child? Language suitable only for a barroom, I swear. And you standing there, allowing it to go on."

Zach agreed; this had definitely gone on long enough. He moved down a step and placed himself in front of Kate. She touched his sleeve, a silent warning to keep his temper, he felt sure. As if he needed one. Getting his ass kicked wasn't exactly high on his list.

"I think maybe you'd better make dust, Blakely."

Blakely jabbed a finger at Zach's nose. "You'll burn in hell for lusting after that little whore. Mark my words."

That cut it. Zach planted a fist square in the man's mouth. Blakely toppled like felled timber, landed flat on his back, and then just lay there for a moment, staring blankly at the sky.

"Oh, dear God!" Kate cried as she hurried to join Zach on the lower step. "Oh, dear God, Zachariah, look what you've done!"

Zach rubbed his knuckles, feeling unaccountably proud of himself. Just look, indeed. Not half bad for a man who could scarcely walk.

Blakely regained his senses and rolled to his feet. Spitting blood and dirt, he dusted wildly at his pants, clearly beside himself with rage. Nudging Kate aside, Zach braced himself for a charge, knowing full well that he couldn't hold his own if Blakely came at him.

"That's it!" Blakely fumed. "That does it, Kate! I'll be back, next time with the sheriff. I'll find Joseph's body, or die trying, and with the law on my side, you won't be able to stop me."

Kate clutched Zach's arm. In a frantic voice, she cried, "I could lose Miranda if he starts stirring trouble. Oh, Zachariah, what have you done? I've no way to prove he's lying."

Even though Zach couldn't imagine anyone's listening to such craziness, he couldn't discount Kate's terror. By striking Blakely, he supposed he had tossed fuel on the fire. Still, the thought of backing down didn't sit well. Blakely had called her a whore, and where Zach came from, words like that got shoved back down a man's throat.

"You'll rue this day!" Blakely scrambled for his hat.

"Apologize," Kate pleaded.

"Apologize?" Zach gaped at her. "The son of a—" He broke off. "He called you a—"

"Just apologize, please. Oh, please, Zachariah."

"Damn it to hell," he said under his breath. "And I get accused of having a filthy mouth? I can't believe this."

He watched Blakely stumble in the direction of his horse. Kate tugged frantically on his sleeve. Zach swallowed. Apologize? He'd be damned if he would. She tugged again. He refused to look at her. He knew if he did, he'd lose his resolve.

"Zachariah . . ." she wailed.

Zach finally turned to look at her. She looked back at him through sparkling pools of tears.

"Please?"

He heaved a disgusted sigh. "Hey, Blakely?"

The man whirled.

"I sort of lost my temper there for a minute." That was sure as hell the truth.

"There'll be more than tempers lost around here!" Ryan sputtered. "We'll see how quick you are to throw punches with the sheriff standing by."

"Why bring the law into it? We're all reasonable adults." Zach clenched his teeth on that. "Kate's got nothing to hide. You can dig to your heart's content."

"You've got that right!" he cried, emphasizing each word with a jab of his finger. "And I will. The likes of you certainly won't stop me. My brother's whoring wife is going to pay for what she's done."

This second slur on Kate's character heated Zach's blood all over again, but out of regard for her, not to mention his trembling legs, he didn't run down the steps to deck the crazy bastard. Instead he resorted to sarcasm.

"Well, don't talk it to death. Start digging! To plant a

man, a little gal like Kate'd have to find an easy spot to shovel." Assuming a thoughtful frown, Zach glanced around the farm. "That narrows the possibilities considerably. The vegetable garden, maybe? The earth's well-turned there. Or why not try the rose garden? That'd be easy digging."

Kate gasped. Zach took one look at her and grabbed her arm to steady her, afraid she might faint.

His blue eyes glinting maniacally, Blakely threw a disgusted glance at the flower bed. "As if you'd point me in the right direction!"

With that, he staggered the remainder of the way to his buckskin horse. After one false try, he dragged himself up onto the saddle. Wheeling his mount, he cried, "I'll be back. Next time with digging implements!"

"I'd say. If you think I'll let her lend you a shovel, think again!" Zach retorted. As Blakely rode off, sending up a cloud of dust behind him, he whispered, "Crazy bastard." He turned toward Kate, concerned by her chalky pallor. "Come on. Let's get you inside."

"Why couldn't you simply apologize?" she cried.

"Because I would have choked on it."

"You've no idea what you've done!"

"I know what I didn't do. I should've knocked his teeth down his throat."

As if in a daze, she allowed him to lead her up the steps and into the house. Zach aimed for the kitchen. After seating her on a chair, he stepped to the sink and pumped her a glass of water. When he turned around, he saw she had her hands cupped over her face and was shaking violently.

"Honey, you shouldn't let a lunatic like that upset you so." He hunkered beside her. "Here, drink this. You'll feel better."

Making a visible effort to regain her control, she accepted the glass with tremulous hands and pressed it to her lips. After taking one sip, she set the water aside. In a hoarse voice, she whispered, "Zachariah, I truly do think it's time for you to go."

Go? Not on his life. "He might come back."

"I'll handle him. You've only made matters worse."

He stared at her. "Kate, is Ryan Blakely the one who—"

"Just go! Can't you see that I don't want you here?"

Using the edge of the table for leverage, he pushed slowly to his feet. "Well, I guess you can't put it much plainer than that."

"I'm sorry. I don't want to hurt you. Please believe that. But you don't understand what he's like."

"Then enlighten me."

She pressed the back of her wrist to her temple. "Just go, Zachariah. It's for the best, believe me."

He conceded with a nod. "All right, I'll go. But understand one thing, Kate. If I see him out on the road, riding this way, the devil himself won't keep me from coming over here."

"No! You've done enough damage! Just stay out of it. The more enraged he becomes, the more he'll spout off in town. I can't afford that. Can't you see? I could lose my child!"

"The hell you could. No one in his right mind will listen to that nonsense."

She fastened huge eyes on his. "I'm not willing to bet my daughter on it."

Defeated, Zach turned to leave and spotted Nosy sitting near the door. With a heavy sigh, he crouched to scratch the animal's ears, remembering all the evenings he had sat by the fire in an empty house, Nosy his only companion. But then he also recalled all the times the mutt had gotten loose and gone in search of excitement. Nosy had finally found his heart's desire, something Zach could never give him, a child to love.

"Tell Mandy Nosy's my gift to her." He glanced around, not wishing to go without telling the child good-bye. "Maybe it'll make my leaving a little easier on her."

"No," Kate whispered raggedly. "He digs in my roses every time my back is turned. I don't want him here."

Incredulous, Zach stared at her. Up until now, he had never heard Kate say no to anything that would make Miranda happy.

As if she read the accusation in his eyes, she cried, "Just last night! You saw him! He's nothing but trouble."

"Miranda adores him. Surely you can put up with a few holes in the roses, Kate. What are a few flowers?"

"I said no!"

As he rose to his feet, he saw that she had tears in her eyes. "Kate—"

"Just take your dog and leave!"

"It'll break her heart."

She angled an arm over her eyes. "I don't want the dog. And I can't risk your being seen here. At least not for a while. I'll explain everything to Miranda as best I can. I'll make her understand that you'd like to come but can't."

The silence in the kitchen seemed oppressive. Zach's boots felt as if they were glued to the floor. She looked so . . . Words couldn't describe it. Frightened. Frantic. And so alone, so terribly alone. His arms ached to hold her. Even if it was only as a friend.

After Zachariah left, Kate folded her arms on the table and rested her forehead on her wrists. Tears threatened, but she blinked them back. Miranda might come in at any second.

Zachariah . . . If she lived to be a hundred, she would never forget the look in his eyes right before he left.

Wounded, that was the only way to describe it. If only she could explain. Not that it would change anything, but then he'd at least understand. As it was, there was no telling what he thought.

His feelings weren't her problem. God knew, she already had enough to deal with. She just hated to hurt him. He didn't deserve that, especially not from her. She owed him for every breath Miranda took.

Taking a deep breath of her own, Kate pushed erect. Miranda. It was anyone's guess where she was hiding, bless her heart. Kate could only hope that when she found her, there wouldn't be a repeat of what had happened after Ryan's last visit.

"A fat little pig was dancing a jig, for he had got out of his pen. With a high diddle diddle, the fife and the fiddle was played by a cat and a hen!" Leaning on her shovel, Kate peeked over the partition at Miranda and winked. "It's your turn, little miss."

Miranda, who was sitting on a fresh pile of straw in the adjacent stall, glanced up with a gloomy expression on her face. "I don't recollect any rhymes."

Kate sighed. "My, what a long face. If I recited the one about the pet kitten, would that cheer you up?"

"I don't got a pa to go git me a kitten, so why would it?"

Defeated, Kate folded her hands over the end of the shovel. Zachariah and Nosy had been gone for over twenty-four hours, and Miranda had been pouting every minute since except for when she slept. "You know, Mandy, I—"

Miranda shot up from the straw. "Don't call me Mandy. That's Mr. Zach's special name for me. I gave it to him on official, and it's only for my best friend."

"Aren't I your friend, too?"

Miranda balled her hands into fists and rubbed her eyes. Kate could see her mouth quivering. "You made him go home. I heard you say it. You made him go, and you made him take Nosy with him. I hate you!"

Kate felt as though she'd been slapped. "Oh, Miranda, you don't mean that! Nosy dug in the roses. No matter how closely we watched him. You know I couldn't let him stay."

With a sob, the child wheeled and ran—straight into a man's braced legs. Ryan Blakely seized the child by the shoulders to keep her from falling. "So you hate your ma, do you?"

Miranda shrank beneath his touch and threw her mother a panicked glance. Kate was equally startled. She hadn't heard anyone ride up. "Ryan," she said softly. "What a surprise."

"I'll bet."

He regarded Miranda for a moment, as if weighing the advantages of keeping a hold on her, then finally set her free.

Even though the child fled from the barn, Kate moved her hands down on the shovel handle and got a steady grip. Not that she dared use it. The only thing that would induce her to do that would be if he threatened Miranda. Her own well-being didn't matter. Not anymore.

"How are you today?" She knew that was a stupid question, but she couldn't think of anything else to say.

He touched his split bottom lip. "As you can see, I've been better. But I'm back. And this time, I brought digging implements."

Striving to keep her expression calm, Kate worked her grip on the shovel. It wouldn't do for Ryan to guess how he unnerved her. His blustering was just that, a lot of bluster. What alarmed her was the possibility that his wild accusations might cast suspicion on her. If, in his raving, he let it slip how brutal Joseph had really been, people might begin to wonder.

Only Joseph's riding gear and coat had been found along the banks of the river. His body had never been recovered. Without evidence so she could prove accidental drowning, Ryan might sway opinion against her enough to win custody of Miranda in a court battle.

It couldn't come to that. She wouldn't let it.

She could handle Ryan, just as she had Joseph. She wouldn't think about the times she had failed in that. Not right now. "Ryan, can't we please bury the hatchet? With Joseph gone, I need your support. You're the only friend I can truly count on."

"You have a *friend,* Kate. I take it he left?"

She moistened her lips. "He planned to leave anyway. We discussed it the night before you came. It wasn't at all like you thought." She tried a smile, praying it didn't appear as forced as it felt. No matter what it took, she had to defuse this situation. "I know it looked bad. I had already begun to worry about that myself. So I asked him to leave. I swear it."

"Really?"

She didn't like the expression in Ryan's eyes as he walked slowly toward her. Her gaze darted to the barn doors behind him. Even if running were an option, which it wasn't, she'd never manage to get past him.

"Of course, really," she said with an assurance she was far from feeling. "Joseph dead barely seven months. Do you truly believe I'd take up with someone else so soon?"

"Obviously, I do." He stopped at the entrance to the stall, his breadth filling half the opening. "I hope you didn't take what I said too lightly yesterday. I meant every word. Joseph asked me to watch after you and Miranda."

"I know." She searched her mind for something, anything she might say to pacify him. "The last time you came, I'm afraid I was a little abrupt."

"Abrupt? You told me to leave the house. My brother's house."

Kate swallowed. "I was exhausted. Short-tempered."

He said nothing. The silence gnawed at her nerves.

"How did your move from Seattle go?" Kate heard the fear in her voice and tried to slow her speech. "Did you get all your things down here this trip?"

He didn't seem to hear her. "If you refuse to marry me, I'll find a way to get custody of my niece. I promise you that."

"Ryan, please. I've done nothing to deserve this from you."

After closing the distance between them, he brushed a strand of hair from her cheek. The cold rasp of his fingertips made her think of reptile skin. "You and I could raise Miranda together, you know. If only you'd cooperate."

She yearned to shove him away. Instead, she gripped the shovel more firmly. "Perhaps I will . . . in time. Can't you give me that, Ryan? A little time, out of respect for Joseph?" The remainder of what she intended to say clogged in her throat. She pushed the words out, because she had to. "I loved him. I can't bring myself to be with someone else so soon."

"You know you're beautiful, don't you, Kate?"

He wasn't listening to a word she said. Beauty, the unforgivable sin, and one over which she had no control. She stared into his eyes, afraid of him as she had never been. He had slipped beyond her reach, his mind ensnared in the same twisted dementedness that had so often afflicted Joseph.

Even as frightened as she was, Kate saw the irony in that. Two brothers, both fine-looking specimens of manhood, yet so horribly flawed within. *Train up a child in the way he should go; and when he is old, he will not depart from it.* Proverbs 22:6, if she recollected right, and so true. Both Joseph and Ryan, trained up to walk a path of self-righteous madness.

14

Like a voice from out of a nightmare, Ryan's droned on, curling around Kate like slimy tentacles. *Madness.* It was a word people used too lightly. She doubted most knew what real madness was. There would be no saving herself this time. She could only thank God that Miranda had escaped and that the child had a penchant for hiding. There was no need to worry that she might see or hear something she shouldn't.

"You use your beauty to your advantage, don't you, Kate?" he continued. "Bringing men to heel like dogs after a bitch."

"What men? Ryan, you're imagining things."

"I saw the look in McGovern's eyes."

Kate recoiled from the brush of his fingertips along her neck. "Please, don't touch me," she whispered. "Regardless of what you might think, I'm not that kind. I don't— no one but Joseph—surely you can understand that— please, Ryan?"

He curled his fingers around her throat. When she fell back against the wall, he followed. "Joseph left you to me."

She closed her eyes against the insanity of that. "In time. Please give me some time."

"If anybody's got a right to put his hands on you, it's me." He dipped his thumb under the edge of her collar and gave her skin there a slow caress. "Does McGovern touch you like this?"

Kate flattened herself against the wood, scarcely able to breathe because he had left her so little space.

He moved closer and settled his other hand on her waist. "I know what you're trying to make me want." Digging in with his fingers, he whispered, "Oh, yes, I know. You want to play me like an old, out-of-tune fiddle. To laugh at me like you laugh at all the others."

Kate shook her head in mute denial.

"Oh, yes. Only you can't, can you? Not with Joseph, and now not with me. That's why you don't want to marry me. Because you know you won't be able to control me. I'm too much like my brother. I'll resist you and save you from yourself while I'm at it." He rubbed his thumb across her mouth. "And you don't want to be saved. Satan has his talons in you."

"Ryan." She gasped as his fingers dug more deeply into her waist. She knew he was trying to inflict pain. And he was succeeding. He saw it as her just punishment because she kindled desire within him, desire that he believed would condemn him to hell. Nausea rolled through her stomach and then up her throat, bitter as gall. "Stop it! I'm your brother's wife."

"And he gave you to me. McGovern's the one you've got your eye on, though. You can bring him to heel with what's between your legs. Pleasures of the flesh. That's all you care about, all he cares about. You want him so badly, you can't stand it."

"No. Nothing has happened between us. Nothing."

He shoved hard against her, driving the breath from

her lungs. Before she realized what he meant to do, he grabbed for her skirt. "Let's take a look-see, shall we? Then let's hear you tell me you don't want him."

Trying to hold him off, Kate jammed her arm against his throat, then twisted to one side to evade his clawing hand. "Stop it! Don't, Ryan, please!"

She felt his fingers seize hold of the drawstring waist of her bloomers. Panic gripped her. She almost swung at him with the shovel. Then an image of Miranda's little face flashed in her mind. She swallowed a sob, let the handle of the digging implement slip from her fingers, and forced her body to go limp. If she fought Ryan, it would only enrage him. She couldn't risk that. Nothing mattered but Miranda. Nothing. Not even this.

"Joseph told me," he said with a grunt, struggling to unfasten the drawstring. "How you tried to tempt him, night and day, no matter what you were doing. One time even while he was reading to you from the Bible. A Jezebel, that's what you are, doomed to burn unless a God-fearing man disciplines you. Those times when you tried to lure him into sin, who had you been thinking about Kate? Some other man? God knows it wasn't Joseph. Because you despised him!"

Kate averted her face and tried to stifle the sounds coming up her throat with her fist. Her legs weak, she slid down the wall and fell sideways. Ryan came down on top of her, his elbow wedging her thighs apart, his hand tearing at her underwear. He was going to touch her. Because of Miranda, she could do nothing to stop him.

She closed her eyes. The pressure of her fist against her mouth made her teeth cut into her lip. Images slashed across her mind, and another sob welled within her, cutting, tearing its way up from her belly as if she were vomiting ground glass.

She felt his clammy fingertips on the inside of her thigh. She couldn't bear it. Oh, God, she couldn't bear it. In that instant, she forgot everything and cried out in protest. Curling her fingers, she clawed wildly at the air, found her mark, and dug her nails into his face.

Then, as if he'd been plucked off her by a giant hand, he wasn't on top of her anymore. Kate blinked and rolled to her knees. She saw four booted feet, two pairs of legs. Someone else had entered the barn. The sickening sound of a fist connecting with flesh over bone resounded in her ears.

Using the rails of the stall, she pulled herself upright. A tall, broad-shouldered man was scuffling with Ryan. Kate stared. Then relief made her feel weak. She hooked an arm over the rail to hold herself erect. Zachariah. He had come, just as he promised. And she was safe.

Her relief was short-lived. *Fists hitting bone.* She blinked to bring her eyes into focus. Zachariah was tearing into Ryan like a wild man. Kate staggered toward them.

"Zachariah! Stop it!" She pressed her hands over her ears to block out the sounds. It didn't help. "Stop it! Please!"

The two men had fallen backward across the aisle and into the opposite stall. Zachariah sandwiched Ryan into a corner, grasping his shirt with one hand while he pummeled his face with the other. Kate ran up behind him and grabbed his arm.

"Please, please . . . Stop it before you kill him!"

With a roar of rage, Ryan shoved out from the corner. Zachariah stumbled backward, knocking Kate into the stall rails. He turned to look at her, and while his gaze was averted, Ryan took advantage, ramming a fist against his temple. Zachariah toppled and hit the dirt with a *whoosh* of breath. Ryan leaped on top of him and grabbed for his throat.

Horrified, Kate struggled to right herself. Zachariah's face went red. Then purple. He clutched at Ryan's wrists.

She could see he didn't have the strength to shove him off. She screamed and ran toward them.

"Ryan! Ryan, look what you're doing!"

She grabbed her brother-in-law's arm. As she pulled to break his grip, he turned an enraged face toward her. Before she realized what he meant to do, he released his hold on Zachariah's throat and dealt her a stunning blow to the side of her head. Everything went black. The earth slammed into her.

Zachariah bellowed, "You miserable son of a bitch!"

Kate heard a dull thud. Ryan grunted. The sounds of boots scrambling for purchase filled her head. Heavy breathing. The straining of muscular bodies, manifested by low moans in male throats.

Slowly her vision cleared. Ensnared in a strange feeling of separateness, she watched, still unable to make her body move. Zachariah had regained his feet. Weak, yes. Staggering, yes. But magnificent in his anger. He dove at Ryan, burying his head in the other man's middle. Ryan's lungs expelled his breath in a whining rush as he fell backward. His head cracked audibly against a support post, and he slid limply to the ground, a stunned expression on his face, his eyes oddly blank.

Zachariah circled him, the quivering muscles in his long legs bunching under the denim of his jeans, his boots scuffing the dirt as though he hadn't the strength to lift his feet.

"Get up, you slimy bastard. I'll teach you to hit a woman." Ryan didn't stir. Zachariah planted a foot on his rump.

"Get up, I said. I'm not finished with you yet."

When Ryan still didn't respond, Zachariah swore and grabbed the back of the unconscious man's jacket. "Offal to throw on the dung heap," he said with a grunt, and began dragging Ryan toward the doors.

Kate locked her elbows and pushed dizzily to her

knees. Through the open barn entrance, she watched as Zachariah pulled Ryan along behind him toward the buckskin horse. Once there, he let the unconscious man drop to the ground and executed a drunken sidestep to stay on his feet. Kate pressed her wrist to the side of her head, wincing at the pain, willing herself to stand.

Zachariah braced his hands on his knees and leaned forward, drawing in shuddering gulps of breath. After resting a moment, he bent and grabbed Ryan by his collar and the seat of his britches. With one mighty heave that clearly took all his remaining strength, he tossed the man across his saddle and then slapped the horse's rump. Startled, the buckskin sprang forward into a gallop, nearly tossing his limp burden.

Zachariah braced his hands on his knees again. Kate wanted to go to him, but couldn't. Instead, she huddled there in the dirt and bowed her head.

This wasn't real. None of it. It couldn't be real. A bad dream. Yes, that was it. A horrible dream that had no end. Seven months—seven long and endless months of insanity.

A warm, heavy hand settled on her shoulder. A little at a time, she raised her eyes. Large boots, faded denim, blue chambray. Zachariah, Miranda's hero. When he knelt on one knee, she allowed him to draw her against him, yearning to be absorbed by his hardness and heat. No more Kate. She'd just melt into his strength and not exist anymore. It would all be over. All of it. And she'd never feel afraid again.

"Katie . . ."

His voice flowed over her like ladled butter. *Katie.* Her father had called her that. A name for a child. Someone little and helpless and loved. His arms came around her. Even atremble with weakness, they felt like she imagined heaven must feel. Velvet over steel. And so safe. She wanted to remain there, pressed against him forever.

She buried her face against his shoulder, found the limp stay of his collar, burrowed past it to the hot hollow of his neck. Ah, yes. She breathed in the smell of him, sweat and leather, grass and dust, faint traces of some lemony soap he must use for shaving. Zachariah. Miranda's hero. Surely it couldn't hurt if she borrowed him for just a few seconds.

"Did he hurt you?"

Kate couldn't reply. *Hurt.* Such an ambiguous word. By what measure did one gauge pain? Physically, she was all right, but inside, she felt lacerated. Those horrible moments when she had lain there beneath Ryan, not fighting. In all the endless months since Joseph's death, for strength she had clung to her pride, and now she had lost even that. Zachariah had seen her lying there, allowing Ryan to grope under her skirt.

Did shame qualify as hurt? Oh, yes. A hurt of the worst kind. Because the reality was that she couldn't melt into Zachariah and cease to exist. Because eventually she would have to lift her head and look him in the eye. *A finer lady I've never met.* What did he think of her now? How could she explain? Even if she told him everything, he would never understand.

Kate wished she could die. But even that was denied her. Because she couldn't leave Miranda. . . .

"I'm fine," she managed to say.

Away from him. She could do it. Just by putting the heels of her hands against his shoulders and pushing. Away from him, and back to being Kate. Kate, who wasn't a child. Kate, the mother. Kate, who was strong because she had no choice.

He didn't resist when she drew away. His hands slid from her back to her arms. Large hands. Bigger than Joseph's. His palms and the splay of his long fingers stretched from her elbows nearly to her shoulders. Hands that had been fashioned to take, yet so gentle. Hands that a woman wished would cup her cheeks. Wide, leathery thumbs that had been fashioned to brush away tears. Tears she couldn't cry.

She forced herself to lift her gaze to his. And felt naked. The questions were there in his eyes. She looked at him as long as she could bear it. For the space of a heartbeat.

"Katie," he moaned. "Honey, let me help you. What is it that he's holding over your head?"

"My child," she whispered.

It wasn't enough. She had known it wouldn't be. He didn't understand, would never understand. It was her burden to bear alone. Keeping her gaze averted from his, she raised her chin. Even those stripped of pride could pretend. What he thought didn't matter. Nothing mattered but Miranda.

She had to remember that. For an instant, there in the barn, she had forgotten and started to fight Ryan. That had been her mistake. Fighting him, forsaking her daughter. And for what? To keep her flesh inviolate? What of Miranda's flesh? Kate cherished every precious inch. And she would do what she had to. The devil take Zachariah McGovern and his opinion of her.

To his credit, he didn't voice an accusation, but it lay heavy in the air, a silent indictment. *Why?* After pushing to her feet, Kate turned her back on him and stumbled toward the house. She heard him coming up behind her. His hand clamped around her arm, bringing her around to face him.

"Talk to me, for God's sake," he said hoarsely.

"There's nothing to say." She couldn't meet his gaze again. It hurt too much, and she already felt raw. Instead, she stared at a button on his shirt. Stared at it until her eyes burned. "I asked you not to come back here. You should have listened. You've only made a bad situation worse."

She heard his breath catch. "What? The bastard was trying to rape you! If I hadn't come—"

"I would have survived," she interrupted. "Go home, Zachariah. You've no idea what you've done. If he wasn't out for blood before, he will be now."

He tightened his grip on her arm. "That's insane, Kate. Where I come from, no man worth his salt stands by while a woman's attacked."

"Then go back where you came from."

She tried to wrench free. Her strength was no match for his, and he held her fast. Kate could feel the anger emanating from him. In the face of it, she felt dwarfed, yet oddly unafraid.

A wind had come up, and it tossed his dark hair. His face above hers was drawn with anger, burnished, and lined with white, the usually unnoticeable scars on his jaw now a pulsating crimson, his full lips pulled back over straight white teeth. The blue expanse of his shirt eclipsed the barn behind him.

He looked angry enough to shake her, and she had no doubt he could snap her neck if he gave in to the urge. With a trembling hand, she tried to pry his fingers from her arm.

"I have to find my daughter. Please, let me go."

For a moment, she thought he'd maintain his grip. Then he reluctantly released her. Set free at last, she whirled and ran toward the house.

If this wasn't a hell of a pass, Zach didn't know what was. He stood in the open doorway of the barn and gazed out across the valley. His body felt like a piece of chewed jerky. A cool wind puffed against his jaw, drying the sheen of sweat that filmed his skin. He plucked weakly at his shirt where it stuck to his chest.

In his mind, he relived everything that had transpired in the last thirty minutes. Seeing Blakely on the road. Riding here, hell-bent for election, to help Kate if she needed it.

Jesus H. Christ! He'd never forget the rage that had rushed through him when he walked in and saw that miserable bastard on top of her. Or the look on her face. Dear God, she had lain there under him as though she had no choice, her expression a blend of defeat, resignation, and revulsion. Why?

He wasn't sure which had taken the worse beating, her pride or his body. He closed his eyes and pinched the bridge of his nose. Damn it, win or lose, he'd done the right thing by stepping in. At least he'd stopped the son of a bitch. Kate was out of her blooming mind. Either that, or scared to death. But of what?

Zach was too exhausted to search for an answer. He gazed numbly at the rolling hills that rose from the green sweeps of grassland. Beyond them, layer upon layer of forested mountains reached into the infinity of a gray sky. He studied the black clouds that hovered to the north. It looked like one hell of a storm was brewing. That suited him fine. In his present mood, the blacker the clouds, the better.

And wasn't that just like Oregon, sunny one hour, pouring buckets the next? Pneumonia weather, his ma had always called it, steamy hot then turning cold.

Above the gusting wind, Zach heard something. For an instant, he thought it sounded like a litter of kittens mewing, but when he listened more closely, the hair of his nape prickled. Miranda. Damn it to hell. How much had she seen or overheard?

Following his ears, he circled the barn and found the child huddled behind a barrel near the pigpen. Nosy sat beside her whining. She had her arms wrapped around her knees, her dark head buried in her lap. As she rocked to and fro, she shook horribly. Zach crouched in front of her.

"Hey, half-pint?"

Without looking up, she continued to rock and make those awful sounds, half moan, half wail, deep within her narrow chest. He settled a hand on her curls.

"Mandy?" When she still didn't respond, Zach pried her chin up to look in her eyes. It was as if she didn't see him, as though she heard nothing. The wind cutting through his shirt seemed to turn colder. "Mandy . . ."

Suddenly, as though launched from the ascending end of a teeterboard, she threw herself into his arms and clung to his neck. "Mr. Zach!" she sobbed. "Oh, Mr. Zach."

He enfolded her in his embrace, fighting back a flood of tears himself. Dear God, how he loved this child.

"My Uncle Ryan comed agin!"

"I know, pumpkin. But he's gone now."

"Only 'cause you came," she whispered in a thin little voice. "Oh, Mr. Zach, I'm so glad you comed back. Don't leave no more. Please don't leave me no more."

Ignoring the mud that oozed out from under the rails of the pigpen, he sat with her on his lap, aching because he knew he had to do just that. This moment they had together couldn't last. Pressing his face to her hair, he breathed deeply and committed the scent of her to memory.

Why had he let himself come to care so much? About her or her mother? In the beginning, he had never imagined it hurting like this. And that wasn't the half of it. What of the child?

"Don't leave me no more," she repeated. "Please don't leave."

The plea tore at him. "I can't stay, sweetheart. I wish I could."

She squeezed his neck so fiercely that he had difficulty

breathing. "But he'll come back! He'll come back and git me! Please don't let him. Please."

Zach felt as though a knife was twisting in his guts. Thunder rumbled in the distance, and he felt her flinch. "Honey, if I see him out on the road, I'll come over. That's a promise. You won't be alone if he comes again."

She shrank closer to him. "But what if you don't see him? He'll hurt me and my ma! She ain't big enough to make him stop."

Zach tightened his arms around her and swallowed to get his voice. "I won't let him hurt you or your ma. I promise."

Even if he had to station a man near the road twenty-four hours a day as a lookout, that was a promise Zach would keep. In an attempt to soothe Miranda, he expressed that intention. "So you see? There's nothing to worry about. You'll be just as safe as if I was here."

The frantic clutching of her arms relaxed. "For sure?"

"For sure."

She burrowed against him, her sharp elbows and knees digging in as she positioned herself more comfortably. When she finally grew still, Zach moved one of her knees to a less vulnerable spot on his lap and rested his chin on her head. Lightning flared above them. He narrowed an eye at the tumultuous sky. One hell of a storm was coming, that was for certain. He could smell the rain in the air.

"Miranda!"

Kate's voice sounded faint, and frantic. Zach stiffened. "Your ma's looking for you, half-pint."

"I don't want her to find us. She'll make you leave."

Zach heaved a weary sigh. "She's worried though. Listen."

Kate's voice rang out again. Miranda turned to catch the sound. Zach brushed his jaw against her cheek. After a moment, she stirred and raised trusting eyes to his.

"You'll watch the road?"

Zach extended his hand to her. After regarding it for several seconds, she finally crossed his palm with her small fingers. As they shook on it, she whispered, "Now it's on official."

With that, she scrambled from his lap. As she gained her feet, thunder shook the skies again. She paled and glanced up.

"I'll watch until you and your ma get safely in the house."

Her eyes clung to his. Then she nodded. Her mother's voice drifted to them on the wind again. Zach angled a leg under himself and stood. Miranda gave him a little wave and ran toward the house. With a heavy heart, he walked out from behind the barn. He saw Kate running to meet her child, heard her cry of relief and then her scolding tone as two of them hurried toward the front steps.

Once on the porch, Miranda turned to look back. Even from a distance, Zach felt the impact of her eyes. Kate pivoted and cupped a hand to her brow. He saw her body go rigid as she followed her daughter's gaze and spotted him.

Farewells had never been easy for Zach. This one came particularly hard. The two most important people in his world, and he was turning his back on them. He raised a hand to wave. Then he directed his steps toward his horse.

It was the longest walk of his life.

15

As Zach expected, the storm turned out to be severe, a deluge that lasted three days. Fearful that his tender new vines would never survive the onslaught, he spent every hour of daylight on the slopes, trying to shore up his plants and redirect the water flow so the topsoil wouldn't be washed away.

On the fourth night, the storm turned violent again, as if in finale, with thunder and lightning ripping across the heavens. Still not up to snuff after his recent illness and feeling indescribably weary after an endless day of work, Zach sat near the fire, absorbing the electrical tension in the air, his skin prickling as the windows and walls shook with thunder.

If the storm unnerved him, how might it be affecting Miranda? He hadn't had time to go by and check on her and Kate since the bad weather had hit. How were they? An awful sense of foreboding filled him. As irrational as he knew it was, he couldn't shake it. Something was wrong. He felt it in his bones. What with all the rain, things had been hectic here at his place. What if, in the confusion, the man he'd stationed to watch the road had missed seeing Ryan Blakely ride past?

The thought brought Zach to his feet. He moved to a window and stared out into the lightning-slashed darkness. He didn't relish the thought of riding in this deluge to reach Kate's, and he knew she wouldn't appreciate the sacrifice if he did it. If he had any brains, he'd sit tight.

But since when had he laid claim to brains?

Leaving Nosy to cuddle near the fire, Zach dragged on his sheepskin coat, planted his old leather work hat on his head, and let himself out onto the back stoop. Wind buffeted him. He turned up his collar, hunched his shoulders, and stepped off the porch into ankle-deep slop. He wouldn't win any popularity vote from Dander for doing this, that was for sure. But he wouldn't get a wink of sleep if he didn't. He had to assure himself that Kate and Miranda were all right.

As Zach rode up the road to the Blakely place, he couldn't believe the evidence of his own eyes. When lightning bolted across the sky, he thought he saw Kate in the illumination. Kate outside? In the rose garden?

Peering through the sheets of rain, Zach rode closer and dismounted, leaving Dander's reins dangling. As he drew near he saw her dilemma. As had happened in his vineyards, the heavy and ceaseless rain had trenched the well-turned earth in her flower garden and was washing away the soil in rivers. She was working frantically with her hoe to mound dirt back around her plants.

"Katie! What in hell do you think you're doing?" he called. "You'll catch your death out here."

She gave a violent start and whirled to stare at him. Zach stared back. Her face was smeared with mud. Her gray skirt and white apron were soaked with brown clear to her hips. She must have been out here for quite some time.

Crazy, so crazy. For a bunch of damned roses? He threw a disgusted glance at the battered petals that eddied atop the currents of runoff. It was then that he saw it.

A man's boot.

He fixed his gaze on the sole protruding from the flooded earth. For several endless seconds, his mind refused to register what his eyes were telling him. Then he looked back at Kate. Lightning flared. Her skin was so pale it shone blue-white. She looked as dead as the man buried in her rose garden.

Zach felt as if a horse had kicked him in the guts.

She stood there staring back at him for what seemed an eternity. Then, as if all the fight in her had drained completely away, she dropped her head, let the hoe fall to the ground, and turned toward the house.

Zach remained rooted where he stood, his gaze on Kate as she slipped like a wraith up the steps. A feeble shaft of lantern light spilled across the rickety porch when she opened the door to let herself inside. In his peripheral vision, the boot seemed to loom. Rain sluiced off the brim of his hat in streams, ribboning his vision, trickling down his neck. He couldn't stir himself. Ryan Blakely's insane accusations hadn't been so insane, after all.

Holy Christ.

He finally pried his feet loose and followed Kate into the house. He found her sitting on a straight-backed chair in the room off the kitchen. Head tipped as if to listen, her hands folded demurely in her lap, she gazed sightlessly at the fireplace hearth. Muddy water dripped from her skirt onto the floor, forming a pool around her.

Zach came to a stop several feet from her. With a searching glance, he assured himself that Miranda was nowhere in the room. Since he hadn't seen her as he passed through the house, he supposed she was upstairs asleep, which was just as well. This wasn't going to be a conversation for a child to overhear.

"I think I deserve an explanation for this."

She didn't look up. "There's nothing to explain," she whispered in an expressionless voice. "You saw with your own eyes. I killed him and buried him in the rose garden."

Zach couldn't believe he was hearing this. "But—" He jerked his hat off. "He drowned! I thought he drowned."

Still completely motionless, she whispered, "I threw his saddle and some of his clothes into the river to make it appear that he had. It isn't uncommon for the bodies of drowning victims never to be discovered. As I hoped, Joseph was pronounced legally dead." Her mouth twisted. "If not for Ryan and you, that would have been the end of it."

He started to pace, his wet boots squishing as they thumped an erratic tattoo on the floor. Memories rushed at him. Serena, the house ablaze, his frantic efforts to reach her, the accusations later. Though these circumstances were completely different, there were similarities, and every instinct he had told him Kate was as innocent as he had been. Trapped in a nightmare, yes, but that didn't make a person a murderer.

Finally he halted, raked a trembling hand through his hair, and said roughly, "I don't believe it. You don't have a violent bone in your whole body. You couldn't even bring yourself to hit Nosy, for Christ's sake! Don't sit there and tell me you killed him. There's more to this than you're saying, and I want to hear it."

She finally lifted her gaze to his, her eyes haunted with memories he could only guess at. "You'd like me to tell you what you want to hear, that I'm somehow innocent? That it wasn't premeditated, maybe? Or that I regretted doing it later?"

"I want to hear the truth," he came back raggedly.

She blinked. "If I'd had regrets, they wouldn't bring Joseph back. And the truth, if you're really set on it, is that I considered murdering him at least a dozen times. Once I nearly drove my scissors into his back. If he hadn't turned at the last second and caught me, I would have."

Zach's throat felt raw. "Is that how you did it, with the scissors? Jesus, Mary, and—" He broke off, folded his arms across his chest, and put a hand over his face. "How, Kate? How did you do it? I can't believe you have it in you to stab someone."

"Trust me, I do. I wished him dead a hundred times," she replied in that horribly hollow voice. "The fact that his death, when it actually occurred, was accidental doesn't alter that." She dragged in a shaky breath. "I can only pray that—I can only pray Miranda doesn't do penance with me."

The pain he heard in her voice at mention of her daughter drew Zach toward her. Instinctively, he knew that fear for Miranda had been at the root of everything. Tossing his hat onto the floor, he hunkered beside her chair. "How did it happen, Kate?" he asked gently.

She turned her gaze back to the fireplace. "It happened on a night like this. There was a storm, and I brought Miranda in here to keep her warm by the fire. Joseph didn't let me tell her stories other than those I read to her from the Bible, so to pass the time, I was doing mending while she sketched at the hearth." Tears filled her eyes. "While I wasn't watching, she found a sliver of kindling, and she was touching it to a hot coal, blowing and trying to make it catch. Joseph walked in and saw her."

Zach's heart had begun to pound. He forced his eyes toward the hearth, an awful coldness filling him.

"As he often did, he began to scold. 'Don't you know what happens to little girls who play with fire?' That was what he asked her." Kate made a strangled sound. "That's how it always started. 'Don't you know what happens to little girls who play on the steps?' 'Don't you know what happens to little girls who play with scissors?' And then he would show her."

Zach closed his eyes. Dear God in heaven, he didn't want to hear this.

"He was given to fits of anger," she whispered. "To doing outlandish, obscene things to drive home his point. Once when she snitched a bit of cornbread, he crammed an entire piece in her mouth and slapped her until she finally tried to swallow and choked. Once, when he found her dipping cream, he shoved her head in the pail. I finally succeeded in dragging him off her, but he nearly drowned her before I did."

Zach felt as if he were drowning himself, in a horrible sickness that penetrated his bones. But the words kept pouring from Kate, descriptions of one incident after another, as if she were spewing poison.

Then, at last, she returned to the night when Joseph had caught Miranda playing with fire. "As was his way, he . . ." Her voice shuddered down to nothing but a quavering breath. She pressed her fingertips to her lips and closed her eyes for a moment. "He thrust her hand into the flames."

Silence dropped like a blanket over the room. Zach could hear his pulse throbbing.

"Miranda started to scream," she whispered. "I'll never forget the sound. 'Ma! Ma!' over and over again. I tried to pull Joseph away. He beat me off with his fists and went back to holding her hand in the fire."

Zach fixed his gaze on the hairline scar on her bottom lip.

A sob jerked up from Kate's chest, dry and tearing. "I couldn't make him stop," she cried. "But I couldn't bear to let him continue. I had to do something. And so I grabbed up a length of firewood and hit him across the back. Just across his shoulders. I didn't mean to hurt him, only to stop him. But when he fell, he struck his head on the hearth." She held up her hands in helpless supplication. "He was dead. I didn't mean to kill him, not that time. But he was dead."

"Katie . . ." Zach grasped her shoulders. "Honey, you didn't mean to do it. If you had, you'd have hit him on the head. Why in God's name didn't you go to the sheriff? There would have been a coroner's inquest, and within days, you could have put it behind you. Surely you didn't believe the law would punish you for protecting your child from a madman?"

"I was afraid!" she cried shrilly. "What if they had put me in jail? Even for a few days? Miranda had just been through an ordeal, and she needed her mother. I had no relatives to take her. There was only Ryan, and he's as mad as his brother was."

"She would have survived it for a few days," Zach came back.

Kate's eyes, huge and black in contrast to her white face, fastened on his. "Would she have? You don't know how fragile she really is. I couldn't let Ryan get his hands on her, not even for a single night. And what if, after trusting in justice, I had been found guilty of murder? I would have been imprisoned or hanged, and Miranda would have been in Ryan's custody for years. None of it was her fault! She didn't deserve to be punished, and if she were given to Ryan, she would have been, for the rest of her life. I couldn't risk that."

"So you buried Joseph in the rose garden."

She closed her eyes and nodded.

So many things suddenly came clear for Zach. That first day, and Kate's frenzied attempts to keep Nosy from digging in the flower bed. Nosy's determination to return, again and again, to resume his excavations. Kate's terror that Ryan's wild accusations might stir suspicion against her among the people in town. Her pallor the afternoon he had suggested that Ryan start his digging in the rose or vegetable garden. The list seemed endless. Last, but not least, he finally knew why she had been so eager for him to recover from the snakebites and get out of her house.

There had been a dead man buried in her yard. . . .

Now that she was silent, Kate blinked again and seemed to refocus on reality. She searched his gaze for a long while, then looked away. "You needn't look so stricken," she said softly. "There isn't any question of what you must do. I understand that." Her throat worked as she swallowed. "You'd best get to it."

When he remained hunkered beside her, she hugged herself.

"Go, Zachariah. There's no need to worry that I'll take off while you're gone to get the sheriff. I have nowhere to go, and no money to get there. I know better than to try fleeing with a child in a broken-down buckboard. I tried it a few times, you see, and we never got more than a few miles. The one time I saved enough for train fare, which I assure you I don't have now, Joseph wired ahead and had us detained in Medford."

"By the law?" Zach recalled the afternoon he and Miranda had played dolls, the story she had told him about Sarah and her mother being put off the train in Medford by the conductor. At Kate's affirmative nod, he asked, "Why didn't you tell the sheriff what Joseph was like? And why you were running?"

She lifted her hands. "I tried."

Those two words revealed a world of heartache. From the look in her eyes, he knew a measure of the pain and helplessness she must have felt.

She refolded her hands in her lap, intertwining her fingers, digging into her skin with her nails. "Joseph—he was so respectable looking—so charming. He had everyone here, including the authorities, convinced he was wonderful and that I was the strange one." Her breath caught, and she moistened her lips. "He wired ahead to Medford that I—that I wasn't quite right, and that I'd run off with his daughter. The people there thought I was crazy and that *I* was the one who might harm her."

Her voice became shrill as she uttered those last few words, and she closed her eyes, making a visible effort to regain her composure.

Zach was about to reply when he spied movement from the corner of his eye. When he turned and peered through the gloom beyond the lantern light, he saw Miranda lurking in the adjoining kitchen. On leaden legs, he went to find her, gathered the frightened child into his arms, and carried her upstairs. Under her direction, he located her bedroom and tucked her into bed.

"It's just a storm," he assured her. "Nothing to be afraid of."

She huddled and shivered under the quilt. "Is my ma gonna get took away to a bad place 'cause of what she did?"

Zach realized that she had overheard their conversation and that she understood far more than she should. The accusing look in her eyes tore at his heart. He had no idea how to answer her or to explain what he knew he had to do.

As if she sensed his thoughts, she cried, "My ma didn't mean to hurt my pa. The fireplace hearth did it. People shouldn't oughta be punished for what they didn't do."

Zach tried to swallow. "Mandy, the way the law works is usually fair. It's very unlikely that your ma will be punished for something that was an accident."

"They'll take her away," she accused. "She won't be here with me no more. I'll be all alone!"

Zach leaned over and gathered her close. "No, never that. I'll make sure you're never alone."

"And Uncle Ryan? You'll make certain sure he don't git me?"

Zach stiffened.

"You promised," she whimpered. "You promised, on official!"

So he had. Now it seemed that could turn out to be a promise he'd have to break. Miranda in the custody of her uncle?

Everything within Zach rebelled against that thought. But what could he do to prevent it? A man had been killed. He couldn't turn a blind eye to something so serious. If Kate was detained by the sheriff at all, it would only be for a few days. Just for a few days. He felt certain of that. How much damage could Blakely do to the child in so short a time?

"I'll do everything I can to see to it you don't have to stay with your uncle Ryan," he told Miranda.

"You promised," she whispered fiercely. "You promised!"

"And I always try to keep my promises," he assured her. "Don't you worry your head about it. Everything will work out, Mandy."

That seemed to satisfy her. Such trust. In the face of it, Zach felt humbled. Miranda's hero. But he wasn't a hero. Just an ordinary man, that was all he was. An ordinary man who was obligated to do the responsible thing, which meant he had to tell the sheriff about Joseph Blakely's death.

He drew the covers up under Miranda's chin and smoothed her hair, prepared to stay with her as long as it took for her to drift off to sleep. To his surprise, only minutes passed before her eyes fell closed.

When he crept back downstairs, he found Kate still sitting on the chair, the pool of muddy water at her feet grown larger, her eyes fixed on something he couldn't see. She was shivering, whether from cold or shock, he didn't know. He wished there was something he could say to her.

There was nothing.

Kate heard the front door close softly. At the sound, she shut her eyes and listened to the storm outside. Its anger fed the rage within her and intensified her fear. Despite all she had done, Ryan was going to get his vile hands on Miranda.

After so many months of holding the tears at bay, that thought broke through the dam of Kate's self-control. Sobs tore up her throat, and she didn't try to stop them. Crying was what you did when all else failed, wasn't it? Well, all else had failed. Everything for nothing. The endless tension. The constant fear of discovery. Memories haunting her, day and night. All of it had gone for naught.

Even if she was found innocent of any wrongdoing and set free after only a couple of days, Miranda might never recover from the experience. If just a visit from Ryan made her withdraw, what might happen if she were placed in his custody?

Damn Zachariah McGovern. Damn him straight to hell. She'd begged him to stay away, and he hadn't listened. Now her baby's fate was out of her hands. Completely out of her hands.

Halfway to town, Zach drew Dander to a stop and tipped his face back to catch the rain. Memories, so many memories. And voices clamoring inside his head. Miranda's. Kate's. Ryan Blakely's. Mandy's tiny little hand, burned so horribly. What kind of a man did something like that? If given the chance, would Ryan Blakely do something equally vile to her?

Damn it to hell, he had no choice. A dead man was buried in Kate's rose garden. He couldn't pretend he didn't know. There was only one thing for him to do—what any reasonable, rational adult would do. He had to report her to the sheriff. It wouldn't be his fault if Miranda was given over into Ryan Blakely's custody. It wouldn't be his fault if Kate, by some twist of fate, was found guilty of murder. None of that was for him to decide. That was why jurors were handpicked, to see that justice was done. When people started taking the law into their own hands, there was nothing but trouble.

You promised!

Zach recalled the morning he had found Miranda playing with his knife. *Don't you know what happens to little girls who play with knives?* Dear God, he had echoed her father, almost to the word. *Don't you know what happens to little girls who play with fire?* And then Kate, the look on her face that night when he had asked her to trust him with whatever it was that had her so badly frightened. She had nearly confided in him then. He had seen the longing in her eyes.

And if she had? What would he have done? Zach didn't know. He only knew that their faces seemed to be mirrored in the flashes of lightning, that the wind seemed to carry the whispers of their voices.

Roses. Kate's beautiful roses. Everything else going to rack and ruin, but not the roses. No wonder she had such a fixation about keeping the earth just so. She hadn't buried the son of a bitch deep enough. He kept coming up! And the blossoms. Such a vibrant, blood red. The healthiest crop on the place, and well they should be, as well fertilized as they were.

The thought suddenly struck him as hysterically funny. Instead of pushing up daisies, Joseph Blakely was coming up roses. Zach began to laugh, and once he started he couldn't seem to stop. Sitting there in the rain as he was, it took several seconds for him to realize tears were streaming down his cheeks.

You promised, on official!

What if he just went home? What if he simply pretended he had never seen that boot sticking up out of the dirt? And what would that accomplish? Sooner or later, the inevitable would happen. Another hard rain would unearth the evidence. Or, God forbid, Nosy would. And someone else would make the discovery.

Zach clicked his tongue and nudged Dander back into a trot. There was no sense in delaying the inevitable. No sense at all.

Determined to continue toward town, Zach reined in the horse after going only a few feet. He gazed toward Kate's place. It had been nearly seven months since Joseph's death. The corpse would be badly deteriorated. There was a strong possibility, at this late date, that the findings in a simple inquest wouldn't be concrete enough to prove Kate's story. If the coroner couldn't tell by examining Joseph's body whether he had been struck on the head with a blunt object, like a piece of firewood, or by something sharp, like a jagged surface of a stone hearth, the case would go before a grand jury. If that happened, Kate might be incarcerated a hell of a lot longer than just a few days.

Zach closed his eyes, sick with dread. What might happen to the child if her uncle had custody of her, not for days, but for weeks or months?

What if he went back and finished what Kate had started? No one would ever discover Joseph Blakely's body if Zach buried the bastard several feet deeper. If he did a good job of it, Nosy's sniffer wouldn't tempt him to do any more digging. Rain and runoff would never unearth the evidence. And Ryan Blakely had already sworn that the last place he would ever look for the body would be in the rose garden. It was the perfect spot.

Thoughts of Ryan Blakely brought Zach up short. If the man carried out his threat to search for Joseph's body, he'd stumble across it sooner or later. Then what? They'd be faced with the same problem they were now.

No, not exactly the same. Given some time, there were measures he and Kate could take to make certain Ryan Blakely never got custody of Miranda. Not for a day, not even for a minute. Then, even if Ryan did eventually discover the body, at least the child wouldn't suffer the consequences.

All Zach had to do was convince Kate of his plan.

When the storm finally broke at dawn, Kate was still sitting before the empty hearth, shivering, staring, and listening. A few times during the night, she'd thought she heard something outside, but no one had come to the door. After crying herself half sick, she had been too drained to go and see what caused the noise. What did it matter? Sooner or later, Zachariah would show up with the sheriff. Time enough then to face it. Until that happened, she couldn't muster the energy to do anything more than sit there.

But now . . . Zachariah should have returned hours ago. So where was he? How long could it take to bring back the law and a couple of shovels?

As if on cue, Kate heard the heavy fall of boots coming up her front steps. Her heart leaped and she glanced at the ceiling, praying Miranda wouldn't awaken. It'd be best if she didn't witness this.

The footsteps echoed on the flooring, coming from the foyer, along the hall, into the kitchen. Kate heard water slosh and supposed the men were washing up. She braced herself.

"Kate?"

Zachariah's weary voice. From the corner of her eye, she saw that he had come to stand in the doorway. She forced her shoulders erect and rose stiffly from the chair. As she turned, she searched behind him for the sheriff. The other man was nowhere to be seen. Just Zachariah, Miranda's hero, turned traitor. Not that she blamed him for that. He had to do what was right, and in this instance, that was pretty clear, even to her.

He looked exhausted. Wet through to the skin. Mud had soaked into his sheepskin jacket. The sopped brim of his hat drooped low over his brow, shadowing his eyes and darkly handsome face. So tall, so broad at the shoulders, so safe looking. Only he was Miranda's hero, not hers.

"What happened?" she asked when she saw the state he was in. "Did you get thrown?"

He wiped his mouth with the back of his hand. "You could say that, yes. Thrown." He laughed softly. Kate thought that was cruel of him. The situation didn't strike her as being funny. "Can you step outside with me for a second? I've got something to show you. And then we need to talk. I don't want Miranda overhearing."

Maybe not so cruel, after all. He was still thinking of Miranda, at least. Assuming the sheriff must be waiting on the porch, Kate nodded. "I should get my shawl." Then she glanced down at her filthy skirt. "I didn't think to change. I guess—"

"Katie . . ."

At the husky sound of his voice, she glanced up and tried to read the expression in his eyes. Shadows frustrated her, and she realized the lantern had burned out. The only light came in through the windows. Sunlight, at last. But none for Miranda.

"You won't need your shawl or a clean dress," he informed her. "I didn't go for the sheriff."

"You didn't? But—" She stared up at him. "But why not?"

He crooked a finger at her. "Come on, and I'll tell you."

He seemed awfully pleased about whatever it was. Then, with the same finger with which he had just summoned her, he pushed back his hat. She could see the twinkle in his eyes. A very satisfied twinkle. When she drew up in front of him, he took her arm, his grasp firm, and led her through the house and out onto the porch. He drew her to a stop at the head of the steps.

"Well?"

Well? She frowned, wondering what had gotten into him. Then she spied the rose garden. As if by magic, Joseph's boot had disappeared, and the surface of the garden, beaten by pelting rain, looked as though it had never been touched by her hoe. Kate stared, trying to assimilate what this meant. No boot. No sign of her frantic attempts to cover it up.

"Oh, my . . ." She turned toward him. "Zachariah, what have you—"

He touched a finger to her lips. "The problem has been taken care of."

Kate couldn't quite believe her eyes or her ears. And she had no idea what to say. Tears blurred her vision. "Oh, Zachariah."

She clamped a hand over her mouth, perilously close to making an utter fool of herself by bawling.

Zach turned her toward him. "I suppose you think I've lost my mind," he said. "And I guess maybe I have. But it's done, and right or wrong, I feel good about it. A hell of a lot better than I would have if I'd gone for the sheriff, at any rate."

"I don't know what to say," she managed.

His mouth quirked at the corners. "Thanks?"

She brushed at her cheeks. "Oh, Zachariah. A million thank-yous would never—" She caught her bottom lip in her teeth and bit down hard. It was so foolish to cry when she should be leaping with joy and relief. "It seems I'm once again in your debt."

His hazel eyes warmed with an indefinable emotion. "No, not this time." He cupped her chin in his hand. "This time, Katie, there's a charge for my services."

"Oh?" Her heart caught, for she suddenly knew what it was that she sensed in him, an air of possessiveness. "And what might that be?"

"Your daughter. I want to adopt her."

"My daughter?" she repeated hollowly. That wasn't what she expected. "You want to adopt my daughter?"

"Yes, with all my heart." He feathered his thumb across her cheek. She had been right. His thumbs had been fashioned perfectly for wiping away tears. "If she's legally mine, Ryan can never touch her or get custody of her. Think about that."

She stared up at him, her mind circling what he'd said, but shying away from what it meant.

"She'd be safe, Kate. No matter what ever happened, she'd be a McGovern, not a Blakely. If something happens to me, I've got three brothers who'll see to it she's cared for. I know it's probably a scary thought for you to contemplate, given the way Joseph was and all. You've no guarantee I'm a good fellow, I know. But you have to see that I'm a far better bet than Ryan."

"Is this an ultimatum?" she asked weakly. "If I don't agree, you'll go to the sheriff?"

He sighed and shook his head. "God, no. What in hell gave you—" He laughed softly and released her to lean his elbows on the porch railing. After surveying his handiwork in the rose garden for a moment, he said, "No, Kate, I won't ever breathe a word of this to anyone. You've got my promise on that."

She stared at him. "Then why is an adoption necessary?" she asked in a high-pitched voice.

He turned to look at her. A ray of feeble sunlight slashed

across his scarred jaw. "Because of Ryan. The new depth may stop the rain and Nosy, but it won't stop him. Not forever. If he carries through on his threat to search for the body, he'll eventually find it. When he does, we'll be right back where we are now, with him inches away from getting custody of Miranda until you get all the tangles worked out. God knows what might happen to her meanwhile."

It was true. Kate knew that. But, oh, God, to give up her child? Miranda was her only reason for living. "You want to take her away from me?"

"No. Not unless you insist it be that way."

"But if you adopt her, how else can—" She broke off and met his gaze. Suddenly she knew what he had in mind. An unreasoning panic rushed her. "No," she whispered. "No, absolutely not."

"Why not?" he asked evenly. "Give me one good reason."

"I don't want to be married again," she came back, "not to you, or to anyone."

"I'm not Joseph, Katie."

She squeezed her eyes closed for an instant. "You don't understand."

"Oh, yes. I understand, all right. You're scared spitless to be under anyone's thumb again. That's easy enough to figure out. In time, that will fade."

She gave her head an emphatic shake. "No, never. Marriage is out of the question."

"It's that or give up your daughter. Just you think about that. One way or another, you'll lose her, to me if you're smart, to Ryan if you're not. I guess that's your choice."

Kate's legs felt rubbery. She reached to the railing for support. "How can you dare?"

"Dare what?"

"Try to coerce me into a marriage, using my daughter as a bargaining chip!"

He sighed. "Is that how you see it?" He grew silent for a moment, then gave a humorless laugh. "I guess if I'm honest, the idea of adopting her has its benefits. Namely getting you in the bargain. But that's not my reason for offering." He shot her a look. "I want to protect her. If the only way to do that is to adopt her outside of marriage, I'll do it in a shot. That's entirely up to you."

"I'd lose my child!" she cried angrily.

His eyes held hers. "I didn't cause this situation. I'm just trying to salvage something from it. If you feel that strongly about not marrying, then let's just draw up papers in front of a judge. I'll let you see her any time you like."

"She's *my* daughter, not yours!" Kate wrapped her arms around herself. "I won't give her up. I won't!"

"You will if Ryan finds that body," was his answer.

Kate flinched. His words hung in the air between them, an undeniable truth. But to let him adopt her?

Frantically, Kate tried to think of alternatives such as seeing a lawyer to have Zachariah declared legal guardian for Miranda in the event of her mother's death or incapacitation. She no sooner hit upon that idea than she discarded it. With all his convincing lies, Joseph had succeeded in casting Kate into a bad light with the townspeople, calling her fitness as a mother and her emotional balance into question. To throw suspicion off himself, he had even implied that Kate's mood swings could make her dangerous, to Miranda and possibly others. With those lies as ammunition, Ryan would find it frighteningly easy to make it appear that Kate was of unsound mind and therefore incapable of choosing a proper guardian for her daughter.

Closing her eyes for a moment, Kate struggled for composure. As much as she hated to admit it, Zachariah was right. If she married him and he adopted Miranda, he would have inalienable rights to his wife and child, legal rights that could never be questioned by Ryan or anyone else.

"I love her so much," she whispered raggedly.

"I know you do."

"I can't give her up. I can't."

"I'm offering you another choice."

"Marriage?" she squeaked. "For me, that isn't a choice, it's a life sentence."

He shifted his arms on the railing and gazed down at the palms of his hands. After a long while, he said, "I'm sorry, Kate. It seemed like a good idea when it occurred to me. I guess I just wasn't thinking." He laughed again. "I suppose it'd be more correct to say I wasn't thinking about how you'd feel about it. Marrying you, adopting Miranda . . . that'd make me one happy man. Kind of like a dozen Christmases, all rolled into one."

He pushed erect and heaved another weary sigh. After gazing for a long while at the rose garden, he repositioned his hat on his head and turned up the collar of his jacket.

"Well . . ." He turned to regard her. "It's been a long night, and I'm beat. I think I'll head on home. I left Nosy locked up in the house. He'll be needing out. What I said earlier, about keeping my mouth shut? You can count on that. As far as I'm concerned, I never came here last night."

He started around her.

"I've hurt you," she said. "I didn't mean that the way it sounded—about the life sentence. It's nothing personal."

He touched a hand to her shoulder. "You know where I am if you need me."

Kate watched him as he cleared the steps in two long-legged strides. Once in the yard, he lengthened his gait. Miranda's one hope, and she was letting him walk away. True, entrusting her daughter to him was a risk, but, as he said, he was a far better bet than Ryan.

"Wait!" she cried.

He wheeled to a stop and nudged his hat back to gaze at her, not speaking, his expression impossible to read.

"Can we d-discuss this?"

He slowly retraced his steps until he reached the porch. Planting his feet wide apart and his hands on his hips, he said, "I'm sorry. I thought we had."

Kate didn't miss the sarcasm in his tone. "It isn't easy for me to contemplate getting married again."

"Then don't."

She moved to the head of the steps. "How can I not? Giving up my daughter is out of the question. And you're right. Ryan won't give up."

"Is that a yes?" he asked with an unmistakable smile in his voice.

Kate took a gulp of air. "Wh-What if we drew up the adoption papers, just like you said, only she stayed here?"

He dug the heel of one boot into the mud. "That's a thought. My worry would be that Ryan might contest the legality of it if I didn't actually have custody of her. If she's in my home and happy there, a judge would think twice about annulling the adoption."

She worried her lip. "What if you adopted her, and I moved in as the housekeeper? That Ching Lee fellow, he could get a job elsewhere, couldn't he?"

His mouth lifted slightly at the corners. "There you go. Wouldn't Ryan have fun with that in court. You and I living together without benefit of marriage? All the God-fearing folk in Roseburg would stone us every time we rode into town."

She raised her hands. "There has to be an answer other than marriage."

"Marriage is simplest."

"But I don't *want* to be married. I like being my own person."

"And you couldn't be if your last name was changed?"

"There's a bit more to it than that."

"We're talking about a wedding ring, not a ball and chain."

"We're talking about more than a ring!" she cried.

It was his turn to throw up his hands. "What, aside from accommodating me in the bedroom? You sure as hell wouldn't have as much work to do. And you wouldn't have to filch away every miserable penny you got your hands on, trying to clothe your daughter. Or walk around in the dark at night, afraid to waste lantern fuel. Just what are we talking about, Kate?"

She could only stare at him.

He stepped closer, his hands once again riding his hips. "Let's get a clear understanding here. If I adopt your daughter, and then I turn out to be the bastard you're afraid I might be, your independence will be shot all to hell, anyway." He leaned toward her. "With Miranda's happiness at stake, if I said jump, you'd ask how high. There'd be no end to the leverage I'd have over you. So what the hell difference does it make, married or not?"

She pressed her fingertips against her temples. "None, I guess." She fastened frightened eyes on his. "What about you? Doesn't it bother you, knowing how I feel?"

He shifted his weight to one foot and bent a knee. After gazing at her for several seconds, he said, "I aim to change that. If I didn't think I could make you happy, that'd bother me. But I think I can if you'll give me the chance."

Kate couldn't believe she was about to ask this. "Wh- Where would we live? At your place?"

He glanced over his shoulder. "Not with Joseph planted in your front yard. We'd have to stay here to keep Ryan out of here." He pursed his lips, then exhaled a breath through his clenched teeth. After a long moment, he said, "I thought

JOIN THE
TIMELESS ROMANCE READER SERVICE AND GET FOUR OF TODAY'S MOST EXCITING HISTORICAL ROMANCES FREE, WITHOUT OBLIGATION!

Imagine getting today's very best historical romances sent directly to your home – at a total savings of at least $2.00 a month. Now you can be among the first to be swept away by the latest from Candace Camp, Constance O'Banyon, Patricia Hagan, Parris Afton Bonds or Susan Wiggs. You get all that – and that's just the beginning.

PREVIEW AT HOME WITHOUT OBLIGATION AND SAVE.

Each month, you'll receive four new romances to preview without obligation for 10 days. You'll pay the low subscriber price of just $4.00 per title – a total savings of at least $2.00 a month!

Postage and handling is absolutely free and there is no minimum number of books you must buy. You may cancel your subscription at any time with no obligation.

GET YOUR FOUR
FREE BOOKS TODAY
($20.49 VALUE)

FILL IN THE ORDER FORM BELOW NOW!

YES! *I want to join the Timeless Romance Reader Service. Please send me my 4 FREE HarperMonogram historical romances. Then each month send me 4 new historical romances to preview without obligation for 10 days. I'll pay the low subscription price of $4.00 for every book I choose to keep – a total savings of at least $2.00 each month – and home delivery is free! I understand that I may return any title within 10 days without obligation and I may cancel this subscription at any time without obligation. There is no minimum number of books to purchase.*

NAME_____

ADDRESS _____

CITY_____STATE_____ZIP_____

TELEPHONE_____

SIGNATURE _____

(If under 18 parent or guardian must sign. Program, price, terms, and conditions subject to cancellation and change. Orders subject to acceptance by HarperMonogram.)

GET
4
FREE
BOOKS
(A $20.49
VALUE)

about moving the evidence. My first instinct was to bury him out in the woods somewhere." He paused to gaze thoughtfully across the valley. "The way folks are settling here though, it would have been just my luck to choose a spot that some farmer plans to clear soon. If somebody started digging a well or uprooting trees near where I buried him, they might—" He broke off and swallowed. "Next I considered taking him to my place. Then I thought better of it, for two reasons. One being that the rose garden will be the last place Ryan will look, the other being that I'd be implicated as an accomplice if the body was ever found."

"I wouldn't expect you to take that risk."

"It wasn't my risk that concerned me but Mandy's. If suspicion was thrown on me, we could both end up in jail, and there she'd be with no one to take care of her again. It's better to leave things alone and hope we can keep Ryan away."

"And what if—" She wrung her hands. "What if we can't? What if he finds Joseph and turns me in?"

"Then you go to jail, and Mandy and I wait for you to come home. They aren't going to put you in prison or hang you, Kate. It's not as if you deliberately killed the man."

"I thought about it enough times."

"You can't think a man to death. No jury on earth will convict you."

She closed her eyes. "I murdered him in my thoughts a thousand times. According to the Bible, that's as bad as doing it."

"Bullshit."

"It says it, right in—"

"I don't care what it says. You can't take everything so literally. Three-quarters of the world's population should hang if that's the case. Practically everyone has a violent thought now and again. And you had more cause than most."

She curled her hands into fists. "I didn't have a choice when I married Joseph."

"I guessed as much. You're too intelligent a woman to have made such a rotten choice in a husband."

His admission surprised Kate. It had been years since a man have given her credit for having any brains. "With all the best of intentions, my uncle made the nuptial arrangements shortly before he died. I swore I'd never be coerced into marriage again."

He rubbed his jaw. "I'm trying my damnedest to feel guilty about that."

She stared down at him, wondering what that was supposed to mean. Then he looked into her eyes, his warm with a mixture of amusement and tenderness.

"But the truth is I'll take you any way I can get you. And it's hard to feel guilty about that when I know it's probably what's best for you."

Best for her . . . How many times had Joseph said the same? Kate had hoped to spend the remainder of her days deciding for herself what might be best.

"Is it the physical aspect of marriage?" he asked softly. "Was Joseph—" He broke off and tipped back his head to gaze at the roof. "I know he was a mean so-and-so. Was he ornery in the bedroom, too?"

Ornery? A picture flashed in Kate's head of darkness and the panting sound of Joseph's breath. Hoping Zachariah wouldn't notice how tense his question made her, she shoved the memories away and knotted her hands into fists. If he started to suspect just how *ornery* Joseph had sometimes been, he might demand she give him particulars. Kate couldn't do that, couldn't even contemplate it. There were some things so horrible that one dared not expose them, dared not even think of them.

Reluctant to lie, she temporized, struggling to keep her

voice even. "No, as a rule, he wasn't ornery. Not in the bedroom, anyway." That was the truth, as far as it went. Kate avoided meeting Zachariah's gaze, afraid he might see the unspoken truth in her eyes. "The physical aspect is only part of the reason I feel as I do."

Zachariah looked relieved. "Well, then." He flashed her a slow grin that made her skin tingle. "At least he did something right. I have to admit that was my biggest worry, that maybe things hadn't been—" He broke off and shrugged his shoulders to rearrange his jacket. Running his finger under his collar, he glanced at the rising sun. "If this weather doesn't beat all. It's getting damned hot out here."

"It's July."

He studied the sun a moment longer, his eyes in a squint to block out the light. "Yeah, July. Now I suppose it'll get hot enough to fry eggs, and we'll all wish for rain."

Kate felt like screaming. How could he switch to talking about the weather at a time like this? Her whole life was being decided here. Her thoughts drifted to Miranda, asleep upstairs. Kate imagined the joy on her face when she heard the news. At least her child would be happy. Pray God. There was always the chance that Zachariah McGovern might show a totally different side once he had his fish hooked.

"Wh-When will we do it?" she asked in a tinny voice.

Still rubbing his jaw, he seemed to freeze at the question. After a pregnant moment, he said, "When it feels right, I guess. Do we have to decide that right now?"

Kate lifted her chin and stiffened her shoulders. "If I have to do it, I want to get it over with."

He just stood there, holding his jaw and gaping at her.

She was beginning to feel annoyed. Two minutes ago, he couldn't seem to wait. "Who'll we get as witnesses?"

"Witnesses?" An odd expression crept into his eyes, and then he started to clear his throat and nearly choked on a smothered laugh. "Witnesses." He rearranged his expression to one of solemnity, apparently with great effort. "Of course, witnesses. I don't know where my head went." He pinched the bridge of his nose. "How about Marcus and Ching Lee? I can round them up and have them ready by noon."

"Noon today?" she asked.

He swept off his jacket and swiped his forehead with his shirt sleeve. "Like you said, we may as well do it. I'm not going to feel easy until those adoption papers are signed."

Kate tried to take a deep breath but her lungs didn't want to expand. Men. She'd never understand them. One minute, any old time suited him just fine, and now he wanted to set out at noon? She hated that. Feeling like a ball being bounced about at someone else's whim. "I can be ready."

Hooking his jacket on one finger, he slung it over his shoulder. "Do you want me here with you to tell Miranda?"

Kate couldn't feel her feet. "No. I think it'd be best if I do that alone."

Apparently reluctant to leave, he planted a boot on her bottom step. "I know you're not happy about this."

That was an understatement.

He looked up to eye her eave again. "That roof needs fixing."

The weather, and now the roof? Kate bit down on a wave of irritation. "Yes. Much more rain like we've just had and it'll leak like a sieve, I imagine."

He thumped his heel on the step. "This porch is in sorry shape, too."

"Yes."

His gaze sought hers. "So is your life, Katie."

There was no answer to that.

"I'm handy at fixing things," he said huskily.

With that, he turned away.

16

For Kate, the remainder of that day sped by on winged feet, the hours and events a blur. Going into Roseburg, visiting the judge, the brief wedding ceremony, signing her name to documents, one forever binding her to Zachariah McGovern, the other giving him parental rights to her daughter.

At least there wasn't time to think, and for that, Kate was grateful. Her life loomed ahead of her, once again uncertain, once again controlled by someone else.

As she had expected, Miranda reacted positively to the situation. She was so excited at the prospect of attending the wedding and being adopted that she wasn't even shy around Ching Lee and Marcus on the way into town, which was remarkable. The child seemed to see Zachariah as her bulwark, someone who would protect her from all that she had once feared.

Mr. Zach was going to be her pa! All day long, she kept repeating that, driving Kate half-mad until Zach brought a stop to it by informing the child there was no longer any "will be" to it; he *was* her pa.

As much as it grated on her nerves, Kate had felt more comfortable with "will be." But as the afternoon gave way to evening and she found herself alone in the house with her child and new husband, the reality of her changed circumstances began to sink home. She was Mrs. Zachariah McGovern, no two ways about it. The plain gold band that he had picked up at the jeweler's and slipped onto her finger was a constant reminder of that. The indentation that had been worn into her flesh by Joseph's ring hadn't completely faded yet, and now she wore another.

A circle of gold, the symbol of eternity.

She decided not to dwell on the distasteful. If she pretended hard enough, maybe things wouldn't seem too different. After nursing the man for nearly a month, she was accustomed to having Zachariah in the house. Now he was back. Not much had actually changed.

Except, of course, that he was now at large in her house, a broad-shouldered, looming presence with speculative hazel eyes she couldn't escape. He joined them for supper at the table. And then he remained while she did dishes, reading aloud to her and Miranda from a recent issue of the Portland *Morning Oregonian.* Kate enjoyed that and suspected he knew it.

She tried to ignore the gleam of anticipation in his eyes when he glanced over the top of the newspaper at her. He was making her feel unaccountably nervous. He had fired up two lanterns, which struck Kate as wasteful. The evening shadows in the house had been frustrating at times but restful. With the kitchen lit up as bright as day, she knew he could tell every time she blushed—which was often.

Men. She guessed what he was anticipating. The hour was growing late, and whether she wanted to think about it or not, it was their wedding night. Not that she could see what the big deal was. It wasn't as if she intended to incite his anger in any way, and as long as she took care not to, all should go smoothly. A perfunctory joining in the darkness, a few panting breaths, and it would be over.

Maybe men enjoyed it. Joseph hadn't pestered her but once every few months, but she distinctly recalled a few times when he had given what had sounded like a satisfied grunt after he finished.

As she dried the last plate, she turned to regard Miranda, who was perched on Zachariah's knee and perusing the paper, for all the world as if she could read every word. "It's about that time, little miss."

Zachariah's gaze flew to hers. Kate swallowed, feeling unsettled. She wished he'd get that twinkle out of his eyes. He made her feel like a dish of dessert. She put the plate away on the shelf and dried her hands before hanging up the towel.

"I don't wanna go to bed!" Miranda complained. "It's a special day. Can't we stay up late?"

Zachariah gave her a playful swat. "Off to bed you go. Your ma's tuckered, and so am I. Special day or no, the sun won't come up late in the morning."

Miranda pulled a long face but slid obediently off his lap. Kate took her hand and cast a meaningful glance at her husband. "I think I'll turn in myself. Can you douse the lamps before you come up?"

"Sure." His gaze traveled the length of her, a slow appraisal that made her nerves leap. "I think I'll read a while longer first. That'll give you some time to yourself."

Though he didn't say it in so many words, Kate knew he meant for her to be ready for him when he finally joined her. She hoped he didn't linger down here overlong. After not getting any rest last night, she truly was tuckered. If she had to perform her wifely duty tonight, her one wish was to get it over with quickly so she could go to sleep.

Nosy scrambled to his feet to follow Miranda from the kitchen. Once upstairs, he settled on the rug as though he intended to remain there for the night. Kate wasn't fooled. She gave Miranda a quick scrub at the washstand, then helped her into her nightgown.

"Do I git a story?"

Kate sighed. Her mind wasn't on stories tonight, but she supposed she could come up with something. After tucking the child into the bed, she perched on the edge and searched her mind for a tale to tell.

"I wanna hear one about a little girl who made a magic wish for a new pa," Miranda requested happily.

Kate stifled a groan. But she dutifully began, spinning a tale that sounded uncomfortably autobiographical. As she wound down to a finish, Miranda smiled with contentment and closed her eyes, her expression dreamy. A happy ending, Kate thought. Only it wasn't the ending for the little girl's ma.

Trying not to think of what lay in wait for her, Kate rose from the bed and turned down the lamp. Images encroached, and she shoved them away, refusing to let herself become nervous. A quick, impersonal joining, that was all it would be. If she closed her eyes, it would be no different than when Joseph had come to her.

Wiping her suddenly damp palms on her skirt, Kate said, "Good night, Miranda."

"G'night, Ma."

Turning to leave the room, Kate took a deep, bracing breath. She would simply go to her room, don her nightgown, and wait for Zachariah at the dresser, just as she had a dozen other times in her last marriage. He would come upstairs, finish his business, and go to bed. She doubted they'd even speak. There was nothing to be afraid of, certainly, and no reason to feel embarrassed. She wouldn't think about that knowing twinkle in his eyes.

Zach set a boot on the stair, wincing when it creaked beneath his weight. It'd be his luck Miranda would wake up. As much as he loved the little imp, he had one destination in mind tonight and didn't relish the thought of making any side trips into the child's bedroom.

Kate was waiting. At the thought, Zach's pulse quickened, his body sprang taut, his breathing became ragged, and his throat constricted. If this kept up, he'd be winded before he got out of the gate. She deserved better than that.

Once upstairs, he paused outside her door. He knew it was her door because Miranda's room was down the hall and he could see light coming out from around this one's cracks. Kate was in there, waiting for him.

He envisioned her nude body. Then he backtracked, deciding Kate wasn't that sort. A modest gown would be more to her taste. White muslin, probably. Sleeveless, with a scooped neck and those little pink bows that women liked all down the front. Anticipation filled him, and he felt his hands start to shake.

Whoa, boy.

She was a lady, for God's sake, from the tips of her toes all the way up. If he went in like a bee after honey, he'd unsettle her, not to mention the very real possibility that he might disgrace himself. He leaned against the wall and tried to recall the baseball scores he'd just read in the paper. His brain refused to function. Clearly, thinking about something else wasn't going to dampen his enthusiasm.

He reckoned most men probably had the same problem on their wedding nights. Randy as hell, and tired of waiting.

Not that the knowledge was much consolation. He wanted to make it nice for Kate. Perfect for her, if he could. If he could make this part of their marriage beautiful, maybe she would find it less difficult to adjust to the rest. He had no illusions; she wasn't the least bit happy about being his wife.

At least she hadn't seemed nervous when she'd left the kitchen. Resigned was a better word. Zach smiled to himself. He'd use a slow hand. Give him a month. That lack of interest he sensed in her would become a thing of the past. And eventually she'd begin to see how much better her life could be, married to him. Less work, a nicer home, pretty clothes, and someone to protect her from bastards like Ryan Blakely.

The light shining out around the door began to dim. Zach pushed away from the wall, swamped with disappointment. She had doused the lamp. He had been hoping she'd leave it lit. Now that he thought on it, though, he realized that had been a stupid expectation. Naturally, she wasn't as blasé about this as she pretended to be. He hadn't even kissed her yet. The unfamiliarity between them would make any woman feel nervous.

He took a calming breath. That was fine. He didn't need light. And what man worth his salt couldn't work his way past a little initial shyness? He grasped the doorknob and pushed slowly into the room.

In the dying illumination of the lamp, he saw Kate standing at the dresser. Modest didn't describe her gown. She was covered chin to toe, fingertip to shoulder in white muslin. Yards and yards of muslin. Her dark hair hung in silken, unbraided ripples down her back. He closed the door behind him but she didn't turn to look at him when the latch clicked into place. He supposed a woman had nightly rituals to perform, even on her wedding night. She'd probably been brushing her hair.

He walked slowly up behind her and grasped her shoulders. As his fingers curled around her arms, he half expected her to stiffen, but she didn't. He pressed his face to her loosened tresses and inhaled. Lord, she smelled wonderful. So sweet and wholesome, not at all like the lilac-doused whores he'd been forced to settle for these last few years.

Roses and cinnamon, yeast and vanilla. She was enough to make a man salivate. He sniffed his way to her neck, only to be frustrated by the high collar of her gown. Pearline Washing Compound. He smiled and closed his eyes.

"Can I help?" he asked softly.

"With what?"

"With brushing your hair."

"I'm finished."

She leaned slightly forward and braced the heels of her hands on the dresser's edge. Swathed in moonlight and folds of white muslin, she looked childlike, her insubstantial frame diminished by the fabric and shadows.

Her forward movement pushed her soft rump against his thighs, reminding him of the womanly curves that he knew were concealed under the cloth. His lower regions snapped to attention. A muted groan caught in his throat.

Thankful for the restrictions of his britches, he ran his fingertips lightly down her arms. Now he knew where the saying "keep your pants on" had originated. He intended to do just that—as long as he could bear the agony. If it was the last thing he did, he wanted to make this a night she'd fondly remember.

His lips found the velvety nape of her neck. Lord, she was so incredibly, impossibly sweet. He trailed his fingertips over her hands where she clasped the dresser, then back up to her wrists. The fine network of her bones tantalized him. He'd never touched a grown woman so delicately made.

Beneath his lips, chill bumps sprang up on her neck,

and he heard her breath catch. He nipped the silken lobe of her ear, and she quivered. Images of how she might react when he captured an erect nipple in his teeth made his own breathing become labored.

He dipped his tongue under the collar and lapped seductively at her skin. God, he wanted to taste every inch of her. She made a strangled sound in the back of her throat and crossed her arms to capture his hands where they caressed her shoulders. He hesitated, not quite sure how to read her. Was she frightened, after all?

"Katie, if you'd rather wait . . ." He could do that, couldn't he? Just at the thought, his body throbbed in protest. "I don't mean to rush you. Exchanging vows and signing a piece of paper . . . If you need some time, all you have to do is ask. Just because we're married doesn't mean you don't deserve to be courted a little. Anything that'll make this easier for you."

As he spoke his breath washed over her skin, and she shivered again. "No, it isn't necessary to wait," she replied tremulously. "I'd just like to get on with it. That's all."

Zach didn't need to be asked twice. Turning her slightly, he bent to catch her in his arms. She squeaked as he lifted her. When her head fell back, he settled his mouth at the hollow under her jaw and drank of the throbbing pulse-beat there. Feeling the frantic rhythm of her heart clear to his toes, he imagined thrusting into the wet, pulsing heat of her, and another moan issued from his chest.

He carried her quickly to the bed. As he settled her carefully on the mattress, he moved a hand to the bodice of her gown. Buttons, not bows. Two dozen, at least. The itty-bitty kind, fashioned by females, he was sure, to drive men mad. They extended from her waist to her high-necked collar in a frustrating line. First thing tomorrow, he'd go over to his place and get his new Montgomery Ward catalog so she could order some decent gowns. Or maybe a more appropriate description would be less decent. She wasn't a nun, for God's sake.

As he freed buttons, Zach followed the trail of his fingers with his lips, nibbling softly at the silken flesh he bared. When he found the swell of a breast, she whimpered low in her throat and grabbed handfuls of his hair.

"Wh-What are you doing?" she asked in a panicked little voice.

Her tone splashed over Zach with the same shocking coldness of ice water. He drew back, perplexed by the confusion and uncertainty he heard in her voice. In the dim glow of moonlight, he could see that her eyes were huge and filled with alarm.

"What am I doing?" he repeated hoarsely.

Until that instant, he had thought he was making love to an experienced woman. Now he was no longer so sure. She looked as scandalized as a virgin, her face white, her lips parted to emit shallow breaths. Her fist closed on her gown to hold the front plackets together. He had a feeling he'd have a battle on his hands if he tried to pry those slender fingers loose.

By way of explanation, which he couldn't believe was necessary, he said, "I'm making love to you."

She swallowed hard. "Wh-Why can't you just do it the regular way?"

"The regular way?" He closed a hand over hers, and sure enough, she had her fingers clenched on her nightgown in a death grip. "What way is that, Katie?"

"A-At the d-dresser."

He shot a glance through the darkness at the piece of furniture. Granted, she didn't have scent bottles and a lot of other feminine accessories on the dresser top like most women, but the available space still didn't look suitable for what Zach had in mind. Knowing her as he did, he couldn't quite believe she had suggested such a thing. Ten years into marriage, maybe, when new spots and different positions kept the excitement high. But now? Their first time together?

He gently massaged her clutched fist, hoping to relax her fingers and get back to where he'd left off. "I reckon we can do it wherever you'd like." He bent his head to kiss her whitened knuckles. "First, let's get this nightgown out of the way."

She brought up her other hand to grab another handful of muslin. "It doesn't get in the way. You—you can just raise it up in back. That's what Joseph always did."

In back? Zach remembered how she'd pressed her bottom against him when he'd come up to stand behind her, and a warning bell clanged inside his head. He studied her taut features.

"Katie, how, exactly, did Joseph make love to you?"

She licked her bottom lip. "He, um . . ." She jerked her gaze from his. "He just did it."

"How?" he prodded cautiously. "From the back? With you standing?"

"Sort of."

"Sort of what?"

Even in the moonlight, he saw her face flush crimson. "Sort of standing. I bent forward."

Zach curled his fingers more tightly over hers. "And did you like it that way?"

"Like it?"

From her tone, he could tell that her preferences had never been a priority. His guts knotted on an awful suspicion. "Didn't Joseph—" He broke off, a little uncomfortable with the turn of this conversation. How did a man go about asking these sorts of questions? "Didn't he kiss you and touch you?"

She looked scandalized. "Lands, no."

"'Lands, no?'" he echoed.

"He was always very polite."

Polite? How in the hell could a man make love to a woman properly and be polite about it? Zach knew he was gaping at her, but he couldn't seem to stop. "Honey, didn't he try to—to make it nice for you?"

She seemed to shrink into the feather mattress. "I'm not removing my nightgown," she informed him in a quavery voice.

Zach could see that concessions on his part were indeed in order. He tried a smile, hoping that might reassure her. "That's fine. Like you said, I can work around it."

She looked none too thrilled by that thought. He sat up and began unbuttoning his shirt. She watched him with unmistakable wariness. "Relax, Katie."

"Wh-What are you doing?" she demanded to know.

"Taking my shirt off." He tossed the garment in question toward the foot of the bed and then leaned over to unlace his boots. Toe to heel, he prized each of them off.

As he stood to take off his pants, she wiggled over to the far side of the bed and bolted upright. In an accusing tone, she cried, "You're undressing!"

That was fairly obvious. His fingers froze on the fastening of his jeans. "Joseph didn't?"

Her eyes huge in her pinched face, she stared up at him. Of course Joseph hadn't undressed, Zach realized. How could a man be polite if he was bare-assed naked? He decided his first inclination had probably been more appropriate for the occasion; he'd best keep his britches on. Angling a knee onto the bed, he braced his fists on the mattress and leaned toward her. She reared back.

"Katie, don't be frightened."

"Kate, not Katie. And it's absurd to think I'm frightened!

I'm a grown woman with a child! But if you think I'm going to do it naked, you have another think."

Zach had already had another think. Several of them. Steadying his weight on one arm, he reached to trace a finger along her cheek. "I said we could work around the nightgown. No problem. And I've still got my trousers on."

As he spoke, he brushed his lips lightly over hers. Her breath tasted as sweet as honey blossoms. He ran his hand into her hair. "Ah, Katie," he whispered. "My precious Katie girl. Don't be nervous."

"I'm not nervous."

As his lips descended to her throat, he felt the rigidity in her. Not nervous? That was the biggest understatement he'd ever heard. Cupping one hand behind her head, he used his other to knead the stiffness from her. Every place on her back that his fingers probed, he felt her muscles retract.

With a muffled little moan, she finally relented and dropped her head back. Zach had a feeling tonight might prove to be far more memorable for her than he had guessed. Polite? *Jesus H. Christ.*

He kissed his way down her lovely throat to where her fists clenched her nightgown together. Not wishing to alarm her by forcing her hands down, he waged his assault on the exposed *V* of her chest and then went to work on her fingers, nibbling and suckling her knuckles. She shuddered, and he felt her hands spasm. The result was that she loosened her grip a bit.

"Zachariah?"

"Hmmmmm?" He found an opening in the cloth and invaded with his tongue to lick at the warm swell of flesh beneath. She jerked her wrist down to cover the spot. He circled and found another. "Lower your hands, Katie," he urged huskily. "Don't be afraid. It'll feel nice, I promise."

"Nice?" She executed another frantic maneuver with her wrists. "I'm not that kind of woman—"

He found more skin, and she broke off with a startled murmur of protest. Her wrists shifted again to intercept, and in her attempt to frustrate him, she left a length of unfastened plackets unprotected. Like a magnet drawn to the head of a nail, his mouth went to the crest of her breast.

"Wha-What are you—?"

She never finished the question. Zach caught the erect tip of her nipple between his teeth and flicked it with his tongue. Her spine arched, and she let loose of the night-gown to grab his hair. A low wail came up her throat as he drew sharply on her.

"Zachariah?"

He rolled her lightly between his teeth, exerting just enough pressure to drive all thought from her mind. She shoved halfheartedly against him and gave a ragged sob. Then her fists relaxed, and she ran her fingers into his hair, cupping her palms to pull him closer.

"What are you doing?" she finally managed.

In response, he drew all of that wonderfully taut cone of flesh into his mouth. She cried out and arched up to meet him, her throat issuing breathless little cries each time he dragged his tongue over her. The tension in her changed, and instead of trying to ward him off, she bowed her body into his and clutched him close.

Confident now of making her his, he nearly smiled at the jolts he felt running through her. As he worked her, Zach slid a hand along her hip, down her thigh, his busy fingertips gathering muslin until he found warm, silken skin. He lowered her onto the pillows and shifted his body to lie beside her, his mouth never relinquishing possession of her breast. Soft inner thigh. He grazed a palm upward, seeking the tantalizing center of her.

Just as his hand found its mark, she gasped and started scrambling to pull her nightgown down. The change in her came so quickly and with so little warning that for an instant, Zach tried to hold her. Then he realized she was struggling in earnest against him.

The fear in her was unmistakable. He drew back and listened with growing puzzlement to her frantic attempts to convince him she was innocent of any wrongdoing.

"I haven't been thinking anything bad. Honestly I haven't!" She finally managed to shove his hand back down to the region of her knee. Gulping for breath, she said, "Not one lustful thought, I swear it. The same urges came over Joseph sometimes. Once when I was washing dishes! I didn't do anything. I wasn't even aware he was in the room." A high-pitched, nervous little laugh punctuated that. "Isn't that crazy? No rhyme nor reason to—" Her voice broke on a dry sob. "P-Please don't be angry, Zachariah. Please don't. I can't seem to help it."

Her grip on his wrist was frenzied, her nails digging into his skin. All because he had been about to touch her? Confusion jumbled his thoughts, and on the heels of that, anger lashed him. A cold, mind-numbing anger that made him feel half sick. Dear God, what had that madman done to her?

"Katie," he whispered. "Shhhhhh, honey. It's all right."

Gathering her close, he pressed her face against his shoulder and felt her hot tears against his skin. His passion spiraled downward, splatting like a cold griddle cake in the pit of his stomach. She was trembling, trembling horribly. And by that he knew a measure of her fear.

That bastard. That miserable, no-good bastard.

Zach considered just holding her. Finishing what he had started was out of the question. He had never forced himself on a frightened woman in his life, and he didn't intend to start now. On the other hand, though, problems never got solved by pretending they didn't exist.

He tightened his grip on her knee. "Katie, is your body ready for me? Is that what you're afraid I'll be angry about?"

"N-No!"

He braced his arm to resist her tugging hands and inched his fingertips up the inside of her thigh. "Let me feel."

"No, I don't—"

His strength won out. His fingertips encountered a molten heat and wetness that made his belly contract around a knot of longing.

"Katie . . ." He searched his mind for something he might say to soothe her. "Have you any idea how sweet and beautiful you are, how precious you are to me?"

"A person can't help how she looks."

Zach circled that. He hadn't meant the compliment as an accusation.

"I didn't mean to tempt you!" she cried. Her eyes sought his, huge and filled with fright.

Growing more bewildered by the moment, Zach drew her closer and buried his face in her hair. "Honey, you'd tempt a man in your sleep."

"But Joseph—"

She broke off with a sharp intake of breath when he moved his hand. Zach wasn't certain he could speak. His body clamored for release. After a deep breath and a determined swallow, he managed, "I think we need to have a long talk. This morning when I asked if Joseph was ornery in the bedroom, you weren't entirely honest with me. Were you?"

Still trembling violently, she lay there in the circle of his arm, her spine curled to keep distance between their bodies. An endless moment of silence passed.

Zach could see that she had no intention of answering. Toying with her hair, he gazed thoughtfully at the wall behind her. "Katie, how can I ease your fears if I don't know for certain what he did to you?"

Her voice little more than a high-pitched squeak, she cried, "I can't talk about it. Please, don't ask me to."

He closed his eyes on that. "No matter how hard it is, you have to try."

A violent trembling shook her.

He tightened his embrace, hating himself for pressing her, yet convinced he had no choice. "Did Joseph punish you for making him want you?"

"It wasn't my fault. He said it was, but I never did anything! Not a single thing."

Her defensiveness was answer in itself. He gazed sightlessly into the shadows, trying to put together everything she had unwittingly revealed to him tonight, to make sense of it. He recalled her initial calmness when he first approached her at the dresser, then her sudden rigidity when he started to caress her. Moments later, when he had begun to remove his clothing, there had been no mistaking her alarm.

Piece by piece, the puzzle began to come together, and the overall picture sent Zach's mind reeling. A beautiful woman who drew her hair into a severe braid and wore threadbare dresses, so somber in color that he had mistakenly thought they were widow's weeds. Not so, he realized now. Joseph had been dead only six months, not nearly enough time for her to have worn the sleeves of her gowns thin at the elbows and cuffs.

Katie . . . Sweet, precious Katie who had done everything in her power to look plain because her late husband had punished her for being beautiful.

"Sweetheart . . ." He bent his head, trying to see her face. "Can you look at me?"

"I'm not going to talk about Joseph," she whispered fiercely.

Despite the seriousness of the moment, Zach bit back a smile at her bravado. "I'll do the talking. All you have to do is listen."

Her chin came up a notch, but not nearly far enough to let him see her face. Not a man to split hairs, Zach contented himself with that.

"There's no sin in being pretty," he whispered. "I don't know what Joseph said to the contrary, but trust me. You can no more control how you look than you can the beating of your heart."

"But Joseph said—"

"I don't care what Joseph said. The man was an idiot."

He rolled up on his arm so his face was above hers. She looked so young lying there, her eyes huge and luminous in the moonlight. He wished he could simply let the subject drop. But he couldn't. If left to fret over it, she'd probably grow upset every time he grew amorous. Which was bound to be often.

He tried a smile, but she didn't seem to relax much. Gazing down at her pinched face, he ran a finger lightly along her cheekbone. "One of the first things about you that I fell in love with was your beautiful face. Your skin is like fresh cream, and your features in profile are as perfect as a cameo. You don't have to encourage me to make me want you."

She lowered her lashes, clearly uneasy. Zach bit the inside of his lip, then plunged ahead, convinced that even a bungled attempt at easing her mind was bound to be better than letting her continue to believe the bullshit Joseph had told her.

"Katie, a man can get aroused just by watching a woman walk into a room," he whispered.

At that proclamation, her eyes widened with horror. "Are you saying you don't want me to walk in front of you?"

The suggestion was so preposterous that if any other woman had made it, Zach would have felt certain she was joking. Not so with Kate. She clearly wished to avoid enticing him, no matter what lengths she had to go to. It was also equally obvious that she hadn't the faintest notion what aroused the opposite sex.

"Of course I'm not saying I don't want you to walk in front of me," he replied patiently. "I'm just trying to make you understand—" He broke off, his heart catching at the way she hung on his every word. "Katie, sweetheart, what I'm trying to say is that a woman is seldom responsible when a man becomes aroused. It just happens."

"She isn't?"

"Take walking, for instance. It might be the way her skirts cling to her hips. Or the way she moves. She can be totally unaware of him, not even trying to entice him, and he can start to want her."

By the bewilderment he read in her expression, Zach knew she needed to hear this even if it embarrassed her, which it surely would.

"Just by smiling at Mandy, you've made me ache with wanting you." he informed her in as matter-of-fact a tone as he could manage.

"I never intended—"

He rested a finger across her lips. "I'm not laying blame, Katie girl. You're not responsible for the thoughts that go through my head." Her obvious distrust brought a smile to his mouth. "You have fifteen buttons on the bodice of your black dress, fourteen on the brown, and I've imagined unbuttoning each one a thousand times."

She looked completely scandalized at the thought. "You counted all of them?"

"I did." His grin broadened. "The night we quarreled in the sickroom? When you were ordering me out of the house? Correct me if I'm wrong, but I don't think enticing me was foremost in your mind. But I wanted you even then."

She drew back slightly to escape the pressure of his finger on her mouth. "You did? When I was so angry?"

"You're beautiful when you're angry," he replied huskily. "And beautiful when you're not. A man who'd blame you for his own lusty urges ought to be horsewhipped.

"Sometimes when you move a certain way and the bodice of your dress pulls tight, I want you so badly that I ache. Or you bend over and—"

The color that flooded to her face was visible even in the moonlight, and upon seeing it, Zach cut himself off. He smoothed her hair from her tear-streaked cheek.

"You can't change the way God made you," he whispered. "The differences between us, my need to touch you . . . that's natural and right. When we make love, it should be glorious for you, not frightening."

She cupped a shaky hand over her eyes. "Joseph said I was sinful and wicked for making him want me. The most awful part was that I was never certain what he thought I'd done." After moistening her lips, she continued. "He came to me only when—when he was long overdue in performing his husbandly duty—just to beget offspring, like Scripture tells us. When the urge came over him to do more than that, he grew furious."

"His husbandly duty? At the dresser, you mean? Always quick and polite, never so much as touching you?"

She gave a nod.

"And what of those times when he wanted to do more? Did he?"

Her response this time was a negative shake of her

head. Then, in a ragged whisper, she added, "He believed anything more was a sin and that I must have deliberately seduced him if those wicked urges came over him."

Very gently, he drew her hand down. "Sweetheart, what did he do? Those times when he got angry, what did he do?"

Where seconds before her face had been flushed with embarrassment, it now went deathly pale. She slid her gaze from his. Her throat worked with the effort it took for her to speak. "Some things—" She took a shaky breath. "Some things are so awful they can't be put into words. Please don't ask me to try. Please don't."

Pictures flashed inside his head. Pictures of Kate at the dresser, as she had been earlier, the man behind her not him, but Joseph. The possibilities made his guts clench. Aching for her, he bent his head to kiss the tears that had spilled over onto her cheeks. As she said, some things were so vile, so appalling, a person couldn't describe them, and he would be a callous bastard if he forced her to try. The haunted look he had seen in her eyes conveyed enough. He only hoped he could be as eloquent, in the way he touched her, in the way he held her—that with unfailing gentleness and patience he could heal the wounds Joseph had inflicted.

"Katie, sweetheart, I—"

Before Zach could finish the sentence, he heard the doorknob click. All memory of what he intended to say fled his mind. He jerked Kate's nightgown down and twisted to look over his shoulder. Hinges squeaked, the door swung open, and there stood Miranda, a tiny white wraith in the darkness.

17

When Kate saw Miranda and Nosy standing in the doorway, her body became electrified with a new kind of fear. One of Joseph's rules had been that Miranda should never open their bedroom door without asking his permission. The few times the child had forgotten, Joseph had become enraged and punished her—most times severely.

When Zach spotted the pair, he swore under his breath, which convinced Kate he was furious. When he shifted to leave the bed, she reacted instinctively, crying out and grabbing his arm.

"No! She didn't mean—" Kate scrambled to her knees, yanking at the folds of her nightgown so she could move. "Don't hurt her! Please! I'll make sure she doesn't do it again!"

Miranda fell back against the wall and started to wail. Nosy began to bark. Kate scurried to place herself between her angry husband and her child. Zachariah scotched that plan, seizing her by the shoulders.

"You stay put," he ordered in a gravelly voice. "I'll handle this."

"No, please . . ." Kate grabbed his arm with both hands. "Please, Zachariah. She didn't mean it."

He jerked free of her grasp and hissed, "Stop it, Kate. You're scaring her to death."

With that, he shoved up from the bed. To Kate, he seemed a giant, a broad-shouldered, muscular giant. And her precious baby looked so small, so terribly small. She sobbed and leaped to her feet. Zachariah wheeled, clamped his hands at her waist, and lifted her back onto the mattress as if she weighed no more than the child. Helpless against such strength, Kate hugged herself and sobbed, daunted by the realization that not even Joseph in one of his rages had been able to overpower her so easily.

"I said I'll handle this," he repeated. "You stay put and keep quiet." He snapped his fingers at the barking dog. "You, too, you no-account mutt."

His tone brooked no argument. As he traversed the floor toward Miranda, Kate pressed her hands over her mouth to stop herself from crying out, prepared to intervene if she had to, terrified of what he'd do if that became necessary. With strength such as his, one blow from one of his massive fists would probably shatter her jaw. Regardless, if he became violent, she'd have to face him. Better her than her daughter.

Miranda shrank against the wall, her wail turning to a shriek when Zachariah reached for her.

"Hey," he said silkily, as he lifted the child into his arms. "What is this? We're best friends, remember?"

Miranda gulped and tried to arch away from him but her strength was no match. Nosy whined anxiously and nudged his master's pant leg. Kate gaped in amazement as Zachariah began to pace the room slowly, whispering soothingly and stroking the child's hair. Miranda's terrified shrieks gave way to ragged sobs, and those soon diminished to exhausted catches of breath. At last, the child hugged his neck with her tiny arms.

"There, that's better," Zachariah murmured. "Old Nosy was about to chew my leg off, afraid I was hurting you. Since he knows I wouldn't, he's in a fine state of befuddlement."

Miranda sneaked a peek at the dog, gulping down a sob. "I'm okay, Nose," she managed.

Zachariah drew up at the window and stood there gazing out into the moonlit yard, his arms gently jostling the child to lull her. Kate continued to gape, not quite certain she believed the evidence of her own eyes.

"What happened, Mandy?" he finally asked in a low voice. "Did you wake up and want your ma?"

"I gets bad dreams," she squeaked.

"Uh-oh. Those can be scary," he sympathized.

"I waked up and it was all dark."

"That's even scarier," he agreed. "I've done the same thing, and it feels like the bad dream is real, doesn't it?"

She sniffled and snuggled closer. "Yep. But it goes away if my ma hugs me."

Zach glanced over his shoulder at Kate. "Well, let's go get you a hug, then, hm?"

With Nosy as an escort, he turned and walked slowly toward the bed. When he leaned forward, Kate reached for her daughter with trembling arms. Miranda clutched Kate's neck, digging in with pointed elbows and knees as she searched for a comfortable position. Kate held her close and hid her face in the child's hair. She felt the mattress sink under Zachariah's and Nosy's weight. The canine's cold, wet nose nudged her cheek.

"You mustn't open our bedroom door without knocking," she whispered. "Do you understand, Miranda? Not ever."

A heavy, warm hand settled on Kate's shoulder. "We'll talk about that tomorrow, Katie."

She glanced up. Belying the gentleness in his voice, his eyes glittered with unmistakable anger in the moonlight. Dread constricted Kate's throat. He was furious with her. And in her experience a furious man was a dangerous one.

Anxious to get her child out of harm's way, just in case Zachariah's temper blew, she tightened her arms around Miranda and whispered, "Let's get you and Nosy back to your bed, little miss."

"She's still upset," he ground out. "Let her stay in here for a while."

Kate hesitated, her thoughts invaded by memories. "Y-You don't mind?"

He shot her a look that spoke volumes and threw back the quilts. "In you go," he ordered, his words clipped and harsh. "Both of you. Morning will come early. Let's try to get some sleep."

Miranda didn't need to be told twice. She scrambled from Kate's lap and dove for a spot in the center of the bed. Zachariah fell back onto a pillow beside her, his dark chest and shoulders covering a wide margin, his eyes still aglitter in his shadowed countenance. Kate stared at the pair of them, her limbs frozen. Nosy licked her hand, as if to comfort her.

"Kate?"

The irritation in his tone spurred her into moving. On shaky knees, she crawled forward, flipped the quilt and sheet out of her way, and lay down, her back wedged against the wall. Miranda sighed and burrowed down in the softness between them. Nosy found a vacant spot at Miranda's feet and flopped down, for all the world as if he was welcome there. Uncertain how her husband might react to that, Kate swallowed, her mouth dry and cottony. She heard Zachariah sigh, the sound filled with annoyance.

Fearful that he still might vent his rage, she managed to croak, "I—I'm sorry."

"We'll talk about it tomorrow," he warned.

A knot of dread formed in the hollow of her belly. She squeezed her eyes closed, trying not to think about it, but unable to ignore his anger, which seemed to electrify the air.

Minutes passed, the seconds dragging as slowly as footsteps mired in wet clay. To Kate, the silence was a terrible thing, so thick it nearly suffocated her.

For Zach, the silence was accusing.

He lay there, his gaze fixed on Joseph Blakely's ceiling. Beside him lay the man's child and his wife. Signed documents couldn't change that. The bastard owned them, heart and soul. Even from the grave, he still had the power to hurt them.

Zach's arm still stung where Kate's nails had raked his skin. The terror he'd heard in her voice clawed at his conscience now. How could he have reacted as he had? At the moment, it had seemed imperative that he be the one to collect the child, if for no other reason than to prove he wasn't the monster her mother clearly believed him to be.

But what of Kate? What of her fear? And what of her feelings? Their wedding this afternoon had forever altered their relationship, putting her into a position of subservience, he into one of ultimate authority. That was the way it went in their society. She was carrying a load of unpleasant memories into this marriage, and he couldn't expect her to trust him immediately simply because he smiled a lot. To her, having a husband was synonymous with hell on earth, and it was going to take a spell before he could show her that it could be different.

He wasn't going to manage that by snarling at her when she grew frightened. Even now, he could still feel the tension in her. There wasn't much he could do about that, not with the child lying between them. He smiled slightly, recalling the time Miranda had told her mother that her ears stayed awake longer than her eyes. Whatever he had to say to Kate was going to have to wait until morning.

Rolling onto his side, Zach curled one arm around Miranda and stretched his other across the pillows to rest his hand on Kate's hair. He felt the jolt of fear that ran through her at his unexpected touch. Threading his fingertips to her scalp, he began a light massage, trying in the only way he knew to let her know he was no longer angry.

As if he had a right to be . . .

"It's going to be all right," he whispered. "We just need time, Kate."

She stirred slightly but didn't answer. He hated to leave her fretting for the entire night, but the child's presence between them limited what he could say. A fine line, that was what he walked, and it wasn't going to be easy. Both mother and daughter were going to need constant reassurance for a spell. The problem was that he couldn't reassure Kate that he would never harm her child without putting it into Miranda's head that he might.

For now, Kate's anxieties had to play second fiddle. As much as he hated that, he also knew Kate would want it that way.

Everything for Miranda, nothing for herself. That's the way it had been for a number of years, he guessed. Another few hours wouldn't kill her.

The next morning, Kate spent more effort on breakfast than she usually did. Ham, eggs, fried spuds, biscuits, and milk gravy, a meal fit for a king. Sometimes, though not often, a particularly tasty meal had appeased Joseph when he was in a foul mood.

When Zachariah came in from doing the milking, Kate stiffened. After stomping his boots clean on the stoop, he stepped inside, the milk pail swinging wide of one lean leg as he turned to shut the door. Dark windswept hair, red cotton, faded denim, leather. Everything about him screamed *man* as he passed behind her to set the bucket on the tripod.

He seemed surprised by the spread she had put on the table. Rubbing his thigh, he lowered himself onto a chair and smiled. "If this isn't the finest breakfast I've ever clapped eyes on, I'll be hornswoggled."

Kate rubbed her hands dry on her apron. "A man needs his nourishment before he starts his day."

"So does a woman, and it looks to me like you've already put in a fair amount of work. Come sit down."

Miranda climbed up onto a chair. Nosy positioned himself beside her to catch any morsels she might drop. Zachariah gave the dog an amused glance. "Such loyalty. I raised him from a pup, and what's he turn toward me now? His south end."

Kate perched on a chair, not at all certain she could eat but determined to make a good show of it. Normality, that was her aim. She tried not to look at her husband, but his was a presence that was difficult to ignore.

Damp curls the rich brown of chocolate fell across his high forehead, and he was freshly shaved. He wore his red shirt unbuttoned at the throat to reveal a patch of bronzed chest and curly dark hair, the sleeves rolled back over his powerfully muscled forearms. When he took knife and fork in hand to slice his ham, it seemed to her he was all shoulders. With his gaze cast downward at his plate, the fan of his mahogany eyelashes shadowed the masculine planes of his cheekbones. Early morning sunshine coming through the window highlighted the bold bridge of his nose and glanced off the stubborn thrust of his squared jaw.

Uncomfortable with the silence, she observed, "Your leg's paining you this morning."

He lifted his gaze to hers. Shot through with sunlight, his hazel eyes gleamed as golden as a predatory cat's. "It'll take a spell to heal completely. Deep wounds often do."

The words seemed to carry a double meaning. Uncertain exactly what he meant, she searched his eyes and couldn't mistake the lambent gleam of desire in those golden depths. Because she knew he must still be angry about her outburst last night, the yearning she read in his expression unsettled her even more than it might have otherwise. How could a man want a woman when he was furious with her? Because Joseph had resented his need of her, he had taken her in anger more times than not. But that didn't mean she'd ever come to accept it.

She bent her head, visions of what had transpired between her and Zachariah last night making her cheeks hot. Did he always remove his shirt? she wondered. The idea seemed scandalous to her. And on the bed? Joseph had never taken her there, and Kate couldn't figure how it must be done—unless, of course, she availed herself on hands and knees. That seemed so animalistic. It would be doubly so if he was in a foul mood when he came to her.

She filled her mouth with potato. The more she chewed, the bigger the mouthful seemed to grow. Through the veil of her lashes, she watched Zachariah eat and wondered if he'd go after her with the same enthusiasm. He wasn't a very refined man. It was the height of his ambition to grow grapes and produce sinner's swill. He hadn't even paused to say a blessing before beginning the meal. He swore so frequently that she scarcely even noticed it anymore. She supposed she shouldn't be surprised if it turned out that he went at coupling like a barnyard beast.

If he did, she wouldn't have a whole lot to say about it. Yesterday she hadn't dreaded the moment when they would mate. Now she did because she had no idea what to

expect from him. *Didn't Joseph touch you and kiss you?*
Kate tried to swallow and choked on the potatoes. Only a
quick gulp of milk saved her from strangling. When she
recovered, Zachariah was staring at her with a speculative
twinkle in his eyes.

Miranda finished her meal first. As she slid from her
chair, Zachariah tweaked her nose and said, "How's about
you gathering the eggs for your ma this morning? After we
get the chores all done here, I've got to go over to my place,
and I thought I'd take you along. Would you like that?"

Miranda squealed with delight and ran to fetch the egg
basket. "I'll gather 'em up lickety-split!"

"No hurry," he said with a chuckle. "I've got work piled
up here that I have to do before we go."

With the basket handle over one arm, Miranda let herself out the back door.

"Slow down, girl. Or you'll bring back scrambled
eggs!" he called.

The door slammed with a wall-shaking bang. Then a
tense silence settled over the kitchen. Kate chased a piece
of ham with her fork, acutely aware that the moment she
had been dreading had arrived.

"About last night," they both said at once.

Kate broke off, and he flashed a white-toothed grin.
"Can I go first?" he asked.

She laid down her fork and knotted her hands in her
lap. "Certainly. Except that I'd just like to say I'm—"

He held up a hand. "You can say your piece in a
minute. First let me apologize."

Her mind tripped on that, and it took her a moment to
regain her balance. "Apologize?"

He hooked an arm over the back of his chair and leaned
back to study her. "Yes. First off, for acting like an ass. And
secondly for letting you fret all night thinking I was mad."

Uncertain what to say, Kate took refuge in silence. His twinkling eyes caressed her features as though she were a painting he meant to memorize.

"I'm sorry I was sharp with you," he said slowly. "After all you've been through, it's natural for you to be protective of your child. I shouldn't have gotten upset with you for that. It was just—" He shrugged. "You scared Mandy, and I couldn't think past that until I calmed down. I wanted to prove a point, and instead I made things worse. Next time I'll try to be a little more understanding."

Kate hadn't received an apology from a man since before her marriage to Joseph. She couldn't quite believe she was getting one now—and a sincere one, at that. To her dismay, she felt tears springing to her eyes. She blinked to dispel them, but more welled up to take their place. Then she felt her chin start to quiver. Embarrassed, she rose from her chair and started scraping plates.

"I didn't mean to make you cry," he said softly.

"I'm not." She swiped angrily at her cheek. "It's that dad-blamed pepper. When I use too much, it—"

The legs of his chair scraped the floor. He stood and stepped around the table. Before she could react, he snaked an arm around her waist and drew her toward him. The plate she held dug into his hard belly. He glanced down at the remains of her meal and narrowed an eye.

"I think something's coming between us."

That suited Kate just fine. He apparently didn't share the sentiment and took the plate from her hand to set it on the table. As he drew her firmly into his arms, it occurred to her that nothing was coming between them now but meager barriers of cloth that acted like heat conductors. Her breasts burned where they pressed against his chest.

"I'm sorry, Katie. I wanted to tell you so last night, but with Mandy listening, I didn't think it was a good idea.

You and me discussing whether or not I might hurt her when I'm mad could put ideas in her head."

"I didn't mean to overreact," she said in a choked voice. "It's just that Joseph—she wasn't allowed to come into our room without knocking, and he got so furious when she forgot."

"I figured that." He curled a hand over the back of her head and nuzzled her temple. "I got a little testy myself."

"I'll make sure she—"

"We," he corrected. "We'll teach her together, Kate. Everything's new to her, and she's only four. It'll take time."

"But if you get testy—"

"I'll just get testy," he said with a rumbling chuckle.

"But unless I take steps, she'll do it again."

"Then I'll get good at diving for covers." He moved back to take her face between his hands. "She'll learn. I'll have a talk with her this morning on the way over to my place and slip it into the conversation sort of casual-like. I don't want a big issue made of it. That might make her afraid to come to our room when she's scared, and we don't want that."

"We don't?"

His mouth quirked at the corners. "No, ma'am, we don't." He bent his head to kiss the tip of her nose. "I can see there are a number of lessons to be learned around this place. Let's hope I prove to be a good teacher, hm?"

Soap bubbles aglisten with sunlight clung to Kate's fingers, making her think of Zachariah's eyes. She lifted her hands to the window and turned her wrists, fascinated by the iridescent hues that glinted back at her. Was that why his eyes seemed to dance when he looked at her? Because, like multifaceted prisms, they picked up every flicker of light?

Her gaze came to rest on her new gold wedding band. Its luster was brilliant now, but she knew from experience that day in and day out punishment would soon dull its surface.

"You have beautiful hands."

The deep voice near her ear made her heart trip over itself, startling her so that she might have jumped clean out of her skin if not for the heavy palms that settled at her waist. "Zachariah," she said weakly.

"Beautiful everything." His lips feathered across her nape, his breath warm and steamy. "I didn't mean to spook you. Since I figured you'd be doing dishes, it seemed like a good time to play teacher."

"T-Teacher?"

"Today I mean to teach you a new meaning to an old word."

"You do?"

Unnerved by his nearness and the mischievous tone in his voice, Kate tried to evade him. The breadth of him pressed against her from behind, a hard, immovable wall that held her fast against the counter. With his hands riding her waist, she knew she didn't have a prayer of escaping him. Not that he needed close quarters as an advantage.

"Wh-Where's Miranda?"

"I've got her building a straw house out in the barn," he said with a chuckle. "Years ago, my pa taught me how. Now I know why."

A shiver ran down her spine. His lips were very skillful in their play upon her senses, so silken yet firm, so light yet demanding. "And why was that?"

He found the small mole on the back of her neck and gently worried it with his teeth. The sensation called to mind other things he had nibbled last night, and a hot, liquid feeling pooled in the pit of her belly. "I suspect he wanted me out of his hair so he could torment my ma while she did the breakfast dishes," he replied in a husky voice. "There's something irresistible to most men about a woman doing dishes." His palms slid warmly up her sides. "I guess because she can't fight back with her hands all wet."

The way Kate saw it, she couldn't fight back bone dry. "She might come in."

"And she might not," was his laughing reply. "We decided her house needed at least seven rooms. That'll take a spell to construct, especially with Nosy being his usual unhelpful self. Besides, if she comes in, we'll hear her in plenty of time."

In plenty of time for what? she wondered.

His fingertips halted their ascent at the underside of her breasts. "Lord, Katie, you are so sweet. I'd like to start out at your toes and taste every square inch of you."

Kate was suddenly having difficulty breathing. She extended an arm for the towel rack, but it was beyond her reach. "H-How do you build a straw house?"

"Slowly," he moaned. "Very slowly." He bent his dark head to brush his lips over hers and then waged a silken assault along the column of her throat. His fingertips began a light, kneading caress on her ribs, not venturing to her breasts but uncomfortably close. "Relax, Katie. After that breakfast, I'm not likely to sink my teeth into you."

"Kate," she corrected.

"And what is that you find so objectionable about my calling you Katie?"

She gulped for breath. He had the oddest effect on her, making her heart slam and her knees liquify. Her body responded to him like a tuning fork, the notes thrumming along her nerve endings, shrill and off-key. "Katie is a child's name. For someone small and—" She dropped her head forward in an attempt to escape his mouth. "I like to be called Kate."

"Ah, but to me you're Katie," he whispered. He splayed his hands, his fingertips meeting below the cleavage of her breasts. "Someone small and sweet, my Katie girl. You can be Kate to everyone else in the world, but to me, you'll always be Katie. It's how I think of you, and I don't think that'll ever change."

Kate gave up on trying to keep her neck away from him. He was so tall that her evasive tactics were useless. He simply hunched his shoulders and followed. Lifting one hand to her collar, he deftly began unfastening buttons.

"What are you doing?"

His voice was tight with laughter. "I've never been so fascinated with a woman's buttons in my entire life."

The plackets of her bodice fell open. "Zachariah, it's broad daylight."

"So it is."

His shoulders curled around her as he bent his head to trail kisses in the wake of his descending fingertips. Hungry and hot, his mouth fell upon the beginning swell of her left breast. The swirling heat in her belly coiled into a burning knot and nosedived to an aching place just above the apex of her thighs.

"I love you," he told her with throbbing intensity. "I think I have since the first second I saw you. Have I told you that?"

Kate blinked and tried to focus. "N-No. Y-Yes. I—I can't remember."

"Well, I'm telling you now. I want that to be the first thing you think of when you wake up each morning and the last thing when you drift off to sleep at night. Will you do that for me?"

"I can try."

"After I brought Mandy up from the well, you said I could name anything I wanted or needed," he murmured.

That's my request, for you to remember I love you. And that I love Mandy. I'll never harm either one of you. I'd like for you to try and believe that."

Kate felt his yearning in the rigidly bunched muscle of his arms, heard it in the urgent pounding of his heart. The liquid sensation in her knees spread slowly over her until she was no longer certain she could stand alone. She grabbed the counter edge for support. What was he doing to her?

"Zachariah?"

He freed more buttons, his tongue making fiery forays under the edge of her camisole. Her nipples sprang taut, as sensitive as if they'd been chafed all day by starched cotton, but instead of shrinking protectively into themselves, they thrust forward, beaded and throbbing. Plucking ribbons loose with a masterful hand, he nipped lightly at her skin, making a beeline toward one aching crest, as though he knew exactly what her body craved.

"Zach-a-riah?"

Her bodice and camisole fell away. He leaned slightly sideways. Kate gasped as the surface of his tongue curled around her. The world shrank into a swirling red dot of sensation, and she was spinning in its hot center. He cupped her breast and lifted it. His mouth closed on her in a hard pull.

When he moved his other hand to ride low on her belly, Kate stiffened reflexively and grabbed for his wrist.

"Don't," he whispered against her skin. "Trust me, just this one time. I swear you won't regret it."

Trust him? Memories rushed at her, all unpleasant. She couldn't count the times that Joseph had cornered her here on this very spot. What had occurred during those confrontations was beyond thinking about.

"I didn't do anything to start this," she informed him

with a firmness that even she knew fell short of convincing.

"Of course not," was his husky reply, but he didn't pause in his assault. "Like I told you last night, all you have to do is be in the same room with me."

"All I've been doing, all I've had on my mind, is doing the dishes."

"Absolutely. It's just that you look so damned delectable when you're doing dishes. I can't resist you. I'll take all the blame."

Despite his reassurances, Kate couldn't discard five years of memories and half expected him to start raving at her at any moment. Panic rushed through her. "Don't, please . . ."

The heel of his palm pressed hard against her and ground in a circular motion that robbed her of what little breath she had left. She felt him gathering cloth, felt the hem of her skirt lifting. A picture of Joseph's face flitted through her mind.

"Zachariah?"

His broad, leathery hand slipped inside the waistband of her bloomers. "Don't be afraid, Katie," he whispered raggedly.

Another rush of fear trilled up her spine. She dug her nails into the wood. He ran soothing kisses up her chest until his mouth found the pulsebeat at the hollow of her throat. Kate knew the thrum was frantic, and that he would know by its pace how frightened she was.

"Promise me you aren't angry?" she whispered.

"Honey, the very last thing on earth I feel is anger. I promise you that. I'll swear it on your Bible if you want me to. You're beautiful and sweet, and I wouldn't change a thing about you."

He trailed kisses along the underside of her jaw, making Kate realize with a vague sense of surprise that she had melted against him, her head thrown back against his shoulder.

"You're perfect. Absolutely perfect. And I want you with every breath I take. That doesn't make me angry, but glad."

An electrical tingle shot through her, and she gasped at the shock of it. "What are you—Zachariah, don't do that, please."

He made another light pass over an incredibly sensitive place, and her body spasmed. "Relax, Katie girl. You've been to hell and back for being 'lustful,' and I don't think you even know the meaning of the word."

Kate could feel her control scattering, and she made another desperate grab for his wrist. Her bunched skirt frustrated the attempt. During the delay, his fingertips flicked the sense right out of her. Her legs buckled and she wilted, her only support the firm saddle of his palm.

"How can anything so wonderful be wicked?" he asked. "When a man and woman love one another, Katie, the longing they feel for one another is beautiful and right and sacred. That's the way God intended it to be."

Shocked by the sensations he sent ricocheting through her, she cried out. *Soap bubbles.* A rainbow of iridescent colors danced before her eyes. As if possessed of a will all its own, her body arched toward his hand. The sensation built and built to a spiraling pinnacle, and then burst within her, so white-hot it seared her whole body. Wave after wave of after-tingles jerked her limp muscles. She sobbed and would have fallen face first into the pan of sudsy water if not for the support of his angled arm.

"That," he whispered, "is what lust is all about. And I'll wager my whole life's savings this is the first time you've ever had so much as a taste of it. Joseph, God rest his miserable soul, was a raving lunatic, and if he were alive right now, I'd send him straight back to hell for whatever it was he did to you."

Hanging there in his arms, Kate could make little sense of what he was saying, only that his tone was angry when he spoke of Joseph. What registered was the strength of his body supporting hers and his gentleness. Not long ago, she had longed to melt into him; now she felt as if she had.

Slowly, measure by measure, reality returned to her. Stark and blinding. A sunlit window. A pan of sudsy water. Dirty dishes. And her bodice hanging open to her waist. No man had ever seen her in such a state. Judging from the way Zachariah stood, she guessed he was looking his fill. She made a feeble move to refasten her dress only to discover his hand was still inside her camisole. On the heel of that realization, she felt his other hand still cupping the softness between her legs.

A wave of humiliation washed over her. "Zachariah, it's broad daylight," she cried.

"I think you mentioned that. And so it is."

Another jolt of sensation shot through her. She gasped and tried to move, which only heightened the friction. "This is indecent."

"No, it's beautiful," he murmured. "You're beautiful. So beautiful. I love you, Katie. Especially when I'm holding you. For me, the hell of it would be if I could never touch you like this. Don't ever forget that."

Kate was vaguely aware of a door slamming in some distant part of the house. Zachariah stiffened and said, "Damn."

He set himself to the harried task of retying the bows of her camisole and refastening her buttons.

"My bloomers," Kate cried and grabbed frantically at her skirt.

He groped along her leg and gave a sharp upward tug on her underwear, then abandoned his hold on her as the kitchen door flew open. "Just stand still. I'll get her out of here," he whispered.

"My house keeps falling down!" Miranda cried. "Will you come help me fix it?"

Kate clutched the counter's edge, so weak in the knees she was afraid she might fall when Zachariah moved away from her.

"You bet I will. We can't have your house down around your ears."

Hang the house, Kate thought. Her bloomers were about to reach her ankles. She threw her husband a horrified look as she felt the muslin slide slowly down her legs and puddle on the floor. All she could do was pray her skirt would hide it.

"Wanna come help, Ma? It's lotsa fun."

"Um, no, not right now, sweetness. I'm washing dishes," Kate said shakily. "You two go on and have—fun."

Zachariah's hazel eyes met hers, his rife with mischief. "I'll get back to you and our vocabulary lesson later."

Numb with incredulity, Kate watched as he followed Miranda from the kitchen, for all the world as though nothing untoward had just occurred between them.

Later? He'd get back to her later? She didn't know whether to laugh or cry, and then decided she didn't have the strength to do either.

18

Over the next week, Kate learned another new meaning to an old word, trust. Zachariah proved himself worthy of hers in a dozen small ways, but the most important one was his unfailing patience with Miranda. The child awoke from nightmares seven nights running and came to Kate's room for solace, timing her arrival to coincide almost perfectly with her parents' bedtime. With two farms to tend, the days were so busy their retreat to the bedroom offered their only opportunity for privacy.

For Kate, the delay in consummating their marriage was a welcome reprieve, but she sensed Zachariah didn't share that sentiment. Incredible as it seemed, he never lost his temper over the interruptions and welcomed Miranda into their bed, his one request being that she remember to knock before entering.

At first, Kate feared his patience was an act and that he would begin to show his true colors as his frustration mounted. But as the days wore on, her anxieties about that slowly faded. Miranda spilled her milk, and Zachariah mopped it up, never indicating anger by so much as an inflection of his voice. When Miranda spoke out of turn, instead of slapping her mouth as Joseph had, he stopped talking to give her audience. When the child grew rowdy inside the house, he joined in, tickling her, romping with her, adding to the overall din. When Miranda wet the bed—in this instance, Kate's bed—Zachariah seemed to sense how frightened she was of the consequences, and he insisted the roof must have sprung a leak even though it hadn't rained in days. Though it was the middle of the night, he good-naturedly helped Kate change the bed linen, then went in search of a dry gown for Miranda, exclaiming over the child's miserable luck. That darned old roof had leaked on her and missed everyone else!

Happy tears. Because of Zachariah, Kate found herself blinking away buckets of them. If he noticed, he said nothing. And because he did, another of her fears melted away. Unlike Joseph, Zachariah didn't chastise her for crying for no reason. If anything, he seemed to find that flaw in her endearing.

Unlike Joseph . . . Those words ran through Kate's mind at least a dozen times a day. And each time they did, she relaxed a tiny bit more and soon found herself enjoying Zachariah's presence in her world. Evenings became a time of celebration, the three of them coming together to enjoy simple pleasures, reading aloud, telling stories, playing games, conversing.

Even if he disagreed with her, Zachariah seemed interested in what Kate had to say. For the first time, she was encouraged to express her opinions. What truly amazed her was when her new husband listened to her opposing views, weighed what she said, and sometimes shifted his stand to agree with her.

The one time Zachariah's patience did seem to grow frayed over Miranda's nightly appearance at their bedroom door, he went down and sat on the porch rather than vent his frustration on the child. After Miranda drifted back to sleep, Kate went in search of him, anxious to defuse the situation if she could. When she joined him on the steps, she didn't know what she was expecting. An outburst, possibly. Perhaps an ugly confrontation. But once again, Zachariah took her totally by surprise.

"Want a swig?" he asked as she perched beside him.

Hugging her knees, Kate peered through the darkness to see what he held in his hand. Shadows frustrated her. "What is it?"

"Fine Kentucky bourbon," he replied in a silken voice. "I'm going to get noodle-legged, rip-roaring drunk."

"Drunk?" Kate's heart tripped on a beat and felt as though it somersaulted. Joseph had railed against the evils of alcohol, claiming it turned civilized men into animals. "Aren't you afraid it might"—she angled a frightened glance at the hemp-wrapped jug—"impair your judgment?"

Tilting his dark head, he took a hearty slug, gave a satisfied sigh, and wiped his mouth with the back of his hand. Kate's gaze fell to the unbuttoned front of his blue shirt and the bare expanse of his chest. With every movement, muscle rippled in the moonlight, testimony to the storehouse of untapped power in his body. Joseph had always come to bed wearing his underwear, so Kate wasn't used to seeing the masculine form.

"Impaired. Now there's a word. Synonymous with stupid drunk, isn't it?"

Kate wasn't sure how to take his mood. The smell of the bourbon touched her nostrils, and she was surprised by the sweet mellowness. It seemed to her that something so vile ought to smell awful, but it didn't.

"Men do irresponsible things while intoxicated," she informed him shakily.

"I reckon some do." He gave her a slightly crooked

grin. "All I do is go to bed. Preferably *with* someone. Isn't that a hell of a note?"

The way Kate saw it, he had an oversupply of bed companions. "I'm not sure I follow you."

"If I thought you would, I'd head for the barn and a nice pile of hay." With a humorless chuckle, he leaned forward and braced his arms on his knees, the jug dangling from the crook of one finger. "Mandy asleep again?"

"Yes."

"I've got to work with that child on her timing. I haven't so much as kissed you in over a week. She doesn't give me a chance."

She smoothed her muslin nightgown around her ankles, glad for the balmy breeze. "I just came down to tell you how sorry I am about that. I've never known her to have nightmares so many nights running."

He gazed intently at something in the moonlit darkness. "It'll pass. I think she's feeling a little unsettled. It's not every day her ma up and gets married."

"It's what she wanted—more than anything."

"Reality is never quite as nice as dreaming." Brushing his knuckles along his scarred cheek, which Kate had long since noticed was a habit of his, he added, "When she was angling for me to be her pa, I don't think she looked ahead to things like us sleeping together and her being excluded. I reckon she's a little jealous. In time she'll realize I'm not much of a threat."

He said the last with some bitterness. Kate dug her nails in at her knees. "Perhaps I should talk to her, after all. I'm afraid if this situation continues that you'll eventually lose your temper with her."

"God forbid," he said with a wry grin.

Kate moistened her lips. "It isn't a joking matter."

"What isn't. Miranda? Or my temper?"

Kate chose to ignore that. "She's an obedient little girl. If I ask her not to visit our room, she won't. Why allow the situation to fester until your patience snaps?"

He took another swig of bourbon, swallowed with a shudder, and drew back his lips over clenched white teeth. "Honey, my patience already snapped. About thirty minutes ago." He gestured at the jug. "Which is why I'm going to get noodle-legged, rip-roaring drunk. Unlike Joseph, when I get to the end of my rope, I drown myself, not my kid."

She winced at that and averted her face.

"That's why you followed me out here, isn't it? Because you're afraid of what'll happen if my temper does blow."

There was no point in denying the obvious, so Kate nodded.

He sighed and leaned back to brace his elbows on the step behind them. The jug clunked as it settled against the wood. "Let me explain something," he said huskily. "If I lose my temper, and I stress the if because I pride myself on keeping it most times, I might yell and raise holy hell. If I really lose it, I may even take the house down around your ears. But when the dust settles, you and Miranda will be standing untouched in the rubble. I'll never lift a hand to either one of you in anger. You have my solemn oath on that."

Kate hunched her shoulders. "I wish I could believe that."

The words were out before she could stop them. She could feel his gaze on her, and his silence unnerved her. When she could bear it no longer, she turned to look at him. The angle of the moonlight fell across his sharply carved features, gilding the thrust of his nose, shimmering in his eyes. To her surprise, his expression was inexplicably tender.

Lifting one arm, he rasped the backs of his knuckles

along her cheek, his touch so light and slow that it made her throat tighten with an emotion she couldn't name.

"I wish you could, too, Katie," he whispered. "If I could have my choice of wishes, that'd be it. I'd be one happy man if I could chase all those shadows out of your pretty eyes."

"Shadows?"

He cupped her chin and tipped her face. "Yes, shadows. Not nearly enough sunshine."

His intense regard unsettled her, made her feel vulnerable, made her yearn for an inexplicable something. "Shadows and sunshine? How poetic. I think you *are* getting drunk, Mr. McGovern," she said with forced lightness.

"And that worries you, doesn't it?" He bounced his jug against the step. "Sinner's swill. Sure to bring out the worst in a man, hm? One of these times, I'd love to argue Scripture with you on that point, but for tonight, rest assured that you can relax. I don't get mean when I drink."

"Never?"

"Never have yet." He gave her another slightly off-centered smile. "I promise not to start with you. So why don't you go on back to bed and leave me to my business?"

"About Miranda—"

"Let's just leave Miranda to settle in at her own pace," he said. "She's frightened when she wakes up from the dreams. It'd be cruel not to let her come to us. If she keeps on having them, there's always another jug where this one came from."

"Where did that one come from?"

He turned a mischievous gaze on her. "The barn. I figured I might be needing a swig and stashed it out there. Better than a night of playing five-fingered stud."

Kate frowned. "Five-fingered stud?"

His lashes drooped over his twinkling eyes. "It's a game of solitaire. Ever played solitaire, Katie?"

"Joseph frowned upon card games of any kind."

His teeth flashed again. "His loss, my gain. I'll have to teach you how to play poker sometime. You can ante out with the pennies in your savings crock."

"Those wouldn't last me long."

"Exactly," he came back in a honeyed voice laced with amusement.

Kate felt very like she had as a child playing keep-away, always too short to compete and mocked for her lack of stature. She lifted her chin and folded her hands atop her bent knees. "I take it you're laughing at some private joke? If you would care to share it, perhaps I'll laugh with you."

His grin broadened. "I did share it."

Kate went back over what had been said. "Would you care to explain, then? I'm afraid the humor has escaped me."

"I've offended you. I didn't mean to."

"I don't enjoy being laughed at."

"I'm not laughing at you, Katie girl, I'm smiling. My pa used to say that the thing he loved most about my mother was her innocence. Since I was the fourth of seven boys, I could never figure what he meant. Now I finally do."

Kate circled that. "You seem to constantly confuse me with a young girl, Zachariah. I'm far from innocent, I assure you."

"By whose measuring stick? You're not exactly worldly, Katie. Not that I'd change a hair on your head."

She went back over their conversation again, and if there was a joke hidden in there someplace, it still escaped her. Finally, she gave up on it and said, "Well, I suppose I'll do as you suggested and leave you to your business."

"I won't come into the house drunk, so you don't need to worry that Mandy'll see me."

"If you're a drinking man, I reckon she'd best get used to it. You needn't hide your bourbon, Zachariah. You're the man of the house. If you choose to partake of liquor, you can certainly do so in the comfort of your home."

"Except for rare occasions, I'm not a drinking man. But if I was, I wouldn't do it in the house because it'd upset you." He shrugged a muscular shoulder. "My aim's just the opposite, to make you happy if I can."

Kate took that promise with her when she returned to bed, and over the next few days she recalled it repeatedly. Happiness? Since her marriage to Joseph, she hadn't had much time to contemplate what that meant to her. To see Miranda smile, yes. But beyond that? She wasn't at all certain there was anything else she truly yearned for out of life. Her child's happiness was her happiness, and when she could ensure that, it had always seemed enough.

Zachariah seemed to sense that. If he had tried to woo Kate, she might have rebuffed him, but she found his wooing of Miranda an irresistible draw. Standing apart, always watchful, Kate saw her daughter blossom into a giggling, light-hearted little girl with stars in her eyes. It was an old saying, but true; the way to a woman's heart was through her child.

From day to day, Kate didn't know what to expect from her husband. He was either a consummate actor or had an unquenchable thirst for laughter. Though he worked hard and always seemed on the go, he was never too busy to play for a while.

One morning when Kate entered her kitchen, she found Zachariah and Miranda engaged in a contest to see who could flip a griddle cake the highest and still catch it with the spatula. The plank floor in front of her Estate stove was polka-dotted with their misses, and Nosy lay amid the mess, his appetite appeased for the first time since she had known him. Kate stood unnoticed by the door, her back to the wall, tears nearly blinding her as she listened to Miranda's chortling laughter.

During dinner one night, Zachariah used his spoon to flip peas at a bowl he had placed in the center of the table. Before Kate knew quite how it happened, she had been drawn into the competition, and peas were flying everywhere, the three of them giggling like fools. The perfect ending to that activity was when Zachariah got down on hands and knees to pick up peas, saying she had enough to do without having to clean up his messes. Joseph had never once helped her with a household task.

Another evening, Zachariah had come home toting a new Montgomery Ward catalog. He insisted on cooking dinner while Kate leafed through it and placed an order for clothing for her and Miranda. Why he bothered with the formality of letting her choose, Kate couldn't imagine, because when all was said and done, he erased every one of her choices and reordered to suit himself, selecting colors and styles and quantities that Kate felt certain would make Joseph turn over in his grave. No more browns and grays and blacks, Zachariah vowed. He wanted his wife and daughter dressed in pastels and brilliant colors, and he didn't want them wearing the same outfit twice in a two-week stretch.

As much as Kate knew she'd enjoy having pretty things, and as entertaining as Zachariah's nonsense could be at mealtime, it was the scores of little things he did that truly touched her. Though she knew he didn't have time to watch after a child, he took Miranda with him over to his place nearly every afternoon. Ching Lee's granddaughter came to visit, and for the first time, Miranda had a playmate her own age.

Every evening when Miranda and Zachariah returned home, he sent her into the house first so she could greet him at the door and get her magic wish—a pa who would toss her way up high in the air and then tickle her with his chin whiskers when he came home at night. Kate was impressed that Zachariah even cared about Miranda's little-girl dreams. But what truly touched her was his willingness to make them come true.

In short, Zachariah made himself irresistible. Kate tried to withstand his tactics, she truly did, but the bottom line was that when he hugged her child, he was hugging her. When Miranda smiled, she smiled.

And when Miranda fell in love, Kate wasn't far behind her.

Oddly enough, the crushing blow to Kate's defenses came when Zachariah finally did lose his temper, not because of Miranda's untimely interruptions each night, as she had feared, but because the child disobeyed him and nearly got hurt.

Unbeknownst to Kate, the hayloft flooring had rotted through in one spot. When Zachariah found the weak boards, he forbade Miranda to play up there until he got them fixed. The hayloft had long been one of the places where Miranda took refuge when visitors came. One morning when the iceman made his delivery, up the ladder she went to hide. As she crossed the loft, the flooring gave under her weight, and she plunged twelve feet to the ground below. The only thing that saved her from breaking her neck was a pile of straw that Zachariah had been forking next to a stall. Interrupted in the middle of the task by the ice delivery, Zachariah had tossed the pitchfork atop the mound, and when Miranda fell, she was nearly impaled by the tines.

Kate's first clue that something had happened was when she heard Zachariah roaring with anger. When she ran outside to see what was amiss, the ruckus led her to the barn where she found her husband, Miranda, Nosy, and the iceman, all in a fine dither. Zachariah had her daughter clutched in his arms, looking for all the world as though he couldn't decide whether to hug her or thrash her. After a quick look at his white-lipped countenance, Kate feared the latter inclination would win out.

"You need a good tanning, girlie!" Mr. Cantrell exclaimed in between Zachariah's ranting. "Disobeying your pappy like that's a good way to get yer neck broke!"

To Kate's relief, Zachariah didn't follow through on that suggestion. Instead, he started to pace with Miranda caught in his trembling embrace, Nosy shadowing his footsteps. Kate could see that Zachariah had gotten the sand scared right out of him.

"Durned near landed on the pitchfork," Mr. Cantrell enlightened Kate. Measuring off a scant inch with thumb and forefinger, the thin, balding man shook his head. "Came just that close. The good Lord had her in the palm of his hand."

Kate's gaze shifted to the pitchfork and boards that were scattered in the hay. Her knees nearly gave out when she realized what had nearly happened.

"The dad-blamed flooring is rotten in the loft. I've told her not to go up there a dozen times," Zachariah informed her in a shaky voice. "I had Marcus put in an order for lumber two days ago. I was going to fix it next week."

Kate watched him pace, understanding now why he looked so unnerved. Miranda had her face buried in the hollow of his shoulder, her frightened wails muffled by his shirt. Kate resisted the urge to grab her child out of his arms. Her reasons seemed idiotic when she analyzed them, but Zachariah had taken the decision out of her hands with his utterance of one word, dad-blamed. She knew very well how colorful his language ordinarily was when he got angry. He was shaking with anger now.

I give you my word. I'll never say a single cussword in her presence. Because he peppered his speech with so many profanities all the time, Kate had long since forgotten his making that promise. But now that she thought about it, she realized that it was a vow he had never broken. Swear though he did at all other times, she couldn't recollect his ever having said anything he shouldn't in front of her daughter.

Trust. It didn't come easily to Kate. But it was now or never. Mr. Cantrell was right. Miranda's disobedience had nearly caused her death, and only an irresponsible parent would let the incident slip by without punishing her. What remained to be seen was how Zachariah would go about it. Kate hugged her waist, determined not to interfere unless she must.

Zachariah withdrew one arm from around the child to fish in his pocket. Without counting the change he palmed, he slapped it into Mr. Cantrell's hand. "Credit me with the extra," he barked.

With that, he strode purposefully from the barn, his footsteps aimed for the house. Kate gathered up her skirt to follow him and then stood her ground. It was the hardest thing she had ever done.

Mr. Cantrell chuckled and shook his head. "That's one little miss whose gonna have herself a mighty tender backside."

Kate managed a painful swallow.

"My Timmy and me went 'round and 'round last week," Cantrell continued. "Got out my shotgun without askin' and near blew his foot off. When I got done with him, he durned near didn't have any hide left."

Kate couldn't reply. She watched as the iceman sauntered toward his wagon. Still hugging her waist, she leaned a shoulder against the barn door and squeezed her eyes closed. She wondered what was happening inside the house, and a hundred awful possibilities flitted through her mind. But she remained where she was, listening to the rattle of Cantrell's wagon as it lurched along the rutted drive.

As the sounds faded, she listened for others, namely Miranda's terrified shrieks. But there was only the whisper of the summer breeze. A peacefulness settled over Kate. Zachariah wasn't Joseph, and she couldn't live the remainder of her life trapped in bad memories. There was no need for her to rush to Miranda's defense, not any more.

With a determined sigh, Kate turned and went back inside the barn to finish forking the straw into the stalls. She had a feeling this was going to be a long wait, and it would pass more quickly if she stayed busy.

Not more than five minutes passed before a long shadow fell across Kate. Without turning to look, she knew Zachariah was standing in the barn doorway.

"What's this?" he asked.

"I just thought I'd finish up for you."

She forked more straw and swallowed the questions that tried to surge up her throat. Her aim was off, and a bunch of straw fell short of the stall.

After a moment's silence, he said, "I don't want you out here doing my work."

"It was my work for a long while. And I don't mind."

"I do, so put down that pitchfork and come here."

Kate did as he asked. When she came to stand before him, he arched a questioning eyebrow at her. "Aren't you going to ask what I did to her?"

An awful, quivery sensation attacked Kate's stomach. "No. I'm sure you did what you thought was best."

He took her face in his calloused palms and tipped her head back. "Thank you," he whispered.

It wasn't necessary for him to clarify that. When he folded his strong arms around her, Kate was more than ready to step into them. And as she did, she found her own small patch of heaven. Once she had wished she could melt into this man and cease to exist. Now all she wanted was to savor the glorious feeling of being alive. To hear the steady thud of his heart beating. To feel the heat of him curled around her. To have his big hands running over her, so light and gentle that her skin became sensitized to capture every elusive caress.

"Oh, Zachariah," she whispered shakily.

"She's all right," he assured her. "I have her sitting with her nose in a corner. And I've told her she can't go over to my place for a week. I figure a week is plenty enough time for her to ruminate on the perils of not minding what I say."

Kate nodded because, for the life of her, she couldn't speak.

"You could have come in the house. I didn't expect you to stay out here, worried sick."

She shook her head and managed to squeak, "There wasn't a need."

Zach closed his eyes on that. *There wasn't a need.* It wasn't a long, eloquent proclamation, but it meant the world to him. He knew what it had cost her to remain out here in the barn. It was a precious gift, her trust. He'd have to spend the rest of his life living up to it, but oh, what a sweet task it would be.

"I love you, Katie."

"I'm beginning to believe you truly do," was her whispered response.

A few minutes later when Kate entered the kitchen, Miranda twisted on the tripod to throw her a gloomy look. Kate concealed a smile.

"What's this?" Kate asked. "A pretty little girl on my milk pail stool? And such a long face! What are you doing with your nose in the corner?"

"I'm ruminatin'," Miranda replied with a sniff.

"Oh, I see. And what are you ruminating about?"

Miranda wrinkled her nose. "About mindin' what my pa says."

Kate stepped to the sink and poured water off a pan of eggs she had just hard-boiled. "That sounds like wisdom to me."

"Only I didn't not mind," Miranda came back. "Papa Zach said I couldn't play up there, but he didn't say I couldn't hide ahind the hay."

Kate paused in cracking an eggshell. "That sounds like a case of splitting hairs to me, Miranda Elspeth Blakely. You knew very well what he meant, and you might have been seriously hurt."

"McGovern," she corrected. "My name ain't Blakely no more."

"Isn't, not ain't. And if you're so ready to take his name, I reckon you'd best take his orders. That includes getting your nose back in that corner until he gives you leave to move it."

Miranda gave a dejected sigh and did as she was told. "I didn't think he'd up and start bein' mean when I 'dopted him."

Kate grinned and plopped a peeled egg in the waiting bowl of water. "Just be glad it was him that got hold of you and not me. I'd 've been sorely tempted to warm the seat of your bloomers."

"I'm gonna mind what he says from now on, for sure." Miranda rubbed the end of her nose. "So can I git down? I've ruminated plenty."

"It's not for me to say."

"You promised it'd be just you and me forever. You said we wasn't never gonna git another pa. And you promised nobody'd never be mean to me again."

"So I did. But you magic wished for him to be your pa,

and you got what you wished for. As for his being mean to you, it looks to me like you fared better than you should have." Kate cracked another egg. "You'd best thank your lucky stars."

"My nose ain't so lucky."

Kate couldn't help but giggle when she turned to look. "Lands! It's as red as a button! I don't think he meant for you to push it plumb through the wall."

Pointing to a spot, Miranda said, "He told me to glue it right there and not move it till he comed back."

"Then you'd better do it."

"He ain't hurryin', and my nose is tuckered."

"Isn't, not ain't. He'll come in due time. Until then, mind what he told you."

"You isn't gonna tattle that I moved, are you?"

"Aren't," Kate corrected, "and I will if you don't get your tuckered little nose back into that corner."

Kate went to gather potatoes from the bin in the pantry. When she returned to the kitchen, Miranda once again had her nose pressed to the wall. Shortly thereafter, Zachariah came in.

Toward dusk, Kate heard a horse approaching the house. Thinking it was probably Zachariah returning from his place, she continued with her meal preparations until the thud of a man's fist against the front door resounded through the house. Wiping her hands on her apron, Kate went to investigate and found Ryan Blakely standing on her porch.

Initially, the sight of him sent Kate's heart into a skitter, as it always had, but then she gathered her composure. She had nothing to fear from the likes of him anymore. No matter what trouble he might cause, he would never get his hands on Miranda. That knowledge made her feel gloriously free.

"Hello, Ryan."

"Is it true?" he demanded.

Kate didn't need that clarified. "I'm surprised it took so long for you to hear. We've been married nigh onto two weeks."

He swept off his hat and shrugged his shoulders to resettle the seams of his suit jacket. "You bitch."

Kate tightened her hand on the door handle. "I don't have to listen to this, Ryan. If you've got something to say, get it said, but keep your name calling to yourself."

"Is it true you let him adopt Miranda? Is it?"

Kate braced herself. "Yes, it's true."

Before she realized what he meant to do, he grabbed her by the hair and jerked her out onto the porch. "I'll kill you. So help me God, I'll strangle the breath right out of you! My brother's child! How could you give her to another man?"

Kate's scalp felt on fire. Tears blinding her, she groped frantically for Ryan's wrist to break his hold. "Stop it, Ryan. Have you lost your mind entirely?"

He gave her hair a vicious jerk. "You're the one who's crazy if you think I'll take this lying down! You'll pay. I swear to God, you'll pay. I'll take you to court. I'll get custody of her, see if I don't. And when I do, you'll never set eyes on her again."

Kate was about to reply when a dangerously silken voice said, "Take your filthy hands off my wife, Blakely."

Ryan stiffened and turned. "You!"

With a violent shove, he threw Kate away from him. She slammed against the wall of the house, barking an elbow as she caught herself from sprawling. Settling her back against the wood, she watched as Zachariah swung down off his horse. An avenging angel in blue chambray and denim, his hazel eyes blazing. Never had she been so glad to see anyone.

"That's right, me," he said calmly as he strode toward the porch. "What did you do? Watch for me to leave? Understand something, you yellow-hearted bastard. If you came here looking for trouble, I guaran-damn-tee you've found it."

"You're not so tough!"

Zachariah stomped up the steps. "Tougher than a woman half your size, I'll warrant. I won't say you can't kick my ass, but you'd best pack a lunch if you mean to try."

Tossing aside his hat, Ryan braced his legs and doubled his fists. "I won't go hitting my head on a post this time."

Zachariah kept coming. "I hope not."

Ryan put up his guard and executed a graceful boxing step. Zachariah planted his hands on his hips and paused to watch. Giving a low whistle, he said, "Damn! That's some mighty fine movement you've got there. Prettiest waltz step I ever saw."

"You'll think waltz about the time you're a mudhole I'm stomping dry. You caught me off guard twice. Not this time." He feinted with one hand. "I fought in the Seattle logging camps. Ring competition. And believe me, no clod buster like you is gonna whip me. You wouldn't make a pimple on a real man's ass. Come on, big boy. Or is your yellow starting to show?"

Zachariah grinned and swept off his hat. Handing it to Kate, he said, "Ring competition? I'm flat outclassed. My pa never taught me how to kick shit fancy." With a sideways glance, he murmured, "Go in the house, Katie girl. I don't want you in the middle of this."

Kate tried to move, but her limbs refused to function.

"You just don't want your little whore to see you get whipped," Ryan said with a laugh.

Zachariah's grin faded, and a dangerous glitter came into his hazel eyes. "Blakely, it's time you learned some manners clod buster style."

So quickly that Kate didn't see him start to move, Zachariah punctuated that proclamation by planting a fist squarely in Ryan's mouth, the force of which sent the other man reeling backward into the porch rail. The rotten wood creaked and then gave with an ear-shattering pop. With a startled look on his face, Ryan swung his arms in a desperate attempt to keep his feet. Then he dropped off the porch like a rock, landing on his back in a cloud of dust.

Zachariah followed his opponent's backward scramble, never breaking his stride. When he reached the broken railing, he leaped to the ground, grabbed Ryan's lapels, and hauled him to his feet. "I don't take kindly to you calling my wife a whore."

The instant the other man had his balance, Zachariah let fly with another punch. Ryan's head snapped back, and he staggered drunkenly. Zachariah stalked after him to bury a fist in his middle, which bent the man double.

"Don't touch her and don't call her foul names. Is that clear, you miserable sack of offal?"

Ryan hugged his belly and moaned.

Zachariah grabbed him by the hair. "Feel good? You like getting jerked around by your hair?"

"I'll bring the law down on your heads!" Ryan cried.

"Good idea. Come back here without the sheriff as your escort, and next time, I'll kill you." As if for good measure, Zachariah gave him a lightning-quick jab to the nose and then threw him away as though the touch of him was contaminating. "Stay away from my wife and child. Come within a mile of this place again, and you'll answer to me."

Ryan scurried a safe distance away, then turned to shake his fist. "I won't give up my brother's child! I'll see her dead before I let you have her!"

"My child!" Zachariah reminded him. "Legal and permanent! Get anywhere near her, and I'll show you what hell is like. Now get on your horse and make tracks before I change my mind about letting you walk out of here in one piece!"

Ryan's fiery blue eyes found Kate. "I'll be back. You can't kill my brother and get away with it. I'll be back."

Those words continued to ring in Kate's head as he mounted his horse and rode away. When Zachariah returned to the porch, she fastened a worried gaze on him. "He means it. I'll never have peace. Not as long as he's got breath in his body."

He spotted Ryan's hat and kicked it viciously. "He's mostly bluster." Planting his hands on his hips, he gave her a careful once-over. "Did he hurt you?"

She shook her head. "No." With a tremulous smile, she rubbed her scalp. "Just parted me from a little of my hair. And you? Did he do you any damage with all those fancy punches he threw?"

His gaze sharpened on hers, then his mouth quirked. "Why, Kate. I do believe you're teasing me."

"I do believe you're right. Not bad for a clod buster, Mr. McGovern, not bad at all."

His eyelashes drooped in a lazy sweep as his lips curved in a sheepish grin. "I sucker punched the bastard. Like I told him, my pa didn't teach me how to fight fancy, only how to win. One hard and fast rule was to avoid trouble if I could, but to be damned sure I threw the first punch if I couldn't. One good hit usually dampens a man's enthusiasm and rattles his head enough to make him easy game."

Kate hugged her waist and swallowed a giggle. "I don't think you followed the rules of polite competition, Zachariah."

A lambent gleam crept into his gaze. "I'm not a polite man by nature, Katie girl. Surely you've figured that out by now."

She recalled their wedding night and felt heat rising up

her neck. Her smile slowly faded, and an odd lethargy invaded her body. Remembering the glorious sensations his hands and mouth had wrought in her, she whispered, "It remains to be seen, of course, but I'm beginning to think politeness can be vastly overrated."

"Really?" His voice held a note of mischievous amusement.

Unsettled by the sensual undertones in their exchange, she took a deep breath and straightened her shoulders. "How did you know to come home? I've never been so glad to see anyone in all my life."

"I had a man watching the road. I'm sorry I didn't get here quicker, but I was out on the slopes."

"I'm just glad you came."

He stepped close and drew her into his arms. "I'll always be around when you need me, Katie. You can count on that."

Kate wanted nothing more than to settle into his embrace, but she was worried about Miranda. Just as she started to pull away, the child appeared in the open doorway, her big brown eyes worshipful as she fastened them on Zachariah.

"You sure taught him! Didn't you, Papa Zach?"

Kate searched her daughter's gaze for any sign of withdrawal and found none. Relief filled her. A wonderful, leaden relief that intensified the weighted feeling that had already invaded her limbs. Deep inside her, the cold knot of fear that had been her constant companion for so long began to disintegrate.

Her little girl was going to be all right. She really and truly was going to be all right.

19

Moonlight gilded the rose garden, etching the blooms and serrated leaves with silver. Kate leaned her arms on the fence and breathed in the evening air. She loved the smells of summer. Grass, clover, roses, and alfalfa, all floating on the light, heat-kissed mist from the river.

A light breeze played in her unbound hair and caressed her body through the muslin of her nightgown. Listening, she bent a knee to rest it on a rail. Rustling leaves, crickets, frogs, and the occasional chirp of a roosting bird. So much beauty, and yet so elusive to a troubled heart. She had lived here five years, and this was the first time in her memory that she had ever come out on a moonlit summer night simply to enjoy the beauty of it.

Peace . . . Kate closed her eyes to savor the feeling. Right after Ryan's visit earlier that day, she'd felt leaden with relief, but now that had given way to a glorious weightlessness.

It's over, a voice within her whispered.

And Kate knew it truly was. Ever since Miranda's birth nearly five years ago, she had spent every waking moment in fear for her. These last seven months, that fearfulness had become a fixation. Now, she was no longer afraid. There was no reason to be. Miranda was safe, perfectly safe, and as long as Zachariah McGovern drew breath, she would always remain safe.

Heroes, and magic, and castles made of dreams . . . Foolish childhood fantasies. Kate could never believe in such things again. Her nose had been rubbed too hard in grim reality for her to do that. But she had spun those fantasies for her daughter, day after day, creating make-believe worlds all trimmed in gold because Miranda had needed a handful of magic. And somehow, crazy though it seemed, the fantasies had become real.

Tears filled Kate's eyes, and a tremulous smile touched her mouth. Miranda's hero, Zachariah McGovern. For a man of heroic proportions, Kate supposed he was a little rough around the edges. His castles were seven-room houses built out of straw. Instead of flowing silk garments, he wore dirt-smudged denim and faded chambray. He had ridden to their rescue on a sorrel gelding named Dander instead of a prancing white steed. And last but not least, he didn't have a magic wand. But he was a hero, just the same. And in his own way, he had worked magic, filling their lives with laughter, making them feel safe when Kate had despaired of ever feeling safe again. Miranda's hero.

And now Kate's. She wasn't sure how it had happened, or when it had happened, but she had fallen in love with him, rough edges and all. Deeply and irrevocably in love. And she wanted a life with him. Tossing griddle cakes in the air. Flipping peas with spoons. She wanted it all with no threats hanging over her head, with no fear that it could all be snatched away.

The faint sound of a door closing caught Kate's attention. She turned her gaze toward the house to see the object of her thoughts emerging from the shadows to stand at the top of the steps. Dressed only in jeans that rode low on his hipbones, he struck an unnervingly male pose, one knee bent, hands at his waist, his muscular chest and shoulders gleaming like burnished silver in the moonlight. When he spotted her, the tension flowed from his body, and he descended the steps in two easy strides.

"Katie?" His voice cut through the gloom, low and whispery, yet gruff. "Why didn't you tell me you were going outside? I woke up, and all I had in bed with me was a kid and a dog."

Before she could form a reply, he stepped on something with his bare foot. "Jesus H. Christ!"

Kate smiled to herself as he gimped his way toward her. Bracing a hand on the wobbly fence, he vaulted over, his body a harmony of motion, the perfect blend of strength and agility. As always, she felt dwarfed when he drew up beside her. Dwarfed, but not threatened. Never that, not with Zachariah.

"Are you okay?"

"I just had some thinking to do, and this seemed like the right place." She inclined her head at the garden. "Good-bye to the old, hello to the new."

He leaned on the fence beside her. The touch of his arm was warm and vibrantly male, making Kate aware of her body as she had never been. His shimmering gaze searched hers for a long moment. "Joseph?" he asked.

She studied her hands, uncertain how to express her feelings. "He's ruled my life for so long, Zachariah. I think it's high time to put him behind me."

"Amen to that."

She nibbled her lip. "I'm afraid you don't understand. I mean really behind me." She looked up, her heart in her throat. "You'll probably think I'm crazy. After all you've done—with the garden and all."

She saw the tendons along his throat convulse as he swallowed. He fixed his gaze on the distant mountains. "You've decided to turn yourself in."

It wasn't a question, and by that Kate knew he did understand, probably far better than she had hoped. "He still has a hold on me. He always will if I leave things as they are." Tears stung her eyes, but she didn't try to blink them away. Not with this man. "I want my life back. I know it's crazy, but I'll never feel free of him unless I—"

"Honey, you don't have to explain. I knew you'd decide to do it sooner or later. I just didn't expect it now."

"Would you like me to wait?"

He sighed. "No. I just—" He broke off and turned his dark head to study her. "What about Miranda? They might lock you up." His voice went hard-edged. "Jesus, Katie, think about this, really think. Do you understand what's at stake? An inquest. If that goes badly, you could be indicted and have to stand trial. It could take weeks, maybe months. Are you ready for that? Is she?"

Kate felt as though someone were closing his hands around her throat. She wasn't all that familiar with court proceedings. No small wonder since Joseph hadn't allowed her much contact with the outside world. "You mean the sheriff can't decide?"

"The sheriff?" His dark face looked harsh and alien to her when he turned to regard her. "Honey, a man's been killed."

"But it was an accident."

"The sheriff doesn't have the authority to decide that."

"You mean I'll have to be in jail and tried for murder?"

He exhaled with a weary sigh and ran a hand over his face. "That depends on the coroner's findings. If he can't tell for sure how Joseph really died, it'll go before a grand jury and be their decision." When his gaze returned to hers, he looked more grim than Kate had ever seen him.

"The grand jury will decide whether or not there's sufficient evidence to make you stand trial. Seven jurors, Katie girl, all men. Most of them with wives who have had reason to clobber them a time or two."

"Husbands?" she echoed hollowly.

"Husbands," he affirmed. Though his eyes glinted with seriousness, his mouth quirked slightly at the corners. "Hopefully fair-minded individuals who won't hand down an indictment. But if you go to trial, you can count on the prosecuting attorney to make it look as bad for you as he can. That's his job, to get convictions."

Kate steepled her fingers and pressed their tips against her lips. "Oh, Zachariah, what do you think I should do?"

He laughed low in his chest, but there was no humor in the sound. "Don't lay that on me. It's too tempting to play autocrat. You have to make the decision. The outcome will have an effect on me, yes, but you and Miranda will suffer most."

Kate gazed off across the valley, swamped by memories. For so long, she had never been allowed to make decisions, not about anything. And now she was being forced to make the most important one of her life. There was a part of her that nearly wished Zachariah would play autocrat. But she knew that was fear raising its head. One of the most special things about him was that he treated her like a thinking individual.

Her decision . . . Kate shoved the fear back and focused on the issues that had brought her out here tonight in the first place. Being free of Joseph, putting all of this behind her. She could never do that until she faced things. In short, risks or no, there was only one thing she could do.

"Miranda will have you," she whispered. "She doesn't need me anymore. Not really."

"Oh, honey . . ." He shifted sideways to brush the tears

from her cheeks. "Of course she needs you. She'll always need you."

"You don't understand. I'm not sad about it. I'm glad, wonderfully glad." Kate caught his wrist and pressed a kiss to his rough palm. "If something happened—if I disappeared from her life, she'd be sad for a while, but she'd be all right. Because she has you. I don't have to worry about what might happen to her anymore. Not the way I used to. That was the one hold Joseph still had on me, and now it's gone."

"What about you?" He twisted his wrist to catch her hand in his strong grip. "What about you, Katie? Have you thought of that? We can leave Joseph where he is. You don't have to take the risk. Having him planted there isn't eating on my conscience any, not under the circumstances. The way I see it, a rose garden is better than he deserves."

"It is eating at me, though," she whispered. "Sometimes, life makes it impossible to choose between right and wrong, and we do what we must. We keep secrets that haunt us because to reveal them might hurt someone we love."

At the words, he averted his face, looking for all the world as though she had struck him.

"Zachariah? You understand what I'm saying, don't you?" she asked anxiously.

"Unfortunately, yes." He rubbed the back of his hand across his mouth. "We all have a secret or two that haunts us, I reckon. And sometimes circumstances dictate." His mouth curved in a grim smile. "Instead of doing the right thing, we do what we feel we have to. I understand. Maybe better than you think."

"Seven months ago, I did the unthinkable to protect my child. Now she doesn't need protecting, and I'm free to do the right thing, even though it's late in coming. It's a loose end for me, Zachariah. Please say you understand."

"Honey, of course I understand. But what if you're

tried for murder and found guilty? Not to say it might happen that way. I don't think it will. But what if it did?"

A quiver of fear attacked Kate's stomach. When she finally managed to speak, her voice came out thin and tremulous. "Then you'll have to raise my daughter. Will you promise to do that?"

"Our daughter," he corrected in a deep whisper. "And yes, I give you my oath. I'll raise her and love her with every breath I take. But given my druthers, I'd like to have her ma in the bargain."

Looking into his eyes, Kate knew in her heart that he would keep that oath, no matter what. Not just for her, but because he loved the child. Magic wishes did indeed come true, and Miranda had gotten hers, a new pa who was really something.

"It's a matter I must tend to," she said softly. "I can't live the rest of my life with the threat of discovery hanging over my head." She moistened her lips. "Don't you see, Zachariah? You can't have me in the bargain, not really. Not as long as I'm shackled to the past."

He touched light fingertips to her temple. "Like I said, it's your decision to make, but that doesn't stop me from being afraid for you. Once you take that step, I can't protect you anymore. You do understand that?"

Kate understood all too well. "I—I know it's a lot to ask, but would you consider going with me when I tell the sheriff? I'd feel better if you were there."

He moaned low in his throat and drew her into his arms. "Honey, I'd walk straight into hell with you." He splayed a hand over her back. "You couldn't keep me away if you hogtied me."

Kate encircled his waist with her arms, realizing as she did that this was the first time she had ever returned his embrace. She pressed a cheek to his bare chest and breathed in the scent of him. His skin bore faint traces of sweat and sun-dried denim, grass and hay, little-girl sweetness and musky dog. Being in his arms, holding him close . . . It felt so right, so perfectly and wonderfully right.

With him beside her, she felt ready to face just about anything, even being charged with murder.

An hour later, Zach lay with Kate in his arms, his gaze fixed on the ceiling, his senses alert to every nuance of her breathing, every spot where her slight body pressed against his. In all his life, he had never tasted such cloying fear, not even when cholera had wiped out half his family, taking both his parents and three of his brothers. That had been fate, something he couldn't prevent. If he chose, he could stop Kate from what she intended to do tomorrow.

Zach had a good mind to do just that. The problem was that he couldn't be sure his motivations were entirely noble. Scratch that. He knew they weren't noble. He felt a little sick when he remembered how he had tried to dissuade her from going to the sheriff. The truth of it was that he didn't honestly feel afraid for either one of them.

He believed in the judicial system, and believing in it as he did, he found it impossible to contemplate Kate's being found guilty of Joseph's murder. Considering what the man had done and what he had been in the act of doing when she struck him, a jury would probably let her off even if she had intended to kill him. No one in his right mind would blame her for defending her child.

If he was honest with himself, brutally honest, what really scared hell out of him was what might happen after Kate faced her demons. Once she was vindicated of any wrongdoing, he was going to be an unwanted element in her life, extra baggage she no longer needed, an authority figure she abhorred. After all she had been through, who could fault her for wanting her freedom?

He had gone into this marriage knowing she didn't love him. They'd made a trade, his name and protection in exchange for her hand. After tomorrow, she'd be well on her way to not needing him. He didn't think she'd thought ahead to that yet. But when she did, it wouldn't be long before she started contemplating the possibility of an annulment.

He thought about spiriting her away to another room. To stake his claim on her flesh, to consummate their marriage so nothing and no one could ever put it asunder. Using all his fragile self-control, he stifled the urge and closed his eyes against a rush of possessiveness.

She wasn't ready for a physical relationship with him yet. All he had to do was look into her eyes to know that. She was becoming relaxed with him, yes. And he felt certain they had forged a lasting friendship between them. Given time to worm his way into her heart, he didn't doubt his ability to arouse her and make sex pleasurable for her. But time was a luxury he no longer had. After she went to the sheriff tomorrow, she would probably be incarcerated until she was vindicated. If he meant to consummate this marriage, he had only a few hours left.

When had he become so desperate that he would actually consider tying a woman to him, her wishes be damned? When had his love for her become twisted into something so unholy that he could look upon her as a piece of flesh to be owned?

Behind his closed eyelids, Zach pictured the expression that would come into Kate's eyes if he used his strength against her. At the image, his stomach knotted with rage, not at her but himself because it would be so horribly easy for him to do it. Or worse yet, to use Miranda as leverage against her. She would do anything to ensure her daughter's well-being . . . anything. A carefully phrased threat from him, that's all it would take.

Tucking in his chin to study her sweet face, Zach traced a fingertip along the fragile curve of her jaw. She murmured in her sleep and pressed closer to him. Every other night since their marriage, they had slept with a child and dog between them. But tonight she had moved into his arms as if it were the most natural thing in the world. All he needed was a little more time. Just a chance to make her love him, that was all he needed. And he wasn't going to get it.

He had two choices, the way he saw it. He could force her hand now, or he could risk losing her. The first came with guarantees, the second didn't.

Carefully, so as not to awaken her, Zach withdrew his arms from around Kate and left the bed. There were other places to sleep in this sprawling house, and if he wanted to like himself in the morning, he had best find one.

The choice to walk away . . . that would be his gift to her.

The following afternoon, Kate sat alone in the kitchen, rhythmically rocking in her chair in an attempt to block out the sounds that floated into the house from outside. Men's voices and steel scraping rock . . . the sounds of a nightmare being unveiled and exposed to sunlight.

When the noises ceased, so did Kate's frantic rocking. Curling her hands around the rocker armrests, she dug her nails into the wood. Sweat filmed her body and, not for the first time, she regretted her decision to visit the sheriff that morning. All for what? To exonerate herself? To give Joseph a sacred resting place? To put the guilt behind her? Those reasons seemed so feeble now.

Marcus had taken Miranda over to Zachariah's place. Her husband was outside overseeing the grim exhumation of Joseph's remains. Sitting here in the shadows, she was getting a taste of the dimness and loneliness that could become a steady diet for her inside a jail cell if she should be convicted of his murder.

The report of heavy boots echoed through the plank floor, and Kate knew Zachariah and the sheriff had come into the house. *I won't be able to protect you any longer. You do understand that?* Since hearing Zachariah utter those words, Kate had sensed his withdrawal from her. For the first time since their marriage, he had slept away from her last night. But it was more than that. There was an evasiveness about him, a detached expression in his eyes, almost as if he were bracing himself to say good-bye. That, above all else, struck terror into Kate.

When had she come to need Zachariah so desperately? She craved the feeling of his warm, heavy hand on her shoulder. She yearned for his gaze, twinkling and full of laughter, to search hers for an endless moment, sending messages that both puzzled her and made her skin tingle. She longed to feel his arms around her, to hear him whisper, "It'll be okay, Katie girl."

She wasn't a child. He couldn't wave his hand and make everything right in her world. Yet, somehow, she had come to count on his magic. Her rational side mocked her for that. *You don't believe in heroes, remember?* But she did believe in Zachariah. And she wanted him to slay the dragons so she wouldn't have to face them. Instead, he was pulling away his support, separating himself from her before she was even gone.

Tears burned in the back of Kate's throat. She swallowed them down. Pain and fear were her old friends. She had learned long ago never to weep with sorrow. When things got tough, you stiffened your spine and gritted your teeth.

"Kate?"

Zachariah's voice lashed across her nerves, and she sprang from the chair. Whirling, her heart slamming against her ribs, she saw her husband and the sheriff coming through the door.

"Sheriff Higgins would like to talk to you," Zachariah said softly.

Kate's gaze slid to the lawman. An individual of wiry build and average height, he looked small standing beside her husband. Because of the heat, he had removed his black serge suit jacket. Sweat ringed the underarms of his white cotton shirt, and his bow tie hung loose at his unfastened collar. In one hand, he held a box camera, which she assumed he had used to take photographs of the corpse. The thought made bile surge up her throat.

"Yes, Sheriff?"

Higgins swept off his hat and wiped his sweaty forehead with his sleeve. His thin gray hair lay over his balding pate in wet strips that looked almost black. "Well, ma'am . . ." He cleared his throat and shrugged his shoulders. "I want you to understand that I sincerely believe what you told me this morning. But—" He broke off and looked at Zachariah. "Well, ma'am, the sad thing is—"

Kate knotted her hands in her skirt. "Yes?"

The sheriff heaved a defeated sigh. "Well, to put it indelicately, the corpse is so deteriorated that it's impossible for the coroner to tell by examining the head wound if it was caused by a blunt instrument or a sharp surface on the hearth." He waved his hat in a helpless gesture. "I was hoping for cut-and-dried evidence to corroborate your story. But we didn't get it. We can't settle this with a simple inquest. I've got no choice but to file charges against you."

Kate flinched and averted her face for a moment.

"Understand that I'd just let it go on your word if I could," he put in quickly. "I'd like nothing better than to end all this as quick as can be. You and the child have obviously suffered enough. But I have to follow lawful procedure."

Kate swallowed and managed to say, "What you mean is that I'll have to go to jail and stand trial for murder."

He cleared his throat again. "The evidence will go before the grand jury first. If things go well with that, there may never be an indictment."

"An indictment?" Kate remembered everything Zachariah had said last night. "That's an official charge, correct?"

"The charges are what's happening right now. The indictment comes if the grand jury decides there's sufficient evidence that a crime has been committed. If the evidence presented against you in a preliminary round is strong, you'll be indicted for murder and have to stand trial. If the evidence is too flimsy, the case will never go any farther."

Kate sought Zachariah's gaze only to find that he had braced his hands on the back of a chair and was studying the floor. "Must I be in jail until the grand jury decides?"

The sheriff shuffled his feet. "Your husband and I have been discussing just that, and I've decided to bend the law a hair. He's given me his word he'll bring you in come morning if I'll let you have this one last night at home. More for the child's sake than yours, you understand. I'd like to make this as easy on her as I can. This will give you a chance to explain things to her and prepare her for your absence. The catch is that I have to have your word you won't—" He studied the crown of his hat for a moment. "I'm sticking my neck out, you see. If you hightail it out of here, I'll be in hot water aplenty for not locking you up, straight off."

Kate nodded. "I understand, Sheriff. And you have my word that I'm not going anywhere. I appreciate your bending the rules so I can be with Miranda tonight."

The sheriff looked relieved and smiled, albeit feebly. "Chances are the judge will set bail and you'll be able to come home in a couple of days."

"I'll pray for that," Kate replied. Then she too forced a smile. "You needn't look so woebegone, Sheriff Higgins. I knew I'd be facing serious consequences when I went to see you this morning. I don't hold you accountable for how the law reads."

"For what it's worth, I don't believe any court in the land will convict you if it comes to that."

"I hope you're right."

It seemed to Kate that those precious few hours she had left with her daughter flew by. She went through the motions of a normal evening, fixing dinner, doing dishes, taking Miranda onto her lap to tell her stories before bedtime, but with every breath she fought back tears.

With a maturity far beyond her years, Miranda took the news of her mother's departure calmly. She had seen the disturbed rose garden, and that evidently had prepared her for the worst. As best she could, Kate explained her reasons for going to the sheriff.

"It was something I felt I had to do," she whispered shakily. "We have a new life now, you and I. We're not alone like we used to be. Even if I have to go away, I know you'll be happy here with Zachariah."

Miranda nuzzled Kate's bodice and toyed with the buttons. "I understand, Ma. It's like in a story, huh? Until ever'thing gets all done with, you can't say it's the end."

Kate rested her cheek against her daughter's hair and

closed her eyes. "That's exactly right. And I want to say it's the end. Until I do, it'll never be completely over. We deserve a happy ever after, you and I."

"Are you scared?"

"Not at all," Kate lied. "My one worry was what might happen to you if I had to be in jail for a while. Now I'm just anxious to get it over with."

"Is jail a bad place?"

As honestly as she could, Kate described a jail cell. "I'll be warm and comfortable. They'll bring me my meals. It won't be as nice as being at home, but it won't be terrible, either."

"I'm gonna miss you a powerful lot."

Kate hugged the child close. "Oh, Miranda, I'll miss you, too. More than you'll ever know. I love you so much. No matter how long I'm away, please don't ever forget that."

"I know how much you love me, Ma. You're in all this trouble 'cause of me."

Kate felt she had to dispel that notion. If things went badly, she didn't want Miranda carrying the burden of guilt. "No, not because of you," she whispered fiercely. "You must never think that, sweetness. My marriage to your father caused all of this, and that happened long before you were ever born."

"Why come did you marry him?"

Kate took a shaky breath. "It's a long story. In short, my uncle Jed arranged the marriage, and I didn't have a say."

"Was he a mean man? Your uncle?"

Kate smiled sadly. "Not at all. He was just—" She broke off and smoothed her daughter's hair. "He was very old, and he worried about what would happen to me after he was gone. He was my only relative after my ma and pa died, you see. When your father saw me in church and took a shine to me, Uncle Jed thought it was Providence. He figured I'd be safe and well cared for if I was married before he passed away."

"Only you wasn't, huh? Pa turned out mean."

"Your pa was troubled, Miranda." There were some things Kate felt she needed to say for fear she might never get another chance—things Miranda needed to hear and remember. "So is your uncle Ryan. If it should happen that you and I never speak of this again, I want you to remember that."

"Am I gonna be troubled when I get old?"

Kate managed a light laugh. "Goodness, no. It's not something catching, sweetness. It's a confusion they were trained up to have . . . by their father. You haven't been raised by him, and when you grow up, you'll be right as rain."

"Why come did their pa train them up confused?"

"Because he was a troubled man, too. Imagine, if you will, loving someone with all your heart and having them run away and leave you. That's what happened to him. His wife deserted him, and left him to raise his two little boys all on his own."

"Pa and Uncle Ryan?"

"Yes, your pa and uncle Ryan. Their ma just up and left one night while they were all asleep. She didn't even tell her family good-bye. Your grandpa Blakely was filled with a lot of pain. Sometimes when we hurt, we turn the pain against the people we love most. That's what he did, I think, though I'm sure he meant well. He didn't want your pa and uncle Ryan to fall in love some day and get hurt like he had, so he raised them up to believe females were wicked."

"So Pa never loved me and you?"

Kate took a deep breath. "I think he loved us, Miranda,

but it was a very twisted and ugly love. Because of the way his pa taught him to think, he was all mixed up inside his head. When we think of him, that's what we must remember."

A sound at the kitchen door caught Kate's attention, and she glanced up to see that Zachariah had entered the room. For a moment, their gazes locked. Then he looked away. Kate was left feeling desolate.

She put a bright face on it for Miranda's sake. "Well, it's about that time. Since you seem to end up there every night, regardless, what say I tuck you straight into my bed so we can snuggle later?"

Miranda seconded that suggestion with unbridled enthusiasm. Without a word, Zachariah turned his back on them and left the kitchen.

20

After tucking Miranda into bed, Kate went in search of Zachariah and found him sitting on the porch. When she joined him on the step, she followed his gaze to the moon that hung like a shimmering china plate above the roof line of the barn. To the left, a giant oak stretched gnarled limbs against the sky, its billowy top glossed with silver and swaying in the gentle breeze.

Kate hugged her updrawn knees, acutely conscious of the distance she sensed in him, uncertain how to breach it. His withdrawal made her feel as if her foundation were eroding. She wished she could tell him that, but Joseph had never allowed her to express her feelings, for one thing, and for another, her emotions ran so deep that it was difficult to strip them bare. Yet she couldn't let the situation ride, either. Time was running out. She couldn't bear the thought of leaving here in the morning not knowing what was troubling him.

"Zachariah," she began, "are you angry with me because I went to the sheriff?"

He braced his elbows on his knees, leaning slightly forward and hunching his broad shoulders so the cloth of his blue shirt stretched taut across his back. The breeze ruffled his dark hair, laying it across his high forehead in glistening waves. "No, honey, I'm not angry. If I hadn't wanted you to do it, I would have said something last night when you brought it up."

She dug her fingernails in at the sides of her knees. "Something's wrong. I've sensed it all day."

He took a deep breath. "I've just got a lot on my mind."

"Like what?"

"Oh, lots of things," he replied evasively. "Nothing for you to worry about. You've got enough of a load."

He turned to regard her. It wasn't lost on Kate that he didn't quite meet her gaze. Her heart constricted around a cold knot of pain. Whatever it was bothering him had something to do with her, but for some reason, he didn't want to share it.

"It sounded like Mandy took the news pretty well."

Kate averted her face, wishing, praying for inspiration so she could say the right things. She didn't want to lose this man. "She took it amazingly well considering how she might have reacted two months ago. You've worked miracles with her."

"I can't take the credit."

"Oh, yes. You've wrought a wondrous change in her." She returned her gaze to his face and struggled to swallow. "You know, it's funny. In the beginning, I was so terrified that you'd break her heart. She was searching for someone bigger than life, for someone to be her hero, and I didn't figure any man could live up to that." Her voice turned thin. "I was wrong, Zachariah. So very wrong. I'm not sure what the definition of a hero is, exactly, but if ever a man was one, you are."

The lines that bracketed his mouth deepened with a bitter

twist of his lips. "Thank you. That's a fine compliment."

He didn't look or sound happy about having received it. Kate fought down another wave of panic. What had she done to turn him away from her like this? "Zachariah, I know you're upset about something. Won't you please tell me what?"

"Like I said, I'm just doing a lot of thinking."

"Does it have to do with me?"

"Some. When you came out here, I was dreaming up ways to break you out of jail." He flashed her a grin that fell short of being convincing. "Not that I believe something so drastic will be necessary. I don't. But if worse comes to worst, I could run with you and Mandy to Canada."

"Canada?"

"France, then. Paris is gorgeous this time of year."

"You've been to Paris?"

He returned his gaze to the sky. "A long time ago. So long ago it seems like it was in another lifetime."

Tears of relief stung Kate's eyes. A man didn't contemplate taking such desperate measures for a woman he didn't care about. "Were you truly thinking of ways to break me out of jail?"

He laughed softly, but there was no humor in the sound. "Crazy, huh? That's a problem with us heroes, you know. We're not happy unless we're rescuing our ladies fair. Everything goes to hell when we realize we aren't needed anymore."

"Not needed anymore?" she whispered. "Oh, Zachariah, how wrong you are. I'm entrusting into your care the most important thing in the world to me."

A muscle along his jaw started to twitch, which told her that he was clenching and unclenching his teeth. Then, with no warning, he pushed to his feet and stepped off the porch with one long-legged stride. "I think I'll take a walk. I need a stretch."

"May I come along?"

He flexed his arms and shook the stiffness out of his legs. "You should stay close to listen for Mandy," he said tonelessly. "I shouldn't be long. If it turns out I am, go ahead and douse the lamps. I'll stretch out downstairs someplace."

"You aren't coming up to bed?" Kate heard her voice going shrill, but she couldn't help it.

"Tonight should be for you and Mandy."

Kate made fists in the twill of her skirt, squeezing so hard her knuckles hurt. "Is that part of what you're angry about? Because I let her go to bed in our room?"

His voice thick with bridled impatience, he said, "I told you I'm not angry about anything, Kate. I just need to stretch my legs, that's all."

With that, he strode away into the shadows. For several seconds, she sat there gazing after him. Then she shot up from the step and ran after him. By the time she caught up, she was breathless. "Zachariah, please, wait! Please?"

He turned back just as she clasped his sleeve.

"Couldn't we walk near the house so I could hear Miranda?"

He broke her hold on his arm by raking a hand through his hair. Tension emanated from him. "I'm not fit company right now," he said in a harsh voice that was totally unlike him.

"We don't have to talk. I don't mind. I'd just like to be with you. This is my last night, and I don't want to be alone."

Closing his eyes, he pinched the bridge of his nose and heaved a weary sigh. "I don't think you're following me.

When I say I'm not fit company, what I really mean is—" He broke off and fixed his gaze on her. "What I really mean is that you shouldn't be around me."

Kate peered up at his dark face, trying to read his expression. "Why shouldn't I be around you?"

"Because I'm not myself right now," he replied raggedly. "If you don't get away from me, I might do something we'll both regret."

"Something we'll regret?" she repeated.

"Yes." He bit out the word.

"Like what?"

"Just take my say for it and cut a wide circle around me for the rest of the night. Please, Kate? I don't quite trust myself to be near you. Not tonight."

"But why?" she asked in genuine bewilderment.

He cursed beneath his breath. "Because I might hurt you, that's why. Do I have to draw you a picture?"

"You, hurt me? You, Zachariah?"

"Yes, me! That's what I said, isn't it?" A dangerous glint came into his eyes, and he swung an arm toward the house. "Go sit on the porch. Go inside and read. Go to bed. Whatever you like, okay? But get the hell away from me!"

His voice snaked around her like a whiplash. Kate had seen Zachariah angry, but never like this, his face rigid with repressed rage, his body tensed as if to do her violence. Instinctively, she retreated a step.

"There's a smart girl. Get away from me while you still can."

The words snapped her back to her senses. Though he loomed over her and looked furious enough to bite through saddle leather, he was Zachariah, a man she had come to trust. She had no idea what was eating at him, but she intended to find out.

"I'm not afraid of you," she informed him.

He planted his hands on his hips and gave a harsh laugh. "You've picked a helluva fine time to decide that."

Feeling diminished by his angry posture, she drew up her shoulders and raised her chin. "I apologize if my timing is bad, but that's the truth of it. I could never be afraid of you."

"When did this revelation strike you. Out of the blue at breakfast? It sure as hell is news to me. I'm telling you, be afraid."

Kate could only stare at him. Stalemate. After doing his best to intimidate her with his glare for the space of several heartbeats, he threw up his hands.

"You know, sometimes I wonder if you've got the brains God gave a gnat." He measured off a scant inch between thumb and forefinger. "I'm about that close to raping your sweet little ass. Is that plain enough for you?"

The words took Kate so aback she blinked. "Why on earth would you consider doing that?"

"Why would I—?" His voice cracked, and he gaped at her with an expression of sheer incredulity on his face. Then, hands back on his hips, he leaned forward to press his face close to hers. "I want you!" he fairly shouted at her. "Is that a good enough reason?"

It took nearly all Kate's courage to stand her ground. He was a large man. Body tensed and poised as if to spring, he struck an intimidating figure. At a glance, she could see the untapped power that roped his body. She couldn't even contemplate what might transpire if he turned that strength against her.

Anyone with good sense probably would get away from him. She guessed maybe he was right, and she didn't have brains enough to know what was good for her. Crazy, so crazy. She was a grown woman who knew from bitter experience that real life was grim and seldom fair, that the strong reigned, and that the weak survived as best they could. She was very likely a fool ever to have allowed this man to convince her otherwise. But he had. And now, if she couldn't believe in him, she knew she would never be able to trust in anyone or anything again.

"If you want me," she whispered shakily, "there's certainly no need to contemplate forcing your attentions on me. I'm your wife and yours to take. I won't deny you your marital rights."

"Take, there's the key word," he shot back. "Forget the rest because it's parlor talk. Marital rights. Forceful attention? I'm not talking about a goddamned waltz, for Christ's sake!"

Kate hugged her middle, determined to stand fast. "Perhaps you should enlighten me, then. What are you talking about?"

He spun and took a pace away from her. When he wheeled to face her again, she could see that he was trembling. In a husky voice that reflected that, he said, "I'm talking about choices, honey. Namely yours, and me taking them away from you."

Kate circled that. "Choices?"

"Your right to annul our marriage once all this is over. The right to walk away from me a free woman."

He planted his hands on his hips again, his stance rigid and threatening. Kate had the awful feeling he was keeping those powerful hands at his waist to stop himself from reaching for her. She recalled the night he had grabbed her and lifted her onto the bed. Effortlessly, as though she weighed no more than Miranda. If he came toward her, she didn't have a prayer of outrunning those long, powerfully muscled legs of his, and they both knew it. Yet he stood there warning her away, thumbs hooked over his belt. If he were truly bent on doing her harm, what held him back? Perhaps he didn't know, but Kate felt she did.

"Why would I want to seek an annulment, Zachariah?"

"Why in hell wouldn't you? You won't need me anymore once this is all settled. No more fear of discovery. Nothing hanging over your head that Ryan can use against you. If he comes around causing trouble, you can just sic the law on him. Why keep me around?"

A suspicious sheen had come into his eyes. Kate guessed it was tears, and the realization hit her like a blow. *That's the trouble with us heroes, don't you know? Everything goes to hell when we realize we aren't needed anymore.*

"Oh, Zachariah."

He swore beneath his breath and averted his gaze. She could see that he was humiliated by the show of tears. And no small wonder. This was a rough and rugged man who lived by the sweat of his brow and the raw power of his muscle. To be brought to tears in front of a woman? She could almost taste his shame, and to know she had inflicted it upon him was almost more than she could bear.

A muscle along his square jaw twitched spasmodically. After a moment, he exhaled a quavery breath and squeezed his eyes closed. "I don't know why I ever roped myself into a situation like this," he whispered raggedly. "I knew from the start I didn't stand a chance with you. And now to be faced with the choice of keeping you or letting you go? I've got a real dark side to my nature, Kate. A side I never knew I had—a side that only cares about me and what I want."

Sensing that he would never get beyond what was troubling

him until he purged himself of it, Kate bit down hard on her lower lip to keep from interrupting him.

He took his time, gazing off into the darkness as though the mysteries of the universe were inscribed there. "It's just as well," he finally said. "I know I'd never be happy married to you, not if I'm honest with myself. Every time my back was turned, I'd be afraid some handsome bachelor was giving you the eye. And stuck with a prize like me, who could blame you for looking back?"

Kate's mind stumbled on that. She went back over what he'd said, knowing it would all make sense if she could clear her head enough to focus on it. "What do you mean, a prize like you?"

He shot her a murderous glare. "Don't play games with me. What is it? You're afraid I'll back out on my promise to take care of Mandy?" An accusing silence fell between them. Then he said, "Is that why you followed me out here? Why you're standing there like the sacrificial lamb? To stay on my good side, no matter what? Well, forget it. Using your child as leverage against you would be as bad as raping you."

"Could you back up and clarify what we're discussing here? You've totally lost me."

"Lost you?" he rasped. "For God's sake, don't play dumb with me. You've got eyes in your head. To pretend you've never noticed is an insult to my intelligence."

"Noticed what?"

"My face!"

Kate stared up at him. Slowly understanding dawned. *I know I'm not much to look at.* She could remember him saying that to her the first time he broached the subject of marriage, but she had been so wrapped up in her own concerns that she hadn't registered what he meant. And the habit he had of brushing his knuckles along his cheek?

Not just a habit, she realized now, but a gesture of self-consciousness and shame.

"Are you talking about your scars?" she asked incredulously.

His gaze still sharp as a blade, he glared at her. "Of course, my scars. What else about my face is objectionable?"

"Nothing," she replied tightly. "Absolutely nothing. And neither are the scars. They're scarcely noticeable."

He made a frustrated sound in the back of his throat. "Right. Scarcely noticeable. I have to beat the women off with a stick. Now, would you please do us both a favor and go back to the house before I drag you into the barn, toss up your skirt, and show you what a bastard I can be if I set my mind to it?"

Kate could scarcely believe the pain she heard in his voice. He truly did think his facial imperfections made him ugly. What was worse was that he obviously believed she wasn't attracted to him. *The truth is, I'll take you anyway I can get you. Marrying you, adopting Mandy . . . that'd make me one happy man, kind of like a dozen Christmases, all rolled into one.* She didn't know how she could have been so blind.

Her only excuse lay in the fact that Miranda's and her wounds had run so deep that she hadn't been able to see past them. Zachariah had come into their lives and become their hero, salving their hurts, bringing them joy, teaching them to trust again. It had simply never occurred to her that someone who came bearing such gifts and who imparted such a feeling of peace might be battling a torment all his own.

She closed the distance between them and placed a tremulous hand over his scarred cheek. "Zachariah, you're a very attractive man. The first time I saw you, I didn't even notice the scars. Truly, I didn't."

He jerked back. "Kate, I'm warning you. I can't trust myself right now."

She caught his face between her palms. "I trust you enough for both of us."

He captured her wrists in a viselike grip. "I'm telling you, don't push me. I'm just that close. I swear it."

"If any other man on earth told me that, I'd run like my life depended on it. But never from you."

His body shook with the intensity of his emotions. "You're a fool then."

"Never, not about you."

His grip tightened until it felt as though the bones in her wrists might shatter. "Dammit, Kate, I love you. Don't you understand? With every breath I take. So much it hurts. It's not something I can work out of my system by renting a woman. I can't drown it in a jug of bourbon. It's you I want. Only you. And the thought of losing you is eating me alive."

"Zachariah—"

"Just shut up and listen, for God's sake. I'm dangerous right now. If I consummate this marriage, you can never walk away. It's not easy turning my back on that. I've got tonight. It's now or never, don't you see? After tomorrow, I won't get another chance."

The pain that emanated from him was all her doing. He had given Miranda and her so much, and she had taken, and taken, and taken, never stopping to think what it was costing him.

"What if I were to tell you that I don't want to walk away?"

His grip on her wrists slackened. "A life sentence, remember? It doesn't have to be that way. You can annul the marriage and be free. I'm trying my damnedest to leave that option open to you."

A life sentence. Having those words thrown back at her hurt, but not nearly as much as she knew it hurt him to say them. Options. Only a man like Zachariah would care if she had any. As he had from the beginning, he was once again sacrificing himself to ensure her happiness. Twice now he had risked everything for her, first in the well to save Miranda and then again the night he had reburied Joseph. Now he was prepared to do it once more by turning his back on everything he wanted because he was afraid his wishes conflicted with hers.

As a young girl, Kate had had the usual fantasies of one day falling in love with a gallant gentleman who would beg for her hand on bended knee. That dream had turned to dust a lifetime ago. Now here stood Zachariah. He wasn't quite what she had once pictured. No three-piece suit. No flowers in hand. No pretty proclamations. But in a roughly tender way, no man could ever be more gallant.

Options . . . How lovely it felt just to know she had them, to know that this man would turn his back on her and walk away rather than deny her the right to make her own choices. He certainly wasn't obligated to give her that kind of freedom. Upstairs in the top bureau drawer, there was a marriage certificate that was more binding than any bill of sale. His wife, his property. No one would take him to task for taking what was his by right of law. But Zachariah didn't see it that way. He didn't see her that way. To Kate that meant more than a whole wagonload of flowers.

"Where would you care to try raping me? The barn, did you say?"

"There won't be any *try* to it," he snarled. "You wouldn't stand the chance of a snowflake in August, and we both know it."

"Really?" As nervous as the thought made her, Kate knew this was one of those times that actions would speak far more loudly than words. She tried to free her wrists, but even his more relaxed grip was unbreakable. She jutted her chin at him. "Are you going to stand there talking it to death all night? You say you can rape a willing woman, I say you can't. Let's see which of us is right."

He released her as though the touch of her burned him. "Jesus H. Christ, have you lost your mind? Don't challenge me. I'm dead serious about this."

"So am I."

She spun away from him and headed toward the barn. Acutely aware of the heavy impact of his boots following along behind her, she hastened her pace, afraid she might lose her resolve. When she gained the building, she ducked into its dark embrace and turned to gaze at the broad-shouldered man silhouetted in the doorway behind her.

"Zachariah, if you intend to consummate this marriage, you'd best get to it before I lose my nerve."

She saw him run a hand over his face. "You're playing with fire. I hope you realize that."

Kate sighed and moved deeper into the darkness. Her foot caught on something, and she tripped. At her squeak of dismay, he stepped after her into the building.

"Did you hurt yourself?"

"No." She glanced back at him. "Are you coming? I'm really not all that good at this, you know. Loving you with all my heart only got me down to about the fifth button of my shirtwaist. And now I'm starting to wonder if maybe you're right, and I have lost my mind."

At her profession of love, Zach froze midstride, scarcely able to believe he had heard her right. A feeble shaft of moonlight fell across her, and he could see she actually had unbuttoned her bodice partway. He could also see that she was trembling. "What did you say?" he asked in a taut voice.

She leaned against a stall. Tears filled her eyes, shimmering like diamonds.

"How could you think I would trust a man I didn't love with the well-being of my child? I know I was wrong not to tell you how I was starting to feel. But how could you not know? Miranda is my life. I may not have said it with words, but when I went to the sheriff this morning, I was telling you all the same. I love you, Zachariah. When this is over, I'll still love you. The very last thing I want is to end this marriage."

Zach didn't move so much as a muscle. He didn't trust himself to. God, how he wanted to believe her. But the fact of it was, she was shaking like a leaf and looking none too enthusiastic. A woman truly in love with a man didn't look as though she were about to face the chopping block when she contemplated making love with him.

"As for your scars . . ." She threw up her hands. "Don't you look in the shaving mirror? You're one of the most handsome men I've ever met."

Anger, hot and searing, crawled up the back of his throat. "That's bullshit."

"It isn't!" she cried. "Ever since you came here, female tongues have been buzzing. I knew all about you before I ever clapped eyes on you. Every young woman in town was aflutter. Until I met you, I couldn't imagine what the fuss was all about. And then I was in a flutter right along with them."

"You look scared to death right now," he observed drily. "So what's your game here? If it's to ensure I'll take care of Mandy, it's not necessary. I told you that."

"My game?"

"Yes, your game," he shot back. "What else am I supposed to think?"

A tide of words came up Zach's throat along with the anger. He knew he should keep his mouth shut until he calmed down enough to think clearly, but knowing and doing were two different things.

"I nearly shoved Ryan's teeth down his throat for calling you a whore," he lashed at her. "Don't prove me a fool by using your body as a bargaining chip now."

Even in the dim light, he saw the color wash from her face. "Is that what you think?" she asked tremulously. "That I'm trying to make a trade with my body to ensure Miranda's happiness?"

The stricken look on her face made Zach feel ashamed for having flung that at her. But it was the way he saw it, and there was too much at stake, for him and for her, to talk in circles. "It wouldn't be the first time, would it?"

She flinched as though he had slapped her.

Zach wished he didn't have to look at her, but closing his eyes on her pain was the coward's way out. "I know that's a low blow. But some things need saying."

"And some things are so vile they should never be said," she came back in a raw whisper.

"It may be vile, but it's the truth. Everything for Miranda, anything for Miranda. I saw you lying under Ryan, allowing him liberties, eating your fist to keep from screaming. If I subject you to the same, there's no one standing in line to kick my ass. So there we have it, don't we? I can take you or I can walk away. I tried to walk."

She raised her chin, looking for all the world as though she was bracing herself for a blow from his fist. "You said you were walking away so I could make my own choices. I choose you. Why must you question that?"

"Why wouldn't I? You were terrified on our wedding night. I understood that, and the very next morning, I confronted that issue. What changed after that, Kate? What do you think I am, the world's stupidest bastard?"

She parted her lips as though to speak, but he cut her off.

"Two weeks we've been married, and I've never seen you in anything but shirtwaists or nightgowns buttoned up to your chin and down to your wrists. Two weeks of four to a bed with a kid and a dog? We could have sneaked to another bedroom after Mandy went back to sleep any one of those nights, but did you ever once indicate to me that you were willing to? Hell, no! Because the truth of it was, you were relieved to be off the hook. Do you deny that?"

"No," she admitted tremulously.

He wiped his mouth with the back of his hand, then bent his head to scuff the dirt with the heel of his boot. "Now, suddenly—miraculously—you do everything but issue me a dare to consummate our marriage? Suddenly you're professing undying love? Saying you trust me enough for both of us, and that you could never be afraid of me? If that's so, why in hell are you shaking like I'm the devil himself?"

She straightened her arms at her sides and doubled up her hands.

Without giving her a chance to speak, he rushed to the finish. "I think what's happened here is that while I wrestled with my demons last night and today, you were wrestling with yours. You sensed that all wasn't right with me, and you panicked. You'd already gone to the sheriff. If I backed out about taking care of Miranda, Ryan would get his hands on her. Isn't that a fairly accurate account? And so we've come to this. The trouble is, you're no great loss to the stage, especially not when it comes to seduction. Sorry, honey, but I don't buy in."

She shoved away from the stall, her gaze fixed on the doors behind him. "I don't think you're the devil, Zachariah. However, you were correct in saying I think you're the world's stupidest bastard. And blind as a damned mole, to boot."

With that, she tried to sweep past him. For an instant, he was so shocked by the language she had used he couldn't move. Then the meaning of what she had said sank in, and he grabbed her arm. "If I'm not reading this right, then tell me so."

Set off-balance by the pull of his hand, she whirled to face him. "The only thing I want to tell you is to go straight to hell," she cried raggedly. She jerked futilely to free her wrist. "Let go of me, damn you!"

In all the time Zach had known Kate, he had never heard her curse. That she was doing so now told him she was seeing red. "I'll let you go when you answer me."

"The things you've said don't deserve a response!"

With that, she took a wild swing, hitting his shoulder with her small fist. The impact of the blow didn't phase Zach, but the magnitude of what it meant did.

"Katie—"

She took another swing, and he missed getting a fist in his eye socket by a narrow margin. "Don't call me Katie! It's Kate to you from now on!"

Zach seized her wrists before she perfected her aim. "I think you'd best calm down here."

"You calm down. I don't feel like it." She threw her weight to one side in an attempt to break his grip. "Let go of me! So help me, if you don't, I won't be responsible!"

Zach stared down at her. "Tell me where I'm wrong, dammit."

She froze and fastened huge, tear-filled eyes on his. "You call me whore, and you ask where you're wrong? You mock me for my modesty, and you ask where you're wrong? You talk to me about my choices, and how important they are to you, and then you see lies in everything I say?"

A horrible sinking feeling came into Zach's belly. "Kate, I didn't call you a whore."

"The same as," she cried. "Do you think it was easy for me to come in here? You talk about wrestling with demons! I was married to one. Unlike you, he didn't give warnings so I had a chance to get away from him. Do you think I didn't remember the feel of his fist when you were threatening to hurt me? Do you really believe I could stay near you, trusting in you, if I didn't love you?"

"Jesus," he whispered raggedly. "Katie, I—"

"Kate!" she shrieked. "I'm not a child."

"I never thought you were."

"Then let me walk out of here. That's my *choice!*"

Reluctantly, Zach did as she asked. Taken by surprise, she staggered slightly, then got her balance. The moment she did, she made a beeline for the doors. He watched her, feeling as though his heart was in his boots.

"If you really love me, you won't turn your back on this," he called. "I may be a stupid bastard, but my heart was in the right place. If I drew the wrong conclusions, it was your doing as much as mine! We should talk it out!"

She reached the doors and disappeared into the moonlit darkness beyond. The sound of Zach's voice resounded in his ears and died away to nothing. He stared at the ground, spotted the length of harness leather that Kate must have tripped on, and gave it a vicious kick.

"And that's another thing!"

He glanced up to see her silhouetted in the doorway again. "What's that?" he asked softly.

"Your scars! Understand that this has nothing to do with them. Don't add to all the wrong conclusions you've drawn by thinking I find you ugly, because I don't!"

He watched her whirl away again, but this time, he did so with a slight smile. "If you don't, get your butt back in here and prove it!"

As he hoped, she reappeared in the doorway. Kate, in a temper. The fact that she wasn't afraid to lace him up one side and down the other told him more than she could know.

"Stay here in the barn all night. It's where jackasses belong. Drown yourself in bourbon and play five-fingered stud! It's what you deserve."

He couldn't argue with that. "I love you, Katie girl."

She started to walk away, then turned back, hugging her waist. "You're an idiot!"

He took a cautious step toward her. "I'm beginning to realize that. Can you forgive me?"

"It took all my courage to come into this stupid barn!"

He took one more step. "And I mistook your reasons. I'm sorry."

"How could you think I'd go to the sheriff if I didn't know you'd take care of Miranda, no matter what? Bargaining with my body?" Her voice rose to a squeak. "I'm not a coquette! I don't even know how to begin!"

"You've got this fish hooked." He moved a little closer. "You going to throw me back?"

He heard a sob catch in her throat, saw her turn her face to one side. His heart definitely wasn't in his boots. The pain in his chest testified to that. "Katie, I said some pretty awful things."

"Yes," she agreed in a thin voice.

Zach stopped some three feet from her, then folded his arms and braced his feet wide apart. "Can you forgive me?"

"You made me feel dirty." Her voice broke, and she cupped a hand over her eyes. "I kn-knew you'd seen me." Her breath snagged, and she gulped. "That time with Ryan. I knew you had. But I never d-dreamed you thought of me as a whore for it."

With a low curse, Zach closed the distance between

them and gathered her into his arms. To his great relief, she wrapped her arms around his neck and clung to him as though she were about to plunge off an embankment and he was her only anchor. The force of the sobs that tore from her frightened him. It sounded as though they were ripping right through bone and muscle. Tears filled his own eyes.

"Honey, I never meant for you to think that. Dirty? God in heaven, you're the sweetest thing in my life." He ran his fingers into her hair, heedless of her braided coronet. "Listen to me. Can you stop crying and listen?"

She gulped again and held her breath.

"Ever since I saw what you were doing that day with Ryan, I've admired you."

She made a sound of incredulity and tried to pull away.

"Just hear me out," he said hoarsely. "I admire you for it because there's no sacrifice so great that you won't make it for your child. Not every mother loves that selflessly. You've put everything you are on the line, heart, soul, body. Everything for her, nothing for you. How could I not admire you for that?"

"But I didn't fight him."

"To protect Miranda," he whispered. "I knew that then, I know it now. I've never thought less of you for it."

"But you said—"

He pressed her face against his shoulder. "I said what I did because I was afraid you were doing the same thing with me, sacrificing yourself to protect her. And I was sorely tempted to take you under those terms or force you if I had to, rather than risk losing you. When I threw it up to you, I was angry and scared to death of what I was feeling. Can you understand that? I never set out to hurt you. If I had wanted to do that, I wouldn't have walked away in the first place."

She pressed closer and continued to weep, her sobs less forceful. Zach just held her and let her cry, knowing somehow that her pain stemmed from far more than just tonight. Tears too long in coming. Tears she had never been able to shed because she'd had to be strong for her child.

As she cried, he felt a change come over her. The stiffness eased from her shoulders. Her spine gave under the force of his arm. She moved her face from the hollow of his shoulder and went up on her tiptoes to press her nose and mouth against the curve of his neck.

From Kate to Katie . . . He knew it was fanciful, but that was how he interpreted the difference. Kate Blakely, who had weathered the storms of hell, dissolved with those tears and seemed to melt into him. The enchanting creature who remained behind in the safe harbor of his embrace was Katie McGovern, more girl than woman, her life experience nil, her surrender to him as shy as a virgin's, her trust so unreserved it humbled him.

Katie . . . He buried his face against her hair and wept with her, for her, unashamed because he held her so close there was no room for it. Tears of sorrow for all she had suffered. Tears of relief because she had forgiven him. Tears of joy because he held his world in his arms.

When at last they had both cried themselves dry, they leaned together like two uprooted trees that had butted up against each other during a storm, each supported by the other, doomed to fall if they drifted apart. Zach felt exhausted, and he could tell by the limpness of her body that she was as drained.

"I love you, Zachariah," she finally whispered.

Zach found the frame of the door and leaned their combined weight against it. He gazed down at her pale, upturned face. "You look like you ran into a hive of bees."

She touched a puffy eyelid and sniffed. "Do I look that bad?"

"You look fine," he whispered. "And I love you, too. Every sweet inch, including your red nose. Want my handkerchief?"

She sniffed and gave him a damp smile. "I used your shirt."

He chuckled at that. "You wash it, I reckon you can soil it." Freeing one arm, he tried to smooth her braid. "I messed you up good. You've got a rooster comb sticking up."

She wrinkled her nose, putting him in mind of Mandy. "You have a way with words, Mr. McGovern. I feel downright homely, thank you very much."

He splayed a hand over her narrow back. "I'd like to make you feel beautiful," he told her huskily. "I think I can if you'll allow me the privilege."

He saw her pulse quicken in the hollow of her throat, but she remained relaxed in his arms, which he took as a good sign.

"It's high time, I reckon," was her response.

He bit back a grin. "Such enthusiasm."

"I'm not unwilling," she clarified.

"But not exactly a filly lunging at the gate?"

She wrinkled her nose again. "No, not exactly. That day when I was doing the dishes was nice. When I get nerved up thinking about it, I remember that and tell myself it won't be so bad."

"The dishes?" His puzzled frown gave way to a mischievous grin. "Ah, the vocabulary lesson." He pressed his hand more firmly against her back, his grin giving way to a tender smile. "You said you trust me. If you do, believe me when I say there's nothing to get nerved up about."

"I believe you. I think."

He gave a startled laugh. "You think?"

"It's just that I have a hunch there may be far more involved than what we did that day."

"True. All nice, as you put it. If you'll trust me to show you, I'll prove it."

"I—I trust you."

"Well, then?"

She peered past his shoulder into the barn. "Now that I think on it, the barn doesn't seem like an ideal spot."

He drew her into a walk. "You can rest easy on that score. I'm not about to throw you down in a goddamned horse stall when there's a perfectly good bed in the house."

"We have company in our bed, if you'll recall."

"Not in the sickroom, and there's a lock on the door."

Kate conceded the point with a relieved sigh. "Let's go inside, then. The stall would be smelly."

"Not to mention so dark I couldn't see my hand in front of my face."

She stiffened. "You don't mean to light the lamp, do you?"

"No, hm?"

"No. I'd rather not."

"I'll settle for moonlight coming through the window."

Kate fixed her gaze on the house, acutely aware of how quickly his long stride was eating up the distance. Once again calling to mind the day he had come up behind her while she was doing dishes, she had cause to wonder just what making love with him might entail.

"Zachariah?" She moistened her lips. "Last time—when we almost—well, you know—on our wedding night?"

He turned to regard her, one eyebrow arched expectantly.

She bent her head. "I, um, I got the distinct impression that you meant to completely undress that night." She looked back up at him. "Was that your intention?"

His white teeth gleamed in the moonlight as he spoke. "I had that in mind, yes."

"Is—is that how you always go about things? On the bed, with no clothes on?"

His mouth twitched at the corners. "Kate, until recently, I've been a bachelor, so I don't *always* do anything. But when I get around to it, yeah, I take off my clothes, and I prefer a bed."

"It seems rather—peculiar, if you don't mind my saying so."

"I'll bear that in mind," he said with a low laugh.

"I'm not at all sure how it can be accomplished on a bed with any hint of decorum."

"Decorum?" he repeated.

"That means dignified propriety of behavior."

His breath snagged on another laugh. "I know what it means. I don't think my ignorance is the problem here."

"Meaning mine is?"

He bent his head to kiss the tip of her nose. "Honey, trust me, okay? I'll be as polite as I can possibly be, and I'll leave your dignity completely intact."

Kate relaxed a bit. "I'm relieved to hear that. Not that I'm the least reluctant, you understand. Just a bit anxious."

"Let me be the one to do the worrying, okay?"

"Okay." As they drew near the porch, Kate slowed her footsteps again and hung back. "Just one request."

Not removing his arm from her waist, he swung around to regard her with a twinkling gaze. "What's that?"

"About the undressing part. Since this is our very first night, are you absolutely bent on that?"

There was a smile in his voice when he replied. "If the thought unsettles you so much, I won't completely undress."

Because of the mischievous expression on his face, she wasn't quite sure she believed him. "You won't?"

"Nope." Before she realized what he meant to do, he bent, caught her behind the knees, and swept her up into his arms. Taking the steps two at a time, he said, "I'll leave my socks on."

21

Much to Kate's amazement and dismay, Zachariah managed to open and close both the front and sickroom doors without releasing his hold on her. By the time she found herself closeted with him in the shadowy bedroom, she felt rather like a piece of flotsam that had been carried forth on a wave. She could feel his urgency in the rigidity of his body, hear it in the quickened pace of his heartbeat and breathing. Consummating their marriage was clearly something that he had been anticipating, and now that the moment was at hand, he obviously wasn't going to waste time in getting the deed accomplished.

Though he bent at the knees and took great care when he finally set her back on her feet, Kate couldn't help but feel apprehensive. When she heard the lock of the door click, her nerves leaped. She pressed her palms against her waist and threw a glance at the bed. When he stepped to the window to open the curtains on the moonlight, she rebuttoned her bodice.

"You know, Zachariah. It just occurred to me that I

don't have my nightgown down here." She moved toward the door. "I think I'll run upstairs and change. I won't be but a moment."

"Don't you dare," he said with a hoarse laugh. "You'll wake up Mandy, sure as the world."

The heels of his boots tapped out a muffled tattoo on the floor as he moved inexorably toward her. Since her eyes were already accustomed to darkness, the moon's glow seemed glaringly bright to her, and she could see him clearly. She felt certain he could see her as well. Her mind shied away from what that would mean if she couldn't go fetch her nightgown.

"I'll be quiet as a mouse," she assured him shakily. "I really do want my gown."

He stepped close and curled his warm, leathery hands around her throat. "You worried about your neck getting cold?"

Kate circled that. "What does my neck have to do with it?"

He ran his thumbs along the curves of her jaw. "Because that's all a nightgown is good for—to serve as a neck warmer."

She clasped his wrists. "How so?"

He bent his dark head to kiss her cheek. "Because if you're wearing one when I make love to you," he whispered, "it'll end up bunched under your chin, that's why."

With a startled little laugh, she said, "Zachariah, you are a caution." She tried to step away. "I'll be right back."

He moved his hands to her shoulders. "You're not going anywhere."

"I'm not?"

"No, ma'am, you're not." His hands began a gentle massage of her tense muscles. "Relax. You're not going to miss that nightgown, I promise."

"I'm not?"

"No, ma'am, you're not."

"May I ask why you're suddenly addressing me as ma'am?"

"I promised to be polite," he said with a low chuckle.

Kate closed her eyes. "Please don't make fun of me."

He slid his lips to her ear. "Katie, love, I'm teasing you. It's a little hard not to. There's nothing to be nervous about."

She moved her hands to his chest. The heat of him radiated through his shirt and seared her palms. "Yes, well . . . I certainly hope not."

"Do you really believe God would have gone to such trouble to design our bodies so the act of love could be as boring and uneventful as Joseph's version?" His breath stirred her hair and her senses. "Or that He meant it to be an ordeal for females?"

"God *is* a male."

He chuckled at that. "Maybe. Maybe not. You may wonder after I'm through with you." He lifted his head to search her gaze. "Tell me honestly, are you frightened? If we haven't accomplished anything else in this marriage, I do think we've managed to become friends. There shouldn't be any secrets between us, not about this. Even if I can't completely allay your worries, discussing them might help."

Kate had the unsettling feeling that he could read far more from her expression than she wanted him to. She swallowed with some difficulty. "I really don't want to discuss Joseph."

"Sometimes we can't get things out of our heads until we talk about them. Look at all the worrying I did about my face. If I had only told you weeks ago how I felt, you could have saved me tons of agonizing."

She could feel his gaze, relentless and determined, on

her face. "I can't," she whispered. "Don't ask me to talk about it. Even to think about it is humiliating and—"

He crossed her lips with a fingertip and bent to press his forehead against hers. A quietness settled over them, and by that, Kate knew he wasn't going to insist she discuss her memories with him. An ache of guilt rose in her throat, for she knew he wanted no more secrets between them. Worse still, she understood why.

She closed her eyes and struggled to speak. "If it's truly that important to you, then I'll—"

"Katie," he inserted huskily, "*you* are what's important to me. Only you. And how you feel. I want tonight to be beautiful for you, and if you're frightened because of things that Joseph did to you, it won't be. I only want to ease your mind. Humiliating you is the last thing I want to do."

Tears escaped from beneath her lashes, and she pressed closer to him, trying desperately to think of a way to make him understand. "Remember the day you held me after Ryan had cornered me in the barn?"

"Yes, but what—?"

She moved closer still, absorbing his heat and strength. "When your arms came around me, I wanted to melt into you and cease to exist. No more Kate. No more nightmares from which I couldn't escape. No more feeling afraid. I just wanted to stay there in your arms and become a part of you." A tremor ran through her body. "Because you made me feel safe."

He curled his arms around her and buried his face in the hollow of her neck. "Ah, Katie girl, you *were* safe."

"I knew that," she whispered tremulously. "Just as I know it now. Only this time, Zachariah, I don't have to pull away. I can make one of Mandy's magic wishes for myself and have it come true."

She felt his mouth curve in a tender smile. "And what wish is that?"

"To melt into you and cease to exist. No more Kate. No more Joseph. No more bad memories. I can leave my old world behind and step into yours where everything is sweet and good and beautiful. Where everything is new." Her voice went taut with emotion. "I don't want to bring any of Joseph's ugliness with me. And if I dredge it all back up—" Her voice cracked, and she dragged in a shaky breath. "For five endless years, he took everything good in my life and tried to destroyed it. Even my daughter. Now I'm free. You understand? Please don't let him ruin tonight for me, too. Maybe I'm a coward. Maybe you're right and the only way for me to ever put it all behind me is to talk about it. But I—"

Cupping a hand over the back of her head, he pressed her face to his shoulder, muffling whatever else she meant to say. The urgency of his embrace spoke more eloquently than words. Relief eased the tension from her body, for she knew by his touch that he understood.

She turned her face slightly. "Oh, Zachariah."

For what seemed an endless time, they stood there wrapped in silence, bodies pressed together so tightly that it seemed to Kate their hearts beat as one. When at last he drew away, he lifted his hands and slowly began pulling the pins from her hair. When that task was completed, he gently loosened her braid with deft fingers. Her hair fell like an untied silken drapery down her back.

"Remember the night you told me how it makes you feel when you see the first rays of sunlight come across the sky at dawn?" he asked softly.

Battling tears, Kate smiled at the memory. "As if I've been reborn?"

He framed her face between his hands. "That's how

you make me feel when I look at you. And it's how I want to make you feel when I make love to you."

Kate closed her eyes on that, touched by the aching sincerity in his voice.

"We can turn our backs on the past," he whispered. "As far as I'm concerned, we never have to speak Joseph's name again. But only under one condition. I want you to promise me if anything I do ever starts to frighten you that you'll tell me. Agreed?"

"Yes, but—" She lifted her eyelashes to look into his eyes. "Oh, Zachariah, I'm not frightened. Just a bit apprehensive, that's all. I'm not certain what to expect from you."

"Ecstacy," was his husky reply.

Very gently, he pressed her back against the wall and put some distance between them so his hands were free to unbutton her shirtwaist. Kate resisted the urge to catch his wrists. Inch by inch, her bodice parted and fell from her breasts, leaving only the muslin of her chemise to shield her from his gaze. Next, he unfastened the waistband of her skirt. Kate closed her eyes when he skimmed his warm hands down her arms to peel away her sleeves.

Cloth rustled and fell to the floor in a whisper. Her heart was pounding so loudly she felt certain he might hear it. A tug on the drawstring at her waist sent her petticoats the way of her skirt. An instant later, she felt her bloomers sliding over her hips and down her legs to lie at her ankles. He knelt on one knee to remove her shoes and stockings. Then he stood and began the task of untying the ribbons of her chemise.

Kate dragged in a searing breath and held it as his fingertips eased the muslin apart. Until now, she had never stood naked in front of a man. With an agonizing slowness, he drew the cloth down her arms, trailing in its path feather-light fingertips that electrified her skin.

"You're beautiful, Katie," he whispered.

Kate exhaled in a rush, longing to press close to him so he couldn't continue to stand there and look his fill. "Zachariah, don't do this to me," she pleaded in a tremulous voice. "I'm not quite ready for this."

"You will be. Just let me get a running start here."

She blinked. "I thought we *had* started."

Chuckling under his breath, he toyed lightly with the tips of her fingers, then drew his touch slowly over the palms of her hands, up to her wrists, then higher to the sensitive bend of her arms. His laughter died as suddenly as it had come to be replaced by an almost worshipful concentration, all fixed on her. The sensations he elicited were so acute, so tantalizing, that Kate could scarcely breathe. He touched her as though he meant to sculpt her, his fingers whispering over the flesh of her arms, tracing the curves and hollows, lingering, then moving on, only to stop and hover again as if to memorize each line. By the time he reached the slope of her shoulders, the V of her collarbone, the tendons along her throat, Kate couldn't form the words to ask him to stop.

When he pressed the pads of his thumbs under her jaw to lift her face, she was shivering from head to toe, and her breathing had become ragged. A dizzying swirl of blacks and grays filled her mind, and she closed her eyes again to keep her balance. Behind her eyelids, the shades spiraled to pinpoints, then blossomed as his silken lips brushed across hers.

"Oh, Katie, you're so sweet. Every time I make love to you, I'm going to be on my knees afterward, thanking God with every breath I take for sending me an angel."

With his lips still a breath away from hers, he trailed

his wondrous touch back down her throat once again to trace the shape of her collarbone. When his fingertips ventured downward from there, Kate caught her breath, her entire being focused on each caress. Slowly, so slowly. Her blood felt as though it were as thick as molasses, slugging through her veins with a resonant thrumming that beat against her eardrums in a hypnotizing staccato.

Dimly, she realized he was playing her as though she were a string instrument, her body his fingerboard, her tautly strung nerve endings the strings from which he plucked his notes. The melody that rose within her made her recall the music her mother had loved and shared with her when she was a child. Attending a symphony, hearing the music, being surrounded by it, feeling it to her bones. That was how Zachariah made her feel, as though she drifted on the notes of a light, graceful allegretto. As surely as she breathed, she knew the moment he touched her throbbing breasts that the pitch would reach a crescendo.

Anticipation stilled her lungs. The room around her fell away, and there was only this man and his clever, masterful hands. Her skin quivered at his every touch. The aureoles of her nipples swelled, the tips pebbled and eager to be kissed by moonlight and the brush of his fingertips. As if he sensed that, he circled those pinpoints of yearning, setting her flesh afire all around them, denying her what he had made her want most.

Kate sobbed at the sheer frustration of it, and mindless with need, she grabbed his wrists to guide his hands. Such wonderful, glorious hands. They cupped her with searing heat, the calloused surface of his palms chafing tender peaks, each electrifying contact stirring another need deep within her that only he could slake.

She leaned against him, forgetting all her preconceived

notions about propriety of behavior. For propriety to exist, there had to be a world, and Zachariah had become her only reality. It felt so wonderfully sweet when he skimmed his large hands along her ribs to test her waist and the softness of her bottom. So wonderfully, wonderfully right when he lifted her against him and settled his hungry mouth over hers.

She moaned. His breath spilled into her in a ragged rush. When he moved in a dizzying circle with her crushed to his chest, she likened it to a swirl in a waltz, the melodious scale to which they danced trilling octave by octave up the cordillera of her spine, each thrum of her heart a harmonious drumbeat.

Need. An urgent need. A longing so poignant, so acute she nearly wept with it. Kate clung to him. When he touched his tongue to her lips, she opened her mouth, willing to engage in yet another new intimacy simply because he had asked it of her.

Only vaguely aware, Kate felt him carrying her toward the bed, felt the bunching of muscle in his chest and arms as he struggled out of his shirt, never once turning her loose. Denim rasped down the front of her legs. Boots thunked. Pocket change clinked and rolled across the floor. And then there was only the silken heat of flesh against flesh. Kate gasped at the shock of it and dug her nails into his shoulders.

"Your wish," he reminded her raggedly. "Melting into me and ceasing to exist, remember? That's what it's all about, Katie girl. Making love, becoming one. No more Kate, no more Zach. Melting into each other, getting lost in one another, until all that's left is the magic."

Kate felt the down mattress pillow around her as he lowered her gently onto it. When she realized where she was, she started to stiffen, but then Zachariah was beside her and everything else moved away. With one sweep of his hand over her body, she was mindless.

"I love you, Katie girl," he whispered. "I want to taste and memorize every inch of you. Every precious inch so I'll have the memories while you're away from me."

With his hands and mouth, he proceeded to do just that. And Kate surrendered all that she was to him. No part of her body was left untouched, unkissed. He traced each line on her palms with his tongue, learned the shape of her ears, the slope of her brows. By the time she felt the silken heat of his mouth at her breast, she was strung so taut with need that she arched toward him like a bow. When he slid a hand up her inner thigh, she raised her hips to meet him.

Zachariah. His name became a one-word lyric to the song within her. She loved him with such intensity she ached with it. When his fingertips found the honeyed center of her, she gasped at the sheer pleasure that rocked through her. When her body sheathed the white-hot shaft of his manhood, the pleasure was intensified by a sense of rightness, and Kate finally understood what loving this man truly meant. Oneness. A sense of completeness. Nothing held back. It was beauty at its most exquisite, so sweet, so perfect that she wept.

Partly buried within her, he froze. "Are you all right, Katie?" he rasped. "You're so small. I don't want to hurt you."

Gazing up at him through tears, Kate ran her hands over the broad shoulders above her, along the rippled arms that braced his weight, over his flat belly. When her shyly seeking fingertips encountered the base of his staff, he gasped and moaned her name.

"Don't," he bit out. "I'm having trouble enough holding back as it is."

Instinctively, Kate curled her legs around his steely

thighs, her invitation as old as womankind. "I don't want you to hold back. I've given myself to you. Now give yourself to me."

"I'm afraid I'll hurt you."

Clutching his shoulders, Kate lifted her hips and took all of him. "I've had a child, Zachariah. You're not going to hurt me, I promise you."

A violent shudder ran through his body. "Are you sure you didn't find her under a cabbage leaf?"

A startled giggle erupted from Kate. At the sound, a smile touched his mouth. He executed a careful stroke, driving gently home. Her little laugh ended with a gasp, and she dug her nails into his skin.

"Are you all right?"

With a muted moan, she arched into him with urgent need. It was answer enough, and he set a cautious rhythm. Darkness and moonlight, limbs intertwined, heat then fire. Kate felt as though she were soaring. The sensation of having him inside her was just as he had once said it should be. Glorious. There was nothing and no one but him. Zachariah, lifting her, pushing her inexorably toward a sweet promise. Ecstacy. With a final series of thrusts, he took her over the edge into a swirling vortex of feeling that went beyond the ecstacy to sheer rapture. Jolt after jolt of it. Rocking through her body, spasm after spasm.

Afterward, Kate was too exhausted to move, and she felt as though her body were buried under a thousand pounds of vibrant, muscular flesh. Zachariah. The heat of him radiated to her bones. His ridged belly convulsed against hers with every ragged breath he drew. The pounding of his heart vibrated through her, muting the patter of hers. She felt a whiskery jaw against her cheek, a padded shoulder under her chin, large hands manacling her wrists, long legs anchoring hers apart. His heavy sex was still buried within her, their skin slick with sweat.

Barnyard beasts. The memory came to Kate from out of nowhere, and she closed her eyes on a surge of joy that brought with it an hysterical urge to giggle. Draping an arm around his neck, she lost the battle and gave a weak laugh.

"What?" He turned his head to nip her ear. "Did I do something funny?"

More wild laughter swelled in Kate's chest. Another giggle escaped from her despite her efforts to hold it back.

"What?" he demanded, his voice taut with stung pride. "Jesus, Kate, you're not supposed to break up laughing after I—"

"My dignity," she managed to squeak. "You promised to keep it intact, if you'll recall, and I'm just wondering where you stashed it. Under the bed, maybe?"

She felt his mouth curve in a grin against her ear. "I slipped it under the pillow," he whispered huskily. "Want it back?"

"Not if you hid your socks under there with it."

He barked with laughter and rolled to one side, carrying her along in the circle of his arm. After draping her naked torso across his, he flashed her a rakish grin. "I did promise to keep my socks on, didn't I? Sorry. I got so wrapped up in preserving your dignity and trying to remember all the rules of decorum, I flat forgot."

Looking into his moon-silvered gaze, Kate lost her smile. With tremulous fingertips, she traced the network of scars along his cheek, then bent her head to kiss them. He clamped a hand over the back of her head.

"If I told you all the things I imagined you might do to me in the marriage bed, you'd be laughing with me," she informed him in a tight voice. "Every time I even thought about it, I wanted to shrivel in mortification. I was terrified you'd go about coupling like a barnyard beast."

He tucked in his chin to meet her gaze. "What in hell did you think I meant to do?"

Her voice went even tighter. "Exactly what you did."

For an instant, he lay perfectly still and silent beneath her, then she felt his chest jerk. A strangled laugh came up his throat. Then another. Kate pressed her face against his neck and laughed with him. Until she was weak. A laughter that cleansed and healed as tears never could. And in that, Kate found the magic she had long since ceased to believe existed, the miracles she no longer dreamed could happen, and the peace that had evaded her for so long. All because this big, powerful, absolutely wonderful man held her close and laughed with her—at the nightmares, at the pain, at the heartache—helping her to bid it all good-bye, forever.

"I love you, Zachariah."

"I'm beginning to believe you truly do," he whispered, and turned his dark head so her lips settled over his. After a long, drugging kiss, he asked, "Would you mind if I left your dignity stashed under the pillow for a while longer, Mrs. McGovern?"

"Just what, exactly, do you have in mind," she queried in a throaty whisper.

Clamping his large hands at her waist, he drew her upward on his chest until her breasts were within easy reach of his lips. A little shocked at her brazenness, Kate braced her arms to accommodate him and moaned softly with pleasure as the velvety wet heat of his mouth closed over her nipple.

After tormenting her for several delicious moments, he drew back. "Well? Make your choice," he said with a devilish grin. "Me or your dignity. You can't have both."

As far as Kate was concerned, that was no choice at all. He made love to her again, slow, languorous loving that was so sweet, so incredibly fantastic, that Kate's mind reeled at the sheer wonder of it.

Afterward, he reared up on an elbow, planted a light kiss on the end of her nose, and whispered, "Thank you, ma'am."

Kate giggled and nipped his lower lip. "That isn't nice."

His teeth gleamed white in another rakish grin. "I don't want to completely abandon all decorum and shock you."

Laughing with him again felt nearly as wonderful as making love with him had. She wiggled a toe along the arch of his foot. He bent his leg to escape and lowered his head to nibble her ribs, which sent her into instant fits of shrill giggles. He muffled her mouth with his hand and continued to tickle her until she lay weak beneath him. Completely sated, completely content, and happier than she could recall ever having been.

One night. It was all they would have for a very long while, and Kate half expected Zachariah to spend it making love to her until dawn. And he did. But, as he had from the beginning, he never did things exactly the way she expected. After physically taking her a third time, he threw on his jeans, helped her into her chemise, and led her in a tiptoed ascent of the stairs. For the remainder of the night, they lay four to a bed with a child and a dog, him holding her tightly to the powerful planes of his body, one hand across her midriff, his other resting lightly on her daughter's silken curls.

Kate snuggled against him and learned yet another new meaning to an old word. Love. It went beyond the joining of two bodies, as wonderful as that part was. It meant sharing and caring. It meant embracing a child together. It meant whispers in the darkness, and smiles that had no meaning yet meant the world. It was knowing another's deepest feelings without being told. It meant making sacrifices simply to please. Love, Zachariah, the two were synonymous, and over the course of that one night, he taught her that lesson well.

By dawn, Kate felt filled. As though she had lived and loved for a lifetime. No matter what the day brought, she would never feel cheated. One night with Zachariah. It was enough. She wanted more, of course, but if fate said otherwise, the beauty of the simple gifts he had given her would last her.

When she rose to face the day, Kate stood at the window to savor the dawn's first light, knowing that she might next see it through the bars of a cell window—if she was lucky. If she wasn't and her cell had no window, she might never see it again until she was released. Unless, God forbid, she was found guilty of Joseph's murder. Then she might see it next from a scaffold, for executions were usually meted out as the sun came up.

The thought saddened Kate, but it didn't frighten her. Since giving birth to Miranda, the meaning of her existence had funneled down to one thing, protecting her child into adulthood. Now that had been accomplished. If it was God's will that her life be forfeited for what she had done, then so be it. She could give herself up to an early end knowing her life had had meaning and that her child would have everything any little girl could want.

Kate wasn't surprised when she felt a pair of strong arms encircle her waist from behind to draw her against a warm, well-padded chest. A smile touched her mouth because to share the dawn with Zachariah made their one night together absolutely and perfectly complete.

"A penny for them," he whispered next to her ear.

"I was just thinking if I never get to come back home that this night has been so wonderful, I won't have any regrets."

His embrace tightened. "Don't think that way, Katie. You'll come home, if for no other reason than I don't think I can live without you."

"You'll have no choice. Because I'm leaving behind my reason for living. It's a sacred trust."

He nuzzled her neck. "I'm not worried. I lay odds they throw the case out of court. You'll come home. And I'll spend the next fifty years preserving your dignity under your pillow while I shock you from the tips of your pink little toes right up to your blushing hairline when I make love to you."

Kate grinned. "After last night, I'm well past being shocked."

"That's what you think," he whispered huskily.

Kate stirred to look over her shoulder into his twinkling hazel eyes. The knowing laughter she read there made her skin tingle. "You mean you left something out?"

He bent his head and whispered to her of the things she hadn't yet experienced, his voice so thick with passion that her own rose in a hot tide within her.

"You wouldn't!" she whispered.

"I will," he promised with a chuckle.

Kate's mind filled with shocking images, and she felt a blush rising up her neck. "I would never let you. That's scandalous."

"Delicious."

The blush turned scalding and flooded into her face. "I would never participate in something so—so base."

"Heavensent," he corrected.

"I don't want to talk about this."

"You're right. I'd rather just do it. Come downstairs with me before Mandy wakes up. We'll lock the sickroom door, and I'll give you something to remember me by." He flicked the tip of his tongue against her nape, sending chills the length of her body. "Just like that, Katie girl. You'll think you've died and gone straight to heaven. I swear it."

Her body felt heavy, her blood hot and thick. She settled back against him, seduced by the sultry promises he whispered in her ear, unable to resist the magnetism of him. "I'll think I've died of humiliation, that's what."

"Never with me. Nothing I do to you will ever bring anything but beautiful feelings, sweetheart, because what's between us is blessed."

"No. Maybe one day."

He chuckled and bent to scoop her into his arms. "No woman should face a murder charge without that experience under her belt."

"Zachariah!" she squeaked. "I'm not going to let you do something so—"

He cut her off with a kiss that made her senses spin, a long, hypnotizing kiss that robbed her of everything, including her certainty that what he had suggested was shameful. Out the door, down the stairs. He stubbed his toe and cursed. Kate giggled and tried to pull down her chemise. He carried her into the sickroom, locked the door, proceeded toward the bed.

As he lowered her onto the mattress, he pinioned her with a gaze that gleamed with equal parts tenderness and determination, and Kate knew she was lost.

"I—I really can't contemplate doing something so improper," she tried one last time.

He stretched out beside her and ran a heavy, thorough hand up her body, setting her skin afire. Bending his head to hers, he nibbled gently at her earlobes, her throat, her mouth. "I swear, I'll do it proper. And you won't be able to think, Katie girl, let alone contemplate."

As it turned out, he was right in more ways than one. His technique was perfect. She didn't have a thought in her head. And before he was finished with her, she felt as though she had indeed died and gone straight to heaven.

22

Kate remembered that one little taste of heaven for the remainder of the day. It got her through her last breakfast with her daughter, through the wagon ride to town, through the humiliating experience of going to the county jail and allowing herself to be locked inside a cell. It got her through that first endless day of imprisonment and that first lonely night of darkness and shadows, uncertainty her only bedmate. But most importantly, it helped her survive the memory of telling Miranda good-bye.

"I love you, Ma."

The words echoed in Kate's mind all night long. A hundred times she recalled how her daughter had felt in her arms, so small and helpless, so trusting and sweet. A hundred times she remembered the smell of her hair, the silken brush of her lips against her cheek, the clinging of her hands as Kate pried them away so she could leave.

I'll guard her with my life, Katie. Zachariah's promise, Kate's only comfort. No matter what fate befell her, Miranda would be safe.

Morning came. There were times during that first night

when Kate doubted it would. But despite the fact that her world was upended, daylight followed darkness, and the town awoke to go about its business. The delicious smells of perking coffee and frying bacon wafted from the houses perched on the nearby hillside. Occasionally she heard the hinges of a door creak. Dogs barked to herald the new day. Roosters late in rising crowed halfheartedly at the sunlight. The deputy, a lanky, sandy-haired fellow named Russell, brought Kate her breakfast of eggs, toast, blackberries, and milk.

The outside window of Kate's cell looked onto an empty yard. After forcing down as much of her meal as she could, she stood with her fists knotted around the bars, her face pressed to an opening between them. She breathed deeply of the fresh air, determined not to think about the bare gray walls that closed in around her. The reality of it made her panicky and breathless, knowing she was locked in, that she wasn't free to leave, that her world had been condensed to nothing but a cot, a small table, and a chamber pot. Her clothing felt suddenly tight, and the friction of the cloth against her skin raised goose flesh. She couldn't leave here. If a fire broke out, her fate depended upon someone else's remembering to release her. She was trapped.

Don't dwell on it, she commanded herself. A fire wasn't likely to break out. It was foolish to conjure horrible images and be frightened of what might never occur.

She could see a horse-drawn buggy parked behind the courthouse next door. Scattered houses dotted the hillside behind the jailhouse, most painted pristine white with matching picket fences bordering the yards. When she listened closely, she could hear voices coming from the street out front, and she imagined ladies pausing to chat on the sidewalks as they went from store to store to do their shopping. In the distance, she saw a woman out hanging laundry on her line. Kate wished she were at home doing wash. Doing anything.

She spent the morning sitting on her cot, back rigid, hands folded in her lap, ears strained to catch the voices that filtered in to her from the sheriff's adjoining office. Zachariah had promised to see the judge first thing this morning about hurrying lawful procedure. Afterward, he was supposed to come by the jail to let her know how things had gone. Kate waited, and she waited. Every minute seemed a year long. Her only solace came from the knowledge that Zachariah had never broken a promise to her yet. He would come.

The noon meal came and went. Kate couldn't eat. One o'clock rolled around. She knew because she asked the time whenever she glimpsed the sheriff or deputy through the little barred window of the cell block door. Two o'clock. Three. Dusk finally fell. And Zachariah still hadn't come. Kate didn't touch her evening meal. After it was taken away, she lay in the waning light, dreading the darkness, wondering where Zachariah was and why he had failed to visit her as he had promised.

A dozen possibilities ricocheted through her mind, all of them horrible, for only something catastrophic would keep him from coming, she knew. He had been hurt. Miranda was sick. The house had burned down. Ryan had caused trouble. The list seemed endless, and each item on it made Kate tremble with dread.

Darkness fell. The moon came up. And Kate wept. She knew it was weak to lose her grip so completely, but all the things in her life that had given her strength had been stripped from her. She wept until her eyes burned dry, until it felt as if her lids were stuck open, until her throat felt raw, until her head pounded with pain. And then she just lay there on her cot in a huddle of misery, still tortured with worry.

"Katie?"

The husky whisper sent a shock of joy through Kate, and she jackknifed to a sitting position to peer into the shadows.

"Katie, love. Over here."

Kate glanced up and saw a broad-shouldered silhouette at the outside window of her cell. She threw herself from the bed. "Zachariah! Oh, Zachariah, where have you been?"

She grabbed the bars, dug a toe into the wall, and hoisted herself up to meet his urgent, hungry mouth with her own. He shoved his arms between the bars until they wedged at the biceps. His hands clutched almost frantically at her. His kiss told her how much he loved her. Kate sobbed with relief and wanted to melt through the wall so she could feel the strength of his body pressed against her own.

"Miranda?"

"She's fine," he said between frenzied kisses.

"You?"

"I came as soon as I could." He pressed light lips to her swollen eyelids. "Oh, honey, you've been crying. Are you all right?"

"I am now. I was so worried, Zachariah. You said you'd come this morning."

"Everything took longer than I thought." He moved his feet, and she heard paper rustle. "And then I went shopping for some things to bring you. By the time I got done with that, I had to go back home to eat dinner with Mandy and tuck her into bed. I didn't think it'd be good for her to be without either one of us tonight. She's more upset than she's letting on. It took five stories to get her to sleep."

Kate laughed with relief. "You knew five, I hope?"

"Hell, no. I made them up. With her help. She's a

fussy little minx when it comes to her stories. If I said a gray kitten, it had to be black with spots in designated places, which seemed to take hours for her to choose. I was ready to wring her neck by the time she drifted off."

Kate pressed her forehead against the bars and closed her eyes, serenity slowly eating away the panic, her senses lulled by the sound of his voice. "Did you finally get the spots right?"

Curling a hand over her nape, he pressed his mouth to her cheek. "Exactly right. The entire time knowing you were probably wild with worry. I'm sorry, Katie love. Fatherhood is a trial sometimes. My only consolation was that I knew you'd want me right where I was, choosing kitty spots."

Kate giggled. "You're here now. That's all that matters."

"I'd like to be in there."

Kate seconded that, but only in her thoughts. Zachariah had burdens aplenty without her woes being added to the list. "Any news?"

"It goes before the grand jury next Monday. That's the quickest. Notices have to be sent out, a jury selected."

Six endless days. Kate swallowed down a protest and forced herself to look on the bright side. He could easily have said six weeks or six months. Practically speaking, he had worked a miracle by getting things rolling so quickly. "So soon? Oh, Zachariah, how on earth did you convince him of that?"

"I lied and said you were pregnant."

"What?"

He pushed one arm farther between the bars and curled it around her. "You could be. It's not that big a lie, Katie. Then I went into a big explanation about Mandy and how difficult this was for her. By the time I got done with him, the poor bastard was as anxious to get you out of here as I am. For some reason, he was reluctant to set bail, but he did recommend a defense lawyer, and I've got him on retainer."

Kate sensed there was something he had left unsaid, and the worried look in his eyes bore that out. She knew from bitter past experience how successful Joseph had been in swaying public opinion against her. *Not quite right,* people whispered behind cupped hands. *Unpredictable when those spells come over her.* It made her feel sick to think Zachariah might have been told all those horrible lies. It made her feel even sicker to think she might be kept in jail because of the fear of her that Joseph had planted in people's minds.

A danger to Miranda and possibly to others? If that was why Zachariah looked so stricken, if that was why the judge seemed reluctant to set bail, Kate couldn't deal with it. Not right now.

"How much did retaining a lawyer cost?" Kate hadn't thought of the expense until now but she was eager for anything that might distract her. "Was it dreadful?"

"How much doesn't matter. Jesus, Kate, I'd sell my place to get you out of here. My place *and* yours. Not that I'll have to. I've got savings."

"I don't want you to squander it all on me!"

"What else should I spend it on? You're a good investment."

"And then you went shopping?" she scolded. "What on earth was so important that you'd go spend more money? Zachariah, you must have a care. You've already spent a small fortune on that catalog order. There's nothing I need so desperately that you must buy it now."

"Will you let me be the judge of—" He broke off and tugged on his arm. "Son of a bitch! I'm stuck."

Kate tried to help him dislodge his arm. "Oh, my, Zachariah, you *are* stuck." She giggled again, vaguely aware that there was a note of hysteria in the laughter. "Now I've got you where I want you."

He curled the imprisoned arm back around her. "I don't give a tinker's damn. This is where I want to be anyway." And with that, he kissed her, a long, soul-searching kiss that made Kate forget where she was. "I love you, Katie," he whispered as their mouths parted. "Do you have any idea how much?"

Shakily she replied, "I'm beginning to get an inkling."

He went back to trying to dislodge his arm. Finally, with a mighty heave, he broke free, nearly losing his balance in the process. Then he began shoving packages to her through the bars.

"What on earth *is* all this?"

"Christmas in July. Decent clothing. Books. Lots of books because I wasn't sure what you'd like to read. And sewing stuff galore so you won't go mad in here. And a little something special to remember me by when you get to feeling lonesome."

Despite her concerns about his spending money too freely, Kate couldn't squelch a wave of curiosity. "Something special? What, Zachariah?"

"Wait until daylight and see. It's a surprise. Just be sure to read the inscription."

Kate tugged the last package through the bars. Then she curled her hands over his where they gripped the steel. "I wish you could stay."

"If wishes were rainbows, Katie girl, I'd do just that. But there's another little lady in my life, and she comes first."

Tears filled Kate's eyes, and she nodded, unable to speak. She wouldn't have had him feel any other way.

"She might wake up," he said hoarsely. "I need to be there in case she does."

Kate kissed his calloused knuckles. "I can almost see the two of you all cuddled up together."

"Three. Don't forget Nosy."

She smiled and caressed her cheek on the back of his hand, then breathed deeply of the scents that clung there, loving every one. Horses, and leather, hay, and earth. A man as elemental as the soil he cultivated. She loved every rugged inch of him.

"We'll all three miss you," he whispered. "The bed'll feel downright empty."

"My place?"

"I figured that was best. I moved Ching Lee over. I swear, he's got a hundred pots, and he won't cook without every single one at his disposal. I carted a wagonload of stuff to your place. After all that, he discovered he didn't have a dutch oven. I had to make a trip back to my house to get the damned thing. But now he's all set up, and Marcus is sleeping in the sickroom, so he's there to take care of Mandy until I get back."

"It would have been simpler to take Mandy to your place."

"She's going through changes aplenty without adding to them. It'll be jarring enough for her to hear Ching Lee yelling, and to make matters more hair-raising, he hammers on a pot while he's at it. I told him I'd castrate him if he scared Mandy with his pot banging, but he's so set in his ways, I might as well talk to a wall."

"She won't be frightened if she's with you."

"You haven't heard him calling us to breakfast."

Kate burst out laughing. "Oh, Zachariah, I do love you. Somehow, you can always make me smile, and tonight, that's an accomplishment."

"That's my goal in life, Katie girl, to make you smile."

With that promise to bolster her, he pressed a fleeting kiss to her mouth and disappeared into the darkness. For a long while after, Kate clung to the bars and gazed at the moon. Oddly enough, she no longer felt so alone.

At dawn, Kate opened the packages Zachariah had left with her. Two changes of clothing, from the skin out. She could only smile at the colors of the gowns, one a vivid blue, the other a brilliant russet, both embellished with lace and ruffles. The petticoats even had flounces of lace. And bright red garters? Kate blushed when she saw those. When she opened the next box, her expression turned almost reverent. New shoes. Not high-top boots like she'd always worn, but shoes—beautiful patent leather, low-cut opera pumps. In the next box, she found a vial of rose cologne, a bar of scented soap, a hand mirror and brush, a toothbrush, a tin of saleratus, and a packet of hairpins. As far as the necessities went, he had thought of everything.

When Kate turned her attention to the luxury items, tears of happiness filled her eyes. Books, he'd said? He'd bought her a blooming library. Three volumes of poetry, two recipe books. Her hand froze over the next. *The Scandalous Mistress Novak.*

Fascinated, she flipped it open and began to leaf through. It wasn't long before she came to a section that lived up to the book's title. Her eyes widened, and she snapped the cover closed. Heat flared to her cheeks. Zachariah McGovern was a caution, and that was a fact. She inched the book open again and read a few more lines. Then a few more. Absorbed, she scooted back to brace her shoulders against the wall. Mistress Novak had indeed been scandalous!

Kate's eyes widened even more as she read on. With tense fingers, she turned the page only to be distracted from the story by a neatly folded slip of parchment that had been placed between the pages. She dislodged it from the crease, unfolded it and stared at the distinctly masculine scrawl. *Boo!* it said. Nothing more. Just boo? Her mouth tugged at the corners. Then she smothered a laugh. It was no use. Hysterical giggles erupted. She had only seen Zachariah's handwriting once, and that had been on their wedding day, but she knew as surely as she breathed that he had written the note, such as it was. The one word was eloquence in itself. She could almost hear him saying, "I caught you, Katie girl! Shame on you!"

Convinced that this was the inscription he had mentioned, Kate tucked it away inside her bodice, treasuring it far more than she might have a laboriously composed love poem. *Boo!* He had known very well which part of the book she'd leaf to first, and even away from her, he was teasing her. Kate wanted to draw up her knees and continue to read, but other packages beckoned.

She set herself to the task of opening them. More books. Embroidery cloth, hoops, and threads in a rainbow of colors. The last and smallest package bore the local jeweler's logo on the wrapping. With trembling fingers, Kate tore away the paper and opened the hinged box to gaze with aching eyes at a beautiful gold locket etched with roses. As she lifted it from the silk lining, her fingertips felt engraving on its back, and she turned it over to read, "Forever, my love, Zachariah." Below it, the year 1890 had been inscribed. Kate closed her hand around it and pressed her knuckles to her mouth. She sat like that for a long while before she returned the locket to its case.

* * *

Time passed in an endless, uneventful blur for Kate. Sometimes she feared she might go insane, and at other times she became convinced she already had. Day into night, night into day. For longer than she could remember, she had spent every waking minute of her days working. Now she sat. Or she paced. When she lay down at night, sleep refused to come.

Those black, lonely hours of darkness that came right before dawn were the worst. It was then that her fears came calling, some irrational, some all too real. It was then that she faced the chilling possibility that she might remain locked in a cell for the rest of her life.

Monday came, at last. And Kate's most chilling fears became a reality that had to be faced when she was indicted for murder. In a daze, she moved through that day, speaking, listening, but feeling as though she had been dropped into a foreign country where everyone was babbling, including her. Too many questions in the minds of the jurors were unanswered, her attorney explained.

The trial was finally set for Tuesday, August 26th, nearly a month away. Kate's attorney, Charles Defler, immediately petitioned for bail, but the request was denied. When Zachariah brought Kate that news, she listened in bewildered silence.

When he finished speaking, she whispered, "But why? It's not as if I'm a danger to anyone or anything."

She noticed that he avoided looking directly into her eyes, that he couldn't seem to keep his hands still. When he gave a low curse and pushed up from the chair, Kate's heart constricted with fear.

"Zachariah?" she said shakily. "You're frightening me."

He took a steadying breath, paced to the wall, then turned to look at her. Gazing up at him, she saw that the flesh and muscles in his face were drawn taut over bone, that his mouth had thinned to a hard, bitter line.

"I don't mean to scare you, honey. I'm just upset, that's all." Making a fist, he slugged his palm. The sound made her jump. "It's Joseph again, damn him to eternal hell."

Kate pressed a hand to her throat. "Joseph? I—I don't understand."

"The stories he told about you," he came back harshly. "About your being unbalanced? While you've been in here, old gossip has been rekindled, with Ryan Blakely stoking the blaze." He threw up his hands. "If you tried to harm your daughter in the past and ended up killing your husband, you might be a danger to someone else. 'Bail denied.'"

Kate closed her eyes and strove to keep a grip on her self-control. Zachariah was already upset; if she went to pieces, it would only make this more difficult for him.

In a hoarse voice that shook with anger, he said, "I swear to God, Katie, if they convict you, I'll break you out of here. We'll leave the country."

Kate stiffened her spine. "Don't talk that way, Zachariah. You can't do something so foolish."

"Foolish?" he rasped. "My God, you're my wife. I won't let them do this to you. I'll be damned if I will."

Kate struggled to swallow. When she felt certain her voice wouldn't quiver, she said, "I entrusted my child into your care. I'm counting on you to raise her. You can't do that if you're arrested and thrown into prison."

The silence that followed told Kate she had struck a chord. When she looked up into his eyes, the pain she read there nearly undid her.

"We must pray, Zachariah. For a fair and just decision. Somehow, we'll get through this, and laugh about it one day."

Somehow, we'll get through this. Brave words. Sometimes Kate doubted her ability to carry through on them. But just when she thought she couldn't bear another day of endless nothingness, she dug down within herself and found enough strength to face another. And another.

And the time passed, slowly, with relentless sameness, carrying her inexorably toward the day of her trial.

23

The morning of the trial was uncomfortably warm, and the courtroom felt stuffy, whether from the insufferable heat or from so many bodies being packed into inadequate space, Kate couldn't be sure. She only knew she felt as if she might suffocate while she waited for the procedure to get underway.

It seemed that everyone in town had turned out for the event, which made her feel like a bug on display. She tried her best to be charitable. After all, it wasn't every day a woman was charged with murdering her husband, especially not in a small town like Roseburg.

Zachariah was seated with Marcus several rows behind her. She wished she could turn and look at him, just once, but with so many eyes riveted on her, searching to find fault, judging her, she felt the less attention she called to herself and her new husband, the better.

She drew comfort from touching the locket at her throat, remembering the warmth of Zachariah's hands as he had draped the delicate chain around her neck and fumbled with the tiny catch at her nape. Zachariah. She soothed herself with memories of him, so few, but all the sweeter now because it seemed like a lifetime since she had been home. Flipping peas. Giggling softly in the dead of night. Making love in a moonbeam.

When the judge finally took the bench and convened the courtroom with three raps of his gavel, Kate flinched with every sharp report. Nervous sweat filmed her brow. The lawyer Zachariah hired had spent all last evening with her explaining what to expect, but she had little recollection of what he said. All of this seemed so foreign to her, so ridiculously formal. She wanted to scream that this was her life on the line. But she remained silent, her spine rigidly straight, her hands knotted in her skirt.

When the prosecuting attorney gave his presentation, Kate couldn't separate the words, couldn't make sense of what he said. Then Charles Defler gave his opening statement. *Family way . . . pain and suffering . . . a four-year-old child to consider . . . innocent victims.* Kate heard, but didn't hear. Because none of this was real. When Defler returned to the defendant's table, he gave her arm a comforting squeeze.

"Most of the jurors have children. I fought like hell for that, and it will definitely go in your favor," he whispered with unmistakable satisfaction. "We have a sympathetic ear."

The fathers of children usually had wives, which meant they were husbands. Kate wasn't so sure that weighed in her favor. *A right to trial by a jury of one's peers?* She couldn't readily recall where she had heard that, but realistically speaking that inalienable right clearly applied only to white males, not to those of other races, nor to women. She wanted to see housewives in the jury box—women who might understand what Joseph had put her and her daughter through.

"You're doing wonderfully. Just keep it up," Defler whispered.

Kate clenched her hands. She wasn't doing anything but sitting here, feeling scared to death. She fixed her gaze on the judge. Prayers whispered in her mind, bits and pieces, all disjointed. She gulped for breath, feeling faint.

The coroner was called as a witness. There was a roaring sound in Kate's ears that drowned out everything he said. How could anything be worse than this? Kate wondered wildly. Her head felt fuzzy, and beneath the fuzziness was a horrible swimming sensation. Her ears echoed. Nausea grabbed her middle and wouldn't let go. She slid her hands to grasp the seat of her chair.

"You're supposed to go up!" Defler whispered. "Mrs. McGovern? Mrs. McGovern, you have to take the stand."

Kate blinked and tried to focus on the swirl of polished oak before her. The stand? It looked a hundred miles away. A blurred figure came toward her from the county clerk's table. A gentle hand closed on her arm and helped her to rise. Kate stuck out one foot, managed to place her other in front of it. Walking, one step at a time, through a cloud of cotton. Placing her hand on a Bible. Swearing to tell the truth, the whole truth, and nothing but the truth. Walking up some steps.

Was this what it would be like to climb a scaffold? Kate's toe caught and she pitched forward, only to be saved from falling by a steadying hand. She sank weakly onto hardness, felt the arms of the chair bump against her elbows. Faces, everywhere faces. Accusing eyes. *Murderess!* they seemed to scream at her.

She looked from one relentless and grim countenance to another, panic welling within her. The men in the jury looked the most judgmental, and her worst fears were realized. Many of them might believe her to be exactly what Joseph had always claimed, an unbalanced and uncontrollable wife given to violent behavior. In their minds, if she were allowed to go unpunished, her case might set a precedent and encourage other wives to engage in outrageous conduct.

Kate wanted to bolt from the courtroom. She should never have come forward. Never! She should have left Joseph buried in the rose garden and taken her chances. At least then she might have had a chance.

In her frantic search for just one kindly face, Kate's gaze collided with hazel eyes. She looked into them, became lost in them, embraced by them. Aching hazel eyes. Windswept dark hair. A face that had been chiseled on her heart. She took a deep breath. The upside-down courtroom righted itself. She gripped the arms of the chair. Hazel eyes. She riveted all her concentration on them. *Jesus H. Christ, don't faint!* they seemed to say. *It'll be all right, Katie girl.*

Suddenly Kate believed it really would.

You're right up there with heroes and fairies and mystical unicorns. Can you live up to that, Mr. McGovern? Kate now knew that the answer to that question was and had always been yes. As long as she could look into his tender gaze, she'd be all right.

She lifted her chin. A glow came into his eyes, and she realized he was proud of her. Actually proud of her. For the life of her, she couldn't think why. She was shaking like a leaf, on the verge of collapse, about to keel over in a dead faint. And he was proud of her? She was the world's biggest coward. Couldn't he see that?

His lips tipped in a lopsided grin. Then he mouthed the words, "Give them hell, Katie girl."

Kate read the message and nearly giggled, albeit hysterically. Only Zachariah would dare to be so irreverent in a courtroom. She glanced nervously at the judge, afraid he might have seen, but his concerned attention was fixed only on her.

The state's attorney, Roger Wilcox, approached the witness stand, his expression one of concern. "Are you all right, Mrs. McGovern? You're looking a little pale."

Kate met his gaze and realized his concern was all pretense. This was a stage, the jurors their audience. He wanted to establish himself as a kindly and caring inquisitor when all he really meant to do was draw blood.

Kate moistened her lips. The truth, the whole truth. If she stuck with that, he couldn't trip her up. "I—I'm fine. Sort of fine. N-Nervous, very nervous."

"That's completely understandable, Mrs. McGovern. I must say you've shown a great deal of courage coming forward as you have. As reluctant as I am to admit it, I'm not at all certain I would have been as brave."

Kate struggled to swallow. "I—I'm not feeling very brave right at the m-moment. I'm so terrified, in fact, that if my legs would hold me up, I th-think I'd skedaddle out of here."

Several chuckles erupted from the spectator area, and Kate was relieved to hear that some of them were distinctly male. She relaxed a bit. Clearly, not every man in the room saw her as a threat. The prosecutor's gray eyes took on a polished hardness, belying his good-natured smile.

The judge's expression softened, however, and Kate had the feeling he wanted to give her a fatherly pat. More of her fear fell away.

"Are you up to answering a few questions?" Wilcox asked. "I understand your condition is delicate."

Kate met his gaze. Though she hadn't burdened Zachariah with the news as yet, his outrageous lie hadn't turned out to be a lie after all. She had missed her monthly curse, and since she had always been regular, no matter how much stress she was under, Kate felt certain that meant she was pregnant. "Yes," she echoed, "delicate."

The attorney turned toward the spectator area and, raising his voice a bit, said, "I have to commend Mr. McGovern. An amazing bit of work, that." He walked over to his table and leafed through some papers. "When were you married? Ah, yes, a month and a half ago."

"Nearly two months if you count the weeks," Kate came back.

She felt heat rising to her face. The implication was that she might have lain with Zachariah before their marriage. When Wilcox turned around to face her, the polished hardness in his eyes had become a glint of satisfaction. His first shot had been a bull's-eye.

"You are, I take it, feeling well enough to answer a few questions, though?" he repeated.

Kate licked her lips. "I—I can certainly t-try."

"I think the first and most obvious one—at least in my mind—is what led you to come forward? As I understand it from the sheriff, your late husband's body was safely concealed. He was believed to have drowned. If you had left things as they were, you wouldn't be going through this today. So, why? What made you come see the sheriff?"

Kate moistened her lips again, longing for a drink, afraid to ask for one. "Honestly?"

Another wave of laughter burst from the spectators. The judge's mouth twitched. "Mrs. McGovern, that's the general aim here," he clarified. "Nothing but the truth."

Kate felt another wave of heat rise up her neck, and she wanted to kick herself. Of all the stupid things to have said. She pressed a hand over her abdomen, feeling as if she might be sick. "It's just that my reasons are going to sound rather silly," she rushed to explain. "Fabricated reasons would probably sound more sensible."

The quirks at the corners of the judge's mouth turned into a smile. "You don't have to sound sensible, Mrs. McGovern. Just tell the truth," he inserted.

His expression conveyed more eloquently than words that women, feeble-minded creatures that they were, couldn't be expected to make good sense. Kate took a shaky breath. The truth? As much as the judge's attitude rankled, her mind drew a horrible blank. The truth, she thought frantically. She'd had her reasons; she knew she had. And at the time, they had seemed like very good reasons. But for the life of her, she couldn't remember them now.

"I—I think it would be simplest to explain it to you as I did—my daughter," Kate told the prosecutor shakily. "It's rather like in a story, if you don't mind my making the comparison. Until everything is satisfactorily concluded, one can never say 'the end,' and I felt very strongly that my daughter and I deserved a happy ever after. Until I did the right thing, that bad part of our life would never be over."

A deathly silence fell over the room. Kate's heart felt as though it stopped beating. But, of course, she knew it hadn't. If and when she drew her last breath, it wouldn't happen on the witness stand. She could almost feel the noose tightening around her throat.

Lifting her hands, she made another appeal. "I couldn't live the rest of my life with that horrible a secret. And I didn't want my daughter to, either. She has suffered enough."

The attorney stepped to his table and jotted something down. Then, tapping his pen on the paper, he brought his gaze back to her. "I think your reason makes perfect sense, and very eloquently put, I might add." He pursed his lips and regarded her for a long moment. "Now for my second question, and this time, as difficult as it may be, I'd like you to answer it with a yes or no. Do you regret Joseph Blakely's death?"

Now Kate felt absolutely certain her heart had stopped. "It isn't very fair to put it to me like that. So much played into it. Even Judas had regrets."

More laughter erupted. With a chilling sense of dismay, Kate knew she was sounding as feebleminded and idiotic as the judge thought her to be. The attorney's gaze sharpened on hers. "Being absolutely fair is the aim of this court, Mrs. McGovern. Please answer the question, yes or no. Do you regret killing your husband?"

"Objection!" Defler yelled. "Your Honor, that's a deliberate attempt to lead the witness!"

The judge rapped with his gavel. "Sustained." He leveled a gaze on Wilcox. "Rephrase the question, please."

Wilcox smiled. "Certainly. Mrs. McGovern, do you regret your late husband's passing? Yes or no."

Kate squeezed her eyes closed. The truth, and nothing but the truth. "No," she said faintly.

"I'm sorry. I didn't catch that."

"No!" she repeated more loudly.

The silence gnawed at her. Slowly, Kate opened her eyes.

"Thank you for that," the attorney said softly. "Your answer tells me two things, that you've come forward prepared to tell the absolute truth and that you're equally prepared to accept the consequences, no matter how grim."

He jotted another note. Then he glanced back up at her. "Why don't you regret his death?"

"Because he hurt my child," Kate said. "Again and again and again!" Tears blinded her, and her voice turned shrill. "I tried to run away with her, but he always caught us and brought us home. I can't be sorry that he can't hurt her anymore. On another level, I know my feelings of relief that he's gone are very wrong, but—" Kate shrugged. "She's safe from him, and I can't get beyond that."

The attorney repositioned the paper he was writing on and cleared his throat. "I realize that you claim his death was accidental." He pushed erect and strolled toward her, his manner so kindly that Kate wanted to slap him. "But I'm curious. Did you ever consider deliberately killing him?"

She dug her nails into her hands. In all her wildest imaginings, she had never dreamed that the prosecutor's questions might be this vicious. An honest answer might prove fatal. Her lawyer jumped up. "Objection, Your Honor! If people could be tried for their thoughts, we'd all hang. That question is completely out of line."

The judge leveled a relentless glare at Kate's attorney. "Objection overruled. To establish intent, this question is completely acceptable." Returning his gaze to Kate, he said, "Please answer the question, Mrs. McGovern. Did you or did you not ever consider deliberately killing your late husband?"

"I refuse to let my client answer that question on the grounds that her reply may incriminate her!" the lawyer cried.

Kate threw a frantic glance at Zachariah. His eyes held hers for a long, endless moment, and during that moment, she remembered all her many reasons for coming here. Namely, she wanted her life back, and to accomplish that, she had to put the past completely behind her. No more secrets. No more lies. No more being haunted by memories. Unless she answered the questions, honestly and without holding back, she would never be entirely free of her past. Never.

Kate fixed her gaze on the judge. It had been so long since she had trusted in the goodness of human nature, five years that had seemed like an entire lifetime. She could stay caught in that trap for the rest of her life.

Turning toward her attorney, Kate said, "It's all right, Mr. Defler. I have nothing to hide. If I did, I never would have come forward." Then to the prosecutor, she said, "The answer to your question is yes, I considered killing Joseph Blakely at least a dozen times and probably in every conceivable way you can imagine."

A gasp rose from the spectator seating area. The prosecutor looked taken aback for a moment. He clearly hadn't counted on that being her answer. As his gaze rested on hers, Kate thought she saw a spark of sympathy in those gray depths. "Can you give me one instance?"

"Objection!" Defler roared. "Don't answer that question, Mrs. McGovern."

Kate ignored him. "Once I nearly stabbed him with my sewing scissors. If he hadn't turned at the last second, I would have."

Charles Defler threw up his hands in a theatrical gesture of defeat and returned to his seat.

Wilcox pursed his lips and clasped his hands behind his back. "On the night of Joseph Blakely's death, when you walked up behind him with that piece of firewood, did he turn around?"

Kate stared at him, knowing he had set the trap and that she was about to step in it. She squared her shoulders. This was a courtroom. The aim here was to see that justice prevailed. She had to believe that. "No, he didn't turn around."

"Then what prevented you from hitting him on the head, Mrs. McGovern? According to your deposition, he was torturing your child. She was screaming. You had tried, unsuccessfully, to drag him off of her. At that last second, as you lifted that piece of firewood, you must have considered killing him!"

"I just wanted to make him stop!"

"Permanently?" he fired back.

"Yes, permanently! Of course, permanently."

"No more questions," Wilcox snapped. "The prosecution reserves the right to recall the witness."

Thinking she was finished, Kate pushed to her feet, only to be told to sit back down. Charles Defler rose and walked toward her, clearly agitated. Coming to a stop before the witness stand, he raked a hand through his hair.

"How are you doing, Mrs. McGovern? Would you care for some water?"

Kate nodded and gratefully accepted the glass that was handed to her by a court clerk.

Defler paced, then turned. "You've admitted to nearly stabbing your husband with your sewing scissors. Was he abusing your child when you made that attempt?" he asked gently.

Kate's lips felt glued to the glass. She nearly choked as she swallowed the mouthful of water. Lowering the tumbler to her lap, she replied, "Yes."

"What was he doing to her, Mrs. McGovern?"

She wrapped her hands around the glass. "He was sh-shoving the tip of a knife under her fingernail."

Defler resumed his pacing and directed his footsteps toward the jury box. Scanning the jurors' faces, he said, "A knife under her fingernail? A brutal, unthinkable punishment, surely, but not fatal. Some might wonder why you felt compelled to stab the man. Can you explain that to us?"

The ensuing silence seemed deafening. Once again,

Kate scanned the spectators' faces, looked into their eyes, read their emotions. This time instead of seeing accusation reflected there, she saw shock and revulsion and pity. These people hadn't turned their backs on her; they simply hadn't realized. Kate could forgive them that. Joseph had been a clever man who had hidden his true nature under a cloak of respectability, charming when he chose to be and always treacherously convincing, able to shift moods with honeyed ease as only the truly mad can. These people had been hoodwinked, just as her uncle Jed had been, just as she had been until Joseph revealed his true character to her.

Kate took a deep breath, determined to get through this. Remembering was never easy. To put those memories into words was nigh unto impossible. "She was sc-screaming for me to make him stop, but h-he wouldn't. Nothing I s-said, nothing I did—he wouldn't stop—and so I tried to stab him."

Kate once again panned the courtroom, but now no one seemed able to meet her gaze. Except one man. She looked into his hazel eyes and yearned to feel his arms around her.

Another awful silence fell over the courtroom, broken only by occasional coughs and the sounds of people fidgeting in their seats.

"What had your daughter done to provoke your husband into meting out that sort of punishment, Mrs. McGovern?"

Kate passed a hand over her eyes. "She, um . . . She had taken a piece of bread without first asking his permission. We were late having lunch that day, and she was hungry, and I—" A break in Kate's voice forced her to pause and swallow. Afraid she might spill the water, she set the glass aside on the railing. "I told her she could have a bit of bread to tide her over. When Joseph saw her with it, he assumed she had snitched it, and before I could tell him otherwise, he was in a high temper. Once he got riled, there was no stopping him."

Another silence. "One final question, Mrs. McGovern, and then I'll allow you to step down. On the night Joseph Blakely died, did you consider dealing him a fatal blow with that piece of firewood?"

Kate closed her eyes, struggling for composure. At last she found the courage to meet her attorney's gaze. It seemed a damning question to her, but she could only trust that he knew what he was doing. "Look at my little girl's hand, Mr. Defler, and estimate how long it must have been held in the flames to cause burns so severe."

"Objection!" the prosecutor cried. "This is an obvious ploy to gain juror sympathy!"

The judge rapped sharply with his gavel. "Overruled! Continue, Mrs. McGovern."

Kate ran a finger under her collar and cleared her throat. "I—I can't remember the question."

Defler repeated himself. Kate grasped for what she had been saying, then resumed her testimony. "Anyone who looks can see that her hand had to have been held in the flames for a long while." Her voice quavered. "Imagine, if you will, how she must have screamed. Faced with those same circumstances, show me a mother who wouldn't have considered killing Joseph Blakely, and I'll show you a woman who isn't fit to raise a child."

"That doesn't answer my question," he said softly.

Kate took a bracing breath. "Yes, I thought about hitting him on the head. I nearly did."

"What prevented you?"

Kate felt her face twisting, felt tears welling in her eyes. But she couldn't regain her composure. "I'd like to believe that at the last second something noble in my character held me back." Bracing herself against a violent trembling that had invaded her body, she gripped the chair arms. "But deep in my heart—" She moistened her lips and swallowed back an unbidden little moan. Then, cupping her hands over her face, she cried, "The honest truth is that I was too spineless to do it!"

"Katie, no!" Zachariah burst out. "You have more courage in your little finger than anyone else in this room."

Kate hunched her shoulders, wishing she could melt into the gleaming wood of the witness box and disappear. Sobs choked her. The memories clawed at her, too horrible to remember.

"Defler, that's enough," Zachariah cried.

The judge rapped wildly with his gavel. "Order in the court. Mr. McGovern, take your seat and refrain from speaking out of turn!"

Kate felt Zachariah's strong arm come around her. She turned toward him and clutched his shirt.

"Mr. McGovern, take your seat!" Defler cried.

"This has gone on long enough," Zachariah said. "No more questions. Not without a recess or something. She's too upset to answer."

"Maybe the jury would like to hear the truth!" someone roared from the back of the courtroom.

Kate flinched at the sound of that voice. Ryan! Zachariah swore beneath his breath. A gasp of surprise rose from the spectator seating area.

"She's a lying bitch!" Footsteps clumped toward the judge's bench. "And you, McGovern! You're a murdering bastard! I told you I'd do some digging. Only I didn't use a shovel. After I heard about the indictment, I went to the Applegate Valley. From the first minute I saw you, I suspected you had helped her bury Joseph's body. All I needed was proof of your flawed character. Now I have it!"

Kate felt Zachariah's body snap taut. "That has no bearing on this trial."

"No bearing? No bearing!" Ryan gave a maniacal laugh. "You murdered your wife and her lover, and you claim it has no bearing?"

"Order in the court!" the judge cried.

Kate gasped. "Ryan, how can you say something so obscene! Mr. McGovern didn't even live in the area when Joseph died."

Ryan's blue eyes glowed with red as his gaze met hers. "Birds of a feather flock together. He burned his wife and her lover to death. Found them in bed together and set the house ablaze! Look at his face! How do you think he got those scars? The fire went out of control when he set it, that's how!"

Kate glanced up. The expression on Zachariah's face made her blood run cold. When his hazel eyes met hers, she read the truth. Ryan wasn't making this story up. It had happened. It had actually happened.

"No charges were ever filed against me," he said weakly.

"Enough!" the judge roared. "Back to your seats!"

Ryan ignored him, his attention riveted on Zachariah. "The only reason you were never charged was because they couldn't gather enough evidence, you miserable bastard!"

Shocked and appalled, Kate drew back from Zachariah, begging him with her gaze to deny it. His mouth settled into a grim line, and his jaw tightened.

"A jealous husband's retribution!" Ryan ranted. "Punishment by fire. Wasn't that how it happened, Mr. McGovern? Your wife was unfaithful to you—you came home from a cattle-buying trip and caught her in the act— and in a fit of rage, you murdered her and her lover!"

"No," Kate whispered. "Oh, my God, no."

Ryan began to laugh, a horrible, mad-sounding laughter. He leveled a finger at Kate, tears of twisted mirth streaming from his eyes. "Let her go free! What worse punishment can there be than to be shackled to a cold-blooded killer? You claim Joseph was cruel, Kate? Well, now you'll see what real cruelty is, won't you? Every day for the rest of your life. The perfect punishment!"

The judge rapped his gavel again. "Order in the court! Mr. Blakely, take a seat or be held in contempt!"

"That'd be fitting because I am in contempt!" Ryan's laughter faded as abruptly as it came. "My brother was a fine and honorable man! How dare this court allow his murderess to sit up there saying such vile things, sullying his good name when he's no longer alive to defend himself? Handmaidens of Satan, that's what she and her daughter are!"

The judge hammered wildly. "McGovern? Blakely! To your seats!"

Zachariah released Kate and stepped down from the witness box. Ryan threw him a contemptuous look, then rounded on her. "You and that child deserved everything my brother did to you!" he cried. "Both of you! He was only trying to save you from yourselves. Wicked, that's what you are. Wicked and sinful!"

Gripping the arms of her chair, Kate leaned slightly forward and cried, "My daughter is four years old! Only four years old! Say what you like about me, but she hasn't a wicked bone in her entire body! Your brother was a twisted, insane monster!"

"And you're a treacherous, lying whore!"

Kate shrank back against her chair. Blurred figures ran forward, but all she could see was Ryan. He shook away the court attendants as though they didn't have substance.

As if in a dream, she saw him leap at her. She tried to evade him, but she couldn't move quickly enough even though everything seemed to happen around her with a crazy slowness.

Ryan floating toward her, his hands clawing, his blue eyes wild. His weight slamming against her. And then an awful pain in her throat.

From that point on, everything occurred as swiftly as liquid being sucked down a funnel. A gargling gasp, which she dimly realized was her own, and a pounding sensation inside her head. Falling. A body on top of hers. A frantic need for breath. Black spots. And Ryan's voice. *You deserved it, you ungrateful bitch. You and that miserable brat. He had no choice but to discipline you! No choice!*

Kate heard screams. Not hers because she couldn't breathe. Male voices. Shouting. All of it seemed to come to her from a great distance away. Something at her throat. She clawed frantically to breathe, but the bands around her neck wouldn't slacken. Then she heard Zachariah, roaring with rage. More shouts. More screams. Suddenly, the strangling pressure on her throat let up. Air. Kate clawed at her collar, her need so great she barely registered she was on the floor of the witness stand.

Air, she had to have air. Her lungs grabbed frantically for breath, but it felt as if something was in her throat, blocking her wind. Blackness encroached, an awful, blanketing blackness.

24

As Zach followed the deputy along the cell-block corridor, he felt as though he were walking toward the executioner's block. Katie. If he lived to be a hundred, he'd never forget that look he had seen in her eyes this morning when Ryan burst into the courtroom. Oh, God, why hadn't he told her? *We can't have secrets between us.* His own words came back to haunt him now, making a mockery of everything he had worked so hard to build between them.

Trust. Kate had finally given him hers, and if he'd had any sense, he would have rewarded it with honesty. He had nothing to hide, after all. Now, after hearing it from another's lips, she was never going to believe him innocent.

As he and the deputy approached her cell, Zach steeled himself for a battle. She probably wouldn't like the idea of being locked in with him. Not that he blamed her. Free of one nightmarish marriage, and now ensnared in another.

Swallowing his dread, Zach straightened his shoulders. No, she wouldn't like the idea of being locked in a cell with him. But that was just too damned bad. He wasn't about to play the gentleman, not this time. He had too much to lose, namely her, and by God, he'd fight to keep her.

A single lamp hung from a ceiling hook inside her cell, and its sputtering wick sent out a feeble glow. He glimpsed her lying flat on her back on the narrow cot, fragile face waxen, her hands clasped at her waist like a corpse laid out in a coffin. The instant the key grated in the lock, however, she sprang erect and discarded the damp cloth that had been draped at her throat.

In the dim light, he couldn't read her expression. The deputy swung the door wide, and Zach stepped into the enclosure, wishing for the first time in his misbegotten life that he were a man of smaller stature. The lamplight threw his shadow against the wall, a huge, hulking shadow that reminded him of how big a man he was and how intimidating he must look.

He regretted that. But then tonight he was filled with regrets, and there didn't seem to be a whole hell of a lot he could do to rectify any of them. Her eyes, which had always seemed to him the biggest thing about her, looked like gigantic splotches in her pale face. Her mouth was drawn and colorless. As she perched on the edge of the cot, she kept her tautly folded hands in her lap. "Zachariah," she whispered.

Even in the dimness, he could see the bruises along her throat. Her new russet-colored gown was ripped at the shoulder, and a bit of torn lace dangled from her bodice. Doc Willowby had given her a sedative, and he could see the lingering effects of that as well, mainly in her eyes, which were still dilated and slightly unfocused. Damn Ryan Blakely to hell. He hoped they kept the bastard in jail and that he rotted there for the remainder of his days. Zach had pressed charges of assault, a pitiful vengeance when what he really wanted was to throttle the maniac. At least the man wouldn't be able to bedevil Kate for a few days, and that was something.

"How's the throat?" he asked.

That wasn't what he wanted to ask. The doctor had already given him an account of her condition, for one thing, and for another, a few bruises were the least of her problems.

She worked her hands free and touched trembling fingertips to her larynx. "Better, much better. I slept nearly all day."

"That's what Doc Willowby said." Zach hooked his thumbs over his belt and shifted his weight. Bending his head to shuffle the toe of one boot, he saw that he was wearing his red shirt and wondered, vaguely, why in hell he hadn't chosen blue. Red for rage, red for passion. Blue was a gentler color, and right now, he needed all the help he could get. "I tried to see you earlier. He didn't want you disturbed."

He forced his head up, met her slightly bleary gaze, wished she'd say something, even if she screamed it. A hundred different words crowded into his throat. "Ryan's locked up. Were you told?"

She blinked and frowned slightly. Passing a hand over her eyes, she murmured, "I remember something about it." She shot a worried glance at the corridor. "Not near me, though. Right?"

Zach wanted to grab her up in his arms and promise her no one would ever hurt her again. At the moment, though, she probably saw him as her biggest threat. "He can't get anywhere close to you, Katie. The sheriff saw to that. That's one of the benefits of having a lot of drunken loggers to lock up every Saturday night, I guess. Plenty of space."

The stiffness eased from her shoulders. Zach struggled to swallow. Moonlight came in through the window behind her, creating a nimbus of silver around her. She looked like an angel sitting there. On a jail cot. Jesus, she didn't belong in here. The realization that she might spend the rest of her days locked up—because of him—nearly sent him to his knees.

He made throbbing fists over his belt. No. He wouldn't think like that. The jurors were fair men. They wouldn't allow Zach's past to affect their decision regarding Kate's future. If Zach hadn't believed that with all his heart, he already would have been planning ways to break her out of here. And if that wasn't crazy, he didn't know what was. But, then, it seemed a time for craziness.

"Kate, I . . ." His voice trailed off, and he stared hard at the floor, wanting nothing more than to drop to his knees and beg her forgiveness. It was with a feeling akin to horror that he heard himself say, instead, "If you've been considering getting a divorce, get it straight out of your head. I'll fight you on it to my last breath."

She said nothing, and he finally gathered the courage to lift his gaze. The bewildered expression on her small face caught at his heart.

"I don't like using strong-arm tactics with a woman," he rushed to add, "but if it's that or give you up, I will. Don't think I won't. You're my wife. I guess maybe you're not too happy about that right now. And I'm real sorry you've got to go through this. But there you have it."

She curled trembling fingers around the locket he had given her. Lifting her gaze to his, she whispered, "You know, Zachariah, you have a very bad habit of bringing up divorce or an annulment every time we hit a rough spot."

Zach felt as if a two-hundred pound man had punched him in the guts. Mentally, he staggered back a step, trying to read her expression. Her mouth quivered at the corners. Peering through the wavering light at her face, he decided her eyes definitely looked unfocused, and he realized she must still be under the effects of the sedative.

Still clutching the locket he had given her, she said, "Just for the record, if you decide to leave me, I'm going with you. So all this talk about strong-arm tactics is uncalled for."

The starch went out of his legs. He took an unsteady step toward her. "Katie, are you all right?"

As he drew close, she tilted her head. As she did, her body nearly followed, and he grabbed her shoulders to catch her from toppling. "I'm fine," she assured him in a wobbly voice. "It's just a little upsetting when you go on about divorce. You can't change wives as casually as you do your socks."

She sounded so put out with him that Zach nearly smiled. The unfocused look in her eyes forestalled him. "Honey, do you remember everything that happened this morning at the trial?"

The question made her look all the more disgruntled. "Of course I remember. How could I forget?" She pressed her lips together in an obvious effort to stop their quivering. "I'm in a world of trouble, aren't I?"

Zach's heart caught at that. She did remember. "Yes, and it's all my fault." He sat beside her on the cot, keeping one hand on her shoulder to steady her. "Aren't you angry with me?"

"For what?"

His throat ached with the effort it took to get his next words out. "For not telling you—about Serena."

"Serena . . . Your wife?" She blinked and frowned slightly. "Of course I'm not angry."

"I should have told you straight off." Zach couldn't quite believe what he was saying. He had come here with every intention of arguing his case, not the opposite. "The fact that I didn't is unforgivable."

She passed a hand over her forehead. "At first I was angry. I'll admit that. I couldn't understand how you could have kept something so serious from me."

A heavy silence fell between them. Zach could almost feel her tension and knew she had to force herself to look up at him.

"It seemed to me," she went on, "given your insistence that we have no secrets between us, that you owed me the truth."

"Kate, I—"

She held up a hand. "I figured there had to have been plenty of opportunities for you to broach the subject."

Zach couldn't think of a single thing he could say to defend himself. "I wanted to tell you," he inserted quickly. "A dozen different times, I tried to think of a way . . ." He looked into her eyes, heartened by the warmth he saw there. In a ragged voice, he said, "Honey, I know it was wrong. Can you find it in your heart to forgive me?"

Her mouth tilted in a quavery smile. "Forgive? I think understand would be a better word. Once I tried to put myself in your shoes and really thought about it, I realized there probably wasn't a good time for you to have told me." She wrinkled her nose, putting him so much in mind of Mandy that he nearly hugged her. "Right after you discovered Joseph's body would have been a great time—immediately after I told you Joseph had held Miranda's hand in the fire, perhaps? I can almost hear you. 'Not to change the subject, Kate, but my wife burned to death, and a lot of people think I set the blaze.' Or on our wedding day, maybe, when we were rushing to town and signing papers?" Her mouth curved in a slight smile. "Or maybe later? Right after Miranda burst into our bedroom would have been an ideal time. 'By the way, Kate, I forgot to mention that I was once suspected of murdering my wife. Not that I want to alarm you, or anything.'"

A startled chuckle erupted from Zach's throat, and he followed through on his urge to hug her. When she came willingly into his arms and snuggled against him, he got a taste of what heaven must be like. "Katie McGovern, you are priceless," he whispered shakily. "I've suffered the agonies of the damned all afternoon and evening, worried sick that you'd never forgive me. I really did intend to tell you. I swear it. But there just never seemed—It's not easy to talk about at the best of times."

She looped a slender arm around his waist. "I know."

He pressed his face against her hair and inhaled the scent of her. Roses and vanilla, his sweet Katie girl. There had been times today when he had wondered if he'd ever hold her like this again. "I was afraid you'd think I was guilty, that I would have told you if I didn't have something to hide."

She nuzzled closer. "Never. And it was silly in the extreme for you to think such a thing. You aren't a violent man, Zachariah. And I do love you, with all my heart."

The fear that had been gnawing at him all day slowly fell away, and he absorbed the feeling of her pressed against him. After a long while, he finally found his voice. "I think I should tell you about Serena now so you won't get any more ugly surprises thrown at you."

She touched a gentle hand to his scarred cheek. "It isn't necessary. I know everything I need to know about you."

Zach believed she truly meant that, and the fact that she did touched him as nothing else could. He remembered how humbled he had felt by Miranda's unquestioning trust in him; he felt the same way now. If he tried the rest of his days, he wasn't sure he could ever measure up to it, but he could make a good start tonight.

"I want to tell you about her. But, God help me, I don't

know how to start."

She turned up her face and brushed her lips across his throat. "At the beginning, that's the only place to start."

And so he began. Zach felt separated from himself as he talked, hearing his voice, but not quite sure it was really him speaking. Serena—beautiful, witty, and gay. Himself—young, handsome, with the world just waiting for him to grab it by the tail. The perfect match, everyone had said. Yet in a twinkling, their marriage had become the perfect hell instead.

Zach never knew why. That was the worst of it. The heartbreak of it. The torment of it. He had come home one day to find Serena sipping sherry while she cooked supper. He had poured a glass of wine and joined her, never dreaming he'd rue the day, never dreaming that Serena had a weakness that would destroy her, and him along with her. Within months, his lovely young wife had become a drunk and an adulteress. A staggering, slurring, slobbering drunk who would go to bed with anything in pants. The hired hands, her friends' husbands, even the preacher who had come by the house to pray for her.

"At first I thought it was a failing in me. I guess, if I'm honest, I still wonder about that. I thought maybe I wasn't providing well enough for her. Or that maybe I wasn't spending enough time with her. Or that I wasn't a good enough lover."

Listening to him, Kate blinked away tears. The puzzle that was Zachariah slowly fell into place. Tightening her arms around him, Kate sought to comfort him the only way she knew how, with her love.

"I started getting up earlier so I could put in a longer day without cutting our evenings together short," he went on. "I built another house, a bigger one. I used the money left to me by my folks and took her on a second honeymoon trip to France." His voice turned thick with humiliation. "I even spent a night with the local whore, not for the obvious reasons, but to pick her brain. I went home with a dozen new tricks up my sleeve, guaranteed to make me a better lover."

Kate pressed her cheek hard against his chest, remembering how sweetly he had made love to her. Her pulse quickened just at the thought. "Oh, Zachariah, it wasn't you. Trust me."

She felt his arms quiver as he drew her closer. "I was convinced otherwise. If you'd known her, Katie, you'd understand. Before we got married, you couldn't have met a nicer person. And then, overnight, she changed. It was as if the bottle sucked her dry, draining all the good out of her and leaving only her flaws. She wasn't the same person."

She ran a hand up his chest, tracing the ridges of hardened muscle, aching for him. "Yet you still loved her."

"For a long time," he admitted. "The irony of it was that every once in a while, when she sobered up, I could see in her eyes that she still loved me. She'd promise not to drink anymore, and I'd believe her. She'd swear never to trifle with me again, and I'd forgive her one more time. Then I'd come home and find her drunk, sometimes with another man, sometimes not, and we'd go through it all again. After years of that, the love turned to hate, and then the hate to detachment. I finally reached a point where I no longer cared. The problem was that before I finally did, she and I aired our dirty laundry in public one too many times, and everyone in town knew about our marital problems. And about the rows we had."

Kate sensed that he was about to tell her of the fire, and she set her hands to the task of kneading his tense back muscles, recalling the many times he had done the same for her.

"The night she died, I came home from a cattle-buying trip and caught her in bed with one of my hired hands." His breath caught, and he exhaled with a bitter laugh. "He was just a kid, skinny as a rail with more freckles than he had sense, drunk as a skunk, and her right along with him. When I walked in and saw them together in my bed, I didn't feel anything but disgust. I know that sounds hard to believe, but it's the truth. I hadn't touched her myself in months. I was tired from the trip. And I just didn't have it in me to start a quarrel. Can you understand that?"

Kate recalled the emptiness she had felt the night she buried Joseph. Beyond anger, beyond pain, beyond regret. "Yes, Zachariah, I do understand."

His voice turned thin, and by that she knew how difficult it was for him to go on. "I grabbed a blanket and went to sleep in the barn," he said hollowly. "That's the honest-to-God truth. I went to sleep, and the next thing I knew, I woke up and the house was ablaze. Our bedroom was on the second floor. I could hear Serena screaming up there."

With a suddenness that startled her, he began to sob, a great, soul-shaking cry that wracked his large body and sent tremors through her own. Kate twisted to put her arms around his shoulders. When he buried his face against her neck and she felt his tears, her heart twisted for him.

"I still loved her," he said brokenly. "Not the way I did at first, but I still cared. I had hated her for so long I didn't think I felt anything for her, but all it took was hearing her scream. When I ran out of the barn, I saw her at the window. I tried to get her to jump, but she panicked. Either that or she was too drunk to think clearly. She kept screaming my name."

Kate realized she was shaking as badly as he was. "And you went in," she whispered.

Knowing Zachariah as she did, that wasn't a question.

She touched her fingertips to his scarred cheek, picturing that night, and his frantic attempts to reach his wife through a blazing inferno. It was so easy for Kate to visualize, and no small wonder. He had gone through a pit of rattlesnakes to save her daughter.

"I couldn't get to her," he whispered. "I tried, and the second I hit the stairs, they started to collapse. My shirt caught fire, and I ran back out to roll in the dirt. Then I climbed the porch post and got onto the roof. Before I could reach her, the fire—" He broke off and swallowed. "It was like a blast. It exploded out all the windows, blew me clear off the roof. Just that fast, and the whole house was afire. There was nothing I could do but watch it burn."

"Oh, Zachariah, it breaks my heart to think you kept this to yourself, afraid to tell me. I'm so sorry."

He gave a dry laugh. "You're sorry? You could end up being convicted of murder because of it, and you're sorry? Jesus, Katie, I feel bad enough as it is. Don't make it worse."

"It isn't your fault. None of it."

"I could have at least told you the kind of man you were tying up with and let you make your own choice, but the honest truth is, I never dreamed Ryan would go snooping into my past. I was never charged with anything, and when I left the Applegate Valley, I thought I left all the gossip behind me. I'd never have hurt you."

Kate ran a hand over his hair, loving the thick texture and the way the waves curled around her fingers. "I knew exactly what kind of man I had tied up with," she told him fiercely. "If I had it to do over again, knowing what I know now, I'd still marry you, Zachariah. The devil take the trial."

"You can't mean that."

"I do mean it. For better or worse, remember? The gossip about you wasn't your fault when it happened, and it isn't now. We'll simply have to weather it, that's all, and pray the jury isn't swayed by irrelevant hearsay."

A peaceful quiet settled over them. For a very long while, they sat there, enfolded in each other's arms, the only sound the unsynchronized thrumming of their muted heartbeats. Kate wished their shared closeness could go on forever. She felt so safe and secure with his arms around her, confident against all reason that everything would come out fine in the end. It was an impossible wish. Eventually Zachariah stirred, and she felt the tension flow back into his body.

"There's one thing more I haven't talked to you about. Something I have to ask you."

Kate craned her neck to look up at him. "What's that?"

He took a deep breath. "Just don't say no until you think about it. Promise me that? Try to trust me."

"Zachariah, what?" she prodded.

He drew away and gripped her by the shoulders. "The judge has asked to question Mandy. No cross-examination or anything. Just a few gently phrased questions from him."

Kate's heart caught. "No." She gave her head a vehement shake. "No, absolutely not. I won't allow it."

"Kate." He tightened his grip on her arms and bent his head to look her directly in the eye. "Listen to me."

As far as Kate was concerned, there was nothing he could say to change her mind. "Not Miranda. She's suffered enough. I won't allow her to be put through that. I'd rather hang, Zachariah. I mean it."

"The judge said I can go up on the stand with her, and that I can stop the questioning at any time." His eyes held hers, compelling, giving no quarter. "He's not a heartless man, Kate. He promised to go carefully, and I believe he will."

"I don't want her upset," she cried.

"Do you think she won't be upset if she loses her mother over this? Think, for God's sake."

She averted her face. "I don't want her hurt again."

"And you think I do?"

"No, of course not! It's just—"

His grip on her gentled, and his fingertips began a light, soothing massage that turned her muscles limp. "Please, Katie, trust me. I swear to you, if the questioning gets out of hand, I'll bring a stop to it." He pressed a kiss to her temple. "Miranda may be your only chance."

"She's so little. All of this has been so hard on her."

"I know it has. Let's not add to the nightmare of it all by letting her lose you. What can a few questions hurt, Kate? If she starts to get upset, I'll get her out of there."

Kate closed her eyes. Miranda, on the stand? Just the thought made her blood run cold.

25

Holding Miranda snugly on his lap, Zach encircled her with one arm. Kate and all unnecessary spectators had been escorted from the courtroom for fear their presence would influence the child's testimony, which left Zach as the little girl's only security. The responsibility of that rested heavily on his shoulders, and he shot the judge a warning glance before the questioning began.

The judge smiled slightly. "Your name is Miranda, I'm told," he began gently. "That's a very pretty name."

Miranda glanced around the courtroom and shrank against Zach's chest, plucking nervously at the lace on her pretty new dress. Robin's-egg blue, with lots of icicles on her underskirt. A firm believer that all ladies, however young, felt more self-assured attired in something they liked, Zach had turned the town upside down the day before trying to find a tiny petticoat layered with icicles. He had finally taken a plain underskirt to the dressmaker's and had eyelet lace sewn on. Lots and lots of it, so much that Miranda's eyes had shone when she saw it.

"My name's Judge McGilroy," the judge offered. "You

can call me Judge or Mick or Gil." When Miranda didn't respond, he chuckled and added, "I also answer to Hey, you."

Miranda fastened accusing brown eyes on him. "I ain't gonna talk to you."

Startled, Zach leaned forward to look at his daughter. The judge arched a bushy eyebrow and smoothed his thinning gray hair. "I see. Is there a particular reason you don't plan to talk to me?"

Miranda drew her lips together in a grim little pout. "Papa Zach said I don't gots to if I don't wanna, and I don't wanna."

The judge shot Zach an inquiring look. Zach gave a bewildered shrug. Miranda had seemed tense all morning, but he had laid it to nervousness. Her refusal to talk with the judge was a new wrinkle and one that he hadn't expected.

"Don't you like me?" Judge McGilroy asked.

"Nope."

Someone in the room tittered. The judge cleared his throat behind his hand. Zach saw the twinkle in his blue eyes and relaxed slightly.

"Can you tell me why you don't like me?"

Miranda rubbed her chin on her pretty lace collar. "You nailed my ma up on the wall."

Several of the jurors burst out laughing. Zach's stomach dropped. With a feeling akin to horror, he remembered saying those exact words to Marcus last night. Miranda had obviously overheard him and, as was her way, she had taken him literally. He gave her a jostle on his knee and bent his head. "Mandy, honey, your ma didn't *really* get nailed to a wall. That's just an expression that means she was asked some very difficult questions. And the judge didn't ask them, the prosecutor did."

Miranda looked unconvinced, and she folded her little arms across her chest. The judge pretended to be writing something down, but Zach could see his shoulders shaking. A smile touched his own mouth, and once again, he relaxed. Unless he missed his guess, Miranda was about to make another conquest.

Judge McGilroy sighed, laid down his pen, and folded his hands. "Is there any other reason you don't like me?"

"You gots on a dress."

More laughter erupted. Zach propped an elbow on the arm of the chair and cupped a hand over his eyes.

"This is called a robe. All judges wear them to the courtroom." McGilroy scratched his nose and refolded his hands. "Sometimes little girls misunderstand things they overhear. I assure you that no one nailed your ma to the wall."

"Then how come do you gots a hammer?"

The judge started at that. His mouth twitched. "This is a gavel," he explained as he picked up the object in question. He rapped lightly with it. "I use it to call court to order."

"It's a hammer," Miranda insisted. "I think you're a mean man, and I ain't gonna talk to you."

"Very well." The judge smiled and rubbed his chin. "I can't say I blame you." He took a deep breath. "I can see that you are your ma's champion."

"I'm her little girl," she corrected with innocent acidity. "And if you didn't nail her on the wall, why'd you hide her?" When the judge didn't come up with an immediate answer to that, Miranda's eyes filled with tears. "I think you was afraid I'd see the nail holes, that's how come."

The judge motioned to a court attendant. "Please escort Mrs. McGovern back into the courtroom for a moment."

His chest aching with pent-up laughter, Zach settled back in his chair. An instant later, Kate was led to the bench. The judge leaned forward. "Mrs. McGovern, there seems to be some question in your daughter's mind about my treatment of you yesterday. She has somehow gotten the idea that I nailed you to the wall."

Kate's eyes widened, and she threw a nervous glance at Zach. He grinned. Miranda scooted off his lap, ran down the steps, and launched herself into her mother's arms. While Kate spent the next couple of minutes hugging and reassuring her daughter, Zach watched Judge McGilroy's expressions as he observed mother and child. The poor man didn't stand a prayer. Zach knew the feeling.

After Kate was led away, Miranda returned to Zach's lap and turned to face the judge. "My ma says you didn't nail her up no place, so's I guess I'll talk to you for a little bit even if you do gots on a dress."

The judge smiled. "Thank you, Miranda. That's generous of you." He toyed with his pen. After a long moment, he met her gaze. "Do you know why you're here today?"

"'Cause you want to talk to me."

"Have you any idea what about?"

Miranda fidgeted for a moment. "I think you brung me here to ask me questions." Zach felt her body tense. She glanced nervously over her shoulder. "About my old pa, I think, and whether my ma hurt him on accident."

The judge followed her gaze. "No one here will hurt you, Miranda. There's no need to feel afraid."

"I know. Papa Zach won't let nobody hurt me."

Once again, the judge smiled. "I'm sure he won't." He assumed a thoughtful expression. "I understand that you suffered an accident that scarred your hand."

Miranda burrowed closer to Zach. "It weren't on accident."

The judge fixed his gaze on the angry red scar tissue that

marred the child's fingers. "I see. How did it happen then?"

As if she expected Joseph to appear, Miranda threw another panicked look around the courtroom. "My old pa done it."

"Can you tell me about it?"

Zach hunched his shoulders around the child and hugged her tight. Bending his head close to hers, he whispered, "There's nothing to be afraid of, Mandy. I'm here."

Clutching Zach's sleeve as though her life depended on it, Miranda recounted the events that led up to Joseph's death. In a clear, tremulous little voice, she clearly stated that her mother had struck her father across the back with the piece of firewood.

Judge McGilroy seemed to consider that. "If your pa was bent over you, holding your hand in the fire, Miranda, how can you be sure your ma didn't hit him on the head?" he asked gently. "Could you see where she hit him?"

"Nope."

Zach's heart nearly stopped at that. But he had told her to tell the truth, and he knew Kate wouldn't want it any other way. Zach stifled an insane urge to jump up, fetch her from the other room, and run like hell.

The judge pinched the bridge of his nose. "Sometimes we hear a story told a certain way so many times that we begin to believe it actually happened that way. Could it be that your ma told you so many times that she hit your father on the back that you became convinced you saw it yourself?"

Miranda wrinkled her nose. "My ma never 'vinced me of nothing. She don't talk about it."

"Never?"

"Nope."

The judge sighed wearily. "I can only conclude that you didn't actually see your mother hit your father. Is that right?"

"Yep." Miranda sniffed. "I couldn't see 'cause she was ahind me."

"So your ma could have hit him on the head, and you wouldn't have seen."

Miranda pressed her cheek closer to Zach's. "Nope, I wouldn't of seen. But I know she didn't."

Judge McGilroy flashed a sad smile. "I can see that you love your ma very much. I promise you that we'll all bear that in mind."

Zach's stomach knotted, and he closed his eyes on a wave of dread. Miranda squirmed and blurted, "I said my ma didn't hit him on the head, and I ain't lyin'. I couldn't see, but I know 'cause she didn't hit me."

That gave the judge pause, and he fastened his gaze on the child, his eyes sparkling with rekindled interest.

"What do you mean, Miranda?"

"My head was right aside his head." She reached up and touched Zach's cheek. "Like my head's aside Papa Zach's right now. If my ma had hit my old pa on the head, she would've hit me on the head, too, and she didn't."

"I see," McGilroy said.

Miranda straightened within the circle of Zach's arm and fastened her gigantic brown eyes on the judge's face. "People ain't s'posed to be punished for what they done on accident."

"No, they aren't," he agreed. "That's why we've had you here to talk with us today, so we can determine if your father's death was indeed an accident."

"My ma told you it was, didn't she? My ma don't lie, and neither do I." She shot an accusing look at the jurors. "Only ornery folk'd keep her in jail for somethin' she didn't mean to do. And my ma says you ain't ornery."

The judge smiled again. "We certainly try not to be.

Thank you for coming, Miranda."

Zach could see that he believed the child, and for obvious reasons. With Miranda's penchant for taking everything literally, which she had clearly demonstrated upon taking the stand, she was obviously too young as yet to be capable of formulating such a complex lie. He nearly whooped with joy and relief. Exercising all his self-control, he managed to sit there while the judge concluded his questioning with a few friendly overtures, clearly aimed at making Miranda's experience on the stand a pleasant one.

Afterward, Zach carried Miranda down from the witness box, handed her over into Marcus's care so she could be removed from the courtroom, and reclaimed his seat. Within minutes, Kate and the spectators were brought back in.

After taking a moment to compile his notes, the judge leveled a somber gaze on the jury. "It is my feeling that the testimony we've heard in this courtroom yesterday and today has been sufficient for you good gentlemen to draw a verdict. In view of the disruptions yesterday, I feel I must remind each of you that it is the primary goal of this court to arrive at a fair and just decision. Bear in mind that the vicious accusations made yesterday by Mr. Blakely must be stricken from your minds. If there is anyone amongst you who feels he cannot do that, it is your duty to step forward now so a substitute juror can take your seat."

The judge paused, waiting. None of the jurors raised a hand. After several tense seconds, he called a recess, and the jurors filed into the jury room to begin their deliberations.

Fully expecting the jury to be out for several hours, at the very least, Zach and Charles Defler stepped down the street to have lunch. Before their meal was even served,

Defler's assistant, who had stayed at the courthouse to await any news, poked his head in the door and yelled, "They've reached a verdict!"

Zach and the attorney immediately tossed out money to cover their orders, pushed away from the table and left the establishment. On their way back up the street, Zach said, "Is such a quick decision good news? Or bad?"

Defler cast him a solemn glance. "I've seen it go both ways. All one can really be certain of with a quick verdict like this is that the jurors weighed the evidence and reached an immediate, unanimous decision."

Zach couldn't be put off that easily. "What's your gut feeling? You've defended a number of clients. How do you think the deliberation went, for or against?"

Defler's lips thinned. "I can't make a call like that."

Zach curled his hands into fists. "You think they've found her guilty, don't you?"

Defler straightened his hat and accelerated his pace. "I pray not, Mr. McGovern, but when one examines the evidence, the fact is that a man is dead and your wife's only defense is her own testimony and that of her daughter. As heartbreaking as Miranda's testimony was, she's just a child, and her perceptions of the events that transpired that night may be questioned."

Zach bit down hard on a curse. Struggling for control, he said, "You felt Kate had a good case when all this started."

"That was before Blakely burst into the courtroom yesterday." The lawyer took a deep, bracing breath. "Never fear, though. If worse comes to worst, I'll use that unfortunate incident to petition for change of venue and a retrial. She won't go to prison, that I promise you."

"Another trial? Wouldn't a petition and all that take a long time?"

"Not in comparison to the alternative, which could be a

life sentence or execution."

Zach missed a step. A life sentence or execution? To hear those words uttered in regard to Kate seemed to him a sacrilege. She was such a sweet, gentle person. It hardly seemed fair to Zach that she had been victimized by cruelty for so long and now might be victimized yet again. "How long? A month, two? If that happens, how long will she be locked up?"

Defler tugged on his jacket sleeves and straightened his cuffs. "I'd say six months at the longest."

Six months. Those words echoed inside Zach's head while he sat in the steadily filling courtroom, waiting for court to reconvene. When the door to the judge's chambers finally opened, his brow was beaded with sweat. Not Kate. Six more months of being locked up would kill her.

When she was led into the courtroom, Zach had eyes only for her. From the rigid set of her shoulders and her ghostly pallor, he knew how frightened she was. Pride welled within him at the way she held her head, chin lifted, gaze fixed straight ahead, her steps sure and measured. He saw her searching for him, and then their eyes locked. Though he had to dig deep, Zach found the strength to smile at her.

After calling the court to order, the judge began the proceedings. "The defendant will please rise and face the jury."

Looking as though her legs didn't want to support her, Kate placed both hands on the defendant's table and pushed to her feet. Rather jerkily, she pivoted to face her judges. Her eyes, huge splashes of vivid brown, and her bright blue dress struck an almost startling contrast to the bloodless white of her pinched features.

One of the jurors stepped forward and unfolded a piece of paper. After regarding it for a long, seemingly endless moment, he lifted an unreadable gaze to look at Kate. Zach held his breath. In all his life, he had never been so afraid for anyone as he was for that small woman standing at the front of the courtroom. He imagined her being condemned to a life of imprisonment, or worse yet, to hang. And in that moment, he knew he would do anything on earth to prevent it, even if he had to break the law. She was innocent, dammit. If the judge couldn't see that, if the people in this godforsaken town couldn't see that, then to hell with all of them.

The juror cleared his throat. "We, the jurors, find the accused, Kathryn McGovern . . ." He paused, as if to draw out the moment, and Zach wanted to strangle him for it. Couldn't the pompous ass see how terrified she was? The juror's mouth tipped up at the corners in a smile. He cleared his throat. "Not guilty."

Zach couldn't feel his feet, and his knees threatened to buckle as he stood up. He gripped the back of the chair in front of him. *Not guilty.* Joy burst within him, electrical and numbing. Tears sprang to his eyes. Not guilty! He shoved toward the center aisle, his legs bumping into knees, his feet tromping toes. Not guilty!

The judge called for order, then appealed to Zach by name, saying, "Please, Mr. McGovern, not so fast."

Zach froze where he was, effectively blocking the view of the overweight woman behind him. Not so fast? It was over, wasn't it? A verdict of not guilty! Didn't that mean Kate was free to go? He stood there, heart in throat.

Judge McGilroy folded his hands and scanned the courtroom with a troubled expression on his lined countenance. After looking several of the spectators dead in the eye, he said, "Ryan Blakely's unexpected outburst in the courtroom yesterday brought several things to light, mainly in regard to Zachariah McGovern's past, which has absolutely no bearing on this case. I mention it now only because it is my hope that all those present in this courtroom yesterday will discount his slanderous accusations as the ravings of a man who is obviously unbalanced."

A moan of relief tried to surge up Zach's throat, but he swallowed it down, afraid to believe until the judge finished speaking.

"It is clear to me, and I hope to everyone present here today, that Kate and Miranda McGovern have suffered enough, not only at the hands of Joseph Blakely, God rest his soul, but at the hands of this community." Once again, he looked directly at several people. "There isn't a one of us in this courtroom who wasn't aware, at one time or another, that all wasn't well out at the Blakely place. It is with sincere regret that I extend my apologies to both mother and child in behalf of those individuals who were instrumental in foiling Mrs. McGovern's many attempts to flee to safety with her daughter. We can only hope to have learned a bitter lesson in retrospect, that everything is not always as it seems to be."

Zach saw Kate clamp her hands over her mouth, saw the stifled sobs jerking her slender shoulders. Forgetting courtroom protocol entirely, he once again began pushing his way toward the center aisle, his one thought to reach her.

Judge McGilroy saw him and waved him forward. "Come ahead, Mr. McGovern. I think it's high time you collect your wife and take her home." With that, he gave three sharp raps with his gavel and pushed up from his chair. "You heard the verdict, ladies and gentlemen. Not guilty. The show is over. I suggest you all go home so this couple can reunite in privacy. And from this moment on, I suggest we make it a community effort to give them some smooth sailing for a change."

Zach had a vague sense that he was moving. Instead of reaching the aisle, as had been his first intention, he grew frustrated and vaulted over empty seats, then cleared the bar in a mighty leap. With a whoop of joy, he caught Kate up in his arms and whirled in a circle with her.

The judge chuckled and tossed down his gavel. "If it would be at all possible, I'd like to shuck this *dress* and buy Miss Miranda a celebratory fountain drink. Do you suppose she might be convinced to fraternize with an eccentric old man if he showed up wearing britches?"

Zach stopped twirling his wife long enough to laugh and accept the invitation, then he buried his face in the sweet curve of Kate's neck, not giving a damn who might see them. In a distant part of his mind, he heard people yelling the news outside on the street. "Not guilty! They found her not guilty!" The words filled him with an inexpressible joy and a relief so intense he wanted to weep.

People gathered around them. Defler and his assistant. The sheriff and his portly wife. Several married couples whom Zach had never formally met hung back, clearly eager to offer best wishes. "They reached the only possible verdict." "We're mightily pleased things have turned out so well." "That's a precious little girl you two have there. It took a lot of courage, her giving that testimony!"

Zach kept his arms vised around his wife, ignoring the hands that were outstretched toward him. Pleasantries and good manners be damned. Now that he had her clutched close, he never wanted to let her go.

"Sheriff!"

Russell, the deputy, lurched into the courtroom, looking none too steady on his feet. Recognizing the panic in his voice, Zach lifted his head. The deputy jerked off his hat and swiped at his mouth with his shirt sleeve. His eyes had a wild, half-focused look. "I never thought—He must have heard them yelling the verdict out on the street! I heard him raving, but by the time I got back there to him, it was too late."

The sheriff drew his arm from around his wife's waist. "Slow down, Russell. You aren't making any sense. What's happened?"

"Blakely!" Russell cried. "He hanged himself with his bedsheet!"

Zach heard Kate gasp. A tremor ran through her body. Then she slumped against him. Still stunned by the news, he barely tightened his arm around her shoulders in time to catch her. Her legs folded beneath her. With a detached feeling of disbelief, Zach realized she had keeled over in a dead faint.

Moonlight bathed the rose garden, gilding the blossoms and serrated leaves with silver. Kate leaned on the wobbly fence and lifted her face to the gentle summer breeze, inhaling the scents of the summer night. A deep sense of peace filled her. Her thoughts turned to Zachariah, and she smiled. They had come full circle since the last time she had stood here in the darkness.

The sound of a door closing drew her gaze to the shadowy front porch, and, as he had once before, the object of her thoughts came to stand on the top step. Wearing only jeans, he cut a fine figure, his broad chest and muscular arms silvered by the moon's soft glow, his tousled hair gleaming nearly blue-black. When he spotted her, he stiffened, then came down the steps with two long-legged strides.

"Kate, honey, if you were coming outside, why didn't

you say something? I woke up, and all I had in bed with me
was a kid and dog." As he came toward her, he stepped on
something with his bare foot. "Jesus H. Christ!"

Tears of joy streamed down Kate's face as she watched
him vault over the fence. With the lazy, loose-hipped
stride she had come to adore, he moved up beside her and
leaned his arms on the fence. When his shoulder brushed
hers, her body tingled with awareness. Man and woman.
Lovemaking. Because of him, Kate now knew how incredibly sweet and right such things could be.

"What are you doing out here?" he asked huskily.

"I needed to do some thinking," she replied, "and this
seemed like the right place." She inclined her head toward
the lovely blossoms. "Here, in the rose garden. Good-bye
to the old, hello to the new."

He lifted a leathery hand to brush the tears from her
cheek with his broad thumb. "Is there anything I can do?
I'm a good listener, if nothing else. I know it can't be easy
to accept what Ryan did, Katie, but you mustn't blame
yourself. He obviously couldn't accept the truth about his
brother—or about himself. As heartless as it may sound,
maybe he chose the best way. Maybe in death he has finally
found some measure of peace."

She smiled at the concern she heard in his voice. "Oh,
Zachariah . . ."

"I'm serious," he insisted. "I don't want you agonizing
over this. It can't be good for a woman in your condition."

Recalling his joyous expression earlier when she had
told him about her pregnancy, Kate pressed a kiss to his
knuckles. "I don't blame myself, and I pray you're right,
that Ryan and Joseph have found peace. God knows their
lives were nothing but torment, for them and everyone
around them."

He heaved a shaky sigh. "As horrendous as they both

were in life, I don't think it was by choice. If we can't forgive, at least we can try to understand. Sometimes people's personalities are molded by forces beyond their control."

Kate sighed and nodded. "There's a place within me that will always mourn for Ryan and Joseph, not because of who they were, but because of who they might have been. It seems such a waste, such a terrible, sinful waste. It's frightening to think what power we wield as parents. If not for their father, things could have been so different for them."

He bent his head to catch one of her tears with his lips. "That all happened long before you met Joseph."

"Yes," she agreed, "and that's why I came out here, to put it behind me. As sad as the outcome is, I refuse to waste another day—not even another moment. It's over. And I'm free to go on with my life."

"With me?" he asked gently.

Kate gave a mute nod, not at all embarrassed that another rush of tears welled in her eyes. That felt absolutely wonderful. "Did I ever tell you that Joseph said my happy tears were caused by female hysterics?"

He bent his head to catch another shimmering tear with his lips. "At the risk of repeating myself, Joseph was an idiot. You can cry buckets of happy tears, Katie McGovern, and never hear a word of complaint from me. I've never met a stronger, more resilient woman."

Kate pressed her forehead against his jaw, her chest aching with so much love she couldn't possibly express it. Very gently, he captured her face between his hands. "Good-bye to the old, hello to the new," he whispered. "Here in the garden seems like the perfect place to make you a promise I've been meaning to make."

In a choked voice, Kate asked, "Really? And what might that be?"

He feathered his lips lightly over hers. "From here on out, Katie McGovern, everything in your life is coming up roses. No more sadness."

Kate clutched his wrists, went up on her tiptoes, and lost herself in the twinkling hazel of his eyes. His silken lips settled over hers, the contact so sweet, yet filled with sensual promise. He lowered a hand to her waist, then slid his palm downward to press it lightly over her womb. The possessive touch of a lover, the protective gesture of a father. A man capable of giving both kinds of love . . . fiercely, simultaneously, holding nothing of himself back. With a sense of wonderment, Kate felt a trace of wetness on his cheek, touched her fingertip to it, and realized it was a tear. When she leaned back to see his face, he made no attempt to hide it. The emotions that rocked him were reflected plainly in his gaze.

Magic, and heroes, and castles made of dreams. Perhaps she believed in them, after all.

AVAILABLE NOW

COMING UP ROSES by Catherine Anderson
From the bestselling author of the Comanche trilogy, comes a sensual historical romance. When Zach McGovern was injured in rescuing her daughter from an abandoned well, Kate Blakely nursed him back to health. Kate feared men, but Zach was different, and only buried secrets could prevent their future from coming up roses.

HOMEBODY by Louise Titchener
Bestselling author Louise Titchener pens a romantic thriller about a young woman who must battle the demons of her past, as well as the dangers she finds in her new apartment.

BAND OF GOLD by Zita Christian
The rush for gold in turn-of-the-century Alaska was nothing compared to the rush Aurelia Breighton felt when she met the man of her dreams. But then Aurelia discovered that it was not her he was after but her missing sister.

DANCING IN THE DARK by Susan P. Teklits
A tender and touching tale of two people who were thrown together by treachery and found unexpected love. A historical romance in the tradition of Constance O'Banyon.

CHANCE McCALL by Sharon Sala
Chance McCall knows that he has no right to love Jenny Tyler, the boss's daughter. With only his monthly paycheck and checkered past, he's no good for her, even though she thinks otherwise. But when an accident leaves Chance with no memory, he has no choice but to return to his past and find out why he dare not claim the woman he loves.

SWEET REVENGE by Jean Stribling
There was nothing better than sweet revenge when ex-Union captain Adam McCormick unexpectedly captured his enemy's stepdaughter, Letitia Ramsey. But when Adam found himself falling in love with her, he had to decide if revenge was worth the sacrifice of love.

HIGHLAND LOVE SONG by Constance O'Banyon
Available in trade paperback! From the bestselling author of *Forever My Love*, a sweeping and mesmerizing story continues the DeWinter legacy begun in *Song of the Nightingale*.

COMING NEXT MONTH

ONE GOOD MAN by Terri Herrington
From the author of *Her Father's Daughter*, comes a dramatic story of a woman who sets out to seduce and ruin the one good man she's ever found. Jilted and desperate for money, Clea Sands lets herself be bought by a woman who wants grounds to sue her wealthy husband for adultery. But when Clea falls in love with him, she realizes she can't possibly destroy his life—not for any price.

PRETTY BIRDS OF PASSAGE by Roslynn Griffith
Beautiful Aurelia Kincaid returned to Chicago from Italy nursing a broken heart, and ready to embark on a new career. Soon danger stalked Aurelia at every turn when a vicious murderer, mesmerized by her striking looks, decided she was his next victim—and he would preserve her beauty forever. As the threads of horror tightened, Aurelia reached out for the safety of one man's arms. But had she unwittingly fallen into the murderer's trap? A historical romance filled with intrigue and murder.

FAN THE FLAME by Suzanne Elizabeth
The romantic adventures of a feisty heroine who met her match in a fearless lawman. When Marshal Max Barrett arrived at the Washington Territory ranch to escort Samantha James to her aunt's house in Utah, little did he know what he was getting himself into.

A BED OF SPICES by Barbara Samuel
Set in Europe in 1348, a moving story of star-crossed lovers determined to let nothing come between them. "With her unique and lyrical style, Barbara Samuel touches every emotion. The quiet brilliance of her story lingered in my mind long after the book was closed."—Susan Wiggs, author of *The Mist and the Magic*.

THE WEDDING by Elizabeth Bevarly
A delightful and humorous romance in the tradition of the movie *Father of the Bride*. Emma Hammelmann and Taylor Rowan are getting married. But before wedding bells ring, Emma must confront not only the inevitable clash of their families but her own second thoughts—especially when she discovers that Taylor's best man is in love with her.

SWEET AMITY'S FIRE by Lee Scofield
The wonderful, heartwarming story of a mail-order bride and the husband who didn't order her. "Lee Scofield makes a delightful debut with this winning tale . . . *Sweet Amity's Fire* is sweet indeed."—Mary Jo Putney, bestselling author of *Thunder and Roses*.

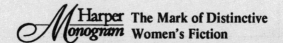

Harper Monogram The Mark of Distinctive Women's Fiction

ANALISE

Analise Caldwell was the reigning belle of New Orleans. Disguised as a Confederate soldier, Union major Mark Schaeffer captured the Rebel beauty's heart as part of his mission. Stunned by his deception, Analise swore never to yield to the caresses of this Yankee spy...until he delivered an ultimatum.

ROSEWOOD

Millicent Hayes had lived all her life amid the lush woodland of Emmetsville, Texas. Bound by her duty to her crippled brother, the dark-haired innocent had never known desire...until a handsome stranger moved in next door.

BONDS OF LOVE

Katherine Devereaux was a willful, defiant beauty who had yet to meet her match in any man—until the winds of war swept the Union innocent into the arms of Confederate Captain Matthew Hampton.

LIGHT AND SHADOW

The day nobleman Jason Somerville broke into her rooms and swept her away to his ancestral estate, Carolyn Mabry began living a dangerous charade. Posing as her twin sister, Jason's wife, Carolyn thought she was helping her gentle twin. Instead she found herself drawn to the man she had so seductively deceived.

CRYSTAL HEART

A seductive beauty, Lady Lettice Kenton swore never to give her heart to any man—until she met the rugged American rebel Charles Murdock. Together on a ship bound for America, they shared a perfect passion, but danger awaited them on the shores of Boston Harbor.

■ HarperPaperbacks *By Mail*
BLAZING PASSIONS IN FIVE HISTORICAL ROMANCES

QUIET FIRES by Ginna Gray ISBN: 0-06-104037-1 $4.50

In the black dirt and red rage of war-torn Texas, Elizabeth Stanton and Conn Cavanaugh discover the passion so long denied them. But would the turmoil of Texas' fight for independence sweep them apart?

EAGLE KNIGHT by Suzanne Ellison ISBN: 0-06-104035-5 $4.50

Forced to flee her dangerous Spanish homeland, Elena de la Rosa prepares for her new life in primitive Mexico. But she is not prepared to meet Tizoc Santiago, the Aztec prince whose smoldering gaze ignites a hunger in her impossible to deny.

FOOL'S GOLD by Janet Quin-Harkin ISBN: 0-06-104040-1 $4.50

From Boston's decorous drawing rooms, well-bred Libby Grenville travels west to California. En route, she meets riverboat gambler Gabe Foster who laughs off her frosty rebukes until their duel of wits ripens into a heart-hammering passion.

COMANCHE MOON by Catherine Anderson ISBN: 0-06-104010-X $3.95

Hunter, the fierce Comanche warrior, is chosen by his people to cross the western wilderness in search of the elusive maiden who would fulfill their sacred prophecy. He finds and captures Loretta, a proud golden-haired beauty, who swears to defy her captor. What she doesn't realize is that she and Hunter are bound by destiny.

YESTERDAY'S SHADOWS by Marianne Willman ISBN: 0-06-104044-4 $4.50

Destiny decrees that blond, silver-eyed Bettany Howard will meet the Cheyenne brave called Wolf Star. An abandoned white child, Wolf Star was raised as a Cheyenne Indian, but dreams of a pale and lovely Silver Woman. Yet, before the passion promised Bettany and Wolf Star can be seized, many lives much touch and tangle, bleed and blaze in triumph.